INTRODUCTION

There are signs that Richard Aldington is returning to the notice of the Anglophone world. That he is thought highly of in the Soviet Union can be confirmed by a visit to the *Dom Knigi*, or House of Books, in Leningrad, where his fiction may be bought complete and annotated, like that of Jack London and A. J. Cronin. He is taken by the Russians to be a loud and bitter voice of disaffection with the capitalist system. Needless to say, they read only his novels and autobiography, neglecting his work as an Imagist poet, anthologist of Provençal literature, and superb if quirky biographer of Norman Douglas and the two Lawrences.

It was his iconoclastic life of Lawrence of Arabia that earned him opprobrium in England. He demolished the legend of the scholar and man of action who had become a national hero and presented T.E. Lawrence as a homosexual masochist, a poseur, an Arabophile whose Arabic was defective and whose political meddlings in the Arab world were irresponsible and ultimately harmful. Winston Churchill was an admirer of Lawrence, and his response to Aldington's biography was one of outrage which found expression in vindictiveness. To read the book at all was an unpatriotic act, and Aldington was pilloried as a traitor. The popularity of his work in the Soviet Union was interpreted almost as a political defection, and evidence of his alleged hatred of England was easily culled from such novels as *Death of a Hero* and the one you now have in your hands. Not that it was easy to find copies of these and his other novels: the bland British have a habit of neglecting, which means letting fall out of print, such books as disturb their complacency.

Aldington has, since his death in 1962, made enemies in a narrower field than that of the British patriots. He was married to the poet H.D., or Hilda Doolittle (a name which she rightly considered more Shavian than poetic), who was glorified by Ezra Pound as the first of the Imagists. In her recently reissued novel *Bid Me to Live*, she presents her relationship with Aldington with a candour that the fictional form does nothing to disguise, and, to those militant feminists who have added H.D. to their pantheon, Aldington has become a mythical male enemy. If we are to take *Death of a Hero* as partly autobiographical, it has to be conceded that Hilda Aldington is libelled in the character of Elizabeth. More than that, Aldington had an excessively sharp eye for the deficiencies of women in general – as this present book very uncomfortably shows – and he knocked them off their self-elected pedestals with the same relish as he brought to the smashing of the T. E. Lawrence ikon.

It is helpful to consider Aldington in the light of the other Lawrence, whose centenary we are celebrating as I write (September 1985). His life of D. H. Lawrence – *Portrait of a Genius, But* . . . – is probably the best of all the memoirs of that uncomfortable novelist, poet and prophet, though this is a judgement difficult for the reader to confirm: like so many of Aldington's books, it has been allowed to slide out of print. To understand Aldington's position vis-à-vis his and Lawrence's native country, it is necessary to appreciate the impact of the mind of the Nottinghamshire miner's son on the bourgeois boy from Portsmouth. Lawrence had the febrile energy of the consumptive, and this was directed against the reactionary forces of the British bourgeoisie, in whom he found such unamiable properties as sexual hypocrisy and artistic philistinism. He had suffered from the British in many ways. He had run away with the wife of his French professor at Nottingham University College and thus established himself as a low-born adulterer. His work, from *Sons and Lovers* on, was regarded as being unhealthily obsessed with sex, and his masterpiece, *The Rainbow*, was proscribed. The reputation of pornographer pursued him to the end of his life, and his *Lady Chatterley's Lover* was made available to the public only as late as 1961, thirty-one years after his death and a year before Aldington's. Aldington may be regarded as Lawrence's chief disciple, a mere moon of the master, but the greater man less taught him rage and disgust than confirmed him in attitudes that were already there and helped him to find techniques for expressing them.

Lawrence's tragedy was to love England and yet to hate what England was making of herself. It was during the First World War that he observed, suffered from, and recorded (chiefly in his letters but also, most memorably, in the novel *Kangaroo*) the ultimate degradations of a society in which jingoism, cynical profiteering, sadism, wholesale lying, and rank intolerance and repression freely rioted. Aldington saw these too, or was taught to see them. But whereas Lawrence, despite being humiliated by army medical examinations that inevitably pronounced him unfit for service, saw the war only from the viewpoint of a civilian, Aldington suffered life in the trenches, first as a private soldier, later as an infantry subaltern. The war impinged on Lawrence's soul at a remove from the bloody actuality and drove him to near-dementia. Aldington had more cause for dementia than his master, and it is in suicidal madness that *Death of a Hero* ends. He became, in a sense, more Laurentian than Lawrence himself.

Disgust with England drove Lawrence out of it, and made him seek a country which had not yet been defiled by industrialism and the fear of sex. He tried to settle in Italy, Ceylon, Australia, New Mexico, to set up a pantisocratic community which he called Rananim, but he died in France unfulfilled and dissatisfied, having found his ideal way of life in a race already long dead – the Etruscans. Aldington was neither so visionary nor so ambitious. He merely left England to settle in France, where – after a sojourn in America during the Second World War – he too died. He was drawn to French culture, and in all his writings there is evidence – in the odd literary citation, even in the odd French phrase (where English would have done quite as well) – of a Gallic allegiance which his British readers must have regarded as unpatriotic. It was enough, anyway, for him to live out of England the better to attack it. But his exile was not as immediate as Lawrence's. He did not settle on the Côte d'Azur until 1928, when he began the sequence of novels that began with *Death of a Hero* and continued with *The Colonel's Daughter*. He needed contact with a rather unlaurentian writer who should teach him less a technique than a social philosophy. This was Ford Madox Ford, Lawrence's first editor and conceivably the best literary editor of the century. He was also a superb novelist.

The finest war novel ever to come out of England is undoubtedly Ford's *Parade's End*, whose philosophical distinction lies in its capacity to see the First World War as a symptom rather than the cause of the breakdown of European society. In a sense, it is not primarily a war novel at all, for it shows human suffering as a constant which war merely exacerbates. The protagonist, Christopher Tietjens, has his chief enemies at home, whose onslaught on his decency and intelligence has begun in peacetime, is given new weapons by the war, and continues unabashed when the war is over (though the British edition of *Parade's End*, thanks to the editorial misguidedness of Graham Greene, omits its post-war segment). What Aldington undoubtedly learned from this book was the significance of the Great War as a mere phase in the collapse of English society. His George Winterbourne is broken by this society, which merely transfers its instruments of destruction to the battlefields of France. *Death of a Hero* attacks the stupidity and wastefulness of war, but, far more, it attacks the moral standards of an England which is unwilling to outgrow torpid Victorianism. 'The old bitch gone in the teeth' for which, in Ezra Pound's poem, the young have to die, is as much a monarch posthumously exerting a murderous influence as a metaphor for the *patria*.

The Colonel's Daughter is a novel that has to be read (and undoubtedly will be by those newly discovering Aldington) in conjunction with *Death of a Hero*. The novel of 1931 is a genuine sequel to the more startling one of 1929. If there is violence in it (there is not much in the physical sense) it now belongs to the most private of the private sectors, but the horror and indignation of the philistinism, hypocrisy and sheer mindlessness of life in an English squirearchy are, if anything, more forcefully expressed than in the previous work. Spandrell in Aldous Huxley's *Point Counter Point* reminds us that there are three kinds of intelligence – human, animal, and military. Aldington-Winterbourne met this last in his army service, but only on the sidelines – in the form of a doddering old imbecile saluting his brigade as it goes off to be minced, in the invisible planners of the staff chortling over the prospect of some new mass homicide. Now he looks at a typical military family full face. He sees how imperialist fatuity ruins private lives by attrition as much as by incompetent staff work. It is the ghastliness of moral atrophy and total brainlessness in a sweet pastoral setting with which he seeks to appal us.

He succeeds, of course, but some readers might complain that the targets are too easy. Because they are so easy, they do not call for a technique of demolition much above the reach of a comic columnist. It is hard to know whether to call Aldington a satirist or not. He borrows from his master Lawrence – chiefly from novels like *Aaron's Rod* – the device of the straight 'yah!', the sarcasm of the clever sixth-form boy who considers that he has grown up and that official adulthood is really senility. He uses, again in the manner of the sixth-form boy who has had Homer as a set text, the device of the mock-heroic:

Tell me, O Muse, the Saga of Smithers, sing me a song o'sixpence of the son of Mavors. Dark mist rolls from the mountains. The spirits of the slain yell in the gale. Give me my harp, let the strings tremble! Oscar is no more, gone are the sons of Fingal!

Macpherson's Ossian as well as Homer. It works, but we are no longer impressed. The more popular media of radio and television have assumed the clever tricks of the sixth-form boy, with the addition of the obscenity of our permissive age. Aldington may not even say: 'Colonel Smithers, get stuffed.'

There is difficulty, with such a verbal register, in taking with sufficient seriousness the eponym, Georgina Smithers. She is a victim of Sandhurst and the Empire, but she lacks the brains to recognise what has been done to her and the vision and energy to get out. On the other hand, she does not want to get out. Shown the bigger world of intellectual dilettantism by the effete rentier Mr Purfleet, she is both appalled and mystified. Her dream is marriage to a Lochinvar of the same imperialist background and brainlessness as her own father and mother. She meets him, and Aldington, having already exploited the possibilities of the type with Colonel and Mrs Smithers and Coz, can do no more than add the qualities of the Empire-sustainer (that is, the plantation manager on a horse) to the Empire-defender. That Georgie is to be disappointed we naturally foreknow. She is well-built but rather an ugly girl. And she is too lacking in brains and sensibility to deserve the attentions of a fiction writer, whose job, after all, is to show the capacity of human character to change under the impact of circumstance. The book is too much a static picture to be altogether a success as fiction.

What is needed is a personage who shall embody the qualities of the bigger life that subsists outside a rentier village and the decaying villa of a retired military intelligence. When we meet Mr Carrington the vicar we think we may have found him, but, knowing Aldington's attitude to the Church of England, we recognise that he cannot sustain the role and, having given an ill-advised sermon on the Woman Taken in Adultery, will be forced out of his living. As for Mr Purfleet, our hearts lift when we meet what sounds like a genuine intellectual who has read the books that Aldington has read, but he is, if anything, worse than the Colonel and his lady. Mrs Smithers can ride to hounds and assume, however ineffectually, the duties of a hospital matron. Colonel Smithers has learned something of the humanity of a battalion officer and, however slyly, has retained a certain concupiscence in his late sixties. Purfleet has no talents and no trade. Literature, even in French, has taught him nothing. He is capable of a certain bloodless sensuality but is fundamentally an epicene poco-curantist of a type we have already met in *Death of a Hero*.

Aldington's detestation of the English intellectual was quite as savage as that of Lawrence. Even his intellectual friends had to undergo the Lawrence treatment of excoriation in his novels. T. S. Eliot is Waldo Tubbe in *Death of a Hero*; in this sequel his name comes perilously close to being spelt out in a gratuitous sneer. Purfleet writes neither verse nor prose, but he will stand for a kind of Eliot, brain stuffed with books, accounts kept in order, anaemic and frightened of life. Life as sexual adventure is typified in the Bright Young People, with their local representative Margy Stuart, whose 'skirts were shorter than ever and showed quite an acreage of pretty silk stocking'. But sexual adventure is lesbian or homosexual, and even when Margy Stuart's social life is intellectualised with poets and barristers, these are always posturing failures. Can Aldington show us salvation anywhere?

If it shines at all from the rural forelock-touchers, it is only in the sense that they are close to the cocks and hens and will copulate at the drop of a pair of old-fashioned bloomers. Georgina is given a couple of lessons in the fornicatory life of the hedgerows: the family maid is, to the delight of the scandalmongers (which means everybody), put in the family way; a woman with gypsy blood appears on the village scene and breaks up two marriages, besides selling her body to help support her complaisant husband. The notion of being 'unclean' is shocking to Georgina. The lessons are wasted. It would have been helpful if Aldington, in the Lawrence manner, could have taken the country copulatives more seriously than he does. But they too, servile and full of aitchless rural lore, are among the lost.

The substructure of this village hell – nobody is purged: it lies deeper than purgatory – is the squirearchy represented by Sir Horace Stimms, Bart. He is given the full treatment in a surrealist epilogue over which a pair of Russian clowns preside.

Bim wore a Harlequin shirt, plus-fours, and white tennis shoes. Bom sported a red hunting coat, running shorts and football boots. In further deference to English taste each had on the ordinary clown's white cone hat. Bim's was inscribed 'H.M.S. Knarr'; Bom's 'K.O. Borderlines'. They were hungrily eating sandwiches from paper bags, and drinking bottled Bass à même le goulot.

They are sitting under the goalposts that Sir Horace has donated to a grateful helotry. Bim and Bom foretell the ruin of the British state, but Aldington's Russian readers totally misunderstand him if they think that its regeneration will come from Bim and Bom's fatherland. Aldington could be a shrieking or sarky moralist, but he was fundamentally unpolitical. Lawrence could at least (*at least,* for God's sake?) find a solution for England's problems in the sensual revolution anticipated by William Blake, but Aldington can only be humorously bitter. He is full of the negative resentment – a hysteria kept under by sarcasm – of a man just out of the trenches back in filthy Blighty. The old soldier's resentment lasted all his life.

How do we, in the Eighties, take this portrait of a segment of English life in the Twenties? We would be unwise to find the satire exaggerated. The brainless army philistine and his brood outlasted the Great War and the brief peace, and were still going round in the vestigial colonial empire to which I lent my inadequate services in the 1950s. Aldington is not speaking (and it is Aldington speaking all the time, not some ventriloquial faceless narrator) of a phase of history that has long departed. We are still a hypocritical people and we are given a lead in philistinism by the royal heads of society. We are not as scared of sex as we were, but we have not come any closer to accepting the Lawrence panacea of tenderness. The squirearchy may have been subdued, but there are other modes of terrorisation and expropriation. The characters of this novel are recognisably all too English. Perhaps only the protagonist Georgina has ceased to exist. Colonels' daughters are not quite like that any more. They no longer have an Empire to grow up in, and they have lost their virginity without too much fuss while still at their decent and not too expensive girls' school. That both male and female pretension and stupidity are still around we do not need to be reminded.

What we have to be reminded, and the admirable proposal to reissue more of Aldington's work will fulfil the obligation, is that here we have a very considerable writer, a frank speaker-out who suffered for his frankness as his master did, a fine manipulator of prose – witty, allusive, sometimes brutal – and a free being who did not give a damn. The society he trounced punished him. If we are living in a more enlightened society, he is one of the writers who helped to create it.

Anthony Burgess, Monaco 1985

PART I

I

GEORGINA SMITHERS, daughter and only surviving child of Lt.-Col. Frederic Smithers and Alvina his wife, was in a pet. Mother had never been a particularly memorable housekeeper, though in her youth she had ridden to hounds with enthusiasm. Never in all her huntin years had Alvina forgotten the place, time and hour of a meet, but rare indeed were the weeks when she remembered everything for the house. As she got older, and had less to do, she forgot more. On this particular Saturday, Georgie had just discovered that Mother had not only forgotten the Bird's Custard Powder and the pound of Danish butter, but the indispensable leg of New Zealand mutton as well. If therefore Sunday was to pass off without grumbles from Father, who still maintained his military ferocity by eating nothing but meat, and from Cousin Robert (an elderly Will Wimble relative of Alvina's, living with the family and known as ' Coz '), who insisted on custard with his prunes, it was up to Georgie to bicycle the seven miles into Cricton and back to fetch the missing matters.

At twenty-six, Georgie was just beginning to resent, dimly and with qualms of a C. of E. conscience, that her part in life was chiefly limited to acting as Mother's little errand-girl and Father's dear little bottle-washer. Georgie honoured her Father and Mother, particularly her Father, who was quite a dear, and still had rather graceful ways with nearly all women except his wife. But when you were doing something important, such as hemming a new petticoat or reading a serial, it *was* rather bothersome to be roked out to go to Cricton. Besides, Georgie hated biking.   A family in their position ought to have a car, even if it was only a Ford or a baby Austin runabout.   So it was not wholly surprising that, as she stood in front of the mirror to put on her hat, she found herself scowling slightly.

Not that she had been doing anything exciting or anything in particular.   In fact, she had been sitting by the smouldering log fire in the drawing-room, which occasionally smoked disagreeably as the wind played some imp's prank in the chimney, doing nothing and thinking how dismal January can be when all the fun of Christmas is over.   Still, even if you are only thinking a trifle drearily, it is nice to have *some* of your time to yourself. Something exciting might happen at any minute, though, Georgie admitted with a slight shock of surprise at her own rebelliousness, it very seldom did ; but perhaps the new Vicar from Cleeve might call—she wanted to see him—or Kitty Colburne-Hosford to arrange a Girl Guide Rally.   So it *was* annoying when Father opened the door and she saw at once by his face that Mother had forgotten something again.

By one of those conventions so common in domestic life, each of the parents acted as Orderly Sergeant to the other in announcing orders to Georgina.   If the Colonel wanted Georgie to come and tidy up his room (a privilege affectionately conferred on her alone) or if he had got his fishing tackle into such a devil of a mess that only female fingers could unravel it, then Alvina would bounce into the room like an Amazon with a ' Father wants you, darling.   Run along at once.'   On the other hand, when Alvina had forgotten something, Fred had to be exhumed from whatever he was doing to convey the glad tidings. Whatever their dissensions and dis-agreements—and these were frequent and endless—they very rarely failed to render each other this service.

Georgina's hair had not been cut. Father and Mother agreed that the ' new fashion ' (already some ten years old) was both unfeminine and ugly. So she parted it in the middle and wound it into a rather uncomely bun at the back. Georgina tugged her hat down carelessly. It was old and unfashionable. That she knew. What she didn't know was that it never had been becoming. Her taste in dress was not so much bad as totally un-formed and childish. Father and Mother believed in ' keeping Georgie young '—a most convenient means, very common in all classes, of avoiding the responsi-bilities of education—and this meant in fact a perpetual servitude *in statu pupillari*, with the result that with the body of a woman Georgie had the mind, habits and feel-ings of a child of sixteen. Though she had successfully insisted on an approximation to the current length and fit of skirt, her clothes were oddly childish. With her broad shoes and black stockings, her blue serge skirt and ugly little blouse, she looked as if she were clad in the cast-offs of an overgrown younger school sister. The ' useful ' hat was the last straw, so to speak, in this breaking of the back of coquetry.

Georgina looked at her face with displeasure. It was a frank face, an untormented face, a face which only too obviously hid nothing in particular. The skin was reddish and a bit leathery—winter winds and Spartan ablutions. Georgina's cosmetics were meagre. Beside the silver brush and comb and hand-mirror there stood

none of that litter of pots and tubes and coloured boxes
and glass bottles wherein the soul of Woman naturally
delighteth.   She had one tube of lanoline and one,
nearly empty, bottle of Phul-Nana, the gift of a dissipated aunt who lived in London and saw as little of
the family as possible.   Father, who had a pretty extensive acquaintance with tarts, would have shuddered to
the core of his honourable military soul if he had seen
wife or daughter handling those instruments of damna-
tion—rice-powder and lip-stick.   Why, dammee, Sir,
they 're the mark of a London street-woman !   The
smell of rice-powder and the taste of red were not unfamiliar to the gallant officer—but never in his own
home.   There he put his foot down—If You Please !
A feller may be a bit wild, don't y' know, and all that,
don't y' know, but he keeps his home-life clean, what ?

No, it wasn't a bad face, either morally or even aesthetically.   It was an essentially *healthy* face, in the full
acceptance of the word, especially in its unintentional
synonym for honest stupidity.   The bone-structure was
all right.   The teeth were good and ostentatiously white,
almost as if they had been whitewashed by the Colonel's
own Orderly.   The forehead, the eyes, childish grey
eyes, and the ears, could all pass muster.   But the fact
was that not even Georgie or Georgie's Father could
claim she was pretty.   Why ?   Alas, where had she
gotten those robustious, already slightly pendulous,
trumpet-major's cheeks ?   Even the cheeks would not
have been quite so bad, but for the nose.   That was a
tragedy.   What devilish Puck of midwifery planted that
man's large nose in the midst of a girl's face, a nose
about which she was as sensitive as Cyrano himself,
without his ability to put resentment into action ?   Poor

Georgie! She hated that nose, especially in winter, when it had a tendency to be red and dew-droppy.

Downstairs, the rest of the family had gathered round the log fire for the afternoon. Nobody was expected to tea. With the *Morning Post* slipping gently between his relaxed knees, the Colonel pondered a campaign, his eyes shut and his breathing regular and audible. Alvina sat bolt upright on her chair, as if riding it with a firm hand and the determination that the beast should take any fence she liked. She was reading a *Daily Mail* account of a plenary session of the League of Nations, with an occasional 'pooh!' or 'umph!' of strong-minded contempt. Coz, the bright one of the family, was regretfully finding that the cross-word puzzle was coming out too easily. Georgie pushed open the door. All three heads were turned to her, the Colonel's eyes blinking rather rapidly and vaguely.

'I'm off now, Mother.'

'All right, dear. What a long time you've been! I hope it won't be dark before you get back.'

'No, of course not. Are you sure that's all I have to get, Mother?'

'Yes, of course.'

'Quite sure? It'll be too late to go again.'

'Of course I'm sure,' said Alvina, very erect and horsewomanly. She laughed a laugh which once might have been pretty, but now was a trifle harsh, forced and cackling. The laugh seemed to imply that though other people forgot—Liberals and tradesmen and Bolshies and that sort—Alvina's memory was a genuine Empire product, incapable of lapses.

'Georgie,' said the Colonel, in his slow authoritative

voice, ' don't go by the main road, there 's too many
of those confounded road-hogs. We don't want you
brought home on a stretcher.'

' All right, Father.'   It meant an extra two miles by
side roads, but never mind.   ' Good-bye.   I must *rush*.'

' Good-bye.   Not *too* fast, dear.'

The door shut, just a trifle impatiently.   How long it
takes to get anything done with old people !   Georgie
wished she knew more young people, but nearly all her
friends were rather old.   It was rather beastly not really
knowing any of the very smart people Margy Stuart
knew—but then the Stuarts were rich—or even any of
the awfully queer and annoying but interesting people
who came to spend week-ends with Mr. Purfleet, the
local intellectual, during the summer.   She trod her
pedals viciously against the streaming pressure of the
wind.   Yes, it *was* beastly being cooped up with old
people, who just wanted to sit about and dawdle and talk
about the past.   Then a pang of self-reproach and compassion hurt her.   It was more beastly for them, though.
In her vague overgrown childish way she felt the pathos,
the horror and pity of age—the hardening of the arteries,
the flesh thickening and slipping to obesity or shrivelling
to show the bone-structure, the lined face settling to
its mask of decay, the once-bright eyes growing dull,
energies and interests waning, waning, the whole being
dwindling in a long tragic diminuendo of activity, losing
touch, becoming obtuse, obstinate, unheeding.   Georgie
shivered, as she pedalled harder to forget her thoughts.
How short a time they had left !   How base of her to
grudge them her life, to long so often to get away, see
new faces, meet new people, talk and drive and dance
and enjoy life, and perhaps—she blushed a little, though

only talking to herself—marry some nice man and have children. After all, they *were* kind to her, they loved her. She had her Guides, she could ask anyone she liked to tea, she had pocket-money, she went to stay with her relatives—also rather old, unfortunately—she had—oh, all sorts of things. And then she was wicked enough to be cross, simply because the days were dull and she felt blue and Mother forgot and Father and Coz were always asking her to do little things for them—not that they really needed her help, but just out of affection and because they liked to be with her. As if biking into silly old Cricton and back for someone who loved you was such an awful penance !

Georgie pedalled on, almost in a frenzy of repentance and self-oblation. She felt all the comfort of self-depreciation, and determined that this Sunday she *would* get to early morning Service, even if it rained and blew great guns, and *not* stay in bed as she had done for two, no ! three, Sundays running. . . .

Five minutes after Georgie had left, Alvina broke the silence by slapping her bony but Amazonian knee and exclaiming :

'There ! I knew there was something else I'd forgotten !'

The Colonel blinked with some irritation—two interruptions of one's serious after-luncheon ponderings were a bit too much. He spoke a little snappily :

' Well, what is it now ? '

' The bottle of H.P. sauce.'

' Oh ! ' exclaimed Coz reproachfully, ' Alvina ! I told you yesterday *and* to-day to be sure to remember.'

' What you ought to do, Alvina,' said the Colonel irritatedly, proffering as a novelty an idea he had expressed at least once a week for thirty years, ' is to have a little *system* in your housekeeping. You ought to have chits, and keep a list of things required.'

Alvina sniffed very erectly.

' Besides, it 's ridiculous that Georgie should always have to be biking into Cricton at all sorts of times and weathers, simply because you 're too careless to remember things. You don't consider the child enough.'

Like a film Cowboy going at full gallop, Alvina fired from the saddle with pitiless accuracy :

' If there were any *real* consideration for Georgie,' she said, ' half the income of this establishment wouldn't be spent on bookmakers and useless trips to London—and Georgie could have a small car. Moreover . . .'

' Now, now,' said Coz pacifically. ' Now, *now*. You two love-birds bickering again ! '

This pleasantry had first occurred to him some decades ago when a lover's quarrel had threatened the engagement of Fred and Alvina. Coz always prided himself on having smoothed the way to what had proved a decent marriage—upon the whole.

The Colonel looked angrily at Alvina over his glasses, which he had put on for the purpose of this discussion. Experience had taught him that he could not compete with Alvina in domestic invective, whatever his triumphs on the parade ground and in the Field. He removed his glasses, grunted twice as one who scornfully declines an action with a contemptible and routed foe, and returned to his ponderings.

II

Tell me, O Muse, the Saga of Smithers, sing me a song o' sixpence of the son of Mavors.

Dark mist rolls from the mountain. The spirits of the slain yell in the gale. Give me my harp, let the strings tremble! Oscar is no more, gone are the sons of Fingal!

Is the name of Smithers aristocratic? Perhaps it is written in Debrett; certainly it has been inscribed in the Golden Book of the Army List. Yet it has more kinship with the nameless Three Hundred of Thermopylae than with the Four Hundred of New York, the *crème de la crème*. Though 'Smithers' invokes rather the ringing of anvils than the glitter of coronets, yet it is marvellous what two generations of Army can do. Colonel Smithers was undoubtedly a gentleman. As he stamped along with his military gout waddle, invisible spurs jingled at his heels; the very houses sprang to attention and the trees presented arms. The Marcia Reale from a distant barrel-organ immediately became the British Grenadiers. Smithers was pukka Army.

Fred Smithers had been born on a troopship, in consequence of a small arithmetical misunderstanding between Smithers *mère* and Lucina. Never a bright child, he early gave unmistakable signs of his military vocation, signs which filled his parents with honest pride. He delighted to flee away from his *amo* and *tupto*, to the brook, the fell and the butts. The Gradus ad Parnassum was abhorrent to this British Hippolytus. The gun and the rod were the symbols of his deity. With that delicate dissociation of feeling only possible to a born sportsman, he contrived to love horses and dogs with a tender passion while waging ruthless war on all wild things, from grouse to trout, and, in later years, from tigers to foxes. Yet when he had passed his salad days of catapults, he never slew tom-tits and never assaulted tom-cats, however plentiful and tempting the game. Every honourable scruple of the chase was his. For the gentle and timid roe-deer he used a rifle with telescopic sights ; he stuck spears into wild pigs, while disdaining the more succulent porkers of his native heath ; he condescended to execute the mallard with Number 5 shot ; but the fox, albeit cousin to the dog, he disdained to touch and abandoned to fratricidal teeth.

Nor plied he Todhunter and the then unspotted Euclid. Rather would he urge the flying ball than compute the formula of its trajectory. Therefore, the Artillery was out of the question. Too poor for the Guards or the Cavalry, he entered a Line Regiment, and on the plea of some remote and hypothetical Keltish ancestry, was gazetted to a Scottish Battalion. Then did my young master swagger it in kilts or in trews, one of the Queen's braw laddies, to whom She had decreed as a *solatium* for ignominious defeat in the Crimea that ' moustaches shall be worn '.

It was the kilt that caught the eye of Alvina at an Aldershot review. Herself an Amazon, terrifying to quiet men who preferred to have their mutton killed for them, she had vowed to wed none but a real sportsman and a soldier. Of their chaste loves, Georgina was the slightly uncomely fruit. A marvel she was not born with a fox's brush.

Up and down the Empire and to and fro upon it this gallant officer sailed, marched, trained, shot, hunted and fought for his country. He jabbed the butt of a pigsticker into himself and broke two ribs ; he came a purler at polo and broke an arm ; a Fuzzy-Wuzzy nicked him in the ham with a spear, and brother Boer broke his omoplate with a well-aimed Mauser bullet. Yet, although he was always conscientiously two years in debt, promotion avoided him, and in 1910 he retired to the half-pay list, a mere Captain with the consolatory rank of Major.

What then ? For nearly five years he abode at Bath, in a small rented house, while Georgina attended school and learned to keep young. Or rather, learned little, and was kept young.

Der Tag was a great day for Smithers. When he learned that the European War was definitely 'on', he pranced about the streets of Bath on an invisible high horse, while the unseen spurs jingled more evidently than ever. He was in a fever of apprehension lest England should be 'disgraced' by staying out. Not that he had made any close study of British international policy or had any clear conception of how the situation had arisen. His feeling was that England must fight and therefore England would be right, for would not Smithers get a job?

Smithers was rejuvenated by the declaration of War. A Voronoff graft could not have been so magical.. For some weeks he had thought of going over to Ireland to defend the Curragh against Redmond's devils, to act as a sort of Runner to Galloper Smith ; but a European War was far more satisfactory. As he told Alvina on the night of the 4th, when they sat up late, too excited and happy to sleep : ' There 'll be plenty of fun and plenty of pickings. Kitchener will make a long War of it.'

Next Monday morning Smithers was in London, tapping at the doors of a perturbed and anxious War Office, which perhaps was rather more conscious of its responsibilities than capable of discharging them. The more earnestly the War Office resiled from his civilities, the more eagerly did Smithers press them. The War Office knew about him and was not impressed. But they had to take him on. Then came the question of what to do with him? Fortunately, someone recollected the famous Smithers love of animals—demonstrated by many a skin, brush and skull—and he was set to look after remounts, and later given nominal command of a hospital for horses and mules. Oh, Smithers did his bit all right. So did Alvina, who positively hunted men back to health in a hospital. So even did Georgina, who was commanded into a V.A.D., and scrubbed floors and washed dishes for The Cause.

But the best of friends must part. The happy War years at full pay as a Lieutenant-Colonel glided by only too quickly. Smithers was once more *en disponibilité*. Now that Georgie's education was 'complete' there was no point in returning to Bath, so Smithers bought a largish but dilapidated house, just on the crest of the hill at Cleeve. This highly desirable freehold residence, comprising etcetera, with 1 ac. 2 ro. 1 p. of land, cut a monstrous cantle in the estate of Sir Horace Stimms, Bart. Holly Lodge had probably been a dower house, alienated from the Manor in the reckless fashion of the old Squires. When Sir Horace bought the estate, the Lodge was occupied by a very elderly lady, who refused to sell it to him or anyone else, and also refused to have any repairs done. She said it would last her time. It did, but it was in a pretty state of disrepair. This Sir Horace knew, and he was confident that nobody would buy it at the price asked. Commercial astuteness got the better of his land hunger and feudal pride. He bargained ruthlessly. Meanwhile along came the innocent Smithers, saw the place, liked it, and bought it, recklessly but simply, with one half his patrimony.

Sir Horace was both furious and respectful. Smithers's complete lack of commercial astuteness was quite beyond him. It never occurred to him that there were men in the world who had no commercial astuteness, who rather scorned it, in fact. In comparison with Stimms, Smithers at once becomes a sympathetic figure. The financial manœuvres of Horace would have filled him with distaste—if he had been able to understand them. But what was the upshot? Smithers had rendered military service all his life, not very efficiently perhaps, but still he had rendered it, sometimes at the peril of his life. Now, 'in the evening of life', as Insurance Companies call old age, he dwelt in a ruinous nook of England on about £600 a year. Meanwhile, Horace had absorbed at least three estates which had been intended for the nurture and comfort of warriors, defenders of the Throne, and he had done it all on grease. Thus, in fact, all Smithers's hoity-toity never-stooping-to-anything-unworthy-a-gentleman had resulted in his being the paid bravo in the international quarrels of a successful Camberwell tradesman and his pals.

Did this ever occur to him? Probably not. Thinking wasn't a strong point with Smithers. But his relations with Horace were interesting. Smithers liked shooting, but Horace owned the shoot. Smithers liked fishing, but the fish existed by kind permission of Horace. Smithers and Alvina would still have liked to hunt, hoary old vulpicides that they were. But whereas twenty noble steeds champed in the stables of Sir Horace, only cobwebs occupied the melancholy void of Smithers's outhouses. Now, when Sir Horace found that Smithers

had beaten-him-on-a-deal-by-Jove, and learned moreover that he was a pukka Colonel of Regulars, Horace
was impressed. He himself was a Captain or Knight-
at-Arms or a Lord Privy Beefeater or something, but
this distinction was not earned in the field ; it was
camouflage from the recruiting officer, conferred on
Horace by a grateful country anxious to preserve him
and to enjoy his services on the Empire Grease and
Butter Board.

So the impressed Horace immediately invited Colonel
and Mrs. Smithers to dinner. He was at first under the
misapprehension that Smithers was rich as well as pukka
military ; and therefore pukka gentry. He invited
Smithers to shoot ; he gave Smithers permission to fish.
But Horace was not astute for nothing. Through the
long meanders of Smithers's military reminiscences he
soon discovered his poverty—and scorned him accordingly. Smithers might have talked to Kitchener as man
to man, but Horace had diddled smarter men than
Kitchener time and again. Moreover Smithers had the
manners Horace would have liked to possess and couldn't
quite acquire. In their first shoot, he put Smithers at
his right and Coz at his left. It was confoundedly
annoying for Horace to find that he could only hit one
in ten of his own pheasants, whereas Coz bagged three
out of five and the Colonel, blazing away right and left,
got nine out of ten. Horace's own pheasants if you
please, which had cost him at least a sovereign a brace
to rear.

In the simplicity of his heart, Smithers rejoiced over
Horace, and told Alvina he was a toppin feller. He
examined Horace's principles, and found him staunchly
loyal to King, Country, and even Church. Smithers

was not much of a one for Church, but he approved of it as a useful institution for womenfolk and other ranks. So did Horace. Smithers also found Horace very sound on the Labour Question. There was a threat of a strike in the grease business, and Horace was uneasy. He told Smithers that the situation was very serious, that he (Horace) would be ruined and the Country itself would reel to commercial disaster if Horace had to pay his men another two bob a week each. And Smithers said the Country was going to the bow-wows, no doubt about it, and the only thing to do was to shoot all these agitators, fellers like Whatshisname, string 'em up ! And Horace, remembering to drop his ' g ' at the right moment, said that Labour was bleedin the Country white. So Smithers was more and more certain that Sir Horace was a toppin good feller.

But, though Sir Horace did not rescind his permission to fish, he did not invite Smithers to shoot again, and asked him to dinner once annually only. Smithers wondered why. How had he offended Sir Horace ? He was inclined to blame Alvina. But one of Smithers's mistakes in life had been the neglect of the study of commercial astuteness. He did not know that commercial astuteness, however opulent, never wastes money and entertainment on people from whom nothing is to be expected.

Consequently, the evening-of-life as a hawkin, huntin, fishin English gentleman became a dull affair for Smithers. He escaped the dullness by making minute but numerous telegraph bets on certs with a booky—and generally lost. He also escaped by an occasional little-run-up-to-town-and-a-night-at-the-Club. With whom did Smithers spend those nights? He was elderly, but . . .

Alas for Alvina's widowed pillow. Alas for the incomparable attraction of converse with retired Admirals and Generals, who left long hairs on Fred's waistcoats and a suspicion of rice-powder about his sleeves. . . .

And life was dull for Alvina, and very, very dull for Georgie. Where were the Hunt Balls, the country-house parties, the brilliant gatherings of which Georgie had dreamed ? Where were the skating parties, the hunting, the race-going, the County events, the golf, the bridge, the motoring ? Six hundred a year is the answer. And where were the young men who should have come a-wooing the Colonel's lovely daughter, for she is grown so fair, so fair ? Georgie wasn't pretty, Georgie wasn't rich, and thousands and thousands of the young men lay dead in rows, or they lived on a couple of hundred a year with no prospects, or they were rich and she never saw them, or they were flabby and wanted to be kept, or they were scattered from Honduras to Hong-Kong, from Labrador to the Straits administering the Greatest-Empire-in-the-World, or they laboured in unhealthy climates (with one year's leave in three or five) making a thousand a year, and dying, or at best growing yellow and liverish, so that wholesale petrol, copra and coffee, rubber and tea, metals and minerals, might be lavishly at the disposal of Horace the Patriot and his pals. But, even as for the old Colonel there came no Lords and gold-giving Caesars, so for Georgie there came no young Lochinvar.

III

The Smithers ladies had a proper attitude towards Church-going—they considered it a duty *and* a pleasure.

The elementary duty of divine worship, possibly in itself
tedious at times (though the tedium was not to be advertised), was sweetened for them by the opportunity for
observing fashion, for neighbourly greetings and invita-
tions. The Colonel was less assiduous. No more
parades for him, including Church parade. It would be
unjust to describe Smithers as a free-thinker. As a disciplinarian he mistrusted freedom of any kind, and his
abstinence from thought would have been ascetic if
thought had ever been a pleasure to him. When he
attended Church, it was, like Sir Horace, to give countenance to an institution which had its useful side. When
had the Church been backward in patriotic duty, when
had She failed to oppose disorder and the unjust demands of Labour agitators ?

The Reverend Henry Carrington, M.A., had some
experience of new parishes. When he first took Sunday
morning duty at Cleeve he was not surprised to find the
Church nearly full. He did not jump to the conclusion
that he had struck a parish of remarkable religious fervour. True, he had been brought in partly to counter-
act by his Low views the conduct of a distressingly High
Anglo-Catholic (of Congregationalist origins), who had
given offence by the introduction of incense and a
crucifix, and by calling Holy Communion ' the Mahss '.
But Mr. Carrington knew that his large congregation
had merely come to see the new parson. There was not
much brightening of village life in Cleeve, Maryhampton
and Pudthorp. Apart from Saturday afternoon football
or cricket on Sir Horace's valuable field and from a rare
' village concert ' of depressing sentimentality and more
depressing humour, there was nothing to do in leisure
hours but hang about, go to sleep, or gossip. The new

parson was, so to speak, the first bit of fun the parish
had been given for a long time.

Under the unpleasant ding-dong of the solitary bell,
a chill silent decorum hushed the Church when Alvina
and Georgie entered.   There was none of the clattering,
pushing, spitting, scraping of chairs, loud whispering
and generally profane bustle which still so paganly occur
in the southern European dioceses under Romish super-
stition.   Here you were in the House of the Lord, and
Knoxly made to know it.   Falstaff himself would have
become glum and decorous in that lot.   A faint rustle, a
discreet cough, the scandalous flop of a fallen prayer-
book alone disturbed the sacred calm.   Mr. Carrington
came forth from the vestry, in a nicely laundered surplice, and the congregation discreetly, soberly and in
godly wise shuffled to attention.

Georgie Smithers was an incurious soul.   The questions of the How ? and the Why ? or the Whence ? and
the Whither ? never disturbed her, never indeed arose.
The normal questioning of her childhood had been
effectually quenched by ready-made answers or a gentle
discouragement, a kindly but firm ridicule.   Before the
terrific spectacle of a cloudless night sky, Georgie was
never encouraged to murmur : ' The silence of those
infinite spaces appals me ' or even ' There is the grand
enigma '.   She would have been made to feel pretentious
and silly.   But it was not pretentious or silly to say :
' Hullo ! Look at the old twinkle-twinkles, aren't they
jolly bright ? '   That was the right attitude in such a
case—disparagement.

If Georgie had been born a Hottentot she would have
gone through all the motions of Hottentotdom with

docility and incuriosity. There was certainly nothing independent or rebellious about her. Since she had been born into impoverished upper middle class England, she accepted its rules, customs and prejudices without comment and without question. Adaptation to environment, in the flabby sense. She was the kind of person who makes a ' good ' wife and a ' good ' mother, because she would never have asked for anything but what she was bound to be given—*i.e.* whatever the prejudices of her class demanded. And she was not such a confoundedly exceptional fossil as you might be tempted to suppose. In fact, there are more Georgies than Shelmerdines. The Georgies would like to think themselves Shelmerdines, but the fact remains that the Georgies are the somewhat dreary rule and the Shelmerdines the lovely exception. It cannot be too strongly impressed on the world that far more people live outside Mayfair than in it.

What, then, was the correct attitude of a plain Georgie towards Divine Service ? Much the same as that of a pretty Margy Stuart (also present) who was undoubtedly on the fringe of Mayfair—*i.e.* outward decorum and attention, inward indifference. Essentially, Margy was merely a richer and more sophisticated and possibly less chaste Georgie. Margy certainly wore more interesting knickers and frequently displayed glimpses of them ; but, given the chance, would Georgie have despised these things ? The main difference between Georgie the little country frump, and Margy the smart Mayfair fringer, was chiefly this—that Georgie had entirely succumbed to her training as a docile female Empire-builder, because succumbing was the practice in her large sub-section of the middle class, and Margy had resisted because that was the practice in her much smaller sub-section. Each had adapted herself to environment, which meant the prejudices of her particular lot. But it is extremely doubtful whether Margy was any more ' original ', ' enlightened ' or ' up-to-date ' than Georgie. In any case, when Mr. Carrington moved down the aisle with customary reverence and dignity, both Georgie and Margy were thinking of the same thing—clothes.

But as Mr. Carrington proceeded with the service, a certain difference between them came into play. Margy Stuart met lots of men and flirted with a good many of them. Georgie saw few men, and flirted with none. Thus while Margy peddled her sex appeal all round and got a fair response, Georgie's sex was nothing but one large mute demand which she hushed into respectability under a formal stolidity and Girl Guide childishness. But to suppose that Georgie did not want a man is as false as to suppose that she consciously, definitely and precisely acknowledged it. Margy Stuart felt about parsons much as the eighteenth-century great lady felt about footmen—that they were not ' men '. Georgie was too naïve for these high-life sophistications. She did not indeed plan a flirtation with the innocently officiating Mr. Carrington ; still less did she imagine herself in bed with him—she would have thought herself somewhat filthy at imagining herself in bed with any man, except possibly on her wedding eve, an event which, alas, seemed to recede rather than advance with the passing years. No, there was nothing precise and vulgar in Georgie's ' reactions ' to the officiating priest. She merely found Mr. Carrington's conduct of the service

most interesting, even thrilling, and she rapidly revised
the half-hearted, nay, irreverent, attitude towards sky-
pilots which she had acquired from her military sire.
Loyally Georgie still felt convinced that killing is the
noblest work of man—*that* she conceded to filial piety.
But was not the Service of God comparable with His
Majesty's Service ?   Did not the Archbishop stand on
the steps of the Throne ?   And therefore might not
praying be considered the nearest and best substitute
for killing ?   Was not the surplice God's Uniform ?
True, the beneficed clergy now seldom hunted, shot or
even fished ; but that was not from lack of goodwill.
Many of them were as toppin sportsmen as you could
desire to meet, and if they refrained from the sports
which, to all right-minded persons, are the chief sanction
for man's position as the Centre of the Universe, it was
partly due to lack of means and partly because a mis-
guided Public Opinion demanded this oblation.   In any
case, though God was not a God of Sport (strange omis-
sion from those sacred and inspired books) He was
emphatically the God of Battles.   Mr. Carrington, himself a War-time Chaplain, might, had he chosen, have
pinned the M.C. on the left side of his surplice.   God's
warriors were the King's warriors ; and if Mr. Carrington refrained from slaying the Hun and the native nigger,
his predecessors at any rate had burned people for dis-
agreeing with them.   It was therefore plain that Mr.
Carrington was not only a first-rate parson, but a Man. . . .

Outside the Church after service, Alvina and Georgie
became involved in neighbourly greetings.   They were
making for Margy Stuart, who was waiting for them,
when they were intercepted by old Mrs. Eastcourt—one

hundred and eighty pounds of monogamous and matriarchal flab, possessed of an unknown but apparently
limitless reserve of oleaginous spite.   She had dared the
chill January wind, to foster her immortal soul and see
what the new Vicar looked like ; and now held pneumonia at bay, standing beside an eighteenth-century
tombstone roughly engraved with a Death's Head,
scythe and hour-glass (which she ought to have been
under instead of beside), in order to eject the maximum
of slander in the time yet allotted her by an irresponsible
Providence.   She was accompanied by her son, a spineless and squeaky-voiced youth of some fifty winters, the
captive of her will and testament.   Mrs. Eastcourt
affected a whining, oily tone of voice which was meant
to say ' listen to the dear kind benevolent old lady who
has only grown sweeter with age '; but this tone was so
flagrantly contradicted by everything she said and by
the appalling malevolence of her fat witch's countenance
that it deceived no one.   She laid her hand on Georgie's
arm with a clutch which feigned benevolence, but had
something of the implacable Ancient Mariner about it.

' Well, my dear, how are you ?   But I needn't ask.
You look so bright and bonny with your lovely clear
colour ! '

This was meant unkindly, because Georgie's nose and
cheeks were nipped to an uncomely red.   But before the
two indignant ladies could launch a sweetly-smiling
counter-attack, Mrs. Eastcourt changed front with the
skill of an old campaigner.

' And what do you think of the new Vicar ?   He 's
rather *elderly*, don't you think ? '

Georgie's indignation at the slight to her complexion
was now transferred to the account of the Galahad she

had so recklessly acquired during her morning devotions. Mr. Carrington elderly ! Despite his good grey head, he couldn't have been more than forty-five. Georgie spoke with imprudent warmth.

' I think he 's splendid, the only *real* clergyman we 've ever had in either of the parishes. He read the Service *beautifully*, I thought, and his sermon . . .'

Mrs. Eastcourt rarely allowed anyone else to talk much. She only waited for the hint, and then launched her shaft of Philoctetes.

' Yes, *hasn't* he a lovely voice ? But you know, my dear, they say he was an *actor*, and only joined the Church because he couldn't make a living on the stage. But there, they seem to ordain *anybody* nowadays, don't they ? '

Alvina saw her chance, and cackled militantly :

' Well, they haven't got down as low as pork butchers yet, have they ? '

That was a good one—the Eastcourt money, such as it was, came from a small bacon factory. Mrs. East-court leered with staggering malevolence. So expert a tactician naturally disdained a frontal movement in reply. She returned to Georgie, clutching her more firmly as the girl tried to edge away in the direction of Margy, who was plainly growing impatient.

' I *am* so glad you like Mr. Carrington. I 'm sure he 's a good man, and, you know, he 's had *so much* trouble in his life. They say his first wife ran away from him and died of drink, and that *he* had to run away from the second wife—a dreadful woman, a stage dancer. Poor man, we must make it up to him by any little neighbourly kindness we can do him. He 's a widower now, of course. Wouldn't it be *nice* if he married one of our own dear girls in the neighbourhood—I *do* think a country clergyman should have a wife, don't you ? '

Georgie flushed with confusion. The old harpy had read her with Satanic efficiency. Now, of course, Mrs. Eastcourt would inform everybody that Georgie was shamelessly ' after ' the parson ! She was dumb with shame and impotent resentment. Mrs. Eastcourt released Georgie's arm, and lowered her voice to a dramatic whisper.

' But they say he 's got *Money* ! That 's why he can afford to take the living. It 'll save that old miser Sir Horace some money too.'

At that moment Sir Horace emerged from the porch, adjusting his silk hat. Mrs. Eastcourt hastily good-byed the Smithers, and waddled almost amorously towards the Stimms millions. As they hurried after Margy, who had gone, they heard Mrs. Eastcourt say :

' How do you do, Sir Horace ? I was just speaking of your *generosity* to the parish. . . .'

Alvina and Georgie almost ran to overtake Margy Stuart, who was a distinctly bright spot in their none too luminous lives. Margy's good-natured father—rubber boom, retired on the proceeds—let her do very much as she liked. She had plenty of money and her own car. Mrs. Stuart went out and entertained a lot in London, but Margy really liked the country and the large house and garden her father rented from Sir Horace. Even in the winter she motored down for week-ends, generally bringing friends with her. She was fair-haired, pretty, well-dressed and twenty-two—just too young to have been directly affected by the War, which for her was one with Babylon and Tyre. She only went to Church be-

cause Daddy asked her to, and Daddy only asked her
because it was essential to keep in with Sir Horace.
Sir Horace was always emphatic that the upper classes
should set an example of duty, in all respects, including
religion.

Margy was walking with a young man of about
twenty, who was languidly but unmistakably sulky at
having his morning immolated. She caught sight of
the Smithers, and stopped.

' Hullo, how are you ? How did you manage to get
away from Granny Silvertongue ? ' Then, without waiting for an answer, ' What a crashing bore that man
Carrington is ! I thought he 'd never get done with his
droning.'

This second brick dropped on the placid surface of
her pool-like day-dream was almost more than Georgie
could bear. Mrs. Eastcourt—naturally ! But Margy,
the kindly, the good-natured, the tolerant, and, what is
more, the smart and social Margy—that was dreadful. Could it be that Mr. Carrington was less distinguished, less *attractive* than she had thought ?
Or had everybody ' guessed ' already, and was Margy
pulling her leg ?

Completely unconscious of the havoc caused in
Georgie's heart by remarks meant to mollify the young
man, Margy rattled on :

' I read in a book the other day about some people
who had novels bound as prayer-books. If this old slow-
coach stops, I think I 'll have to do that.'

Alvina and Georgie were electrically pained by this
blasphemy. Alvina hastily changed the subject.

' Are you down for long ? '

' No, only the week-end. Oh, I 've forgotten to intro-

duce Mr. Brock !   This is Mrs. Smithers and Georgie
Smithers.'

The young man was chillingly ungracious.   Georgie
noted that Margy's skirts were shorter than ever and
showed quite an acreage of pretty silk stocking.   Her
fur coat was open, and Georgie almost yearned at her
novelty five-guinea hand-bag, which Margy treated as
if it had been a two-shilling purse.   They came to the
cross-roads and the expected moment.   Margy hesitated,
and then her good-nature got the better of her common
sense.

'Oh, I 'd forgotten !   Can you both come to tea to-
morrow afternoon ? '

The Smithers accepted with almost unseemly swiftness and gratitude.   They *loved* Margy's tea-parties.

'Who are those two fantastic frumps ? ' asked Mr.
Brock, as soon as the frumps were out of hearing.

'Retired Army.'   Margy was already repenting.   Odd
how we attach ourselves to people by doing things for
them which we don't really want to do—vanity of
patronage.

'I didn't know such people still existed ! '

'Oh yes, they do, lots of them.   You don't know of
them because you never poke your nose out of your
own set.'

'They must be intolerable bores.'

'Why, yes, they are, I suppose.'   Margy half agreed.
'I rather like Georgie, though.   She 's really a nice girl,
but terribly shut in, and *inhibited*, of course.   I 'm sorry
for them all.   Daddy says Colonel Smithers has given
his life to the service of the Empire and got nothing
for it.'

Mr. Brock sneered.

' Does he still have his chutney sent from India ? '

' They 're awfully poor.   Daddy says they can't have anything like even a thousand a year.   How on earth they live *I* can't imagine.'

' How too interesting !   But why must you play Miss Matty and ruin to-morrow afternoon by asking them to tea—after ruining this morning as well ?   It 's too Cranford.   You give horrid week-end parties, Margy.   I can't think why I come.   Your loathly sex appeal, I suppose.'

IV

When Sir Horace Stimms took possession of his estate, he was horrified by the spectacle of a clergyman driving an ordinary farm cart from the station.   This was the unlucky Rector of Maryhampton, whose 'living' was ninety pounds a year, plus thirty pounds from Queen Anne's Bounty.   Since the Rector had a wife and three children, and was unwilling to see them starve, he did a brave and sensible thing—rented some land and worked it himself.   Why Sir Horace should have been so frozen with horror may seem strange, since holy men from St. Peter (who was a fisherman) and St. Paul (who was a tent-maker) down to the religious orders of to-day have worked with their hands yet lost nothing in sanctity. But in Sir Horace's scheme of things, the clergy were merely part of an ingenious system for keeping the rich rich, and in his opinion manually working clergy were less efficient than gentlemanly ones.   Sir Horace solved the problem with characteristic energy.   He persuaded the aged and comparatively wealthy Vicar of Pudthorp

to resign.   He repaired the Rectory and got permission
to unite the two livings and let the Vicarage, thus bringing the Rector up to £310 a year, to which he added
£90 annually, on condition that the farming was given
up.   It was given up, gratefully, but the Rector found
to his dismay that he had merely exchanged toil for
servitude—Sir Horace meant to get his money back in
servility.

Remained Cleeve, where the living was somewhat
better—about £150.   Sir Horace added £100 a year
and gave it to an ex-Congregationalist, who was malle-
able because the poor devil was glad to get any job.
But, such are the aristocratic traditions, nobody liked a
parson who wasn't a gentleman, especially since he tried
to hide his plebeian origins with all the Anglo-Catholic
clobber he could acquire.   The insurance system didn't
work here, because the working people went to Chapel—
and hence might drift into the Liberal interest—and
the gentry stayed away or went to Maryhampton.   Sir
Horace was chagrined, but not defeated.   He wangled
a transfer for the Anglo-Catholic Congregationalist, and
then found he could get no substitute.   £250 a year,
plus Sir Horace, scared the few candidates who presented
themselves.   Finally, Sir Horace saved the situation—
and himself £100 a year—by appointing Carrington,
who had a private income, and was a widower.

Were Mrs. Eastcourt's delicate insinuations accurate ?
Was he a professional actor ? Well, as an undergraduate
he had belonged to the O.U.D.S. and the Debating
Society, whence he had acquired (and kept) a good
speaking voice.   And it was true that he had been
married twice—but on each occasion to a lady of unblemished reputation.   One had died in childbirth with

her child ; the other had been killed not long before in
a motoring accident.   Carrington threw up a promising
career—he was practically certain of a Canonry—and
retired to the country, with the hope that he would soon
join his wives where there is no marriage or giving in
marriage.

When Margy Stuart rang him up on Monday morning and asked him to tea, he at once accepted.

This act of Margy's exasperated Mr. Brock to vain
recriminations, but as Margy had dished the afternoon
by her thoughtless generosity in asking the Smithers,
she had determined to make it an omnibus tea for all
the local bores.   Get it over, and have a few week-ends
in peace.

Mr. Brock wailed despairingly :

' But, Margy, *why* must you ask these appalling
creatures ? '

' Because, if you live in the country, you 've got to
know everybody or nobody, and Daddy thinks we ought
to know them.   They 've got to be invited occasionally,
or they 're offended.   The difficulty is to know them
without getting involved in their fiddling but hideously
vicious little feuds and scandals.'

Mr. Brock sighed.   He felt he would have to drop
Margy, or at any rate her week-ends in the country.

As might have been expected, the tea-party was
hardly a success.   The local people did not like Margy's
London guests, who treated them in a very superior
manner.   Margy's girl friends were unfeignedly amused
by the Smithers's tailor-mades and 'ignorance.'   The
doctor and Sir Horace's agent did their best, but were
conscious of a certain constraint.   Alvina was scandal-

ised to see 'young people' drinking cocktails at half-
past four, and she found the remarks of Mr. Brock
utterly incomprehensible. She said, trying to be sympathetic :

'I suppose you get plenty of cricket and football ? '

'Good God, no ! Had enough of that at Winchester
and Oxford.'

'Oxford ? Ah, I know, you 're a rowing man ! '

Mr. Brock looked round wildly for help.

'You should get Sir Horace to ask you down for his
shooting—my husband says it 's excellent.'

In desperation, Mr. Brock abruptly tried to change
the subject :

'What do you think of the Sitwells ? '

'The sit-wells ? ' said Alvina with a puzzled cackle.
'Do you mean these comfy arm-chairs ? '

Mr. Brock gasped with horror, and fled from the room
with a muttered, 'Excuse me, left my handkerchief upstairs', and did not return. Alvina reflected that young
people were getting very odd and out of hand. In his
flight Mr. Brock had kicked over someone's cocktail
glass which was standing on the floor, but he neither
paused nor apologised. Alvina turned to Margy, and
asked if she were coming to the Jumble Sale. Miss
Lenton, a strong-minded old maid of small but independent means who lived alone in a cottage, endeavoured
to get a free consultation from the doctor on the plea
that 'Doctors are such fine self-sacrificing men ' and
that 'she loved to be told about their work '. The doctor
parried this with the skill of an old practitioner, and suggested that she ought to drop in to his surgery one day
and be 'overhauled '. Margy's friends had got into a
little group, and were frantically talking Russian Ballet,

Josephine Baker, Riviera, motoring—anything to make conversation.   Georgie, who looked a little pale and had dark rings under her eyes, obediently listened to the land agent, who was inveighing against the intolerable habits of tenants.   Margy hovered about in a state of acute nervousness, praying that it might soon end.   At that moment the door opened, and the servant announced Mr. Carrington.   Everybody looked up, even Mr. Purfleet, who was trying to explain psycho-analysis to a thick-headed but sweet young thing who plied a fascinating lip-stick.

Georgie's stolid demeanour now served her well.   She had not expected to meet Mr. Carrington so soon, and her heart gave a flop when she saw him.   She watched him, as she pretended to listen to the prosing of the agent—an art in which she had acquired much skill from the infliction of Father's multi-told military yarns. Mr. Carrington was a *little* older than she had thought, but he seemed even more handsome and distinguished than in Church, and his deep controlled voice was, she thought, bell-like and thrilling.

Presently Margy brought Carrington over and formally introduced him.   Georgie flushed and abruptly stood up.   At first nervousness made her inarticulate.   Then Carrington's almost professional calm influenced her, and she talked volubly—for her—about Girl Guides and local affairs.   Carrington watched her with curiosity. He had a vague feeling that the girl wanted something from him.   What could it be ?   Anyway it was his duty to help her if he could.   A pity a girl with such a fine figure should be—well, she wasn't very pretty.   But obviously, she had retained her girlish purity.   That was much in these days when the youth of England had

fallen into lamentable pagan laxness.   What *could* she
want of him ?   He asked at random :

' Have you done any Church work ? '

Georgie flushed again.

' No—well—that is—of course I go to Church quite
regularly—but—I should like to do Church work, if I
could.'

Her embarrassment puzzled him.   He felt a mild joke
might be helpful.

' We must see what can be done.   But you can't join
the Mothers' Meeting yet, can you ? '

Once more Georgie flushed painfully.   It was now
Carrington's turn for embarrassment.   He felt that his
remark not only sounded silly, but was rather improper
in a clergyman.   Georgie plunged :

' Oh, but I should love to do something for the
children.   I *adore* babies ! '

Sex was never discussed in the Smithers household,
except under the most veiled and delicate camouflage.
The possibility that Georgie might want a husband was
never mentioned, but it was a Smithers convention that
' Georgie adored babies '.   Was this intended as a would-
be subtle indication that Georgie would like one of her
own, eligible young men please note ?   In any case it
indicated that the only thing a young woman should
hanker after in the Stygian fields of sex was a dear little
baby—legitimate, of course.   That sanctified everything.   Smithers purity was always maintained at an
impressive level.   At one time Alvina noticed with displeasure that Coz's bantam cocks were making indecent
assaults upon her Rhode Island hens.   This, thought
Alvina indignantly, with true Regular Army knowledge,
this will make the hens lay little eggs.   After much hem-

ming, she bashfully asked Fred to ask Coz to confine his
feathered Lotharios ; an embassy duly and gravely performed. Since the bantams were much too small to
give any effect to their libidinous enterprises, the whole
situation was eminently grotesque.   Mr. Carrington, of
course, knew nothing about the bantams, but he was on to
the baby fiction. Clergymen had to be. Although many
of them were regrettably forced by poverty to practise
birth control, the baby fiction was still kept up—one of
a host of fictions which make immense areas of English
life appear to outsiders such a dreary and trivial blague.

Carrington was flustered by the naïve pathos of that
' I *adore* babies '. For a second the stolid, sportin, girl-
guidin Smithers exterior was reft apart, and a glimpse
of reality revealed.   Carrington wondered if the girl was
being forward or merely utterly and stupidly naïve. A
glance at her flushed ignorant face satisfied him. He
knew that girls like to have someone to promise to buy
them a bunch of blue ribbons, but his own troubles had
prevented his observing the empty lives of the girls of
her sort. It flashed across his mind that there must be
thousands and thousands of Georgies, whose possible
husbands lay dust under the monuments of Glory. He
felt the same kind of impotent pity and questioning of
God's goodness that he had experienced when it was his
daily duty to bury the lost husbands of these lost girls.

This pause of terrific mutual embarrassment lasted
nearly a minute, while the implications of that ' I *adore*
babies ' ringed out across his mind in swift wavelets.
Carrington spoke hesitantly :

' I think, I feel sure we can find you—you can find—
I can help you to find—er—work to interest you in the
parish. There is always a great deal to be done—more

than you realise.   But—well, at any rate, will you come
and have tea with me soon, and we can talk about it ? '

' I should love to.'

' When are you free ? '

' Any day except Thursday—I have to take the Guides
at three.'

' Come on Wednesday at four, then.   I think you 'll
like my housekeeper's cake.'

V

Thick rain was swept steadily and wetly down by
the Atlantic winds.   Through the compact hurry of
clouds the weak northern sun diffused a hazy damp light
which soon faded into a dull twilight.   The tarred roads
gleamed indefinitely, and the scattered cars crawled sus-
piciously on their non-skid hands and knees.   The lanes
were mud and puddles, with rutty channels on the slopes
and deposits of grit where they reached the level—a con-
scientious father, anxious about education, might have
improved the rainy hour by pointing out the geological
principles of this miniature erosion.   Georgie missed the
opportunity, as she descended the sunken lane leading to
the Vicarage, mailed *cap-à-pie* in shiny goloshes, thin
oilskin coat and umbrella.   The big drops from the elms
plopped on the tent umbrella like dreary little drum beats.
The early catkins obediently waggled their lambs-tails
in the wind, but their canary-yellow was soaked drab.
Innocent trespassers on Sir Horace's freehold, the young
crinkled leaves of primroses displayed their astonish-
ingly artificial green.   Last year's rose-hips all had a
dew-drop on the end of their red noses, like Georgie herself.   The whole world was soak, drip and slither.

If Georgie was unhappily deaf or blind to Nature's
sermons, she was nevertheless in a religious mood and
was not unaware that there is good in everything.   She
walked hurriedly with her inherited military stride, clutching her umbrella handle with unnecessary and absent-
minded force.   She held her head slightly to one side,
plainly absorbed in a meditation which was carrying
her some distance towards a remote Nirvana.   She was
thinking what she would say to Mr. Carrington, and
wondering what he would say to her.   The lane forked
with the village street.   As if designed by some master of
scandal-strategy, Mrs. Eastcourt's bow-window occupied a position which gave the maximum of observation
with the maximum of cover.   Unkind people, who exist
everywhere, even among folk so neighbourly as the phil-
anthropic Eastcourts, remarked that as Mrs. Eastcourt
sat knitting in the window with saintly resignation to her
infirmities, the window blind was so disposed that she
had a first-rate forward observation post over the whole
village.   Georgie turned her head away from the Eastcourt mansion, and almost ran by.   The knitting continued mechanically, but Mrs. Eastcourt's spectacles
were as good as a Zeiss telescopic periscope. She watched
Georgie along the road, held in view the shiny fringe of
her oilskins as she sped along the tall holly hedge of
the Vicarage, and caught a valuable glimpse of the fold-
ing umbrella as she whipped into the Vicarage gate.
Georgie sighed with unconscious content as she rang the
bell—she had managed to nip past the wily old cat un-
observed *that* time !   Exactly at the same moment Mrs.
Eastcourt called to her son in a voice of exquisite
maternal affection :

  ' Maaar-tin ! '

Naturally, Mrs. Eastcourt had named her son from a Saint renowned for his charity.

' Yes, Mother ? '

The will-and-testament-enslaved youth, who had vainly panted for independence during thirty years, obediently and filially abandoned his ' work ' (he was setting the Thames on fire with his artistic poker-work) and entered the room.

' Make me a cup of tea, dear, and then get me my boots and that nice warm coat dear Mrs. Saxby gave me.   I think a little walk would do me good.'

' Oh, but, Mother, it 's so damp and cold !   You know the doctor said you weren't on any account to risk pneumonia by going out in the rain.'

Mrs. Eastcourt smiled happily at this filial solicitude.

' Now, dear, you must humour your poor old mother. I 've only got a little while more to be with you and look after you, and then all I can do is leave you my poor little property.   I feel it in my bones that I shan't last out this cruel winter.'   (Mrs. Eastcourt had made that remark, almost daily, changing the season with the calendar, since 1905.   She died with the protracted vigour of Voltaire and King Charles II.)   ' It doesn't matter whether it 's this week or next.   And I was thinking of the dear Vicar.   Poor man, he must be lonely and dull in this weather.   It would be an act of neighbourly charity to call on him.   Run along now, dear, and do as I say.'

Martin obediently ran along, wondering what devilry was on now.

When Georgie rang the Vicarage bell, Mr. Carrington was in his ' study ', reading the *Spectator*, a journal he esteemed for the solidity of its views and the decent

gravity of its style. As he said, it was part of his duty
to keep in touch with all the most advanced manifesta-
tions of modern thought. The noise of the bell somehow suggested to him that this innocent invitation,
innocently given and accepted, was in fact a social *gaffe*,
a series of *gaffes*. He ought not to have asked Georgie
to tea alone (when would he remember on all occasions
that he was now a widower ?) as if she were a village
girl in trouble. It was almost an insult to a girl in her
position. He ought to have called on the family, her
father, and then have invited her with her mother.
What earthly reason existed why they shouldn't discuss
her proposed parish work in front of her mother ? He
felt a contraction of his scalp as he perceived that there
was, yes, something almost clandestine . . . The door
opened.

' Miss Smithers, Sir.'

They shook hands and exchanged greetings. Mr.
Carrington was thinking almost frantically. Too late
to ring up Miss Stuart—in London anyway—can't have
tea on the lawn—middle of winter—regrettable contretemps—what will parish say ?—bad start—dear, dear—
make this as short and formal as possible.

He rang the bell, ordered tea, and sat down a long
way from Georgie. She was plainly embarrassed. Mr.
Carrington ran his finger agitatedly round the inside of
his collar. He frantically made conversation.

' Do you find your work for the Girl Guides takes up
much of your time ? '

' Oh no, it 's all very easy to learn, and there 's only
one drill a week. The longest time is in the summer,
when there 's the annual week camping out. But that 's
great fun. Last year we had lovely weather.'

' I should have thought it's a little risky taking children under canvas. Don't they get ill ? '

' Some of the little wretches catch cold, but it's good for them.'

' Catching cold ? '

Georgie stared. Was the Vicar chaffing her, in the style of Coz ?

' No, camping out, I mean.'

The conversation faded, owing to mental inertia. Fortunately tea came in, and introduced the welcome diversion of Milk ? Sugar ? How many lumps ? Bread and butter or cake ? Georgie determined to get down to brass tacks :

' It's awfully jolly of you, Mr. Carrington, to give me a chance to do some work in the parish. . . .'

Mr. Carrington almost trembled. Why, in a gush of unnecessary pity, had he made that insane suggestion ? It was as if the girl had hypnotised him. Difficulty upon difficulty ! How demented of him to suppose that he could publicly work with an unmarried girl of his own class in a small village. . . . What was she saying ?

' You see, I haven't really very much to do, except to help Mother with the housekeeping. I have to bike into Cricton pretty often, but I rather hate that. I talked about it to Mother and Father last night, and they both thought it a splendid idea for me to do some volunteer work, something a lady can do, Mother said. And oh, Mother said, will you come to tea next week, on Tuesday ? '

' Delighted, delighted,' murmured the perplexed man.

' Mother thought I might go and teach the working-class mothers how to take care of their babies. . . .'

Mr. Carrington started. That lamentable topic again!

He wondered vaguely why God had afflicted him with
the desolation of childlessness.

'. . . But it seems rather cheek, doesn't it? I've only
done V.A.D. work, and I'm not sure I can teach them
much.'

'We have the District Nurse,' Mr. Carrington said.
'I'm afraid neither she nor the mothers would like outside advice. One has to be most careful not to offend
the natural susceptibilities of the poor.'

Georgie was a little disappointed and perplexed.
She felt that Mr. Carrington had rejected her plan
almost with relief. And then ' the susceptibilities of the
poor' were not considered in the Smithers household—
a woman who ran a home and was bringing up three
children on thirty shillings a week ought, in the Smithers
view, to show profound gratitude for advice from an
ignorant girl, provided she belonged to the gentry. In
the Smithers social system, ' the poor' civilians were in
much the same position as military other ranks ; all
communications from superiors were to be received at
attention. Georgie went on.

'Father said there must be widows and orphans of
men killed in the War, and perhaps some War wounded.
He thinks they might be glad of help from an officer's
daughter.'

'But what can you do for them ?'

Georgie hesitated, badly stumped. If she had been
capable of self-analysis, she would have perceived that
she had not started from the position of a specific job to
be done, but from an unacknowledged desire to be
brought in contact with the fascinating Vicar, for which
the job was merely an excuse. She was playing the
feminine game with childish clumsiness, made still more

clumsy by the fact that she didn't know she was playing it. The world of accepted fictions, into which Georgie had allowed herself to be fitted, firmly discouraged self-analysis and self-criticism. If Georgie had ever possessed those faculties, they had shrunk to insignificance by disuse. She did not know, and would have furiously denied, that in fact she was only exercising the natural right of a woman to offer herself silently and obliquely to The Right Man. In a world of unlimited choice, Mr. Carrington would certainly not have been The Right Man, but in the miserably limited Smithers world, who else was there ? The man shortage there was even more acute than the munitions shortage in 1914. Nor was there any Ministry of Marriage to make good the deficiency. All this Georgie either had not considered or refused to admit. The situation as she saw it was an unconscious subterfuge—she had been happy at the thought of 'a new interest', and was strangely unhappy that the Vicar did nothing but make difficulties.

Carrington took advantage immediately of her silence. He could scarcely be said to possess a Socratic lucidity of mind, but he had some vague feeling of what was going on. He was a little uncertain how to handle the situation, for hitherto the maidens who took a violent liking for 'Church work' had been easily but competently dealt with by his wife. Man-like, he determined to run away. He said in official tones :

' I have given much thought and prayer to this matter. Naturally, my dear Miss Smithers, I should not think of trying to discourage you from any work of charity. Indeed, it is my duty to gratefully accept any aid you can give in bringing this parish nearer to God. But I am certain it is a thing not to be entered upon lightly or inadvisedly. Excellent as your suggestions may be, I don't quite—er—find them practicable. What I suggest is that you hold yourself in readiness, and allow me to suggest what line your work shall take when I am better acquainted with the needs of this district. I am a stranger here in a strange land, I know little or nothing of the place or people, and I blame myself for my haste, my carelessness, in allowing you to think that I could immediately make use of your services. Pray for guidance in this matter, and be sure it will be sent. If you will kneel down by your chair, we will together pray before the Throne of Heavenly Grace that assistance and light be sent you.'

They knelt. The Vicar began :

' O Lord, our Heavenly Father, Almighty and ever-living God . . .'

At that moment, the new and untrained parlour-maid tapped lightly at the door, and entered. She paused in horror at having thus mundanely interrupted the devotions of the Vicar and a lamb from his flock.

' Oh ! Beg pardon, Sir.'

The Vicar and Georgie struggled to their feet in confusion. The Vicar spoke sternly but kindly :

' What is it, Annie ? '

' If you please, Sir, Mrs. Eastcourt and her son have called to see you.'

Georgie could not have been more dismayed if the Vicar had suddenly changed into a leering Mr. Hyde in her presence. But Mr. Carrington, who knew not Mrs. Eastcourt, leaped at the salvation. A chaperone ! A rescuer ! A female full-stop to this distressing and embarrassing situation !

' Show them in at once.'

Mrs. Eastcourt had gently waddled down the passage after the servant, and had been vainly peering through the door-crack to see what was going on. She now entered, leaning on a stick and looking like the wicked old Fairy come to blast a life in the cradle—poor Georgie's pathetic and callow romance. Georgie's confusion and annoyance were evident. The Vicar himself was in some perturbation, both from the agonies of his previous strategy and from being disturbed when acting as Georgie's ambassador to Jehovah. His hair was slightly rumpled from the energy with which he had thrown himself into that sacred mission. Nothing could have looked more like a guilty pair. Mrs. Eastcourt purred with gleeful malice. These were the moments that made life worth living !

' I do hope you 'll forgive the old woman for breaking in on you, Mr. Carrington,' she said. ' I 'd no idea Georgie was here. I hope your poor mother is not unwell, dear ? '

' No, thanks, she 's quite well.'

Mrs. Eastcourt's beautifully feigned surprise said plainly : Then why isn't she here ? What do you mean by having tea alone with the parson, you hussy ?

She said :

' I 'm *so* glad. Dear Mrs. Smithers is always so kind to me—I wish she 'd come to see me more often. These little acts of neighbourly kindness mean so much, don't they, Mr. Carrington, to people of *our* age ? '

Carrington acquiesced languidly. He was wondering if there were still a chance for the Canonry. Mrs. Eastcourt vaguely indicated Martin and Georgie.

' Whereas these young people '—Martin, by the bye, was older than the Vicar—' always have plenty to do,

and everyone is glad to have them. Growing old 's a
sad thing, Mr. Carrington, isn't it ? '

' It need not be,' said the Vicar firmly, ' if we have
done our duty and retained our affections.'

' How beautifully you put it ! ' exclaimed Mrs. Eastcourt with diabolic ecstasy. ' I 've always felt that, but
could never put it into words. I often say to Martin
that I feel the whole village are my friends. I take such
an interest in everybody, and I believe so firmly in being
neighbourly. Martin and I came to see you, because
Martin thought you might be lonely in this dreadful wet
weather without friends. I didn't know you had made
friends with Miss Smithers so easily. You 're very lucky.
She doesn't often come to see *me* ! '

The Vicar did not like this or the tone in which it was
said.

' Miss Smithers came to see me, at my request, with a
view to taking up Church work. I have . . .'

' Taking up Church work ! Why, whatever makes
you want to do that, Georgie ? I had no idea you were
interested . . .'

The Vicar interrupted :

' I was about to say that, on consideration, I have had
to tell Miss Smithers that I don't see what she can do at
present, but that I will inform her if anything—er—
arises.'

Mrs. Eastcourt produced her well-known angelic
smile.

' But I think it a splendid idea ! I always say that the
clergy are the spiritual lords of the manor of the parishes
and that they always need a helpmeet to look after the
women's side. How lovely if . . .'

Georgie stood up suddenly.

' I 'm afraid I must go, Mr. Carrington. Mother
will be expecting me. Thank you so much for your
kindness and advice. I can quite see now that I
hadn't realised the difficulties in what I wanted to do.
Good-bye.'

' Oh, must you go ? '

' Yes. You won't forget Mother's invitation for
Tuesday, will you ? '

' No, I shall be delighted to come.'

Mr. Carrington accompanied Georgie to the door, and
they shook hands again. There was something valedictory about that handshake, a farewell to Georgie's
little dream, and at the same time a sort of sympathy.
He was quite sorry for the girl.

After throwing a few random shafts, Mrs. Eastcourt
departed too, not wholly dissatisfied with her afternoon's
work, but regretting that the Vicar put up such a poor
fight. Carrington watched her waddling down the road,
leaning on her stick, while Martin held an enormous
umbrella over her. He ruminated for a moment the
Mosaic precept : Thou shalt not suffer a witch to live ;
but dismissed the project as inhumane. Yet what but
the spirit of the Evil One could have prompted the old
lady to make those embarrassing innuendoes ? She must
have seen Georgie go by, so the visit was deliberately
planned. Marry Georgie Smithers! That was obviously
what she had insinuated. Why, he had only seen the
girl twice, and . . . How utterly ridiculous ! Yet if
that dreadful old woman started a chain of gossip, it
would be hard on the girl, and perhaps harder still on
him. . . .

He pondered possible courses of action. Obviously,

he had made a petty but regrettable mistake. The thing
to do was to meet the Smithers as if nothing had happened, and treat them just as any other parishioners.
Yet there was bound to be embarrassment. . . . His
mind wandered off to Mrs. Eastcourt. She was certainly
a living refutation of the theory that one must necessarily
love what one was most interested in. Plainly, Mrs.
Eastcourt was intensely interested in other people and
their doings—how otherwise explain her almost super-
natural insight into their feelings ? But why use that
solely to hurt and make mischief ? Why was such paltry
malevolence hidden under that dear old lady exterior ?
Perhaps Mrs. Eastcourt's intense craving for gossip and
mischief-making was like the drunkard's craving for
alcohol—the better side of him would loath it, but the
craving was irresistible. A gossip-drunkard, intoxica-
tion with sly wounding words and the spreading of false
scandal ! But why ? What secret humiliations and
wrongs was Mrs. Eastcourt avenging on the innocent ?
He felt that could only be known to God—ignoring the
far more probable clues of Mrs. Eastcourt's parents and
husband. What a mystery is God's Providence ! The
Vicar sighed, and returned to his *Spectator*.

Georgie walked home quickly through the rain,
entered the house by the back door and went straight to
her room. Without taking off her hat and oilskins, she
threw herself on the bed and cried. The tears trickled
through her fingers on to the pillow. Presently she felt
better, and wondered what she was crying for. It was
very disgraceful to cry. Especially about nothing. She
bathed her face carefully in ice-cold water, but it still
looked a bit puffy. Fortunately the Smithers had only

oil lamps and were not very observant. She helped
Coz with his evening cross-word puzzle, and went to
bed early.

VI

For the next two or three weeks Mrs. Eastcourt had
a most delightful time, calling on everybody to discuss
what she called ' this disgraceful behaviour ' of Georgie
and the Vicar. Her fecund imagination, which would
have been a priceless asset to a yellow journalist, composed an almost horrific scandal from the very simple
and innocent facts. She varied her relation and com-
ments to suit her audience of the moment, and her lies
were gobbled up by most of them with depressing
alacrity. She usually began by praising her own public
spirit, virtue and ' neighbourliness ', with divagations on
the degeneracy of the age as compared with the spiritual
perfections of the 1880's. As a rule this exordium was
coldly received—people knew Mrs. Eastcourt and had
not been adults in 1880. She then won assent by remarking on the necessity for ' decent behaviour ' in
young women and in old widowers, especially parsons.
She said that Georgie had begun gadding after men
—' so dreadful for her poor parents, I think I must
warn them '—and had set her cap at the new Vicar.
What was one to think of a girl who did that sort of
thing openly in the midst of a decent and neighbourly
Christian parish ? But worse was to come. The dreadful old man, though twice a widower, had spotted this
at once, and taking advantage of the girl had decoyed
her away on a dark rainy evening when he thought
nobody would be about. What might have happened

Heaven only knew, but prompted by her spirit of neighbourliness and by a sense of impending evil (sent no
doubt by Providence itself) Mrs. Eastcourt had felt herself irresistibly urged to go to the Vicarage. Although
her entrance had been violently opposed, she had forced
her way in from a strong sense of duty, and had found
' the couple ' in a most *compromising* situation. No,
she could not describe what she saw. She did not
think a woman should speak of such things, especially
in front of Her Own Son (here Martin's cue was to
titter agreeably), but she *hoped*—mind, she wouldn't be
positive—that her providential entry had prevented the
WORST !

The only person with sufficient courage to say ' Nonsense, Mrs. Eastcourt ' was Margy Stuart, but Mrs.
Eastcourt got back at her with a number of proverbial
dark insinuations about fellow feelings, and pots and
kettles.

Mrs. Eastcourt even called on Mr. Purfleet, whom she
detested and who regarded her as a most lamentable
specimen of lovely woman gone sour and mothery. She
found him having tea with Doctor McCall, a Scotchman
who doubled the usual cynicism of a medical student
with that of a battalion doctor. He cultivated a good
bedside manner, and was more liked by the *châtelaines*
of the district than by the panel patients. It would be
ungenerous to suggest that he more than did his bit
towards solving the problems of unemployment and
over-population, but he did not strive too officiously in
the opposite direction. Purfleet and McCall listened
very coldly to Mrs. Eastcourt's hints that ' something
ought to be done ' about the Vicar and Miss Smithers,
and that they were the people to do it. After a very

sharp contest with Mr. Purfleet, in which honours were about even, she departed, rather disgruntled.

Purfleet came back from the front door, after speeding the unwanted guest, and produced for himself and the doctor the whisky and soda he had carefully hidden from Mrs. Eastcourt. Mr. Purfleet pressed the handle of the siphon with a certain amount of heat, engendered by his recent contest. The soda-water splashed on his hand and the table.

'Damn! What a preposterous old bitch that woman is.'

' Not too much soda. Thanks. She rather amuses me. What a detective the old bird is ! Superb malice. How she enjoyed tracking down the unfortunate Carrington and his little bit of stuff ! '

' You don't think there 's any truth in her pernicious gabble, do you ? '

' I don't know. Smoke and fire, you know. Why shouldn't it be true ? So far as my professional experience goes, there isn't a virgin over sixteen in the working class of this district.'

'Working classes. Very possibly. They have a different code from us middle class. They 're nearly as emancipated as Mayfair is supposed to be. But they 're rather fornicators than adulterers. When a girl 's in the family way, all the possible fathers toss up as to who shall marry the girl. Not a bad plan. If they 're all married men, of course the girl loses her reputation.'

McCall wagged his head slightly as he filled a pipe.

' Yes, it 's not unlike that. But I wouldn't be so sure about the adulteries. Divorce is expensive, and they usually settle those little problems in a rough and ready way.'

' But that doesn't apply to the stuffy upper middle

class, especially when they 're poor. I 've only seen
Carrington twice, but he struck me as a very decent
type of parson. Bit stupid—that 's what he 's there
for—but quite honest. As for Georgie Smithers, I 'm
damned sorry for the girl. I saw her the other day
walking down the road ahead of me, with her fine figure
and cross-country stride. . . .'

' Running off to meet the parson, as our amiable old
viper suggested ? '

' Not a bit of it. But there 's something pathetic
about that girl. She 's not pretty, and she certainly
wouldn't suit *me*, but she 'd make a decent wife and
mother. She 'd be loyal and grateful to any man who
treated her decently—most women are. There she is,
absolutely ripe for a man and children, kept away from
the essential experience of her life by blarney and social
imbecilities. What 'll happen to her ? The ripeness
will go rotten, then wither. She 'll turn into a sour old
maid, and poison the world about her with spite, like
the old bitch-pussy who 's just been here.'

' But do you mean to suggest that she get herself a
bastard ? '

' I think she 's right to live up to her code—it can't
be any too easy—but I don't think the code ought to be
imposed on her and her like. It 's a rotten situation,
McCall. Here 's a thoroughly healthy, decent girl, who
wants comfort and comfort's sequel, a baby. You 've
only got to look at her to see it. Is there anything more
natural and reasonable in a young woman ? She isn't
of the kind that thoughtfully keep french letters in their
hand-bags. She 's a family woman.'

' I 'm afraid it 's a thin look-out for your Georgie.
Statisticians, those lords of jugglery, inform us that there

are at least two million more females than males in these
islands.   Add to that, the tens and scores of thousands
of unmarried women with small incomes who live abroad
in cheaper lands, and hunt sheiks in every tourist resort
of Europe. . . . Georgie's generation is short by a
million men.   Who's going to marry her ?   There isn't
anybody of her class to marry her.'

Purfleet leaned forward and slapped his knee.

' Precisely !   The girls of her generation are in an
almost hopeless position, if they want husbands.   The
working class seem to manage it somehow, but they're
far less inhuman than we are.   No one interferes with
them.   If they have a kid, well, it's bad luck, but they
don't throw bricks.   But Georgie Smithers hasn't a
chance to meet a man in a place like this.   If she did,
she'd be hunted to misery, disgrace and possibly death.'

' Well, what do you propose to do about it ? '

' Damn it, man, I can't do anything.   I wish I could.
I think a healthy girl like Georgie should have at least
a couple of kids.   They mightn't be very pretty, but
they'd be healthy enough, and she'd look after them.
Why, damn it, she ought to be paid and get a medal
for having them.   It would be some set-off against the
miserable hordes of slum children and Roman Catholic
families fifteen-strong and all ailing.   Georgie's a
eugenic proposition.   The rotten thing is—if she had
two thousand a year, there'd be a buzz of young blighters
round her who'd give her what she needs in exchange
for being kept.   Bah ! '

McCall began to laugh.

' If only you could see—how funny you look—raving
like that about the woes of the universe and Georgie
Smithers !   Man, you've no sense of humour.'

For a moment Mr. Purfleet looked extremely angry, then he began to laugh too, though less extravagantly.

' I recognise,' he said, ' that humour is almost entirely confined to the Scots. But you, as a Scot, are naturally deficient of patriotism.'

McCall protested that patriotism was entirely a Scottish virtue, exported to England along with all other virtues in the train of James VI. The Scots, he implied, had organised a futile and backward nation into a great imperial race. But Mr. Purfleet stood firm.

' I said patriotism, not nationalism, McCall. The sentiment of Scotland *über alles* arouses no admiration in me. When I say patriotism I mean patriotism and not nationalism. Patriotism is a lively sense of collective responsibility. Nationalism is a silly cock crowing on its own dunghill and calling for larger spurs and brighter beaks. I fear that nationalism is one of England's many spurious gifts to the world.'

' Ye can't have the one without the other,' said McCall, unconsciously stressing his northern accent. ' If a man has a sense of collective responsibility he 's bound to stand by his country right or wrong. You can't change human nature. As long as it 's what it is, there 'll be wars ; and as long as there 's wars men 'll fight.'

Mr. Purfleet clasped his brows energetically.

' It occurs to me that I 've heard something like this before, McCall. But I can't refute half a dozen errors in one breath. What the devil is " human nature " ? It 's just as much " human nature " to refrain from fighting as to fight. You 'll soon tell me I 'm fouling my own nest, and I shall retort that it 's foul enough without any assistance from me.'

' Very true, but what 's your argument got to do with Georgie Smithers and her unsatisfied longings ?   Have you got to drag in the European War to prove the pathos of another old maid ? '

Mr. Purfleet sighed.

' You 're a good fellow, McCall, but the very devil to converse with.   You start a hare with every sentence, and don't hunt down one of them.'   He paused a moment. ' I believe it was Thucydides who first made the dangerous discovery that states could be personified as " shes " and " hers "—suspicious and embattled females.   My simple proposal is loyalty to the human race, instead of loyalty to an imaginary entity called " England " or " Britannia ", complete with helmet and trident.   I feel more concern about Georgie Smithers, who is a real woman with a real wrong in life, than about an effigy of one of Charles the Second's mistresses.'

' What about Charles the Second's mistresses ? ' enquired McCall eagerly, as one hoping for the revelation of unsuspected scandal.

' Oh, nothing,' replied Purfleet impatiently.   ' A Miss Stuart sat for the effigy of Britannia—I don't even know for certain that she seduced the virtue of Charles Rex. Anyhow Britannia is loaded with laurels, but all the Georgies are dull, discontented and unhappy.'

McCall shook his head cynically :

' The Dominions are independent, South Africa is hostile, Ireland has gone, Egypt is going, India will soon go.   We 've lost our trade supremacy—look at the unemployment.   The British Empire 's done for.'

' And then ?   May I ask why Tooting Bec and Pudthorp should export their sons to tell Allahabad, Cairo and Nairobi what they are to do, think and be ?   And may I enquire, doctor McCall, how much trade supremacy you personally have enjoyed ? When you were a sawbones in France, Britannia graciously allowed you fifteen and a kick a day, plus field allowances, to bind up the wounds of Her Gallant Sons fighting on a couple of daily tanners. Don't interrupt me ! I know what you are going to say—they fought not for money, but from patriotism, sense of duty, love of country. Two minutes' silence ! *You* and the other millions did "your duty". Result: the extinction of a generation of men, the misery of their women, an utterly senseless " Peace ", and the enrichment of noble-hearted men like our old pal Stimms.'

'Well, but I *do* benefit ! ' said McCall. ' Stimms pays me well and promptly for attending to his wife— who, by the way, hasn't much the matter with her.'

' I 'm ashamed of you. Aren't *you* ashamed to be sycophant and parasite to a Stimms ? Where 's your Scotch pride ? Sold it with your King and grouse moor, I suppose. But all this money value is wrong. I only employed the financial argument to bring home the truth to your hard Scotch head. The true wealth of a country lies in its men and women. If they 're mean, unhappy and ill, it doesn't matter how " rich " Sir Horace is—the country is poor.'

McCall yawned and knocked the ashes from his pipe.

' Well, I must be getting off. Yes, by Jove ! It 's nearly seven. I like to hear you talk, Purfleet, not as much as you like to hear yourself talk, of course, but quite a lot. I don't agree with you, but it gives me the illusion that life 's worth thinking about. My own view is that it 's all a mistake, and the sooner we collide with that wandering star the better. Life 's evil.'

'Pooh!' said Purfleet. 'Mere Manicheeism. A heresy out of date fifteen centuries ago. We've got a moment of consciousness in an eternity of the opposite. A little common sense, goodwill and a tiny dose of unselfishness could make this goodly earth into an earthly paradise for us and our successors. There are two sorts of traitors to humanity I particularly dislike. The first are the smug bastards who declare that all is for the best in this best of all possible worlds and pray that our unexampled prosperity may last. The second are the peeving cynics like you, who say nothing's worth while, human nature'll never change, the sooner it's all over the better. I wish you'd all shoot yourselves with a bang, instead of continuing to whimper.'

McCall laughed.

' If you were up for a medical examination of your sanity, Purfleet, I doubt you'd get a clean bill if you talked as you have this evening.'

' Probably not. But I've not yet offended any millionaire sufficiently to be clapped into a lunatic asylum. If I ever do, I'll call on you to vouch for my sanity.'

McCall shook his head, with a smile.

' It'd ruin my professional reputation. Well, we've settled the affairs of England and the universe as usual. Now it's time for roast beef and potatoes, bought for you, my boy, by the Welsh mines and the Lancashire looms.'

' I know it, but it might be better to have bread and cheese off our own fields.'

' But we don't seem to have solved the Georgie Smithers problem, do we ? '

' Georgie's merely one of the victims of the whole mess. She's an oblation on the diabolical altar of Stimmsdom. In an over-populated country superfluous

women have a hell of a life.   The involuntary old maid
is a piteous spectacle.   I 'm all in favour of their indulging in non-fertile copulation.   They can't all have kids
—there are too many anyway.   But if Sir Horace gets
Georgie's possible husbands killed, or exiled to look after
his commercial interests in our far-flung Empire, then I
think that Georgie should diddle Sir Horace by having
a lover, several if she wants them and can get them.
Why have legions of tarts to preserve for Georgie an
imaginary virtue she doesn't want ? '

' I 'm going,' said McCall.   ' You 're the most immoral fellow I ever met.   I should lose half my practice
if it were known that I listened to such sentiments without throwing you through the window.'

Purfleet grinned.

' Good old broad-cloth and bowler !   Chaps like you
are rotten moral cowards.   You 'd lick any spittle for
what you call your living.   In your heart of hearts you
jolly well know I 'm right, even if I do cackle too much
like an old goose.   But you 're afraid to admit it.   And
certainly too funky and apathetic to try to do anything
about it.'

They had walked out to the garden gate, where
McCall's car stood by the roadside.   It was a clear
frosty night.   Purfleet pointed up at the stars.

' They make our mighty intelligences and blazing
ideas look a bit foolish, don't they ? '

McCall was fiddling with the starting apparatus.   The
car was cold and reluctant to start.

' Eh ? '

' Oh nothing.   Farewell, Sir Doubting Do-Nothing.
Good luck to the poison and scalpel game.   I 'm going
in.   Jove, isn't it cold ! '

The engine started with a sudden roar. McCall shouted :

' Cheer-o.   See you again one of these days.'

Purfleet ran into the house, and stood warming himself by the large fire.   Presently he rang the bell, and his man-servant, an ex-batman, came in.

' What have we got for dinner to-night, Curzon ? '

' Soup, Sir, bit of grilled cod, chicken, and sweet.'

' Chicken ?   All right, serve as soon as you 're ready, and warm half a bottle of burgundy, the 1911 Chambertin.'

' Very good, Sir.'

Mr. Purfleet sat for a few minutes by the fire, lost in thought, and filled with optimistic hopes for humanity. He checked himself with the salutary but unwelcome thought that it was possibly easier to be an optimist on chicken and burgundy than on bread and margarine and weak cocoa.   He ate, however, with his usual appetite and critical appreciation.

PART II

PART II

I

O^N fine Sunday mornings, when it was not too cold, Mr. Tom Judd took a short, dignified walk. If it was still fine and warm after tea, Mr. Judd again walked out, with Mrs. Judd and the children ; but the morning was sacred to male dignity and the preparation of dinner by womankind. When Sunday morning was cold or wet, Mr. Judd remained in bed with a dignity peculiar to himself.

Mr. Judd rarely attended Church and never Chapel. The Chapelites, he understood, were no friends to beer, while Mr. Judd, in this alone resembling Boswell, liked to promote a friendly glass. But no one, not even his spiritual pastors and material masters, had ever dared to enquire into the state of Mr. Judd's religious views. There was a dignity in Mr. Judd, an air of more than Emersonian self-reliance, which forbade intrusion and familiarity. Even recruiting tribunals had been impressed, and throughout the War he had remained indispensable. This exemption from military brutality confirmed Mr. Judd's dignity and increased the clarity and coolness of his judgment, whereas less fortunate men were liable to run off the rails amid explosions of just, but unfortunately ineffective, anger.

In appearance Mr. Judd resembled an upright, cleanly and intelligent porker. It is impossible to say whether this was a protective disguise, hastily assumed by the family on Darwinian principles of adaptation to environment, or whether Mr. Judd's Saxon ancestors by long

habitation among pigs had become piggy.   He was at
any rate an unmistakable Nordic blond.   His bristly
gold hair was cut short, his blue eyes gleamed with
the baresark intelligence of the Northmen, and a line
drawn perpendicular to the tip of his turned-up nose
would have plunged some distance into his good round·
belly.

The secret of Mr. Judd's consequence is easily explained.   He was chief foreman and rather more than
half the brains of the small factory at Cleeve.   Without
him or someone like him the whole concern would have
gone phut ;   and it is most unlikely that anyone else
would have displayed so much calm efficiency and responsibility for three pounds a week and a ten pound
bonus at Christmas.   Mr. Judd was on the production
side, and was an optimist.   The rest of the brains of the
establishment was supplied by his clerkly friend, Mr.
Raper, a bitter pessimist struggling gamely against an
annual decline in revenue.   Mr. Judd was not interested in accounts—his job was to produce the goods ;
Mr. Raper was not interested in production—his job was
to balance his books and perform the superhuman feat
of showing a profit.   But together this rustic Gog and
Magog propped up a staggering concern, while the
nominal owner fussed about in a car and performed
upper-class Tartarin feats with Sir Horace Stimms.   A
fair and gentlemanly division of labour.

By some unwritten and unspoken convention Mr.
Judd almost invariably met Mr. Raper on these Sunday
morning parades, and they would walk together in grave
converse.   Like Dons and Regular officers, they never
talked shop on these occasions, but devoted the morning
to mental and moral improvement.   Thus, on a Sunday

in late April, they walked together on the recently-tarred road from Cleeve to Maryhampton, undeterred by the Sabbath cars which turn the country lanes into miniature Piccadillys. Mr. Raper wore his working clothes of threadbare black. He was so scared by the state of his accounts that he dared not spend his own money. His thin, anxious freckled face was seared by a straight though ragged moustache, which at some period must have performed a miracle of twin parthenogenesis, for two smaller but exactly similar strips of hair fringed the upper rims of his spectacles. He walked with his pale freckled hands clasped nervously behind him, an anxious Napoleon of rural industry. Mr. Judd, on the contrary, was clad like Solomon in his glory. He wore a splendid suit of rich brown reach-me-downs with a distinct lavender stripe, a pair of glorious tan boots which proclaimed rather than squeaked his approach, a brown felt hat one size too large, an imitation malacca cane with a false agate handle, and a briar pipe with an extravagant display of pseudo-amber mouthpiece. A large, possibly gold, chain was draped across the swelling curves of his waistcoat, and displayed to an impressed and astonished world two alberts and a Queen Victoria sovereign fantastically secured in a baroque setting.

For a while they walked in silence, Mr. Judd admiring his own splendour and the beauties of spring, Mr. Raper plunged in gloomy arithmetic. They watched with interest the honking impatience of a Ford-load of London gentry involved in the scared plunging of a herd of cows, which were being driven to pasture by a muddy-booted cowherd on a motor-bicycle. When this little episode was over, Mr. Judd took a deep breath of sweet country air (ignoring the petrol) and remarked :

' I see be the papers there's bin another 'orrible murder, Mr. Raper.'

' You mean the one where the wife made the young feller lay in wait for the 'usband be'ind the kitchen door and murder 'im with a bay'net ? '

Mr. Judd nodded with great seriousness.

' I dunno what the country's comin' to. That's the third 'orrible murder we've 'ad this year.'

' Fourth, Mr. Judd. There was the chicken-coop murder, and the race-gang slashin' murder, and then the p'liceman.'

' Oh, ah,' said Mr. Judd, puffing at his pipe with deep enjoyment. ' I was f'gettin' the p'liceman. See. Wasn't that the Anarchist murder in Whitechapel ? '

' No, Mr. Judd, that was jest before Christmas. The p'liceman I mean was in February. You *must* remember. They found 'im lyin' by the roadside out Epsom way, and Scotland Yard 'aven't found the right clue yet.'

' Now fancy me forgettin' that ! ' said Mr. Judd with cool placidity. ' Took a great interest in that murder, I did. You know I got a cousin in the force ? '

' Yes,' replied Mr. Raper a little impatiently, for he had been informed of this interesting fact on nearly every fine Sunday for fifteen years. ' It's gettin' a pretty state of affairs when the 'ole p'lice force of the country can't protect one of their own men, and can't even find the murderer. It wouldn't surprise me, Mr. Judd, if that murderer wasn't bein' protected in 'igh places ! '

Mr. Judd started slightly as a large Daimler whizzed by him rather close, and gazed apprehensively across the placid fields with their rich spring grass and grazing cattle and criss-cross lines of elms, poplars and willows.

' Reelly, Mr. Raper ? '

' Yes, Mr. Judd. The other day Sir 'Orace was in the office with the boss, and I 'eard 'im say : " The interests of the Country are at stake," 'e said, " and if you knew what goes on be'ind the scenes in Parl'ment, you'd think so too," 'e said. It's my belief, Mr. Judd, that there's a foreign plot—them Germans and Bolshies —and some of our own flesh and blood's in it.'

Mr. Judd's very boots groaned apprehension and patriotic grief. But he shook his head.

' No, Mr. Raper, I can't believe that of the Country. Things may be bad, but they aren't as bad as that. But it be'ooves us all to keep a sharp look-out. My own belief is that the constable was the victim of a feud.'

' What feud ? ' said Mr. Raper, a little disgruntled.

' The p'lice,' said Mr. Judd with terrific emphasis, ' are a divided force ! My cousin over to 'Opton . . .'

' But what are they divided about ? '

' Ah ! ' Mr. Judd shook his head again. ' That's tellin', Mr. Raper. My cousin couldn't and wouldn't give me no details, but " mark my words," 'e said, " the p'lice are a divided force." That's why they can't make no arrests—there's one working against another.'

' Well,' retorted Mr. Raper, who grudged his colleague the glory of a relative in the force. ' We can't expect no better, considerin' the kind of men they employ. But all the same they caught them two in the 'usband murder.'

Mr. Judd made no reply, but breathed heavily into his pipe stem.

' I shouldn't be surprised,' Mr. Raper went on, ' if the woman got off. Of course, men like you an' me, Mr. Judd, we know 'e wouldn't 'ave done it but for 'er. But it's against the 'igher instincts of the Country to 'ang a woman.'

Mr. Judd was so much moved that he halted, and gazed at Mr. Raper with deep concern.

' Let 'er off ! Why, she 's just as guilty as the blackguard what ruined that 'ome. Now, mark my words, Mr. Raper, if that woman gets off, there ain't a married man among us 'll rest safe in 'is bed ! '

And with this tremendous tribute to the otherwise unsuspected Borgia tendencies of Mrs. Judd he resumed the walk, darkly oracular.

The end of these morning excursions had been immutably fixed by Mr. Judd at a bridge over a small stream about fifty yards beyond a sharp turn in the road. In Mr. Judd's childhood this bridge was a sixteenth-century stone affair resting in the middle on a large diamond-shaped pile. On each side there had been a triangular recess in the upper wall, where it was pleasant to sit on summer evenings when the old mossy and lichened stones were still warm from the sun. In those days pike and large perch hung about in the deep green shadows under the bridge, and there were chub in the pool farther down. The summer water slipped gently past, and you could watch the Mayflies perpetually hovering over the surface, and hear the sudden watery ' suck ! ' as a chub gulped down an unlucky one. The swallows skimmed up and down, sometimes whipping under the bridge in a sudden dash of flight. Mr. Judd knew the place well. It had been the scene of his youthful fishing exploits (no preserving in those days) and was now used by him for maturer contemplation. Unluckily, the new stream of motors had swept away the old bridge, which was perfectly solid ; and one, Mr. Gould, jerry-builder and contractor, had supplied in its place a clumsy steel bridge resting on concrete. This work was erected so unskilfully that it was constantly going wrong, and cost annually as much as would have been needed to strengthen and repair the old bridge for ten years.

Mr. Judd regretted the loss of his bridge, but he bowed to the onward march of science and transport. He still had one consolation left in four magnificent elms, which in thirty years seemed scarcely to have changed, except to grow more majestic and spreading, more solidly indifferent to the tearing winter gales. Mr. Judd loved his elms. They were not ' his ' in the sense that he could dispose of them, but they were his because he understood and loved and enjoyed them from the first pointed buds to the last leaf of autumn. Even in winter he liked to hear them strain against a high wind or to see their enormous pattern of boughs and twigs sharply outlined against a frosty sky. Mr. Judd was only one generation removed from the land, which he sometimes regretted. Trees, and especially ' his ' elms, were his consolation for that divorce.

On setting out that morning Mr. Judd had reckoned that the first leaves would be on the elms, and looked forward to a pipe and chat with Mr. Raper under their green-gold flickerings. Absorbed in his public-spirited reflections on the lamentable spread of crime, Mr. Judd had forgotten the elms. Suddenly he halted.

' What 's happened to the elms ? Where are they ? ' There was anguish in his voice. Mr. Raper, who was totally indifferent to the spectacle of Nature, replied phlegmatically.

' Cut down by order of the Council. There 's been trouble with the bridge agen, and Mr. Gould 'e told the Council the roots was disturbin' the concrete foundations, and the drip was ruinin' the road.'

Mr. Judd gazed at the ruin now revealed to his eyes. Four tremendous stumps, each large enough to make a table, were rawly visible at ground level. The great trees had crashed to earth, splintering twigs and branches with the force of their fall, and the young leaves were already withering. Mr. Judd felt confusedly as if part of his life had been massacred.

' D'you mean to say that feller Gould got my elms cut down ? I lay a penny 'e 's gettin' 'em dirt cheap for 'is own use. Damn 'im ! '

Mr. Judd swore so seldom, abandoned his dignity so rarely, that Mr. Raper was amazed at this display of feeling. He was also shocked.

' Well,' he said with slightly exultant pessimism. ' What d'you expect with a Council like ours ? There 's two of Gould's relations on the Board, and 'arf the others are in with 'im. I reckon 'e 's 'ad his eyes on them trees for a long while. Nice bits o' timber they are.'

' You can't do nothin' much with elm, 'cept coffins,' replied Mr. Judd sadly. ' It 's murder, Mr. Raper, that 's what it is, sheer murder. A bad day for us it was when Gould went into undertakin'.'

' We got to consider the transport needs of the Country first, Mr. Judd. That 's what the boss said to me. 'E reckons they 'll 'ave to 'ave all the trees down along all the roads of England, and the sooner the better, 'e says, with all the taxes to keep up the roads. Sweep 'em all away, 'e says, and make the nation's roads safe for the nation's motorists what pays for 'em.'

Mr. Judd returned his extinct pipe to a mouth which had hung open in dismay. He turned abruptly on his heel, followed by Mr. Raper, who was still at a loss to understand his colleague's emotion. Mr. Judd

babbled angrily to himself : ' Cutting down the bridge
elms—bin 'ere man an' boy thirty-three years come
Michaelmas—who 's Mr. Gould, I 'd like to know ?—
workus brat stole 'is gov'ner's business—drive all the
way to Cricton under the trees, you could, when I was
a boy.'

They turned up the long slope leading to Cleeve, and
Mr. Judd had to move with more smartness than dignity
to avoid a motor-cyclist and fair pillion-rider who came
round the corner full tilt on the wrong side of the road.
Mr. Judd turned his anger on the motor-cyclists, who
were disappearing in a series of explosions like the firing
of a French 75.

' Young varmints ! Gallivantin' about the roads when
they ought to be 'ome 'elpin' their Mas with Sunday
dinner ! They ought to be put a stop to.'

' That there pillion-ridin',' said Mr. Raper, ' is a
national danger an' is lowerin' the prestige of our women
in the eyes of foreign nations. Showin' off their legs
from Land's End to John o' Groat's. I don't wonder it
took that long to win the War, Mr. Judd.'

Mr. Judd grunted, as one slightly unwilling to admit
a chain of abstruse and abstract reasoning. He lighted
his pipe, and reassumed his air of solid dignity. But
Fate, seldom content with sending one misfortune, was
preparing another and more intimate shock for him.

A figure waddling towards them now definitely took
the shape of Colonel Smithers, keepin fit by marching
down the hill and marching slowly up again. Mr. Judd's
Lizzie was kitchen-maid to the Smithers. Alvina, like
many another of the world's teachers, was ' training '
Lizzie in an art she had imperfectly mastered herself—
household management. But Mr. Judd felt for Colonel

Smithers that ' considerable respect ' which our eminent
naturalised critic, Mr. T. S. Pym, feels for a very few
select native authors.   He—Mr. Judd—knew the real
gentry when he saw them.

As they drew level with the Colonel, the two men
raised their hats.   That is to say, they swung up their
arms as if about to make Court bows, grasped their hat-
brims firmly and then, as if afflicted with sudden para-
lysis, tilted their hats slightly upwards and dropped them
back in sheepish haste.   The Colonel acknowledged this
by touching the front of his hat with the first two fingers
of his right hand, holding the other two and the thumb
at an angle of forty-five degrees—a salute worthy of a
Corps Commander.

' Fine mornin, Mr. Judd.'

The Colonel considered Mr. Judd as somehow senior
to Mr. Raper.

' Mornin', Sir.   Lovely weather, Sir.'

The Colonel passed on.   His appearance peremptorily
reminded Mr. Raper of a difficult and delicate embassy
not yet discharged.   He glanced at Mr. Judd, coughed,
and looked uncomfortable.   Mr. Judd appeared to have
recovered his serenity entirely, and was gazing benevolently at a very forward cow which was vainly endeavouring to secure the attentions of a remarkably sullen and
indifferent bull.   Mr. Raper coughed again ; and led
up to the subject obliquely and diplomatically.

' You didn't know them elms was cut down ? '

' No,' replied Mr. Judd shortly.   He did not want to
be reminded of the elms.

' It 's a rum thing,' said Mr. Raper in a tone of
dreamy philosophical speculation, ' as 'ow things is
always goin' on all over the world as we don't know

nothing about. Fr'instance, take the 'Mericans. We
don't know nothin' about what they 're doin' now.'

' 'Avin' breakfast, I expect,' said Mr. Judd realistically. ' Their time 's be'ind ours.'

' Wonderful trees they 'ave out there,' pursued Mr.
Raper, who was sweating slightly from the violent
mental efforts he was making. ' I often stop to 'ave a
look at them tin advertisements of California Big Tree
Claret—you know, where they 're drivin' a coach an'
'orses through the 'ole in the tree. I reckon that must
be the biggest tree in the world.'

' You can take it from me, Mr. Raper,' said Mr. Judd
firmly, ' that 's jest a bit of 'Merican brag and bounce.
They 're jealous of the Old Country, Mr. Raper, jest as
much as if they was real foreigners, instead of bein' 'arf
English. What 's a picture ? Anybody can make a
picture. We could make a picture of the factory as big
as Buckin'am Palace an' the Zoo all in one. Now, if
the 'Mericans was to send us one of them trees, coach an'
'orses an' all, we might believe 'em. Depend upon it,
Mr. Raper, there 's no trees in the world like English
trees.'

Mr. Judd, who had crossed the boundaries of his
native county on only four occasions, spoke with the
authority of a jaded globe-trotter. Mr. Raper felt that
he was getting farther away from his embassy instead of
nearer to it. He plunged.

' An' it 's a rum thing,' he went on, gloomily pessi-
mistic in manner, ' 'ow things can go on under a man's
own nose, an' 'im not see nothing.'

' Yes ? ' said Mr. Judd doubtfully. ' I suppose there
are fellers like that. No natchral gift of hobservation,
as you might say.'

'Fr'instance'—Mr. Raper was now sweating profusely, 'there's you an' your Lizzie.'

'Why, what about 'er?' Mr. Judd glanced sharply at his companion but failed, for all his implied natural gifts of observation, to notice Mr. Raper's embarrassment.

'She ain't bin well, 'as she?'

'Indigestion,' said Mr. Judd firmly. 'Too much rich food. Bolts it like a 'ungry orphan, as you might say. Consequence is, as I 've bin tellin' 'er, she gets these swellin's of the bowels and can't keep 'er meals down. Dose o' castor oil an' not be so greedy—that 'll put 'er right.'

'But s'posin' it wasn't indigestion?'

Mr. Judd looked mildly astonished.

'What else could it be?'

''Er an' your Missus went up to see the doctor about it yesterday.'

'Ho! Did they!' said Mr. Judd indignantly. 'Wastin' money on doctor's jollop, without tellin' me nothin' about it. Umph!'

'It ain't indigestion,' said Mr. Raper coyly.

'What is it, then?' Mr. Judd was becoming bewildered by these mysterious hints. But Mr. Raper went off on a side track.

'I see Mrs. Judd last night, and she asked me to tell you. She an' Lizzie 's afraid to tell you theirselves, and she 's afraid you might turn 'er out o' doors.'

'Turn 'oo out o' doors?' Mr. Judd's bewilderment was turning to amazement and indignation.

'Lizzie.'

'Turn my own daughter out o' doors! I 'm surprised to 'ear such a' idea comin' from a man with children of 'is own! Turn Lizzie out! I wouldn't do it for a king's ransom, Mr. Raper.'

'You're quite sure, Mr. Judd, that you wouldn't never turn 'er out, no matter what 'appened?'

Mr. Judd raised his hand, as if to take a mighty and solemn oath, but a sudden suspicion flashed into his bewildered mind.

'She ain't been giving Mrs. Smithers any of 'er lip and got the sack?'

'No,' said Mr. Raper judicially, 'I don't know that she 'as. But, mind you, I wouldn't swear that she mightn't lose 'er job.'

Mr. Judd looked a little scared and puffed heavily at his pipe.

'You're not going to tell me, Mr. Raper, as a child of mine is a—a *thief*?'

He got the word out with difficulty. Mr. Raper looked shocked and distressed.

'No, Mr. Judd, no, no. Lizzie wouldn't do nothing like *that*. But what would you say if she was goin' to 'ave a baby?'

Mr. Judd stopped dead, and removed his pipe.

'Goin' to 'ave a *baby*?'

'Yes, goin' to 'ave a baby.'

'Lizzie?'

'Yes, Mr. Judd.'

For about half a minute Mr. Judd contemplated the handsome amber mouthpiece of his pipe with unseeing eyes. This appeared to give him an idea, and he put the pipe in his mouth. He took about a dozen long pulls, and with each pull consternation and surprise seemed to yield to serenity. He walked on in silence for about twenty yards, with the now super-agitated Mr.

Raper at his elbow. Finally, Mr. Judd delivered his sentence with oracular calm.

' Well, 'e 'll 'ave to marry 'er, that 's all.'

Mr. Raper sweated even more profusely. He blurted out :

' But 'e can't marry 'er.'

' Why not ? '

' Because 'e 's a married man with three children ! '

Under this new blow Mr. Judd reeled, at any rate mentally. His outward self continued to smoke and walk with a steady dignified tread, but he uttered not a word. Mr. Raper walked beside him, with anxious glances. Outside the small wooden gate leading to his own cottage, Mr. Raper halted, and his friend stopped mechanically, still sunk in a profound and apparently painful reverie. Mr. Raper tried an appeal.

' You 'll stand by 'er, Mr. Judd, won't you ? You won't turn 'er out ? '

Mr. Judd ignored this remark. Indeed, he seemed not to have heard it. Suddenly he struck the asphalt with his malacca cane.

' What I can't get over is 'ow a daughter of mine could 'a bin so stoopid as not to know what 'ad 'appened to 'er. Indigestion be blowed ! '

And he strode off, leaving Mr. Raper gazing after him in unmitigated astonishment.

II

If avidity for public discussion had been Miss Judd's motive for her illicit amour, she chose well. In the next few days she was nearly as much talked about as if she had been violently done to death or had committed arson or violated the King's Mails or inherited a fortune from a rich uncle in New Zealand or had suddenly been proved a *lusus naturae*, a village Salmasis, a two-headed pig or a maid all hairy. Only such extraordinary and inhuman feats could have obtained her more publicity than the rumour that she was about to become a mother without the kind permission of either the civil or ecclesiastical authorities.

Whom man hath joined together let no god put asunder.

Nothing could show more clearly the avidity for life, the poetic passion for stripping the veil of familiarity from common things, which was so eminently characteristic of the inhabitants of these three parishes, than their passionate interest in this comparatively normal pregnancy. The casual outsider, corroded by the modern spirit of scepticism and cynical indifference (that favourite tit-bit in the cheap daily-maily denunciations of Roman Catholic prelates)—this *blasé* worldling might have felt some surprise at the interminable chit-chat evoked by an event so common, so natural, so well-nigh universal, whereof examples may be found in the remotest abysses of historical time.

Mr. Raper tattled it to Mrs. Raper ; Mrs. Raper tattled it to Mrs. Attwood (who had to do washing because Mr. Attwood was frequently, in both senses of the phrase, prone to the bottle) ; Mrs. Attwood tattled it to the Postmaster's wife, who confided it under the seal of secrecy to the Postmaster, who at once ran out to tell the Postman, who delivered it everywhere along with the letters.

Mrs. Eastcourt heard it before anyone else, either from the mysterious goddess Rumour of Virgil (*snobbice* 'Vergil'), or from some Grimalkin, some affable familiar sprite, whose services may be purchased by a blood-written and terrifying contract with the Prince of Dark-ness—always with the hope, of course, that its validity may be denied by the Judicial Committee of the Privy Council of Jehovah Augustus and Jesus Caesar.

Nor would the impartial enquirer assert that this interest was wholly due to the spirit of loving kindness and generous delight that one more female had success-fully begun those amiable functions on which the future of the human race depends. Did they gather together, with branches of olive and myrtle, with gifts of gold, frankincense and myrrh, crying : ' Behold, a virgin hath conceived, *laeti adoremus* ' ? They did not. Nor even, shunning such rites as barbarous and unhealthy, did they bear her in triumph to the dwelling of Venus Pandemos to the stirring strains of ' *Cras amet qui num-quam amavit, quique amavit cras amet.*'

They condemned her unanimously, and each and every crowded forward to cast the first stone, lest it might be thought that there was even one among them not without sin. So much so, that Miss Judd could not walk the lanes proudly and with swelling port, saying to herself : ' Thine handmaid hath found favour in the eyes of a valiant man of Israel and the Lord hath opened her womb ; blessed be the name of the Lord ! ' On the con-trary, with bowed head and tearful eyes and quaking limbs, she sneaked from the Smithers Valhalla to the desolate hearth of her home, where Mr. Judd sat smok-ing in silence, darkly brooding on the stupidity of a girl who thought she had indigestion when she was only in the family way.

The Postman had a tenderness for Maggie, the

Stuarts' cook. His mind hovered over two topics of
contemplation, as he laboriously pedalled against one of
those frightful winds which seem as if they are trying to
blow the island into the North Sea. He fretfully wondered why the Government couldn't afford a motor-
bicycle for a poor bloody ex-Service regular, who had
to be out in all weathers, and up and down all sorts of
roads. But the chief problem he debated was whether
he should tell Maggie about Lizzie. Obviously, she
would be delighted to hear the news, and he would earn
her gratitude by being the first to tell her. On the other
hand, this disaster to Lizzie rather weighed against his
own illicit suit. Hitherto, he admitted it frankly, the
suit had made small progress. True, Maggie generally
got ahead of either of the housemaids when he knocked
at the back door. But she might merely want to get the
letters first—she received a weekly one which looked like
a young man's—or she might like to vary the monotony
of domestic service by a little chat with one of England's
heroes. She had certainly refused his hints and then
his open request that they should walk out together. He
decided not to tell her.

They greeted each other with all the rigid ceremonial
demanded by their class.

' Morning, Miss.'

' Morning, Mr. Philpot.'

' Lot of wind this morning.'

' Yes, I expect we shall be having some rain soon.'

' 'Ere you are—seven letters, two post cards, and a
book post. What does Miss Stuart do with all them
books she gets ? Can't 'ave time to read 'em.'

' That just shows what a fat lot you know about the
gentry, Mr. Philpot. Why, they have to *find* things to

do to fill up their time.   It isn't like us that have to
work. Why, they 're that helpless, I don't know what 'd
happen to 'em if they didn't have us to look after them.
Miss Margy has to have everything done for her, and a
maid to dress her ! And the goings-on, Mr. Philpot,
her sitting on young men's knees and drinking them
wicked cocktails.   And her so pretty too ! '

Mr. Philpot saw his chance and took it with gallant
clumsiness.

' I don't say nothing against Miss Stuart, but for
looks, well, it 's a sight for sore eyes to see you, Miss.'

Maggie tittered with gratification :

' Now don't start that again with me.   You know you
don't mean it.'

' I do !   Straight, I do.   I see a young lady on the
pictures the other night, Greta Garbo her name is, and
she 's just like you, only not so pretty.'

Maggie made as if to slam the door in the face of
this outrageous compliment.   Mr. Philpot's anxiety to
detain her got the better of his prudent resolution.

' 'Ere, don't go yet, Miss.   I got something to tell
you.   What do you think the Postmaster told me just
afore I started ? '

' What ? '

Mr. Philpot lowered his voice to a tragically conspira-
torial whisper.

' 'Eard about Lizzie Judd ? '

' No, what ? '

' Well, it appears that Mrs. Judd told Mrs. Raper
who told somebody, and they told the Postmaster that
Lizzie 's goin' to 'ave a baby ! '

' Oh, Mr. Philpot !   What a story ! '

' It 's as true as I 'm standing 'ere, Miss.   There 's

all sorts of a to-do about it down at Judd's and up to
Colonel Smithers's.'

'And her only seventeen ! The wicked girl ! '

Mr. Philpot looked and felt slightly uneasy. He
began : ' Oh, well, you know . . .' but Maggie interrupted him, losing some of her carefully acquired service
English in her excitement.

' 'Oo done it ? Isn't he going to marry 'er ? '

' Well, they say it 's the copper over to Dunthorp.'

' What, him ? Why, 'e 's a married man with
children ! '

' They say it 's 'im.'

' The low 'ound ! They ought to turn 'im out of the
force. And as for that Lizzie, bringing disgrace on her
old Dad and Mother, and on Mrs. Smithers too that 's
been so kind to her ! I 'd 'ave 'er flogged at the cart
tail, I would, and then sent to the Union. The *wicked*
girl ! '

And Maggie shut the kitchen door with a virtuous
slam, leaving her wooer disconsolately alone in the
whooping wind.

' Of course, we must dismiss her at once,' said Alvina,
very erect and horsily contemptuous.

' Why ? ' said the Colonel simply.

Alvina gazed at him with a horrified suspicion which
was totally unjustified. The Colonel's ' why ? ' did not
imply that he was directly concerned at all in Miss
Judd's mishap. His somewhat confused old mind was
dominated by the convention that an officer is not concerned with the morals of his men, but should try to get
them out of any mess they fall into. Lizzie, he felt, was,
as it were, up for drunk and disorderly, and he ought to

play prisoner's friend before the austere Court Martial of Alvina.   But Alvina saw the matter differently.

' How can you ask such silly questions, Fred ?   In the first place, it 'll be a scandal all over the village, and we can't *condone* an illegitimate child by continuing to employ the girl.   Then you must think of Georgie —she knows nothing about it, of course, but it can't be kept from her if Lizzie stays.   And I won't have my daughter sleeping under the same roof as a common prostitute ! '

' No, no, by Jove, it 's not as bad as that,' said the Colonel, who was rather fond of Lizzie in a paternal way.   ' She 's been a bad girl, kicked over the traces and all that, I grant you, but it 's very hard on a first offence to disgrace her publicly.   Hard on Judd and his wife too—decent, worthy people, and very respectful.'

' I can't help that.   She should have thought of that before.   I shall dismiss her now.'

Without listening to the Colonel's feeble protests, Alvina made straight for the kitchen.   Lizzie was peeling potatoes for dinner, looking rather pale, swollen and timid.   She was so occupied by disturbing reflections that she forgot to stand up when Alvina came in.   Like a basilisk of Virtue, Alvina held the culprit with a fierce eye.

' Well ? '

Lizzie sprang up nervously, and upset some of the water from the basin.   Alvina ignored this.

' Beg pardon, 'M, I didn't see you come in.'

' I 've come to give you notice to leave at once,' said Alvina, every inch a Smithers in dignity.   ' Here are your week's wages.   You will prepare and serve dinner to-night, and leave as soon as you have washed up.   I

need not tell you *why*. You have disgraced yourself and
your parents, and no decent house will keep you.'

Lizzie uttered a piteous wail, burst into tears, and laid
her head dismally among the potato peelings on the
table. Alvina retired hastily, firing back :

' Understand—you are *not* to sleep here another night.'

Another wail showed that she was understood.

' I wish very much that I could do something to
comfort you in this undeserved sorrow, Mr. Judd,' said
the Vicar.

Mrs. Judd sniffed behind a corner of a handkerchief.

' You 're very kind, Sir,' replied Mr. Judd ponder-
ously, ' but I don't know as 'ow there 's anythin' to be
done. She 's made 'er own bed, beggin' your pardon
for mentionin' it, and she 'll 'ave to lie in it.'

For the third time during the ten minutes that Mr.
Judd had been enduring this painful visit of charity, he
took out his pipe and looked at it appealingly. Then,
feeling it disrespectful to burn shag in the presence of
the clergy, reluctantly put it back in his pocket. The
Vicar noticed this gesture.

' Please smoke if you want, Mr. Judd. I don't mind.'

' Well, Sir . . . Thank you, Sir . . . P'raps I *will*
'ave a bit of baccer.'

And he began to fill his pipe with almost unseemly
haste.

The Vicar went on :

' I 'm sorry to have to bring up this matter, Mr. Judd.
I know your feelings must be very painful, and believe
me, I sympathise deeply.'

Mr. Judd grunted involuntarily with satisfaction as he
got his pipe well alight. Conscious of this slight *gaffe*,

he attempted to cover it by a sententious remark which the Vicar failed to understand :

'What gets me, Sir, is 'er bein' reg'lar stoopid about it.'

' I 've spoken to Sir Horace Stimms about it, Judd, and he is perfectly prepared to—er—make a grant and —er—secure her entry to the Workhouse Hospital at the proper time.'

Mr. Judd listened very gravely and seemed to ponder.

' I 'm very much indebted to Sir 'Orace and to you for your trouble, Sir, but a girl—even when she is stoopid— 'as a right to look to 'er own 'ome. I can look after 'er, and I don't want nothin' from Sir 'Orace or nobody else. I wish she 'd 'a done it some other way, but if a daughter of mine 'as a child, she 'as it in my 'ouse, and not in the Work'ouse. I 've never seen the inside of no Work'ouse, and my children shan't neither.'

Mr. Judd spoke with unusual heat, and the Vicar looked and felt abashed. He began to stammer an explanatory apology, but Mr. Judd puffed it aside.

' Quite all right, Sir. You was only bein' 'elpful. We don't set up to be gentry like some as I know, but we got our pride, Sir.'

And Mr. Judd rapidly smoked himself back to serenity —his dignity he had never lost. The Vicar started on another track.

' I 've seen and talked with—er—the other guilty party. I found him truly penitent, and he has author-ised me to express that penitence to you and to say that he 's ready to make every reparation.'

' The wicked man . . .' began Mrs. Judd, but her husband interrupted :

' Now, you leave this to me, Mother. We don't want no more women mixed up in this.'

Mrs. Judd sniffed resignedly, and corked up her eloquence and wrath with regret.

' I thank you again, Sir,' Mr. Judd said, ' but I don't see as 'e can make no reparations. There ain't bin no War 'ere, and there ain't no War debts.'

' I didn't mean money,' said the Vicar hastily, ' but a genuine effort to repair the wrong.'

' Repair ? ' said Mr. Judd, mystified. ' And what's 'e goin' to repair ? '

' I mean, that if you and she consent, he 'll marry her.'

' Marry 'er ! ' exclaimed Mr. Judd, now completely bewildered. ' An' 'ow 's he goin' to do that ? '

' He 's only got his thirty shillings a week, I know, but he 's willing to marry her now, do extra work, and set up house after the child is born.'

' But . . .' cried Mrs. Judd.

' 'Ush,' said Mr. Judd magisterially. ' An' 'oo is this, Sir, as 'll marry 'er ? '

' Why ! ' said the Vicar, now himself astonished. ' Don't you know ? The father of the child, Tom Strutt.'

Mr. Judd leaned back in his chair, and once more silenced his less prudent wife.

' Tom Strutt, eh ? Well, 'e can 'ave 'er so far as I 'm concerned, and she 'll be a fool if she misses the chance to get 'er name back. Tell 'im to come along an' see me, and perhaps you 'll get out the banns, Sir.'

' But we must ask Lizzie first.'

' She won't 'ave nothin' to say against it, Sir.'

' But you 'll ask her ? '

' You tell Tom Strutt to ask her. If she says No, call me a Dutchman.'

When the Vicar had gone, Mrs. Judd released her pent torrent of words, peppered liberally with ' Well I nevers ' and ' 'Oo 'd 'a thought it ? ' and ' Fancy 'er goin' with two men at once, the 'ussy.'

Mr. Judd smoked out his pipe in complete silence, not listening to a voice which, as he knew only too well, rarely said anything to the point. At last he knocked out the ashes against his heel, and pointed the stem of his pipe at his spouse to emphasise this weighty summary of his reflections :

' She ain't so stoopid as I thought she was ! '

Georgie Smithers looked rather glum and dour as she cycled back from Cricton. The wind had backed to the north-west, was gentler but colder. The horizon in front of her was a mass of broken drifting clouds, superb vapour effigies of a ruined Troy collapsing in fire. Star-lings waddled greedily over the cropped green meadow-grass, and a young cart-horse colt with absurdly hairy fetlocks gambolled heavily before the fatuously maternal gaze of an adipose mare. The sallow blossoms had lost their bright pollen, like little gold women past their prime ; but there were young green leaves dipping and shaking in every copse. Only the great cautious oaks and black-budded ashes still withheld their leaves from the peril of late frosts. And oh, those bird-voices sing-ing under the wide cupola of the sky ! Lovely shrill notes, so pure, so clear—blackbird singing against blackbird and thrush against thrush, heedless of the hungry generation to be hatched and laboured for. The lovely northern spring, which is so cool, so rain-drenched, so virginal, so unlike the sudden sensual warmth of a southern April where all the song-birds have been killed. . . .

But in Georgie this state of mind was mediocre. Her

very slender spiritual baggage was entirely without the
viewless wings. She saw, and did not see ; heard, and
did not hear. The great inscrutable forces gave her an
incomparable performance *gratis*, and so far as she was
concerned they might as well have packed up and gone
home. She might possibly have taken an interest in the
sunset if it had been billed as a military torchlight tattoo,
entrance only half a crown. The gambolling colt, unluckily, was not a hunter, and was therefore pointless.
The thrush-blackbird competition had never taken rank
as a sportin event, and so Georgie failed to register the
phases of the contest. A naturally sportin military soul,
she found almost everything unsportin and unmilitary
alien to her. Even Mr. Carrington, though still vaguely
regretted, was slowly gliding back from his temporary
rank of God's warrior to the humbler but more permanent position of sky-pilot. Georgie had twice spent
churchless Sundays in the last month.

Georgie was no Gea-Tellus, indulging in richly
dramatic and bawdy reveries. At best she now dwelt
in the twilight of Venus. On her was slowly descend-
ing the desiccation of the superfluous and ageing middle-
class girl. Without the money to misuse modern transport in aimless dashing about—the common substitute
for living in the parasitic classes—she was not forced by
necessity to work at an occupation and hadn't the wits
to invent one. Having no life of her own, she necessarily found the world lifeless. Unwittingly but inevitably she imposed her own dwindling commonplace on
all about her. She was too simple-minded, too readily
obedient to the girls-public-school-spirit to take to the
dreary consolation of secret drinking—yet. And yet ?
There was yet something there, some fading glow under

the dull ashes, some spark of life which still might have
kindled to a cheerful if limited blaze under the stimulus
of a kindly male breath. Some deformed but valid
physical instinct still tried to shoot up pallid leaves under
the sunless weight of the genteel life. . . .

Georgie came in by the back door to leave her pur-
chases in the kitchen. A blackbird sang, wild, wild,
unheeded, from the tall elm. The kitchen was dark
under a pale ghostly window. Georgie groped her way,
a little angry—where was Lizzie, why no light, no dinner
preparing ? Suddenly she halted, surprised by a faint
sound of snivelling. She peered and saw a dark mass
collapsed across the table—Lizzie mourning her sins
among the potato peelings. Georgie called sharply :

' Is that you, Lizzie ? '

A sad snivel answered.

Georgie went over to her :

' What 's the matter ? Why are you crying here in
the dark ? '

Lizzie began to blubber in an almost obscene platitude
of repentance and grief.

' Stop that noise ! Stop it at once ! '—Georgie in her
best Girl-Guide-stick-it-for-King-and-Country air of
authority—' Tell me what 's the matter ! '

Georgie shook the girl's shoulder.

' I can't, Miss, I can't,' and Lizzie began to sob with
rather awful vehemence. Georgie was shaken and a
little frightened, as we all are by an animal abdication
to distress. Something a little more humanly tender
pierced through the lobster-like disguise of the Colonel's
daughter. She patted Lizzie's head, saying with her
touch : ' I 'm sorry, I 'm not pretending to be above you
any more, I would like to help.' Aloud she said :

'Poor Lizzie!' Then, after more silent pats: 'Do tell me what's wrong. Surely something can be done? I can't help you if you won't tell me.'

Lizzie lifted her head. Fortunately the darkness helped her—what a fright she must look—if Miss Georgie could see her!

'The Missus just give me notice, Miss. I've got to go—to-night.'

And Lizzie's head plumped down once more on her arms and the cold potato peelings.

'Given you notice! But why? To-night? I don't understand. Shall I go and see Mother at once?'

'Oh no, Miss. Please, Miss.'

'But I shall have to, if you won't tell me why.'

'You wasn't to know, Miss. You mustn't touch me. I'm a bad wicked girl, I am.'

More tears.

'I'm sure you're not a bad wicked girl. It's just one of Mother's tantrums, I expect. Do cheer up, Lizzie, and tell me what it's all about, and I'll make it right with Mother. I'm sure it's all a storm in a teacup.'

'No, it isn't, Miss. You'd make me go too, if you knew.'

'No, I shouldn't. Now, if you don't tell me at once I shall go and get Mother.'

'Please, Miss, please don't ask me.'

'Tell me.'

Lizzie gulped.

'Please, Miss, I'm going to have a baby.'

'But you're not married!'

'No, Miss. I've been a bad wicked girl.'

And Lizzie sobbed once more inexhaustibly.

With a sudden instinctive movement Georgie clutched

her hand to her mouth. This utterly unexpected confession brought her at once to an emotional state only less violent that the despairing Lizzie's. Two Georgies were sharply at war with each other. The social being, the Colonel's daughter, the young lady, the willing victim of the sportin code, shrank from Lizzie as the unclean criminal who had yielded to unlawful embraces and conceived forbidden fruit. The artificial code was strong upon her, forbidding the young lady to pollute herself with sight or touch of the adulteress, even as none of the blessed gods may be polluted by the sight of death. But against this stonewall of acquired beliefs and prejudices there suddenly clamoured all the irregular hosts of suppressed instinct. In the tense darkness of the little kitchen, with its heavy smells, the valediction of innumerable past meals, Georgie felt real emotions. She could feel the beating of her own heart. Something physical in her yearned over the other girl, that panic pity of the female for all trapped in the inexorable law of the womb. Jealousy, envy, pity, repulsion, tenderness struggled within her. She fought against it—but how her own flesh insisted on envying this bedraggled and miserable scullion ! What ! this pig-snouted child with her stupid big blue eyes and wispy yellow hair had been found desirable by a man and had conceived ! Irregular, yes, a seduction, perhaps an abuse of her ignorance, but still she had been desired. No man had desired Georgie. How she would have repelled improper overtures ! Yes, and even now the training would have been too strong, and would still have repelled them. Men knew that instinctively. The young lady must be lawfully married or left to wither. Oh ! pangs of revolt and jealousy ! The Lizzies live on and the Georgies die.

She struggled hotly and ashamedly against the something in herself which whispered so insistently that it
would be far better for Georgie Smithers to be sitting
in the place of Lizzie Judd, shamed, agonised, weeping,
but fulfilled and a woman, than to stand apart from her
and above her, the chaste young lady who repelled improper advances, even before they were made.   Tragic,
perhaps ; but more vital than her own long vista of
genteel nullity, rendered ignominious to herself by the
scrambled furtive pleasures of the Daughters of Albion.
Georgie shivered.   She saw herself as a monstrous
anomaly, an uncloistered unwilling nun, a victim immolated to the Great God Keeping-up-Appearances, a
kind of unwanted commodity in the human mart.   Did
she know that they ordered these things better in
Babylon ?

She leaned forward and touched the girl's head tenderly, and she knew and Lizzie knew that for a moment
at least the human being in her had triumphed over the
young lady.   Lizzie clutched her hand and kissed it.

' Oh, Miss Georgie, Miss Georgie, it's bitter hard to
have all the world against you, and I didn't mean no
harm, I didn't know . . .'

Georgie withdrew her hand, repelled again by the
other girl's freer expression of emotion. *Noli me tangere*,
I am the chaste woman, I have played the game.—Yet
pity was still in her.

' Why does it matter so much, Lizzie, if you have to
leave now ?   You'll have to leave soon, when . . .'

False modesty prevented her from saying ' when your
child comes '.

Lizzie, who had almost cried herself out, was limp
with tears, but calmer.

' But it *does* matter, Miss.   The Missus spoke so cruel like after 'er being so kind and training me.   And if I go home, I shall have to sit in the kitchen with Mother going on at me for a hussy, and Dad smoking 'is pipe and not looking at me and calling me a stupid.   It 's the disgrace, Miss.   Dad doesn't mind so much now, Miss, but he 's wonderful proud for me to work for the Colonel, and if I 'm turned out in disgrace, Dad 'll half kill me, 'e will.'

Lizzie dramatised, for it is certain that Mr. Judd nourished no intentions of parricide against his daughter. But Lizzie felt herself the victim of a whole hostile universe.

' And then, Miss, I thought if I was here for the rest of me time, I could save me wages and start making the clothes for it when it comes, though 'ow I 'm going to do that . . .'

The back-door pull-bell suddenly rang violently above their heads, *tang-tinkle-tinkle-tinkle*.   Georgie started, the noise jangled her nerves.

' What 's that ? '

' Someone at the back door, Miss.   I 'll go and see.'

' What, after you 've been crying like that ?   It 's someone with an acetylene lamp.   Stay still.   Perhaps they 'll go away.'

A silence.   Then, *tang-tinkle-tinkle-tinkle*, more vehement than before.

' Oh heavens ! ' said Georgie.   ' Mother 'll be down in a minute to know why the bell isn't answered.   Sit where you are, Lizzie.   I 'll go.'

Georgie opened the kitchen door, and perceived a vague male form, holding a bicycle with a brilliant acetylene lamp which half-blinded her.

' Turn that lamp away ! What do you want ? '

' Beg pardon, Miss. Can I speak to Lizzie a minute, please ? '

' No, you can't, she 's not very well.'

And Georgie made as if to shut the door. But the vague form was persistent.

' Please, Miss, I must see 'er. Mr. Carrington sent me along, and said I was to see 'er and ask 'er this very evening.'

' Mr. Carrington sent you ! What 's your name ? '

' Tom Strutt, Miss.'

' Why did Mr. Carrington send you ? '

' It 's very important, Miss. I 've got to ask Lizzie now.'

' What have you got to ask her ? '

' Please, Miss, I 'd rather tell 'er meself.'

' Lizzie 's very upset. She 's been crying about something, and I don't think she 'll want to hear even a message from Mr. Carrington.'

Tom Strutt was getting impatient—very thick-headed the gentry are sometimes. In desperation he said :

' Well, Miss, if you must know, Mr. Carrington told me I got to come up 'ere to-night and ask Lizzie to marry me.'

For a moment Georgie was too amazed to speak or act. Then she seized Tom Strutt by his coat, and dragged him over the threshold.

' Come in, come in at once ! Lizzie ! Here 's Tom Strutt come to ask you to marry him. I 'm so glad, I 'm so glad ! '

Georgie lighted a candle with trembling fingers.

' There ! Get rid of him as soon as you can, and then go straight to bed. I 'll put it right with Mother and get the supper. Good-night.'

And to her own amazement and embarrassment, she kissed Lizzie's hot, tear-grimed face.

Thirty seconds later Georgie burst into the dimly-lighted drawing-room, where Alvina as usual was sitting bolt upright with the *Daily Mail*, and the Colonel was profoundly meditating certain aspects of the Afghan Campaign.

' Mother ! '

Alvina and the Colonel both looked up in surprise at the resentment and anger in Georgie's voice.

' What is it, dear ? '

' What do you *mean* by turning Lizzie away in that cruel way ?   It 's terrible of you.'

Alvina felt as annoyed as if a barbed-wire fence had suddenly appeared before her with hounds in full cry.

' I sent her away because she had disgraced herself, and I won't have such a creature in the house.'

' And if she has disgraced herself, is it for us to persecute her, with all the rest of the village against her ? It 's unsportin,. Mother.'

' Hear, hear,' said the Colonel, ' I told you so, Alvina.'

But Alvina rode straight at the fence on a tight rein.

' I am the mistress of this house, Georgie, and it 's for me to decide.   I will *not* harbour a common prostitute.'

Georgie stamped her foot.

' Mother !   Listen to me.   Mr. Carrington has just sent Tom Strutt—I suppose he 's the father—to ask Lizzie to marry him immediately.   Let her stay here the three weeks, and then leave without scandal.   Anyway, she 's not going to-night.   I 've told her to go straight to bed.   Now I 'll go and get supper.'

And Georgie banged the door, leaving Alvina in a high fever of surprise and resentment.

'Hear, hear,' said the Colonel, secretly charmed by this revolution against matriarchy, 'the child's right. Let her alone, Alvina. I'm glad that feller Strutt's done the right thing. Jove, I'll give 'em a joint weddin and christenin present.'

'I understood,' said Alvina scornfully, 'that the father was a married constable. Apparently your *protégée* had more than *one* string to her bow.'

This was said with a meaning glare at the Colonel, who was very properly annoyed. He stood up as briskly as his infirmities permitted, and slapped his thigh indignantly.

'Upon my soul, Alvina, you're gettin preposterous, preposterous!'

And the door banged again.

'Sub Dio,' said Mr. Purfleet, carefully pronouncing *soob deeo*, 'our thoughts are clearer and nimbler, says a seventeenth-century Anglican divine.'

'Ay?' remarked McCall absently. He was busy with a trowel on one of his admirable herbaceous borders. 'What divine was that?'

'I've forgotten if I ever knew. One of those learned and good men—Dr. Henry More of Cambridge, perhaps.'

'Never heard of him,' said McCall, giving his words that shade of disparagement we all try to feel for what we don't know. 'But I was brought up a Presbyterian, and we've no high opinion of the Anglicans.'

'You Scotch,' said Mr. Purfleet severely, 'are so besotten with self-love that you've no opinion of anything but yourselves. I wager you believe God wears the tartan and goes in for secret drinking. There were great men in the Church of England.'

' I 'm not interested in religion.' McCall dragged up a dandelion root as if he had been extirpating a heresy. ' *I* believe in facts.'

' Facts are self-evident, so there's no occasion for you or anyone else to believe in them. You only need faith for what you can't prove. Ha, ha, got you there, McCall.'

The doctor grunted, and went on trowelling.

' But the Jeremy Taylors are no more.' Mr. Purfleet sighed. ' If our friend Carrington delivered a sermon one-tenth as learned, eloquent, passionate and poetic as the Oration for the Countess of Carbery, the village would say he'd gone barmy and Sir Horace Stimms would insist on his resigning. This, however, is a very academic topic, since such a thing is most unlikely to happen. . . . But tell me, McCall, why do you labour in your garden, instead of paying a man and enjoying the results, as I do ? '

McCall stood up and stretched his back.

' I like it. It gives me a bit of exercise. And it saves me the wages of a regular gardener.'

' There speaks Aberdeen ! You could easily afford a gardener, and so spare time to cultivate an otherwise neglected mind. Since Divine Injustice has given me more money than I need, I prefer to give some of it to a man who needs it—namely, Tom Strutt—in exchange for his work, while I employ my leisure in higher things.'

' Pooh ! ' said McCall, with a little spluttering laugh. ' Higher things ! That's good. Why, you do nothing but potter about, and clog the passages of your mind with too many books, and talk more nonsense in a week than all the rest of the village in a year. You 'd be better employed on a little honest work.'

Mr. Purfleet looked up happily at the pale blue sky, and sniffed the pure spring air with relish.

' I shouldn't wonder,' he said reflectively, ' if this insensate grovelling on Mother Earth is imposed on you by her as a penance for loading her bosom with so many corpses. But I forgive you, McCall. These delicate spring days dispose one to charity—and anyhow I 'd rather have a Scotch materialist than a Scotch metaphysician.'

' Davy Hume,' the doctor began seriously, but was at once interrupted by the garrulous Purfleet :

' Talking of charity—by which I mean *caritas*—I met that abominable hag of Endor, Mother Eastcourt, yesterday.'

' Man ! She 's an awful woman, that,' said McCall with a shudder. ' I 'd like to operate on her. What had she to say ? Nothing good, I warrant.'

' She started at once on a most malevolent rigmarole about the unfortunate Lizzie Judd. You 've heard about it ? '

' Have I not ! Everyone I 've met in the past week has asked me if it 's true that I diagnosed her pregnancy, poor girl. I told 'em all I wasn't giving away professional secrets. But I don't mind telling you—you 're not to repeat it—that she and her mother came here, saying the girl was suffering from indigestion. I took one look at her, put my stethoscope down and heard as good a five-months foetal heart as you could expect to get. But they 're all the same. As I 've told you, only you won't believe me, there 's not a virgin over sixteen in the place.'

' I daresay,' said Mr. Purfleet benevolently. ' *Alma Venus genetrix.* But why, on the one hand, pretend it doesn't happen so long as it can be concealed ; and, on the other hand, why make such a fuss when an honest blunderer like Lizzie Judd is found out ?   Hypocrisy 's a detestable thing, McCall.'

' It 's the way of the world, and maybe it 's necessary. After all, life 's a game, and we 've got to have rules to play it.   If people openly break the rules, they 've got to be punished.   If they do it secretly, no doubt it 's better all round to pretend that they haven't broken the rules.'

' I disagree,' said Mr. Purfleet. ' Violently. Life isn't a game, however much the public schools may try to make it one.   Life a game !   My God, what a disgusting and degenerate attitude !   It 's a most extraordinary experience, a unique adventure.   It 's . . .'

' There, there,' said McCall soothingly. ' We 've had this up for discussion before, and I daresay we 'll have it up again, before we quarrel or start pushing up the daisies.'

' I never quarrel,' said Purfleet superbly. ' 'Tisn't worth it.   I have no natural malevolence, or, if I have, it is occult and disguises itself as minding my own business.   I give everyone leave to disagree with me, and I am saddened, not foully exultant in the Eastcourt manner, over the misfortunes of my fellow-creatures.'

' Ay, ay,' said the doctor satirically.   ' If only the rest of the world could reach the pure, lofty and unselfish heights of Mr. Reginald Purfleet, what a paradise it 'd be ! '

' None of your lip, McCall ! ' said Purfleet.   ' But I give you leave to despatch me to the next world in your best professional manner, if you ever catch me doing the Eastcourt, and scattering unnecessary hatred, malevol-

ence and scandal about the world.   What do you think
that abandoned old Alecto said to me ? '

' What about ? '

' About Lizzie, of course.'

' I 've no doubt she went beyond the facts.'

' She did.   She began by telling me with all the chaste
periphrasis of a perfect lady, that Lizzie was in the family
way.   I said I knew.   She leered disgustingly, and said
she had no doubt I *also* knew that Lizzie was a common
little strumpet who had allowed half the men in the
village to make free with her.   I registered that insinuation with calmness, and said it was news to me.   She
then said : That the father of Lizzie's child was a
married man with children, who was being dismissed for
his share in the matter.   Is that true ? '

' I don't think so.   The mother, Mrs. Judd, hinted
something about a police constable, but that didn't surprise me.   Those village Caesars are by no means above
suspicion.   He won't lose his job.'

' Good.   She then dropped a number of confused and
vague hints about you, from which I afterwards gathered
that she meant you had proposed to procure an abortion,
but had failed.'

' By God!' said McCall furiously.   ' That's a criminal
libel !   I 'll have her up for that.   I 'll have the law on
her.'

' No, you won't !   It isn't a libel because it isn't
written.   And I couldn't swear to her exact words, if
you brought an action for scandal.   Besides, what jury
would convict such a benevolent dear old lady ? '

McCall grumbled profanities.   Purfleet went on :

' After that, she got very involved indeed and cautious.
But the insinuation was that the child *might* be Colonel

Smithers's, which (she hinted) was supported by the fact
that Lizzie had not been dismissed immediately, and that
Georgie seemed to be taking an unnecessary and unseemly interest in the matter.   I said old men didn't
have children, any more than old women, and that anyway a gentleman like Smithers wouldn't make love to a
scullery-maid.'

' What did she say to that ? '

' She complimented me on always looking at the
bright side of things, and said " but you men always
stick up for each other—for reasons best known to
yourselves ".'

' Meaning that you as well as Smithers might be
credited with the event ? '

' I suppose so—making poor Lizzie a sort of Pan-
dora's box of illicit amours.   The Eastcourt then hinted
that there had been a plot between Georgie and Carrington—whose own relations, she implied, would not
bear investigation—to entrap Tom Strutt into marrying
the girl, and so hushing the whole thing up.'

' Is Tom Strutt going to marry her ? '

' Well, as a matter of fact he is, but it 's all bunkum
to talk about a plot. He admitted to me that he had
been the girl's lover.   I don't think he knows about the
policeman, and he won't unless he meets Mrs. Eastcourt
or her bright young offspring.'

' I suppose that 's why you 've suddenly taken a dislike
to gardening and an equally sudden interest in the em-
ployment of Tom Strutt ? '

Mr. Purfleet almost blushed.

' Well,' he said apologetically, ' the poor devil only has
the miserable thirty bob a week he wrings from some
close-fisted, pot-bellied farmer.   Someone 's got to help

him. He came and asked if I could give him any
extra work after hours. He told me the whole situation
frankly, so far as he saw it, and said he was anxious to
do the right thing. He said Georgie Smithers was going
to help Lizzie with the baby's clothes—poor Georgie !—
and try to give Lizzie sewing work. I gave him a long
lecture on the population problem . . .'

' You would ! '

' And a lot of sound advice about birth control, and
told him if he 'd undertake to keep my garden in order
I 'd give him another thirty bob a week. . . .'

' Thirrty bob a week for looking after that little garden of yours ? Why, it won't take him two evenings a
week ! Man, you 're wildly extravagant ! You 'll be
raising wages on all of us.'

' A good job too,' said Mr. Purfleet placidly.

' You 're not that well off that you can afford to be
scattering money like that,' said McCall, whose frugal
soul was still shocked. ' You 're too impetuous. Why
didn't you see me or the parson, and we 'd have asked
Sir Horace to do something ? '

' Carrington did see him. And,' said Mr. Purfleet in
a gust of indignation, ' I believe the miserable old skin-
flint offered to pay her expenses to go to the Workhouse !
Damn him.'

' Well, Purfleet, you 're a good lad, though you 're a
scatter-brain and a dangerous anarchist.' McCall hesitated, in the throes of a violent mental conflict. ' I don't
like it all to drop on you, though.' He coughed. ' I tell
ye what—if you 'll limit it to a year or until Strutt gets
a better job—I 'll see him about it to-morrow—I don't
mind contributing five shillings a week to lighten your
financial burden.'

Mr. Purfleet gave a whoop of joy and leaped into the air. He threw up his arms to heaven.

' Hearken, Father Zeus and all ye other deathless gods! A Scotchman offers money for nothing! *Jam redeat Virgo!* Bless thee, McCall, thou art translated!'

And Mr. Purfleet bounded from the garden, still calling upon the gods to witness a miracle. The perplexed McCall could hear him whooping with joy as he strode down the lane.

III

Although Coz had been an athlete, and was indeed a pukka Sahib, he had somehow missed that physical beauty which belongs by divine right to both those summits of the human race. Perhaps, like a good many of them, he had merely gone flabby and whiskyish in maturity. His head looked like a small pink Brancusi egg balanced on a large tweed one. His arms and legs bulged with fat muscles. He had one of those unmistakably aristocratic faces which must be such a comfort to Nietzschean eugenists. His Nordic blue eyes, overflowing with stupidity, had bulgy underlids, like a bloodhound's, and his shaved red jowls imitated those of the nobler animal. A wispy yellow moustache, ominously stained—no philanthropist had ever insisted on his using a moustache-mug—drooped hopelessly over a wobbly mouth which he held moistly half-open with astounding pertinacity. The backs of his aristocratically large hands were almost as hairy as an Ainu's.

Coz, alias Robert Smale, was proud of his blood. He was a thoroughbred. Not a drop of mongrel blood in him. Good breedin, he often said, showed in man and beast, in horse, hound and woman. Nothin like a pukka Mem Sahib, can't beat 'em. Coz was a younger son, one of *the* Smales. Genealogists are still not agreed as to the origin of this aristocratic, though not ennobled, name. Some say it was originally Smirk, changed to Smile in the forties, and since the nineties pronounced 'smale'. Others say it is only Small with an 'e'. At any rate he was pukka gentry, with a small inheritance which, by skilful mismanagement, he had reduced to £150 a year. He had led a life of exemplary uselessness, residing with one or other of the wealthier members of the family. Most of these having perished after helping to swell the statistics of longevity, Coz now resided permanently with the Smithers as a kind of underpaying guest. The Smithers were proud to have him, for his consanguinity increased the pukkaness of their Sahibdom.

Taken in hand early, Coz might have made quite a decent carpenter or stone-mason. Quite how these things happen in families without a drop of mongrel blood, one doesn't know ; but the fact is that he was a kind of perverted craftsman. As a born gentleman, living on his means, he had made no commercial use of his instincts and aptitude. He made his own rods and flies and spinning minnows ; caught his own chub, perch and pike ; preserved them as skilfully as a professional taxidermist, and mounted them realistically in glazed cases of his own construction, with cardboard backgrounds, representing stones and weeds in water, painted with his own hands. He made horses' hoofs into paper-weights, and had been responsible for the initiation of young Eastcourt into poker-work, owing to the universal admiration evoked by his masterly copy of

Frith's ' The Derby Day ' on a deal table.   He made
huge Union Jacks of butterflies' wings, carefully framed
under glass, and for some years had been at work on a
screen of varnished postage-stamps in a series of medal-
lions representing the Royal Family with the attributes
of Their Rank.   Thus he spent his days turning silk
purses into sows' ears, which he bestowed on his relatives as Christmas and birthday presents.   The Smithers
household was littered with these cloudy trophies.   Hence
his reputation as the clever one of the family.

He lived with the ponderous slowness of overworked
manual labourers, but without their hearty brutality.
His brutality took the form of heavy and pointless chaffing.   He was careful not to go too far with Alvina,
because she was a blood-relation of the Smales, and also
because he was not quick enough to parry her tart replies.
But he gave himself every licence with the Colonel and
Georgie, dropping his jests from a lofty height in a
muffled and debilitated voice, too gentlemanly to trouble
about articulation.   He was keen on his meals, and did
his best to keep Alvina up to scratch.   Coz liked to
begin the day with a substantial breakfast—kippers or
haddock, bacon and eggs, toast and marmalade, and
plenty of good strong sweetened tea.   With this foul
barbaric mess inside him, he felt strengthened for his
daily toil.

Teasing Georgie or Fred had become almost a necessary rite at meals.   Georgie, of course, took her chaffin
in the right sportin spirit, yet, in spite of all this excellent education, had not reached the point of callousness
where brutality fails to hurt.   Coz had been the last
person in the three parishes to twig that there was a sort
of unspoken sympathy between Georgie and Carrington,

but when he found it out at last, he ran the topic un-
mercifully. As a personal defence against Coz, Fred
invariably munched his morning way through the newspaper ; but Alvina, sitting straight as a die over the tea-
pot, refused that consolation to Georgie and herself.

' What 's the programme for to-day, Georgie ? ' enquired Coz languidly, but with a fine pretence that
something happened daily in their desiccated lives.

' Nothing much different from any other day.'

' I thought you and your mother were going out to
tea ? '

' So we are ! ' exclaimed Alvina. ' I 'd nearly forgotten it. Georgie, why didn't you remind me we are
going to tea with Mr. Carrington ? '

' Oh, ho ! ' Coz made a feeble attempt to look sly.
' Still after the fascinatin parson, what ? '

Georgie flinched inwardly. Anyone less enslaved to
a futile and stupid stoicism would long ago have revolted,
and have told Coz off as he deserved ; it was a cardinal
Smithers sin to lose-your-sense-of-humour and get ratty
over a bit of chaff. Coz's pin-pricks were administered
with a bent and very blunt pin and Georgie's sense-of-
humour was pretty leathery with misuse, but his constant jabbing really hurt. Georgie wished he 'd stop.
With her habitual incuriosity she failed, however, to ask
herself why people of breedin are so vulgarly insensitive
to other people's feelings. Yet she did occasionally
notice, with some vague surprise, that Coz and Alvina
seemed really to enjoy hurting her, while the disciplinarian
behind the newspaper very rarely intervened to help her.
What especially hurt in this constant clumsy chaff about
Carrington was that it made her so ridiculous. The
whole thing had been so slight, they might try to forget

it, as she had.   But what they couldn't forgive her was
for falling down on the Mem Sahib pose—she had made
a few innocently clumsy advances to a man, and had
been clumsily repulsed.   Stone her !

' I didn't know parsons were such a gay lot nowadays,'
Coz went on, fatuously self-complacent.   ' But in my
young days they were a different type of man.   Church
and State fellers.'

' Mr. Carrington 's a very staunch Churchman,' said
Georgie, ' but he doesn't believe in reintroducing Roman
fripperies which were abolished at the Reformation.'

This—for Georgie—abnormally intellectual phrase
was a quotation from one of her ' serious ' conversations
with her spiritual director.   Coz snickered.

' Roman fripperies ?   Flirtin wasn't one of them, was
it ? '

' He doesn't flirt,' said Georgie.

' Doesn't he ? ' said Coz, with hippopotamus levity.
' Well, I 'm glad to hear that.   *You* ought to know.
Ha ! He ! He !'

' He 's a thoroughly respectable man,' said Alvina
gravely, ' but he was thoughtlessly put in a false
position.'

Georgie flushed slightly.

' Respectable ? ' said Coz, helping himself to an enormous spoonful of marmalade.   ' I question that.   I
don't mean about his morals, of course.   Now we 've got
Georgie's assurance in the matter, *that* 's all right.   But
I say he isn't sound, and I don't believe Sir Horace
would disagree with me.'

' Why isn't he respectable ? ' asked Alvina.   ' He 's
much better than the last one, anyway.'

' Oh, him ! ' said Coz grammatically.   ' He was a dirty

tyke.   Carrington's a gentleman, but there's a bit of
the Bolshie about him.   I happened to meet him and
that howlin cad, Purfleet—can't stand that feller—and
Purfleet was gettin off some of his agitator's twaddle.
He said the housin conditions in the village were infamous, and that Craigie ought to be ashamed of himself
for allowin it and for underpayin his men.'

'No!' exclaimed Alvina.   'Did Purfleet say that?
He oughtn't to be allowed to live here, if he stirs
up trouble!   D'you know, I passed one of the village
children yesterday, and she didn't curtsey to me?   I
gave her a good scolding for it.   But what did Mr.
Carrington say?'

'I was dumbfounded,' said Coz, goggling his watchet
eyes.   'He said: "I don't deny it, but what can we do
about it?"'

'*No!*' said Alvina again.   'He *didn't* say that, did
he?'

'Yes, he did.   And Purfleet said: "If we had any
guts I should go and preach a mutiny, and you'd de-
nounce both abuses from the pulpit."'   And Carrington
shook his head and said: "It's my duty to confine
myself to spiritual things, and above all not to stir up
strife."'

'Quite right,' said Alvina approvingly.   'I'm glad he
told the Socialist off.'

'Well, he didn't quite get the better of it,' Coz admitted
reluctantly, 'because Purfleet said: "Feed my lambs,
eh?   But why feed 'em tripe?"'

'Vulgar brute!' exclaimed Alvina.

'But, Mother,' said Georgie, greatly daring, 'don't
you think there may be something in what Mr. Purfleet
said?   I don't think he ought to be rude to Mr. Carring-

ton, but why shouldn't Craigie pay his men properly?
And some of the cottages *are* very poky and smelly.'

'They get paid quite enough with all the idling and
drinking they do,' said Alvina emphatically, 'and the
cottages are perfectly all right. Do they expect to live
in palaces or gentlemen's houses? And their places
wouldn't be so smelly if they didn't live like pigs.'

'But, Mother . . .'

Georgie was interrupted by the servant, who brought
in the morning's letters on a silver tray. Alvina took
them, and distributed them—a letter for Georgie, several
bills and bookies' communications for the Colonel, a
letter for herself. Coz went on talking to the air, as
the others read.

'All this talk about the workin class and conditions
beats me. They 're better off than we are, haven't got
our appearances to keep up, and they 're always strikin
for more wages. *I* don't go on strike. Supposin we
struck payin 'em, how about that, eh? But we 're too
soft-hearted, and the Government 's afraid of its job.
What are the workin classes for, except to work? 'Pon
my soul . . .'

'Oh!' interrupted Alvina excitedly, 'listen to this!
Geoffrey Hunter-Payne writes from the Colonies that
he 's coming home on six months' leave, and asks if he
may come and stay with us for a time, since he 's an
orphan.'

Everybody looked at Alvina with deep interest—something really had happened, or was about to happen,
after all.

'Geoffrey Hunter-Payne?' said Coz. 'Let 's see.
He isn't related to the Smales, is he?'

'Only by marriage,' said Alvina. 'His mother was

one of the Bedford Hunters, who married Corky Payne
of the Guards, who was a distant cousin of the Admiral's.'

' So he 's a relative of ours ? ' asked Georgie.

' Distant,' said Coz, ' distant.   No close connection
with the Smales.   The Admiral married a Smale, who
was a relative of your mother, Alvina.'

' What are you going to do about it ? ' asked Fred.

' He says,' Alvina went on, ignoring the question,
' that he 's doing very well, but longs for a sniff of the
Old Country again.   He 's going to buy a car.'

' How lovely ! ' said Georgie.   ' How old is he,
Mother ? '

' Um ! ' cried Coz waggishly.   ' The parson's nose 'll
be out of joint.'

Then he almost blushed at the *gaffe* he had committed
in referring to the ' parson's nose '—a vulgarism for the
rear of a cooked fowl.   Georgie didn't notice this.   She
was annoyed, at last.

' Oh, do shut up, Coz !   Can't I know anyone without
you spoiling it and trying to make a fool of me ? '

Coz collapsed and looked foolish with his open cod's
mouth, as he always did when anyone stood up to him,
however feebly.   The Colonel ignored them both.

' We must give him hospitality, Alvina.   He 's working for The Empire.   When does he want to come ? '

' In August or September.   I 'll write to him to-day,
and say we shall be very happy to receive him.   Georgie,
will you come and help me look through the linen-
cupboard ? '

Nothing more was said about Lizzie and her affairs
in the Smithers household.   In fact, public interest in
Lizzie's case (fie upon her !) considerably evaporated as

soon as Tom Strutt appeared.   Since there was to be no
drama, no family indignantly casting forth the fallen
wench, no virtuous employer turning her away at a
moment's notice, no Workhouse brat, no ignominious
exile, but merely an *ex post facto* marriage, the matter
slid back into the commonplace.   While the village outwardly commended Tom, it secretly rather grudged him
the loss of a promising melodrama.   Properly goaded,
Lizzie might have furnished them with the thrill of an
infanticide, or might even have played Ophelia in the
weedy horse-pond.

The promise of legal marriage, followed by the pub-
lication of the banns, also silenced Alvina—much to the
Colonel's delight.   It was nearly two years since he had
managed to score off his stiffly dominant spouse, and he
felt the deep satisfaction of the house-broken male who
manages for once to defy matriarchal authority.   He
even went so far as to stop Mr. Judd on his way back
from work, an honour to which Mr. Judd was highly
sensible.

' Judd,' said the Colonel, in his more benevolent
Orderly Room manner, ' I want a word with you.'

' Yes, Sir ? '

Mr. Judd listened with more respect than he would
have yielded to Sir Horace or even his own employer.

' I 'm very glad indeed that this business has turned
out well.   Confoundedly awkward for the gel if Strutt
hadn't done the right thing.'

' Well, Sir,' said Mr. Judd cheerfully, ' no use cryin' '
over spilt milk.   Least said, soonest mended, that 's
what I always say.   It ain't exactly what I 'ad in view
for 'er, Sir, if you understand me, but better 'arf a loaf
than no bread, as you might say.'

' Umph ! ' said the Colonel, a little disconcerted by
this flood of rustic philosophy. ' All 's well that ends
well, eh what ?   I was going to say that Mrs. and Miss
Smithers will be unavoidably prevented from attending
the ceremony—hem !—but I intend to be there and to
make Lizzie a small wedding present.'

' Now that 's very kind of you,' said Mr. Judd warmly,
' and a darned sight more than she deserves. You 'll
pardon me sayin' so, but if there was more of the gentry
like you, Sir, we should all get on more 'earty like.'

The Colonel was pleased by this very proper and
respectful compliment, but waved it aside.

' Not at all ! Very happy to be of any assistance.'
He lowered his voice a little. ' Of course, in view of my
own daughter's reputation, Judd, I 'm sorry this happened at my house, but I consider myself as at least
partly responsible. Lizzie will not leave at once, because
that might look as if we were turning her away, but will
come home the day before the wedding. Is that all
right ? '

' Very glad to 'ave 'er out of the 'ouse, Sir,' said Mr.
Judd gratefully. ' An' my best thanks to you, Sir.'

' That 's all right, then.   Good-day, Judd.'

' Good-day, Sir, and thank you again, Sir.'

That evening Mr. Judd nearly drove Mrs. Judd wild
with dignified but mysterious references to aristocratic
connections and patronage.   He finally explained, with
some self-importance, that it was entirely owing to the
Colonel's high regard for him (Mr. Judd) that Lizzie
had been spared the disgrace of abrupt and ignominious
dismissal.   Mrs. Judd gazed at him open-mouthed, forgetting to spit on the hot iron she held in her hand.

' Pooh ! ' she puffed with immense contempt. ' You

an' your Colonels ! Why, it was Miss Georgie done it. Lizzie told me so 'erself. An' you goin' on as if you was the Lord 'Igh an' Mighty ! '

Somewhat crestfallen, Mr. Judd searched in his pocket for the unfailing consolation of shag.

But, for Georgie, whose life was such a husk, so pathetically meagre, the matter was not settled by this ignoble peal of wedding-bells. Those minutes beside the weeping girl, shaken with a sordid agony but charged with the mystery, had shocked Georgie out of her aimless apathy. In her dreams she wandered up and down stairways, through innumerable corridors; arched colonnades led her to pools of dark rippling water on which curling water lilies floated. Sometimes she was pursued, sometimes in pursuit. Sometimes she found herself in a room, wearing too few clothes, while Carrington and Mrs. Eastcourt and Coz mocked or scolded her. Once after interminable wanderings she met Lizzie, who gave her sneeringly an old rag doll to hold, and Georgie clutched it with a thrill of shame and gratitude. Or vague male forms pressed against her, in spite of her desperate nightmare-bound resistance, and she awoke with a sharp spasm of relief that it was only a dream.

In Georgie's waking hours, she was obsessed by Lizzie, sometimes with a feeling of prim repulsion, more often with a curious sense of attraction. She spent as much time as she dared with Lizzie, under pretence of giving her good advice or of helping with her wardrobe. That, at least, was how she explained it to her family, and they accepted it, themselves knowing the pleasures of inexpensive patronage. But Georgie knew that some other, less definable reason, attracted her. Once or twice, when everyone was out, she went stealthily to the kitchen and sat and sewed with Lizzie.

Now that she was ' out of trouble ', Lizzie was almost unconcerned.   Her face was a little pinched and pallid, but she ate voraciously, and her plumping body was already too large for her narrow black clothes.   Tom Strutt came to see her for an hour each evening, but she did not appear to look forward to his coming very ardently.   Georgie glanced at her as she sat stitching and humming unconcernedly.   How absurd that very soon this uncomely girl would be a married woman with a child !   Georgie felt as if her servant possessed some important secret which she did not know how to extract from her.

' Lizzie ! '

' Yes, Miss ? '

Georgie was going to say : ' What made them fall in love with you ? ', but shyness got the better of her and she only said :

' Give me the white cotton.'

Lizzie handed it over.

' To-morrow, when I 've finished hemming these, I 'll cut out the other things for you.'

' Thank you, Miss.'

A long pause.

' Lizzie ! '

' Yes, Miss ? '

' Are you—glad that you 're going to be married ? '

Lizzie sniffed and unconsciously wiped her nose on the back of her hand, a habit for which she was always sternly reproved by Mr. Judd.

' Yes, Miss.'

The answer was unenthusiastic, merely dutiful.   Now

that the emotional scene in the darkness was in the past, Lizzie had returned to the customary attitude of submissive stupidity towards the gentry. She was holding Georgie off.

' But I mean, are you really happy and excited ? '

' Yes, Miss.'

Georgie sighed, and was silent. She began again.

' Lizzie.'

' Yes, Miss ? '

' Are you in love with Tom ? '

' Yes, Miss.'

' But I mean *really* in love with him, or are you only marrying him to get out of trouble ? '

' I don't know, Miss.'

' You don't *know* ? '

' No, Miss.'

' But, Lizzie, if you 're not in love with him, you oughtn't to marry him, even in your present situation.'

' No, Miss ? '

' Lizzie ! You know that as well as I do. Do you think you 'll be happy together ? '

' I 'ope so, Miss.'

' But you aren't sure ? You don't sound very certain.'

' Oh, yes, Miss. Tom says he 's sure he can earn three pound a week now that Mr. Purfleet 's give him the extra gardening job.'

' Did Mr. Purfleet give Tom an extra job ? '

' Yes, Miss.'

' But, Lizzie, I didn't mean just having enough to live on. I meant . . .'

Georgie's courage failed her again, and Lizzie made no effort to help her. There was another long silence. Suddenly Georgie burst out :

' Lizzie, whatever made you do " that " without being married, and with two different men ? '

' I dunno, Miss.'

They stitched on for some time in silence. Then Georgie gathered up her materials and went to her own room, where she sat at the window for a long time until the twilight had almost faded.

PART III

PART III

I

LIZZIE'S marriage and induction into a home of her own had surprising side results. The cabals of the two factions were pursued as furiously as the intrigues against Racine or as an American trade War. Only a theological dispute could have been more trivially bitter. The leaders of the pro-Lizzie set were Georgie and the Colonel, Mr. Purfleet, Carrington, McCall, Margy, and all the factory hands who were not rebellious to the autocracy of Mr. Judd. The anti-Lizzie faction included such formidable adversaries as Sir Horace and Lady Stimms, Mr. Constant Craigie, Mrs. Eastcourt and Son, the Rev. Thomas Stearn (the Methodist divine), a farmer who had failed to seduce Lizzie, the constabulary (ever loyal to a comrade), and those of the factory who were ill affected to the Judd *régime*. Here was material for a second Great Rebellion.

The objectives of the Lizzie faction were precise but ambitious. It was required :

1. To obtain for the couple that public consideration which can only be expressed by the banker's adjective ' respectable '—without which village life is intolerable, especially for a labourer.

2. To maintain Tom Strutt in his job, menaced by the disapproval of Sir Horace, the spells of Mrs. Eastcourt and the unfortunate fact that Tom's employer was the identical farmer who had caught Lizzie at a wrong moment.

3. To get them a cottage, in spite of the landowners;
and

4. As a panache, to make the wedding a social success, instead of a hugger-mugger union of fornicators.

In such batrachomyomachias are expended the energies of a great Imperial people.

Tom and Lizzie, thus strangely promoted to the rank
of *casus belli*, endured their fate with stoic stupidity.
They were a gallant little Belgium in this war of the
greater powers.   At first the honours went entirely to
the Central Powers.   Sir Horace's agent was sorry, but
he had no cottage available for the loving pair.   The
three unoccupied ones would soon be required for Sir
Horace's own employees.   The farmer was sorry, but
times were bad, and in order to pay his taxes he felt com-
pelled to give Tom a week's notice.   Mrs. Eastcourt's
womanly purity was shocked at the thought that a light
woman, suspected to be everybody's concubine, should
be foisted on the village as a respectable married woman.
That a section of the gentry should support her cause
was, Mrs. Eastcourt hinted, due to the fact that they had
their own unavowable reasons for keeping Lizzie quiet.
From this came a persistent rustle of ' You know, they
say that Purfleet . . .' and ' There's a reason why the
old Colonel and his daughter . . .'   It looked as if Tom
and Lizzie would start married life with a bad press and
no visible means of support.

Mr. Purfleet, the brains of the Allies, and Georgie,
their moral inspiration, held conferences.   Georgie was
surprised by the unsuspected powers displayed by Mr.
Purfleet.   Hitherto she had always rather resented his
perpetual chatter and bookishness.   His avowed dislike

for killing things, the fact that he obviously preferred
sitting still and talking to running about after balls, had
prejudiced her judgment of his intelligence. Such a
man, Georgie felt, must be spineless and inefficient, if
not actually a degenerate.

It was a worried and rather hopeless Georgie who set
out to consult Purfleet on a pleasant May morning when
dappled clouds roved like browsing deer across the blue
plains of heaven. The fancy did not occur to Georgie
as she closed behind her the front door of Holly Lodge,
but it occurred to Mr. Purfleet who at the same moment
stepped forth from breakfast through french windows to
his garden. The night before, Lizzie had wept her fresh
woes to Georgie, and Georgie had promised to help.
Only her knowledge that Mr. Purfleet was a staunch
pro-Lizzieite drove her to the forlorn hope of asking his
aid. She clicked open the gate, and almost immediately
came upon Mr. Purfleet, in bedroom slippers and a
flowery dressing-gown, caressing his cat beside a flower-
bed.

Mr. Purfleet shook hands rather vaguely, and seemed
not to hear Georgie's formal how-do-you-do. His mind
was occupied with higher things.

' Montaigne,' said Mr. Purfleet musingly, while
Georgie wondered who on earth ' Montagne ' was,
' says that we do not caress them, they caress themselves against us. What do you think ? '

Georgie's apprehension, stiffened by too much Coz
and Colonel, was not quick enough to guess that by
' them ' Mr. Purfleet meant ' cats '. She said :

' I don't know what you mean.'

' It 's very probable,' mused the philosopher, ' and I
have sometimes thought that the same is true of women.

There is an affinity between cats and women, which explains why poets always keep cats, when they are too poor to afford the nobler extravagance. Cats and women occupy our hearths but never admit us to their confidence. Why? They caress themselves against us. You agree?'

Besides being mystified by nonsense, Georgie vaguely apprehended that Mr. Purfleet was working off a dirty French joke on her. She determined not to stand it.

' I don't know anything about such things,' she said, very Girl-Guidey and pure. ' I came to ask you if you can do anything to help poor Tom and Lizzie.'

' Oh, ho!' said Purfleet, immediately dismissing his morning reverie. ' What's up now? Is there another claimant to the putative parentage of Lizzie's embryo Messiah?'

Georgie blushed at the horridness of Mr. Purfleet's expression, but explained the situation as lucidly as she could. Mr. Purfleet listened attentively, asking an occasional and precise question, while his eye aesthetically appraised Georgie, avoiding her features as an unsuccessful effort of the Life Force, but appreciating the lines of her breasts, waist and thighs, the fineness of her wrists and ankles, the promise of athletic loins. When she had finished her account of Lizzie's new troubles—

' Beauty,' murmured Purfleet, ' is a promise of happiness.'

' *What?*' exclaimed Georgie.

' Nothing, nothing,' said Purfleet hastily. ' So the dragons of virtue threaten the miserable enough prospects of our young friends? The corrupting influence of too much virtue is a shocking thing, my dear Miss Smithers. I can't warn you against it too earnestly.

It 's particularly pernicious, as in the present case, when
supported by economic power.'

' You do say funny things ! ' said Georgie, half laughing at a stale nineties pleasantry which was a startling
paradox to her.   ' But what 's to be done ? '

Mr. Purfleet raised a deprecating hand.   He wasn't
going to be done out of his chatter.   If Georgie wanted
his help she must pay for it by listening to him.   It really
did not matter to Mr. Purfleet whether she understood
him or not; what he enjoyed was the sound of his own
voice.   He himself supplied all the applause necessary.

' Patience !   The whole secret of action is a complete
preliminary enquiry into the extent of the problem to be
solved.'

As a matter of fact, Mr. Purfleet already knew exactly
what he was going to advise and to do himself, but he
was not going to miss his fun.

' Yes ? ' said Georgie submissively, rather as she
greeted one of the Colonel's military whoppers.

' Have you ever meditated on the economics of this
community ? '

Georgie's heart sank lower.   What were economics ?
And surely meditation was an Oriental indecency, practised by the lower castes of India ?   Mr. Purfleet linked
his arm benevolently with hers, unconscious that this
simple action caused her a distinct flutter, and began to
walk up and down the smooth-shaven lawn.   Occasionally he gesticulated with his free hand.   Georgie noted
with horror that he had nothing but pyjamas on under
his rococo gown.

' It is an unholy mystery,' said Purfleet in tones of
awe, ' which always reminds me of the elephant which
supports the world standing on the back of the tortoise.

What does the tortoise stand on ?   The theologians of political economy refuse to allow the question.'

' *Do* elephants stand on tortoises ? ' asked Georgie in surprise. ' I should think the tortoise would be squashed.'

' Exactly,' said Purfleet, thinking Georgie had replied amusingly to his analogy, instead of taking it literally. ' One would think so.   But the tortoise isn't squashed, and continues to stand firmly on nothing.   Most amazing.   I live in comfort, you live in comfort, so do McCall, Craigie and Carrington ;   the Stuarts live in solid opulence, and the deplorable Stimms in a bestial luxury worthy of Trimalchio.   A hideous pyramid, Miss Smithers.'

Georgie looked round for the clipped yew-tree, but saw none.   She perceived that Mr. Purfleet had another pyramid in view.

' Oh, I don't think pyramids are hideous.   When Father was in Egypt . . .'

' None of us,' interrupted Purfleet, ' is of the slightest practical use, except McCall who labours earnestly to reduce the population.   I might also except my own modest efforts in the Socratic line, but I prefer to consider myself as useless, quite useless.'

And Mr. Purfleet sighed modestly.

' Oh . . .' said Georgie, in amazement.

' You 're very kind,' said Mr. Purfleet, squeezing her arm gratefully, unaware that she was exquisitely perturbed by this male contact.   ' But no, I am a parasite. I defend myself as being a kind of flea on the body politic and economic, endeavouring to sting it to a salutary fury, whereas our friend Carrington is a leech, and the horrid Stimms an anaconda gorged with an empire.'

' Mr. Carrington isn't a leech,' said Georgie indignantly, ' he does a great deal of good ! '

' A leech of souls, eh ? Ha ! ha ! ' said Purfleet.
' But what I was going to ask you is—how the devil do
we all live ? '

And Mr. Purfleet stopped abruptly in his walk, gazing
at Georgie with an air of triumphant query, as if saying :
' There 's a nice riddle for you ! ' Georgie felt his rather
bony knee pressing against her leg. She moved it coyly
away. Utterly unaware that he had even touched her,
or seemingly had made an assault on her maiden virtue,
Mr. Purfleet continued their walk and his discourse.

' You will of course say : Agriculture,' said Purfleet,
using a favourite figure of speech of orators, ' and, I
grant you, agriculture supports a certain number of us.
But English agriculture is in a bad way, even if you
subtract ninety per cent. from the grousings of farmers.
It 's a fact that Stimms last year lost five hundred pounds
on the Home Farm—about which, by the way, he made
a confoundedly indecent bobbery and tried to pose as a
universal benefactor to humanity. The mingy hypo-
crite genially overlooks the fact that he draws several
thousands a year in rents for farms, buildings and land,
and that if he were not a first charge on the industry the
farmers wouldn't be in debt to the banks.'

' Lizzie . . .' said Georgie, trying to bring him back
to the point.

' But,' Purfleet went on pitilessly, ' what about the
rest, who far outnumber the agriculturists ? There is
Craigie's factory, which incidentally is heavily mort-
gaged to Stimms. This grotesque anachronism, Miss
Smithers, is run on patriarchal lines. That means that
Craigie employs non-union labour (which he can still

get here) and pays his men about half a crown to five shillings more than the standard agricultural wage of the county. He houses them, cheaply indeed, in those two infamous blocks of cottages. Have you observed that at least twenty-five people have to live in an area about one-half the size of Craigie's own house, so huddled together that when a man coughs at one end of the row Granny Burton drops her false teeth with fright at the other end ? '

' I don't know anything about Socialism,' said Georgie. ' Tom Strutt . . .'

Purfleet gently patted the back of her hand to keep her quiet. His fingers were cool. Georgie wondered why she not only failed to resent this familiarity, but even rather liked it.

' Obviously,' continued Purfleet, ' he is able to keep going only because of these peculiar circumstances. A strike would smash the business, which explains why the men don't strike. But he won't be able to survive long. A new factory has just been started near Cricton. That 'll kill his pig.'

Mr. Purfleet now amiably held her hand in his—he always found his thoughts were stimulated by holding the hand of an attentive, even though unintelligent, lady.

' Therefore,' he said, gently waving his unoccupied hand, ' it is quite useless to get Tom Strutt a job with the factory here, even if they 'd take him, which they wouldn't.'

' Oh,' said Georgie, bitterly disappointed that all this pribble-prabble had led to nothing but a negative. ' Then what are they going to do, poor things ? '

He squeezed her hand reassuringly, and still she did not withdraw it.

' The plan of campaign,' said Purfleet, adapting his metaphors to the low level of military understanding, ' is complicated. We must attack on three fronts simultaneously. You, my dear,'—he omitted to add ' Miss Smithers '—' must deal with the billeting of the troops.'

' What troops ? ' asked Georgie.

' Mr. and Mrs. Strutt and expected family. Margy Stuart 's a friend of yours, isn't she ? '

' Yes. But why ? '

' Is she here now ? '

' Yes.'

' All right. Now, listen.' And Mr. Purfleet again pressed her hand, this time with the agreeable realisation that it was a cool and shapely hand, a conductor of pleasant sensations. ' The last time I had to go and play billiards with that genial profiteer, Stuart, I noticed that the lodge cottage was empty. What you must do is see Margy, arouse her sympathies—you know, play on the strings of pathos and patronage—and get her to promise that Tom and Lizzie may have the cottage. Stuart 's away, and once Tom and Lizzie are installed, he 'll have a devil of a job to get 'em out—ha ! ha ! '

' What a good idea ! I never thought of it.'

' Intelligence, my dear, intelligence,' said Purfleet, with fatuous self-complacence. ' It 's our one weapon. We must play the guileful Odysseus against these rustic Ajaxes. Ah ! if only we could abolish that obscene Bible and re-establish the Hellenic tradition ! What a Renaissance ! What an object for a life-work ! Homer ! Homer 's the thing ! '

Georgie was so scandalised that she abruptly withdrew her arm, and then felt confused at having so

pointedly called attention to the fact that they had been
walking hand-in-hand. Mr. Purfleet remained un-
perturbed.

' Have you ever read Homer, by the way ? '

' No.'

' I 'll lend you my Butcher and Lang, if you like.
Come in a moment, and I 'll get it for you.'

Georgie hesitated. In Cleeve morality it was the
wrong thing for a girl to enter a house alone with a man.
The reputation of Margy had been irrevocably destroyed
by such proceedings, though, oddly enough, Margy
didn't care. But Purfleet had already ushered her into
his sitting-room before she knew what had happened.
Purfleet picked the Wardour Street *Odyssey* from his
shelves, expatiating on the glories of Homer. He
opened the book at random and began to read in the
fantastic droning voice adopted by literary gents when
they try to be impressive *à la* W. B. Yeats. By chance
he dropped on a very late interpolation—the episode of
Aphrodite and Ares caught in the net of Hephaestus
amid the huge laughter of the immortal gods. Mr. Purfleet enjoyed reading the passage. But happening to
glance up, he paused abruptly, surprised by the look of
terror in Georgie's eyes. She had not understood much,
but she had gathered that he was reading a description
of *a man and woman in bed together !*

' The goddesses,' said Mr. Purfleet easily, ' stayed
away. I should have remembered.'

And he bowed politely to Georgie, who thought he
really must be cracked. She got up to go.

' Oh, don't hurry off.'

' I 'm afraid I must. Mother 'll be expecting me.'

' How ghastly families are ! ' said Mr. Purfleet with

deep feeling. ' Each member preventing the others
from doing what they want, and they call it love.'

' I do wish you wouldn't say such queer things, Mr.
Purfleet. But you haven't told me how you think we
can arrange the other matters for Lizzie and Tom.'

Mr. Purfleet tapped his nose with a mysterious and
Fagin-like air.

' Don't you worry. I 'll attend to it.'

' Good-bye then.'

' Good-bye. May I come along later in the week, and
tell you what has happened ? '

' Yes, come to tea.'

Mr. Purfleet grimaced.

' I hate tea-battles. I 'll come along about six, and
you can pretend to show me the garden, while I make
my report.'

And with this tacit rendezvous, they parted. Mr. Purfleet accompanied Georgie to the gate, burbling amiably
about phlox and clove pinks and nymphs. He insisted
that Georgie should take the Homer to begin his Renaissance. She held it as if she thought it might sizzle in
baptised fingers.

Just outside Purfleet's gate Georgie ran into Coz, the
last person on earth she wanted to see. He looked at
her indignantly.

' Did I see you coming away from that bounder,
Purfleet ? '

' He isn't a bounder.'

Poor Georgie ! Why was she so ungrateful for all the
loving care lavished on her ? And why was she always
so unable to defend herself ?

' What were you doing there ? ' asked Coz, gazing

fixedly at her. With horror Georgie found she was blushing.

She stammered slightly.

' I—I went to borrow a book.'

That's a lie, she thought.

' What book ? '

' I don't know. . . . This one.'

Coz sternly took it from her, as if he had expected to find the works of the Marquis de Sade, or, more likely, of James Lovebirch, who was doubtless more in Coz's line.

' *Homer !* What on earth do you want that for ? '

' I—Margy wanted it in a hurry and asked me to get it on my way.'

' Umph ! ' said Coz, reluctantly returning the book. ' I s'pose it's all right, but I don't like you associatin with a feller like Purfleet. He's a confounded cad. Why, by Jove, he was in the pub the other night when I passed, laughin and drinkin with Judd and a lot of other workin people. Found his own level for once, I suppose.'

Georgie made no answer. She was thinking that even if Mr. Purfleet was a most eccentric and in some ways improper person, yet he had a certain attractiveness. She felt warm all over, remembering that she had allowed him to hold and press her hand. But Coz, she felt, was an ignorant and domineering person, even though he was a pukka Sahib. She decided to read Mr. Purfleet's naughty book, and find out what it was he liked in it.

II

Like lots of other old women, Purfleet was a congenital busybody. Having ruined what little natural intelligence he possessed, by an indiscriminate gobbling of books, he was almost completely at the mercy of a drivelling sentimentality which he misnamed ' Idealism '. His apparent benevolence was in reality nothing more than a necessity for vicarious experience and emotion. His instinct for self-preservation was so highly developed that he had no occasion for a life of his own ; and a snugly invested patrimony sheltered him from the carnivorous human circus. In the matter of money Mr. Purfleet was, so to speak, priceless. To hear him talk you might have thought he was the gent who asked if money was an 'erb. And yet locked in his desk were careful computations of his investments and income, neatly docketed correspondence with his broker and banker, and a terrific array of annotated company reports. By judicious transference of capital this puresouled idealist annually increased his income ; and his skill in tax-dodging, which he concealed under the seemingly artless pose of a bloody fool about money, took every wicket of the Inland Revenue in the annual test match between bureaucracy and the rentiers. His generosity was fortuitous and emotional, immediately regretted, but made good from vanity. If he had analysed his motives (which he didn't), he would have credited his charities as investments in life. They gave him an opportunity to enjoy the feelings he was incapable of supplying to himself.

The witless inhabitants of Cleeve judged Mr. Purfleet from themselves, and went wrong in consequence. This slightly lachrymose pedant, with his gift of the gab, took them in completely. They despised his learning because they had none themselves ; yet if there is any virtue in consuming mentally acres of classical print, Mr. Purfleet deserved their esteem. While he exploited the rentier swindle with respectable ability, they considered him a dangerous revolutionary. They never paused to consider how averse from any form of work Mr. Purfleet remained. His busy vamping of other peoples' lives they interpreted as Franciscan charity. They never realised that he kept his idealism in the realm of words, while in practical affairs he was a shrewd realist. The tradesmen all had the agreeable illusion that they were over-charging Mr. Purfleet on the higher gentry scale, but through his carefully prompted batman he invariably got the better of them. He lived twice as well as the Smithers on a relatively smaller expenditure. The man who really paid through the nose was the belligerent Smithers, who was convinced that the tradesman who could get the better of him had never been born.

Mr. Purfleet enjoyed his part of Grand Negotiator in the Tom-Lizzie-Georgie drama. As he trotted about on his lawful intrigue, he reflected with pleasure on his situation as the god in the machine who was putting everything right. It was all jam for him. By getting Strutt a job in the Cricton factory, he was saving himself that recklessly proffered thirty bob a week. He was defeating the Eastcourt-Stimms faction by Machiavellian transactions, and at the same time enjoying a gentle titillation by flirting with Georgie. The flirtation hitherto was very nearly unconscious on his part. Mr. Purfleet was faintly homosexual in a benevolent way, but much too cowardly to get down to business. He remained a bachelor and worked off his unclamorous sex by multitudinous flirtations with women, who usually treated him as a warm but unimportant lap-dog whose attentions were not undesirable, *faute de mieux*. This rôle suited Mr. Purfleet to a T. He felt safe with women, and yet got from them as much as he was capable of getting. Mr. Purfleet, who affected an immense discretion in the matter of his amatory fumblings, privately considered himself a public benefactor to the female sex—as indeed he may have been.

After baffling her undernourished brain with the first few pages of the praeraphaelite Homer, Georgie abandoned her first and only flight into Hellenism. She knocked, but it was not opened unto her. However, Mr. Purfleet had so far aroused her sensibilities that she did not immediately abandon all hope of living the highbrow life. She wandered into her father's room to consult him, for, after all, he let her down less frequently than anyone else. This bedroom was a tumult of sporting implements and bizarre souvenirs, in some cases not even clear to the Colonel himself. If the stuffed, inconveniently large and slightly mouldy wart-hog recalled a jungle triumph, what was commemorated by the pimply-looking meteorite, the pair of fans painted with somewhat Europeanised Geishas and the broken ivory back-scratcher ? The Colonel himself would have been flummoxed if sternly required to explain how he acquired them and why he kept them. Shelves and a large table were littered with papers hopelessly involved with such objects as collar-boxes, sharks' teeth, fishing tackle, dum-dum bullets, bills and County Court summonses. Many sheets of paper were covered with names and figures very neatly written. Fred Smithers had once played cricket for the Army *v.* the Navy, and still continued to play that noble and intelligent game vicariously. He kept his own statistics of the batting and bowling averages of the County teams, having once detected a slight but scandalous error in the official figures.   A few volumes were scattered about, including a large exercise book.   For several years the Colonel had been writing a book to be called ' My Life and Times ', wherein he intended to record his feats of arms and sport and to expose the venal folly of the Commanding Officers who had all strangely but unanimously rejected the advice and co-operation of Fred Smithers.   So far all he had written was : ' I was born on   , the 25th of February, 1859.'   Unable to remember which day of the week it was, he found himself checked at the very begin-ning of his important work.   Efforts to borrow an old calendar and to calculate the day had failed, and though he had several times set forth to consult the British Museum records he had somehow never reached Blooms-bury.   But this did not really matter, for when he talked of his book—as he very frequently did—he always ended up by tapping his head impressively and saying : ' It 's all there, all there, my boy.'   And there it remained.

Georgie found her father busily ruling lines on sheets of numbered foolscap.   The cricket season was in full swing, and he had not yet begun his records.   A pile of cricket pages from the newspapers lay at his side.

' May I come in a moment, Father ? '

The Colonel looked round with the slightly vacant eye of a man dragged unwillingly from profound intellectual labours by the materialist importunities of womenfolk.

' What is it ? '

Georgie hesitated, afraid of the almost inevitable ridicule.

' I 've read all the books downstairs and nothing has come from the Library.   Can you lend me something ? '

Like many pure-minded men, Fred Smithers kept a
small but valued collection of pornographic books and
picture post cards, purchased in such different fields of
bibliophily as Gibraltar, Simla and the Charing Cross
Road.   These were carefully locked away in one of the
drawers of an old roll-top desk, which remained permanently shut in a corner of the room.   Alvina, Georgie and
Coz were all unaware of the existence of this treasure.

The Colonel did not offer these works to his daughter ;
indeed, he would have thought it wrong to do so.   He
said :

' There 's several books knockin about here.   You
can have 'em if you like.'

' I want a *good* book,' said Georgie, beginning to
gather together the scattered volumes.

' Eh ?   You 've got a Bible and prayer-book, haven't
you ? '

' I didn't mean that,' said Georgie clumsily.   ' I
meant . . . well, not just ordinary trash, but a good
book, you know.'

' I never read trash,' said the Colonel with rather
severe dignity.   ' You 'll find none here, I assure you.
Trash indeed ! '

' Oh,' exclaimed Georgie with prompt feminine sub-
mission, ' I didn't mean *that*, Daddy darling.   I meant
—would you tell me which of your books you think
would be a good one for me, please ? '

Mollified, the Colonel rose goutily to his feet, and
began rummaging, unsuccessfully.

' Humph !   I wish your mother 'd leave my things
alone, Georgie.   I swear she 's been in here.   Where
the devil is that confounded book ?   It 's a jolly good
yarn, my dear.   Where did I . . . ah ! here it is.'

And the Colonel triumphantly held out a tattered paper-bound book, entitled *The Hunters of the Ozark*, which his daughter obediently took with a grateful :

' Thanks so much, Father.'

It was remarkably warm for May when Mr. Purfleet set forth to make his report to Georgie Smithers. For some reason, which he did not trouble to make clear to himself, he dressed with rather more care than usual in a neat suit of grey flannel with a blue shirt and blue foulard tie. For a moment he considered the possibility of exhuming an old College blazer, but refrained, on reflecting that for him to wear a blazer was low hypocrisy, even to flatter a woman. Not that he had any particular reason or desire to flatter Georgie, but he instinctively adapted himself to feminine prejudices. Besides, it was a useful alibi.

He found Georgie alone in the garden of Holly Lodge. She blushed slightly as they shook hands. He noticed that she had put on her Sunday frock, and wore a little old-fashioned pendant set with seed pearls. Mr. Purfleet was in excellent spirits, which in his case inevitably meant a lot of chatter. They strolled slowly up and down the gravel paths bordered with clipped box, while Mr. Purfleet expatiated.

' Well,' he said with a chuckle, ' I think we 've cooked their goose. It 's all fixed up. Have you managed to get Margy's consent about the cottage ? '

' Yes. She said she 'd write to her father at once, and that Tom and Lizzie can move in as soon as they 're married.'

' Excellent ! '

' But what are they going to do about furniture ? '

Mr. Purfleet gravely considered the question in silence.

' I think that 's more or less up to their respective families. After all, we 've solved the chief difficulties, haven't we ? But I 'm dying to tell you what I 've arranged.'

Georgie was silent. She experienced that feeling of moral deflation which comes upon us all when we have over-anticipated and over-prepared an event. The un-defined expectations aroused in her by Mr. Purfleet's imprudent caresses had skilfully camouflaged themselves as intelligent interest in the fate of Tom and Lizzie. The feelings which had made her fish out the pendant and put on her best dress remained obscure to herself, but she was now conscious of disappointment. She reproached herself for growing lukewarm over the interests of her protégés. Between Georgie and Mr. Purfleet lay an embarrassment, the embarrassment of unconfessed desire. Yet this was mild and modified in them both. Mr. Purfleet's ambiguous lusts were checked by the sober ugliness and non-intelligence of Georgie's face, and she was vaguely repelled by a man who trafficked so shamelessly in ideas, as if her white-robed guardian angel were whispering : ' This, my dear, is *not* the man for you.' Georgie felt there was something satanic, almost Nietzschean, in this self-indulgent and garrulous sentimentalist.

Mr. Purfleet unexpectedly found he was not in his best form. He was acting as his own guardian angel and inwardly warning himself against entangling alli-ances. The excellent spirits in which he had begun their conversation were already checked. Even to him-self his remarks seemed unfunny. But he persisted.

' You might have thought that Carrington would have rumbled me, but he didn't.'

' What's he got to do with it ? ' asked Georgie in astonishment.

' Ha! Ha! In complicated affairs like this, my dear, the best strategy demands that the moral victory shall precede the material. I went to Carrington because I wanted to defeat the machinations of that foul old Eastcourt hag. D'you get it now ? '

' But what can Mr. Carrington do ? ' said Georgie, uneasily remembering her dismal defeat in that quarter.

' A great deal. It took me a long time to wangle it, but I flatter myself we 've made a scoop of Church support. He and I gassed for ages in what he would describe as a heart-to-heart talk. I pointed out to him that the life of these villages is poisoned by senseless and malign gossip. I hinted that he himself had suffered. Then I introduced the topic of Tom and Lizzie, drew a pathetic picture of their innocently amorous gambols— suppressing the bobby, of course—and asked him if their young lives were to be blighted by Eastcourt poison-gas. I was emphatic that he had a sacred duty to perform, both in this special case and for the good of his parish in general.'

Mr. Purfleet grinned in a manner he would have described in himself as puckish, in others as fatuous.

' And what do you think he 's going to do ? Ha! Ha ! '

' What ? '

' He 's going to preach a sermon on human charity and neighbourly love—I particularly insisted that he should stress the "neighbourly", which is such a favourite hypocrisy of our local Ate—and he 's going to read as his text the whole episode of the woman taken in adultery. Ha! Ha! Ha! I wish to God they'd all go out one by one, beginning with the eldest, but that's too much to hope for. Ha! Ha!'

'Oh!' said Georgie, rather scandalised. 'But do you think you ought to have deceived Mr. Carrington like that? We oughtn't to jest with sacred things.'

'Pooh! Who's jesting with sacred things? Is there any harm in his denouncing one of the most obvious and pernicious failings of his parishioners? And if he hasn't the wit to think of it himself, why shouldn't I inoculate him with a few ideas ' It's all in the sacred cause of strategy, my dear.'

Georgie shook her head, but could think of no argument to oppose to Mr. Purfleet's sophistry. Suddenly he guffawed, in a slightly forced manner. He glanced at Georgie's serious face with benevolent malice.

'The cream of that jest is that old mother Eastcourt will go about hinting that he has his own reasons for tolerance in such matters. Ha! Ha!'

Georgie went very red. She felt that Purfleet was rather unkindly hinting at her. But she was unable to break through her embarrassment. At that moment they caught sight of the scarlet face of Coz, under a floppy tweed hat, as he entered the garden.

'Good Lord!' exclaimed Purfleet in consternation. 'There's that crashing bore, Smale. Quick! He hasn't seen us. Let's hide somewhere!'

They sped down a shrubbery which hid them from sight.

'This way,' whispered Georgie, all alert at the prospect of a game of hide-and-seek. 'I'll show you my den.'

At the end of the Smithers's shrubbery, disorderly
through lack of clipping, were several ruined outhouses,
themselves built on the ruin of a large Elizabethan barn.
Nobody ever went there.   The high barn entrance was
made of mouldering planks, and there was a smaller
stout wooden door hanging on one hinge.

Georgie led the way in.   Purfleet found himself in
almost complete darkness, amid a smell of dust, old
straw, cobwebs and mice.   He stumbled over a broken
wheelbarrow.

' Shssh ! ' whispered Georgie.   ' He 'll hear you.'

Mr. Purfleet tenderly rubbed his shin.

' I can't see,' he whispered plaintively.   ' This darkness is like the bottomless pit ! '

' Here ! '   Georgie seized his hand, and guided him
to the far end of the barn.   Behind a ruined farm cart,
which had probably been there for twenty years, a rough
ladder led to an upper story.   Georgie went up nimbly,
followed by Purfleet with his nose almost at her heels.

She took his hand again at the top of the ladder.

' Go easy !   Walk on the rafters.   The boards between
are rotten.'

In some terror Mr. Purfleet trod his rafter gingerly,
supported by Georgie's steady Girl-Guide hand.   They
came to a low arch with a piece of sacking nailed over it.
Georgie pushed this aside, and Purfleet found himself
in a little square room, lighted only by a high barred
window.   There was a rug on the floor.

' There ! '   said Georgie, speaking in more natural
tones.   ' We 're safe enough now.   Nobody ever comes
here.'

' Is this your den ? '

' Yes.   I come here sometimes when I just can't bear

the house another minute.   It 's easy to slip in, and slip
back again.'   She hesitated.   ' You know, I 'm not supposed to smoke, but I sometimes have a cigarette here
on my lonesome.   You won't split on me, will you ? '
she added imploringly.

Mr. Purfleet offered her his cigarette-case.

' I should be a low cuss if I did.'

' And you won't tell anyone about the den ? '

' Indeed I won't.'

' Honest injun ? '

' Parole d'honneur.'

Mr. Purfleet struck a match, and held it cupped for
Georgie.   In the semi-darkness, the match lighted up
her face.   Mr. Purfleet was distressingly conscious of
her large nose, but as her chin accidentally touched his
outstretched fingers he felt it was smooth and pleasant.
They sat down side by side on the rug.   The run through
the shrubbery, the sense of playing a game, and the thrill
of smoking a forbidden cigarette in the forbidden company of an unchaperoned man wiped Georgie's embarrassment away.   She found it almost natural and quite
pleasant to be seated smoking with Mr. Purfleet in semi-
darkness in an old heavy-aired barn.   Their cigarettes
glowed.

' Have you managed to get Tom a job ? ' she asked.
' I think it 's so generous of you to take him as your
gardener as well.'

Purfleet coughed a little awkwardly.

' Yes, I 've got him a job, quite a good one, but I 'm
afraid it means that he 'll have to give up the gardening
idea.'

' Why ? '

' Well, you see, as I explained to you the other day,

it's quite hopeless to try to get Tom a job in the immediate neighbourhood.   The opposition are too strong for us.   But I knew that McCall is very thick with the managing director of the new Cricton factory.   He's even put money in it.   Of course, he jumped at the idea of getting Tom taken on as a hand, and it's arranged. Tom'll get fifty-five bob a week to start with, and a chance of rising to seventy pretty soon.'

'I *am* glad!   But why does that prevent him from doing your gardening.'

'Well,' Mr. Purfleet was obviously in some difficulty with his explanation, ' er—you see, he has to cycle to and from Cricton and he'll be very tired when he gets back.   He won't want to work then, and he's getting an adequate screw.   Of course, if he likes to come in on Saturday afternoons, I'll pay him trade union rates per hour.'

' You *are* kind!' said Georgie enthusiastically.   ' I think you've arranged it all beautifully.   I shall tell Lizzie that she owes everything to you.'

Mr. Purfleet sought her hand and gently pressed it.

' Not a bit.   As a matter of fact, she owes it to *you*. If you hadn't been so much interested in her, I doubt if the rest of us would have been so eager.'

Georgie flushed with pleasure.   It was very seldom indeed that anyone troubled to praise her.   Under the Smithers system she was expected to be grateful if she escaped reproof.   She allowed Purfleet to retain her hand.   Purfleet ground his cigarette out, and then slipped his glasses into his pocket, without loosening his hold. The invisible Senator within him, pleading urgently for no entangling alliances, was entirely ignored.   He could guess rather than feel that Georgie was trembling very slightly. There was a tremor in their voices as they spoke, almost in whispers in the darkness.

' Yes,' Mr. Purfleet proceeded with a purring earnestness rather in excess of the situation, ' if anyone is entitled to credit in this business, it 's *you*.'

Georgie felt rather happy and pleased with herself, as if she had triumphantly vindicated an otherwise aimless life. But the code prescribed that she should immediately check Mr. Purfleet, especially since he might be chaffing her ; while, in fact, she hoped he would go on.

' Oh, I didn't do anything.'

' Yes, you did ! I heard how you stood up for the girl when your mother wanted to turn her out, and I must say I admired you for it.'

' However did you find that out ? '

' Ah ! Wouldn't you like to know ? '

' Do tell me.'

' It was through Judd, as a matter of fact. At first, he thought it was due to your father, but Lizzie said it was all your doing.'

' She oughtn't to have told.'

' Of course,' said Mr. Purfleet seductively, ' I look at these matters from a rather different point of view, you know.' He released her hand, skilfully slid his arm round her waist, and recaptured the hand. She made no resistance. ' That,' he went on, a little tremulously, ' is all the more reason for admiring you.'

' Ye—es ? '

' We live in rummy times,' Mr. Purfleet went on musingly. ' Though I s'pose times always seem rummy to the people who live in them. Take this Lizzie business. It involves the whole matter of sex, you know.'

' Yes ? '

Mr. Purfleet squeezed a little nearer, and went on confidentially.

' A lot of people went off the rocker during the War, and a still bigger lot quietly made up their minds not to be humbugged any more. They 've got to work out their situations. Then there are the Bright Young Idiots, who seem determined to queer the whole pitch to the puritans, by being as vicious as they can, or at least pretending to be.'

Georgie listened to his voice without hearing the words or following the meaning. She was rather like a she-cat unwillingly fascinated by the discordant amatory croonings of an old tabby. Even so, Mr. Purfleet would have attained his object—if he had had any precise object—more effectively by silence than by speech. He talked because talking was really the only thing he knew how to do in life ; he talked because he was one of those people for whom words are the sole reality ; and he talked to give himself the illusion that he had an object. He was not in love with Georgie, he did not even want her, he did not want any woman except in a rather per-verse and superficial way. Without passion or any ardency of desire, he used what attraction he had for women to gratify his vanity and sense of power, and perhaps even a sort of gentle cruelty. The only thing which held Georgie was his physical proximity, but that seemed almost to paralyse her by the intensity of sensation it created in her. Yet she was profoundly un-easy, not so much from embarrassment as from an in-stinctive recoil from Purfleet. She did not really like this verbose if carefully laundered doctrinaire with his bloody flux of ideas which merely disturbed and offended her. Too crudely ignorant to understand herself or this

type of man, she still retained enough vital instinct to
feel a repulsion from him.   Yet, in the darkness of the
old barn, with the warm scented spring air flowing in,
she was powerless against the pressure of Purfleet's arm
and the warm gratifying touch of his fingers on hers.   In
the confusion of her mind, only her senses acted positively.   The guardian angel had hastily retired to more
decorous surroundings, after a frenzied and scandalised
appeal to a daughter of Army and Church *not* to allow
herself to be cuddled by a man whose intentions, if any,
were obviously strictly dishonourable.   Purfleet's voice
went on and on.   To her amazement Georgie found herself wanting to say brutally : ' Shut up, and kiss me ! '
But she said nothing, waiting in a kind of tense daze.

' On the other hand,' Purfleet went on, rather comic-
ally mellifluous, ' there are a great many people, like
yourself, who have been trained in a different and less
rational ethic, and unfortunately still stick to it.'   He
pulled her closer, so that her body half-leaned towards
him.   With apprehension and shamefaced pleasure she
allowed her head to rest awkwardly on his shoulder.
Purfleet was genuinely surprised at this warm easy
yielding, and if he had formulated in words the thought
which sprang into his mind, he would have said : ' Gad !
The wench desires me ! '   He was flattered by this tribute
to his charms.   Or—sudden suspicion—was she merely
having him on ?   Cautiously he slid his hand up to her
left breast.   Jove !   Her heart was beating like a young
dynamo.   Male fatuity, that most contemptible of
vanities, insisted that he should pursue his advantage.
A respectable simulacrum of desire possessed him.

Georgie had lowered her head.   Purfleet drew a deep
breath, made a bold decision, and kissed her neck behind

the ear.   He registered with complacence her little start
of ecstasy.   Since words were essential for him to enjoy
even the most primitive or ordinary sensation, he murmured vaguely :

' Loveliest of all things, pale alabaster ! '

Georgie thought he meant she was lovely, but still
prudently kept her head turned away.   He moved it
gently round, and then kissed her mouth.   Her lips
yielded unresponsively, but she trembled and gave a
little gasp.   Purfleet rather envied her lack of practice.
Obviously she was getting a hell of a kick out of it,
whereas the more enlightened females with whom Mr.
Purfleet became familiar took it all as a matter of course,
and were often displeased by his reluctance to indulge in
finalities.   At this moment he himself remained comparatively unmoved.   What was the next step ?   He
kissed her again, lengthily, to get time to think.   He
registered a response, timid but unmistakable.   Good.

Virtue, Purfleet told himself, is its own reward ; but
how in this case does one reward virtue ?   Like Panurge
I feel the disadvantage of never having known an honest
woman, by leave of their husbands be it said.   A false
step and I shatter the cup of strategy—what a lovely
mixed metaphor !

In this perplexity he fell back upon an ancient gambit
he had tried so often that he was now ashamed of it.
He put up his hand, delicately stroked her cheek with his
finger-tips and murmured with just the right huskiness :

' You have an adorable epidermis.   I should like just
to touch you for hours '—slight, significant pause—' all
of you.   It would be like gathering a bouquet of flowers,
with a rose at the centre.'

Lord ! he reflected, what damn silly things one says,

but they seem to expect it.   Influence of bad fiction on
the arts of seduction.

Georgie said nothing.   Within her the mystic trinity
of the Colonel's daughter, the Church's lamb and the
Girl Guide clamoured with one voice : ' This is disgraceful ! Stop it at once. Push him away. You 've let him
kiss you ! Get up at once, and tick him off ! ' But Purfleet was kissing her again, and her limbs were liquefied
with a strange voluptuousness. They did not want to
move. ' Oh, keep still,' they said. ' Don't let this stop.
Do let him go on.   We 've been waiting for this, so long,
so long.'

Upon my soul, Purfleet reflected amid kisses, I believe
she 's a pukka virgin. *Rara avis*. Were I the egregious
Coz I should cut an extra large cross on my seduction
butt. Has the *jour de gloire* arrived for her ? Better
not advance too far—unnecessary complications. Period
of tentative exploration *à tatons*, so to speak. O her
America, her Newfoundland !

Mr. Purfleet explored, with elaborate precaution.
Surprisingly, Georgie made no effort to repulse him,
even aided the enterprise by a judicious limpness.   Her
eyes were shut.

We are always more careful not to wound their
modesty, he reflected, than they are to preserve it from
affront.   That is why blackguards make the most successful Don Juans.   I myself am a bit of a blackguard.

Wherever he touched her, he felt the flesh delicately
shrink and quiver with a mingling of apprehension and
delight.

' Her heaving embonpoint,' he thought satirically.
Dash it ! I am a bounder. But the golden age is gone
—we no longer do these things simply.

Mr. Purfleet prided himself upon his caressive skill. Minutes passed. Georgie lost sense of time, and felt as if she were gliding up through a clear atmosphere of sensation to some unimagined peak. Suddenly she became tense, all her limbs seemed to contract on themselves, and ' Aaaa ' exhaled from her in a long breath. Purfleet was startled, almost scared. He remained quite still, peering at her white face, almost invisible in the darkness. He felt rather hot, his hair was dismally rumpled, both his arms were aching, and one foot had gone to sleep. He became aware of all these annoyances simultaneously.

An expense of physical energy to no personal end, he thought. Really I am a philanthropist, or rather a philogyne. Will she be grateful ? She ought to be. After all, I haven't Lizzie-ised her. She 's eaten her cake, and still got it.

He was abruptly disturbed in these profound philosophisings by Georgie's pushing him from her and springing to her feet. She stood at the other side of the dark little room, with her hands pressed to her face and her back to him. Purfleet became aware of the mouldy smell of the barn. His foot tingled so much that he limped as he walked over to her. He put his hand on her shoulder, and spoke with paternal fussiness :

' What is it, my dear ?   Do you feel unwell ? '

Georgie snatched her hands from her face.

' Oh ! What have I done ? Why did you do it ? Why did I let you ? '

So this, Purfleet noted indignantly, is virtue ! You ask for cake, pretty obviously ; your humble servant performs the miracle of allowing you to eat it and keep it too, and then you abuse the miracle-worker. No, you

don't, my girl ! I 'm not going to let you get away with
this !

He took his hand deliberately from her shoulder, and
spoke severely :

' Well, you made no objection. I gave you several
opportunities to back out, and you didn't take 'em. You
rather seemed to enjoy it. In fact, I might almost say
you invited it.'

' Oh ! ' exclaimed Georgie, with that deep sense of
outrage we always feel when someone ruthlessly exposes
our real selves. ' Oh ! You *beast* ! '

Insult, Purfleet said to himself, is the refuge of those
who have no case to argue. But I must calm this in-
flamed female spirit. She might make a scene, which
would be distressing. She might go and blurt it out,
which would be embarrassing all round.

Very gently he put his hand back on her shoulder.

' There, there ! ' he said soothingly. ' There, there !
I wasn't trying to hurt you. I was only showing you
that you were being unfair to me. If there 's any guilt,
which there isn't, then we 're both equally guilty. After
all, it was a pure accident that we came in here, and I
swear I had no intentions until you—but never mind.
These things happen, you know.'

' But it 's wrong, it 's dreadfully wrong and degrading,'
Georgie wailed. ' Why did I let you ? '

Purfleet grinned a trifle maliciously in the dark.

' If I were you, darling, I 'd put it all down in the
category of natural and inevitable happenings. After
all, you 've only experienced what most girls experience
long before they 're your age.'

' But,' said Georgie desperately, ' a nice girl should
keep herself *pure* for her husband. We aren't even en-

gaged, and I don't want to be.   I'm not in love with
you.'

Tant mieux, thought Purfleet.   The way out of this
epicene labyrinth will be almost as easy as the way in.
And anyhow I 've only scotched the Minotaur, not killed
her.

' So much the better,' he said aloud with a sort of
post-prandial purr of lechery.   ' You are committed to
nothing, and, as it were, nothing has happened.   You
may rely on my discretion.   Whatever else I may be,
thank God I 'm *not* a gentleman.'

' I feel so degraded, so wrong,' wailed poor Georgie.
' I feel so ashamed.   I shall never, never be able to
forget it.'

A pretty compliment if true, thought Purfleet.   Yet if
this is really her first paddle in the lake of Cythera, she
may remember it.   But this is my cue to make an
end on't.

He put an arm about her, and pulled her, only half-
resistant, to him.

' Nonsense, my dear !   Such shame is not even skin
deep.   And as to forgetting, surely you know that is
Woman's First and Greatest Art ? '

He kissed her, as she made an effort to move away.
And again her Will to Virtue seemed paralysed by this
fragile caress.

' Truly, there is no need for remorse,' said Purfleet.
' I assure you.   'Twas but a tent where takes his one
day's . . .   Don't let it distress you—most natural and
inevitable thing in the world.   Soon more natural than
swimming, and far pleasanter.   Your education has been
neglected, but, if I may say so, you have started in good
hands.   I don't wish to flatter, but you have possibilities,

possibilities.   You must meet people—but avoid women
who seem to take an unnecessary interest in you.   Let
us part friends on this occasion. . . .'

' What time is it ? ' said Georgie.

Mr. Purfleet was vexed.   This it was to cast pearls of
sensation and eloquence before, well, Colonels' daughters.
Like sending a book of poems to the *Daily Mail.*   Nevertheless he looked at his watch.

' Nearly half-past seven.'

' Oh ! ' exclaimed Georgie.   ' It 's nearly dinner-time !
I must go !   What will Mother say ? '

She wrenched herself from his grasp with, he thought,
a haste and indifference which were almost brutal.   The
indelicacy of females !   The power of *que dira-t-on* !

They groped their way hastily and clumsily along the
beams, down the ladder and across the silent, musty,
gloom-filled barn.   At the door Georgie paused and
whispered :

' I *must* go back at once.   Can you find your way out
through the garden ? '

She is as anxious to be rid of me as a sated husband
of his spouse, thought Purfleet.

' Of course,' he said.   ' But do tell me we are still
friends.'

' Yes, yes ! ' she whispered impatiently, turning to go.
He found her hand in the darkness, and kissed it.

' Good-bye, or rather au revoir.'

' Good-bye . . . Oh ! '

' What ? '

' That funny book of yours ! '

' What about it ? '

' I must bring it back to you.'

Mr. Purfleet felt as if his mind had been jaggedly and

violently illuminated by a flash of lightning.   God, he thought, it's true—inevitably they fix another rendez-vous !   She's after me !

'Oh, never mind,' he said casually.   'Keep it—as a souvenir.'

'No,' whispered Georgie, 'I'll bring it back—next Wednesday—at four.'

And before he could speak again, she gave him a peck kiss on the side of his nose, and fled silently down the dark path.

Mr. Purfleet made his way home in the pleasant spring darkness, filled with so many reflections that he regretted no one had invented a mental dictaphone to record all the excellent whimsies which pass through a polished brain in a brief quarter of an hour.   His musings were fragmentary, for several times he missed his path in the darkness.   The long meadow-grass was wet with dew. He felt it soaking his socks above the tops of his shoes. With bitterness he realised that the roll of a superb pair of trousers might be ruined for ever—all because of Virtue.   As he opened the door of his house, he sneezed twice.   Good God, he might even have caught a cold ! But there, he reflected with intense bitterness, it's always the man who pays.

III

On the following Monday the three parishes awoke at various hours with the delighted certainty that the Tom-Lizzie affair was not going to be quite such a fizzle as had seemed probable.

Quite a lot had happened.

The Stimms-Eastcourt faction had heard with fury of
Purfleet's machinations, which had robbed them of the
opportunity of protecting other people's chastity by ruining the lives of Tom and Lizzie.   Mrs. Eastcourt said
that Purfleet ought to be tarred and feathered and then
drummed out of the village.   But, she hinted, public
spirit and the love of morality had died with good
King Edward.

Sir Horace, who was in residence, was really angry.
Tuppenny-'apenny little bounder shovin himself into
village affairs !   It was the business of the aristocracy to
look after the workin people—don't want Nosey Parkers
like Purfleet takin things into their hands.   Upon his
(dingy) soul, Sir Horace was annoyed.   He intimated
the same to Dr. McCall, who, with proven Scottish
loyalty, refrained from calling upon Purfleet for some
time.

Then there was the sermon.

Mr. Carrington appeared in the pulpit, looking a little
stern but otherwise quite unruffled.   In his clear sonor-
ous voice he read the story of the woman taken in
adultery.   He made it sound so impressive that Mr.
Purfleet, who had broken one of his most cherished
habits by going to Church, determined to re-read the
Gospels on the off-chance that there might be something
worth considering in them.

At the end of his lengthy text, the Vicar paused, and
those skilled in sermon strategy vowed that his gaze
dwelt first and earnestly upon Mrs. Eastcourt, then upon
Sir Horace, and then in turn upon other notorious dis-
regarders of charitable speech.

Then he preached a short but energetic sermon, in
which Mr. Purfleet recognised with pleasure the ideas he

had communicated to Carrington in their interview. It was flattering to find that his intellectual seed had not fallen upon barren ground, for once in his life.

The Vicar began by pointing out the beauty and charm of the story, as if the Evangelist, caught up by Divine Inspiration, had risen to supreme heights in communicating a Supreme Message. But what was this Message? It was the Message of Divine and Human Charity, and by ' charity ' he did not mean the letter of charity, the perfunctory or even lavish giving of alms, but the spirit of brotherly love between man and man, the true spirit of neighbourly kindness. (Here Mrs. Eastcourt simpered with conscious virtue.) The speaker regretted to say that he found a lamentable absence of that spirit in Cleeve, despite many ostentatious professions. (Mrs. Eastcourt looked haughty and untouchable.)

Was it not significant, the Vicar continued, that Our Lord had chosen this story of human frailty to impress upon us the duty of true charity in word, thought and act? The Pharisees, the purse-proud defenders of conventional religion, the astute and pedantic practisers of the *letter*, had sought to entrap Our Lord, who had come to show mankind that they must worship God in spirit and in truth. They brought before Him a wretched woman, a sinner, one taken in adultery; and they waited with eagerness for Him to commit Himself—either to a condonation or to a condemnation. What did Our Lord do? He wrote with His finger in the sand, and at first would not answer. Why? Did that not mean a lesson in charity? Our Lord meant us to see that the mere frailty of the unworthy flesh was not so much a sin as the malevolent eagerness of the self-righteous to press hardly upon an erring and unhappy fellow-being. Our Lord,

like the great poet, Dante Alighieri, held that to sin from
excess of Love was less displeasing to God than the sins
which arise from lack of Love.

(Here he made a pause, wherein the silence was broken
by a cough of reprimand from Sir Horace and a sniff of
disdain and contempt from Mrs. Eastcourt.)

' Have we not women taken in adultery in our own
time and village?' Mr. Carrington cried earnestly.
' And do we not find an almost indecent haste of condemnation, a most uncharitable alacrity to cast the first
stone? The Pharisees at least had the grace to listen to
their consciences, which told them that not one among
them was without sin. " They went out one by one,
beginning with the eldest." But we, deeper sinners than
they, have no such qualms. We compete as to who shall
be first in condemnation, hoping thereby to cloak from
Almighty God the sorry screed of our own errors and
sins !

' It is not for me, the humble and sinful servant of my
Master, to question His Wisdom and Justice. Whom
He has absolved, shall I condemn? Nor do I seek to
condone what He did not condone. But I would warn
you that here we have Our Lord's express intimation
that in His sight the sin against human kindness is far
worse than the sins of the flesh. " Neither do I condemn thee ; go, and sin no more." I ask you, my
brethren, to meditate this in your hearts, and to ask
yourselves if during the past few days and weeks you
too have not sinned against the spirit in defence of the
letter, if you too have not made the monstrous claim that
ye are without sin by pressing forward to cast the first
stone against a hapless woman taken in adultery. Be
assured that on the last day it shall be more tolerable for

that sinful but repentant woman than for the Pharisees who condemned her.

' And now to God the Father . . .'

As the sermon ended there was a terrific scraping of feet, rustling of prayer-books and an excited whispering.   Mrs. Eastcourt rose ostentatiously to her feet and, followed by young Master Eastcourt blushing and grinning with embarrassment, tottered indignantly from the Church.   Sir Horace was almost apoplectic with coughing—confound the feller's impudence, preachin at his betters and supportin the lower classes.   The unco guid exchanged glances of superior condemnation. Georgie and Alvina were perplexed, but gamely certain that there must be something in what the parson said. Mr. Purfleet giggled happily into a copy of *Candide*, which he had brought in place of a prayer-book.

When the service was over, Sir Horace, purple-visaged and startled of eye, pursued Carrington into the vestry ; and those parishioners who had stayed behind to eavesdrop were soon gratified by the sound of voices evidently raised in altercation.   Sir Horace emerged, even more beetrooty, but triumphant—Mr. Carrington had announced his determination to resign the living.

A few days earlier he had heard that the Canonry was still vacant, and at his disposal.

But the scandal of the bolshie sermon and the Vicar's ' dismissal ' (so Cleeve chose to regard it) was immediately capped by a more savoury and enjoyable episode, which combined prurience with moral edification in an almost ideal manner.

The whole episode should be considered as a warning

by those who are tempted to preach the Word of God with too loose an interpretation, unchecked by the Wisdom of the Ages and a public school education.

On Monday night, Lizzie, like Niobe, all tears, fled from the Smithers's house, in spite of Georgie's almost abject entreaties to her not to go, and fell sobbing upon the bosom of the embarrassed and indignant Mr. Judd, who more than ever most ardently wished that Mrs. Judd had brought forth men children only.

Fired by a mistaken interpretation of the now famous sermon, Coz that evening had made a determined, not to say brutal, attack upon Lizzie's damaged virtue. If, Coz had argued, even the Church was gettin so jolly broad-minded they didn't mind a skivvie kickin over the traces, there couldn't be any harm in an extra kick or two. Especially with a feller of decent blood and breedin, who could obviously show the girl a thing or two beyond the attainment of mere yokels. After all, damn it, she 'd been carryin on with young Strutt and that policeman feller at the same time. Hot little bit of stuff, evidently.

And so, penetrating into the back kitchen at what he considered the appropriate moment, Coz had signified his male will and pleasure in no uncertain terms. No use beatin about the bush with a girl of that class. To his amazement at first, and then his frozen horror, Lizzie resisted his attempts with an almost ferocious energy, which cannot be too highly commended to all ladies who may find themselves in a similar situation. (He had come upon her so suddenly, like one of the bogey-men of her infancy, that she was scared out of her wits.) She scratched his face and bit his thumb with an animal fury which was not only disconcertin, but extremely painful.

She then clasped the astounded Coz so tightly that he could not move and could scarcely breathe, and uttered the most piercing yells for help.   Coz struggled to get free, exclaiming :

' I say—by Jove—what the—let a feller—breathe— I say—O my *God* ! '

The last exclamation, less pious than agonised, was caused by Georgie's rushing into the kitchen, closely followed by Alvina, and, at a distance, by the hobbling and perturbed Fred.

' Coz ! '

' *Coz !* '

There was so much scorn, reproach, contempt, amazement, horror and condemnation in those two monosyllables uttered by his female relatives that Coz felt himself blush to the base of his spine.   As he afterwards explained to an outwardly sympathetic but inwardly sardonic friend at The Club, it was ' the most dam' awkward situation a feller could find himself in, what ? '   Lizzie suddenly released her grip—so suddenly that Coz staggered—and fell on her back in what Mrs. Judd later described with relish as ' screamin' 'ysterics '.

' What 's the matter ? ' asked the Colonel, who appeared at that moment, hastily averting his gaze from the disorder of Lizzie's dress, which Georgie was ' repairing ' with sisterly solicitude.

' Matter ! ' snapped Alvina, more sportin-erect than ever.   ' Only one of you *pigs* of men again ! '

And she retired, with all the dignity she had acquired from a careful study of the late Queen-Mother.

The Colonel was genuinely distressed—a pretty kettle of fish under a chap's own roof.   He peremptorily ordered Coz to leave the room ; and that bleeding, pant-

ing, unhappy Apollo was only too glad to retreat from
such a virago of a Daphne.   Fred and Georgie then
turned their efforts towards calming Lizzie, but she was
not going to lose such a chance of a real melodrama.
She maintained the hysteria almost beyond the limits
of human endurance, and then insisted upon leaving.
Threats, promises, entreaties, cajoleries, appeals, all were
in vain.   Lizzie had got in one on the gentry, and wasn't
going to be deprived of her lawful scandal.

The Colonel sent Georgie to bed, and retired himself.   As he undressed with his usual slow deliberation,
he mused profoundly, and shook his head frequently.
A bad business.   Most unfortunate that the women
should have seen it.   Have to see Judd and Strutt, too,
and make the gel shut up.   Damned awkward to have
a scandal.   Coz would have to apologise all round.
Better let him go away for a few weeks, until Lizzie and
Tom were well settled down.

But there was a silver lining even to this sordid
little cloud.   It was revealed to Fred just as he was
about to pull back the bed-clothes.   After all Alvina's
hints—and dam' nasty hints too—about him, it was
amusin that Coz should turn out to be the sinner.   The
Colonel chuckled.   One for them and their family pride !
No, no, it wasn't the rather-looked-down-upon Fred
Smithers, Lieutenant-Colonel by the grace of God and
His Majesty's oversight, who was at fault.   It was Coz.
Robert Smale, Armiger.   The pukkaist Sahib of them
all.

The Colonel blew out his lamp, and chuckled again
as he pulled the sheets up to his double chin.   He !
He !   The pukkaist Sahib of them all.

IV

Georgie and Purfleet met again under a cloud of good resolutions.

Mr. Purfleet had been thinking seriously. And on Wednesday afternoon he was still thinking. He owned a very spacious and comfortable arm-chair, which had a device for holding a book open at just the right height, so that Mr. Purfleet could read in voluptuous tranquillity, without the degrading physical effort of supporting the book himself. Before him was a handsomely printed edition of the *Golden Asse* (Tudor Translation, of course—Mr. Purfleet had once corresponded with the late Charles Whibley on a Point of Scholarship), open at the story of Cupid and Psyche. But his eye wandered from the sweetly turgid prose, so gallantly appropriate to the rendezvous set by this very rustic Psyche for her overgrown and reluctant Cupid. Mr. Purfleet was thinking.

No doubt there is something in the misfortunes of our best friends which is not wholly displeasing to us ; but, on the other hand, there is occasionally something in the misfortunes of our worst foes which may hold a warning. Mr. Purfleet was reflecting on the unhappy situation of Robert Smale, Armiger, who had left that morning to hide his shame and humiliation in a small but select East Coast watering-place. Sullenly, reluctantly, disputing every inch of terrain with indomitable pluck, Lizzie had been forced to retreat from her position of outraged virtue, determined to fight for its cause to the last shilling of the last man. Exactly what compensation she demanded was never quite clear, but it was certainly something substantial, to include a criminal prosecution for rape, a civil action for heavy damages, an abject apology as public as possible, and the legal injunction upon Coz to wear some sort of distinctive costume to mark his crime for the rest of his life—some Jewish gaberdine on which pure maidens would spit, or some scarlet letter from which all young matrons would avert their shocked gaze.

Mr. Judd's feelings calmed more rapidly. Whereas in the first outburst of indignation he had boldly asserted that ' 'e ought to be publicly carstrated', he soon supinely assented to the Colonel's suggestions for 'patchin things up and stoppin all the talk'. But the united efforts of Mr. and Mrs. Judd, Tom Strutt, Georgie, the Colonel and McCall (who had been called in to bear medical witness to an outrage whereof, he firmly declared, he could find no trace) were needed to persuade Lizzie to abstain from the revenge naturally demanded by a Woman's Finer Feelings. The weakest point in Lizzie's defence was obviously McCall's determination to stand by his own class, and his bold Scottish refusal to commit himself in any way whatsoever. Great strategic ability had been shown by Mr. Judd and the Colonel in heading off Mrs. Eastcourt, who would undoubtedly have brought a lawyer on the scene in a brace of scandals, and then obviously the Law would have had to take its course until there was no more money to fee It.

But the Colonel, steady, cool, never calmer than when under fire, snatched victory from the iron jaws of defeat. Lizzie accepted Coz's written apology (which she ever afterwards preserved, folded up with her marriage lines, the two indubitable proofs of respectability); she accepted a ten-pound note with naïf pleasure, never having seen the like before or heard of compounding a felony; and she freely and frankly forgave (but never forgot) what after all was but one more compliment, if an outrageous one, to the power of her charms. And on the Thursday she would be duly wedded, tra-la, to Mr. Strutt.

Everybody, especially Mr. Judd, looked forward with an anticipation of extreme relief to the moment when this squint-eyed Helen would be safely married and dumped as a responsibility on Tom Strutt. He, naturally enough, was not consulted in any of the arrangements, except when he was commanded by his future mother-in-law to use what little influence he had over Lizzie to make her accept them.

All these things had reached Mr. Purfleet, though somewhat distorted by the limpid flow of village gossip. And now, as he sat with his unread book before him, anticipating Georgie's coming with a slight pain in his stomach, he pondered them in his heart. As he sat there in his great chair, lightly tapping the arm with the tips of his long drooping fingers, he might have been a model for the bronze statue of Richelieu in the Sorbonne Church—minus the barbiche and the grandeur.

The case against entangling alliances had now become unanswerable. Naturally, a Man of Sense and Feeling would not behave with the bovine brutality of a Coz. But nevertheless there were snares, snares. Georgie was not Lizzie, true, true; but sisters under their skin—a very coarse metaphor even for an Empire Poet, Mr. Purfleet reflected on the side. It was odd, very odd, he mused, how different Sex in real life was from Sex in books. Considering the unscrupulous way women exploit themselves for grossly material ends, it was not at all surprising that a sensitive man like Pierre Vidal (for a moment, Mr. Purfleet identified himself with Pierre Vidal)

should have gone mad, and run uncomfortably about
Provence—a hot and hilly country—imagining himself
a wolf, or was he pursued by a wolf ?   Mr. Purfleet felt
too languid to look up the reference.   And those eighteenth-century seducers—Casanova and the heroes of
erotic French novels—how the devil did they get away
with it ?   Confounded liars.   In Mr. Purfleet's experience, there was inevitably a snake hiding under the
flowers, inevitably something bitter surged up in the
midst of delight.   Women had not the same purity of
intention as men.   He wished . . . Either they treated
you with an insulting contempt as the most insignificant
of pastimes ;   or they blackmailed you in subtle and
annoying ways ;   or they overwhelmed you with embarrassing attentions which proclaimed your intimacy to all
the world and led to horrible complications ;   or they
were so very prudent, you never saw them ;   or, as in the
present case, they actually schemed to marry you.   Mr.
Purfleet shuddered.   He perceived the danger of being
a bachelor.   Would it not be possible to go through a
form of marriage with some female unfortunate who, for
a small consideration (say, five pounds), would then dis-
appear for ever ?   No.   Too dangerous.   Mr. Purfleet
sighed, and wondered if it were now possible to take the
tonsure, as in the Old Régime, without committing one-
self to a life of odious austerity and lack of freedom ?

He got up, sighed, drank a stiff brandy and soda, and
then began meditatively to chew a clove.   He more than
half hoped Georgie would not come—the peace of mind
would be worth the loss of a not highly prized edition of
a somewhat mediocre work.

Georgie's meditations, though briefer and less erudite,

were none the less prudential.   But she was in a curious
state of mind.   The events of the past few weeks had
undoubtedly shocked her, but they had shocked her to
a sort of life.   With amazement she perceived that while
these horrid and repulsive things had been happening to
her and around her, she had not been bored once.   She
scarcely remembered the listless Georgie who biked so
reluctantly and wearily to and from Cricton ; now, busy
with thoughts, plans, emotions, an almost happy confusion, she simply flew over the ground.   Things, she
felt, were happening, and would happen.   She neglected
the Guides.

Yet she had been hurt and frightened by the revelation of what had hitherto been concealed from her—the
furtive desires and mouldy intrigues and aimless spite
which creep their slimy way below the outward decorum
of family and village life.   How beastly men were, how
utterly beastly.   All they cared about was—well, Georgie
didn't like to specify, even to herself, what it *was* they
cared about—and then they simply *despised* a woman.
The way they treated women was horrid.   Think of poor
Lizzie !   And Georgie worked herself up to quite a
passion of indignation over poor Lizzie.   Either they
were like Mr. Carrington, so reserved and cautious and
selfish ; or they were like Reggy (Georgie already called
Mr. Purfleet ' Reggy ' in her meditations, a fact which
would have filled him with acute apprehension if he had
known it), they were frivolous and sensual and evasive
like Reggy, with no notion of what made for serious and
permanent happiness in life.   Or—but here Georgie was
forced to limit her examples of male shortcomings, for,
after all, she had no more examples to recall.   So once
more she reviewed their conduct, particularly Reggy's. . . .

One thing she was certain of—she would never permit any renewal of what had happened, once, through some inexplicable accident.   It was wrong, it was degrading, it was . . . She forbade herself to think about it any more.   Wrong, degraded . . . She went over the whole scene again, in a kind of day-dream. . . . Of course, if Reggy were serious, if *only* he were serious.   They could be awfully happy together.   They could live in his house —after a little economical trip abroad for the . . .—and that would be so convenient, for she could see Mother and Father every day.   They could get rid of that great silent brute of a man-servant and have a neat maid to open the door and wait at little tea and dinner parties— she could get a lot of hints about entertainment from Margy.   And she would superintend *all* the business of the house and the tradesmen and the garden and every-thing, so that Reggy could be quite undisturbed and read and read and read.   And she would see that the books were all carefully dusted and make him a catalogue so that he could find any book he wanted at a moment's notice.   And they would cut the Eastcourts, but she would *make* Reggy be polite to Sir Horace and to Mr. Craigie—after all, we 're here to be friendly and brighten everyone's life, aren't we ? ' No, Sir Horace,' she im-agined herself saying, dressed in a plain but most refined evening gown, ' my husband doesn't dance, but I *know* he likes me to dance, especially with *old* friends like yourself.'   And, of course, Sir Horace would invite them to shooting-parties, and Reggy would love it, any man would love it.   And if she were very, very careful with the housekeeping, they might even have a couple of hunters.   She felt sure that at heart Reggy was really a *sportsman*.   It 's in every Englishman's blood. . . .

But, of course, if he wasn't serious, there would be an end to it.   She would stand no nonsense from him.   No more degradation.   But he *must* see—how could he fail to see ?—that it was better to be serious.   How could he go on living there in lonely unhappiness, never brightened by a gun or a fox, very likely mixing himself up with impure and degraded women, when solid happiness was tapping—so discreetly but so obviously—at his very door ?

Thus it was that while Purfleet hopefully and thankfully beheld a steady downpour of rain set in soon after lunch, Georgie felt dismayed, as if God were refusing His benediction.   How could she pretend she wanted to go for a walk if it was raining ?   Thank goodness, Coz was away, so she could probably slip off unseen.

Once more the umbrella, the oiled-silk raincoat, the strong practical shoes and goloshes, came into action. Once more she walked through wet lanes, where the full leafage fluttered in the light wind and swished down little broken cataracts of raindrops.   The buttercup meadows had turned from gold to a sort of drenched drab mustard, but all the tangle of green things which ran under the hedges like a wave breaking into ragged white foam of umbelliferae seemed richer and darker in the soft wet light.   Passing the woods, she noticed that the bluebells were over.   Fortunately, this time she did not have to pass Mrs. Eastcourt's abode of love, since Purfleet lived in another direction ; but it would scarcely have mattered if she had—Mrs. Eastcourt and Purfleet were not ' on terms ' nowadays.   It was hoped that a universal boycott by village society would determine Purfleet to leave altogether.   But, so far, the experi-

ment had not proved much of a success, since Purfleet
was unaware that anyone was cutting him, and only
thanked the gods that none of the bores had called
recently.

Was Georgie one of the bores ? Distinctly, he reflected, oh most obviously a bore, especially under the
present circumstances. Then, why encourage her ? Ah,
why indeed ? What a terrible encumbrance good-nature
is ! More than half the difficulties of life are caused
by not being selfish enough. I am far too altruistic,
thought Purfleet, pulling the snug coverlet of his rentier
bachelordom about him, far too altruistic. I must make
a slogan of it—not Buy British Goods but Be More
Selfish. What an excellent plan ! He began to look
comfortably through a recent catalogue of second-hand
books from a bookseller who specialised in uncut review
copies. Like so many British book-lovers, Mr. Purfleet
always bought his books second-hand, no doubt to encourage authors. The saving of the thirty shillings a
week was an irresistible temptation to spend twice as
much on himself. Through the half-open window he
heard the steady gentle whisper of the falling rain, and
the louder splashy drippings from trees and eaves. How
fortunate that it was raining !

Suddenly he heard the click of the gate, which somehow sounded louder and more imperative through the
subdued murmur of a world of rain. A few seconds
later he saw an umbrella top pass the window. It was !
It was ! The determination of the female on the sexual
war-path, the determination ! And Mr. Purfleet raised
his hands mutely to heaven in supplication, as he thought
of the determination of the female. A sharp suspicion
darted its unworthy poison into his mind—did she know

that Wednesday was Curzon's half-day off ?   (Curzon was the name of Purfleet's butler-batman.)

He opened the door himself.   Real courage, he knew, would have made him look stony and say ' Not at home ! ' and then shut the door, quietly but firmly.   At the last moment he lacked courage, and instead clasped both her hands—umbrella handle and all—in his, saying with a heartiness which greatly surprised him :

' Come in, come *in* !   I *am* glad to see you.   How kind of you to bring me your sunshine through this dismal day.   Stockings not wet, I hope ?   Come along, then, come along.'

Georgie had so worked herself up with a picture of Mr. Purfleet—or rather, Reggy—living in dismal bachelor misery, that she was surprised and rather hurt to find him looking so cheerful and comfortable.   Especially so comfortable, since the cheerfulness might have been attributed to joy at the coming of The Woman, who would tinge all his days with gold.   Mr. Purfleet was wearing the costume of a Benedictine monk, which he affected on occasions ; and this almost crude declaration of celibacy impressed Georgie unfavourably, almost as a rebuff.   It was also a little depressing to find how very snug and *settled* both he and his room looked.   There was a gentle fire of logs on the raised hearth, just enough to ward off the damp of a late spring day.   The aroma of an excellent cigar dwelt in the air, and a tray beside the piano displayed a coffee-pot and one cup (used), de- canters of port, brandy and sherry, and a bottle of Bene- dictine.   There was one liqueur glass (unused) and a large balloon goblet of very thin glass with a shallow gold deposit of brandy still in it.   The room was sur- prisingly neat—far neater than any of the cluttered

rooms under martial law in which she dwelt—and the
books were almost indecently free from dust, and meti-
culously arranged.

Conversation did not come easily.   Purfleet, bustling
about to fill the gap, found her a cushion she did not
want, offered her drinks—brandy ?   No ?   Sherry or
port ?   No ?   Drop of Benedictine ?   No ?   Well, what
about a cocktail ?   No ?   He did not offer tea, and
Georgie was dying for her cup of tea.   (She did *not*
know that Curzon was away.)   However, she accepted
a large Turkish cigarette, and they sat opposite each
other in arm-chairs, smoking, and desperately making
conversation.   More than ever Georgie felt that Reggy
was not serious.   And yet . . .

And yet gradually the icy atmosphere thawed.   The
almost canine stupidity and suspicion with which they
started the meeting—sniffing at each other, so to speak,
with bristling hair, starting eyes, inaudible growls and an
inane wagging of tails—gave way to a more companion-
able warmth.   Mr. Purfleet took a sherry ;   Georgie
changed her mind, and took a sherry too.   That she
was unused to wines, especially in the afternoon, soon
became apparent from her flushed cheeks, bright eyes
and unusual loquacity.   Mr. Purfleet took another sherry.
Georgie felt that although Reggy was not serious, still,
there *was* something very pleasant and attractive about
him—but, of course, there would be no more degradation.   That was flat.   And Purfleet ?   He could not
help noticing, with a certain amount of complacency,
how greatly the girl improved in intelligent society—
seemed really to understand and see eye-to-eye with him.
And, really, with her hat off and her back to the light,
she was quite passable, quite passable.   Once again, he

noted with appreciation the agreeable curves of her body
—in the matter of significant feminine form Mr. Purfleet
was no Cubist. But, of course, there was to be no
entangling alliance, no more love's labour lost, so to
speak. And yet . . .

And yet, somehow—impossible to say why or how—
Butcher and Lang were degraded to the status of Gale-
otto. Somehow—why? how?—Mr. Purfleet found he
had shut the window and drawn the curtains, and the
degradation of the barn was repeated, more fully and
more comfortably, in Mr. Purfleet's large arm-chair.
The guardian angel gave very little trouble—possibly,
like Curzon, off duty. The (alleged) Boucher Diana
who hovered above Mr. Purfleet's mantelpiece, elegantly
sprawling among nymphs with engagingly pink opulen-
cies, smiled and waved her little silver bow as if ironi-
cally cheering the Triumph of Chastity. The red heart
of the fire glowed with sympathetic warmth, and then
collapsed with a bright orgasm of sparks.

Came the inevitable pause, the change of the tide, the
backward surge of the wave with its dismal rattle of
shingle like the dying breath of desire. Or rather, Purfleet reflected, like the rattle of peas in a fool's bladder.
He was amazed at his own stupidity and the ease with
which he had been preyed upon. Why had he allowed
his altruism to get the better of prudence, why had he
given these dangerous alms, why so foolishly hoisted the
Jolly Roger on a peaceable and ugly craft? ' Obfuscation,' he murmured to himself, ' obfuscation of the intellect.' He repeated the phrase to himself several times,
as if it were an incantation potent enough to wipe out
the past, to levitate Georgie from his knees to her own
room, and leave him calmly uncompromised. Un-

fortunately, nothing happened. Georgie did not levitate, and he began to find her weight an unusual and indeed painful strain on his femurs and tibias. His gluteus maximus trembled slightly, with fatigue, with nervousness, with the wan exhaustion of having given what he didn't get back. A situation, he felt, both ridiculous and unpleasant. Never again. What a weight! Ten stone? Eleven? A ton! He wished to God she'd get off. He glanced at her face. She seemed asleep, her eyes shut, her cheeks very flushed, her lips slightly apart. Her nose was awfully conspicuous and indeed repulsive at such close quarters and at such a moment. A line of Heywood rushed into Mr. Purfleet's mind from the stores of his memory : ' O that 'twere possible to undo things done ! '

Georgie stirred, and he hastily averted his eyes. He felt he could *not* meet her gaze at that moment, he would positively hate her if she looked possessive. What was she saying ? What had she whispered ?

' Reggy ! '

A chill fear seemed to strike fever into him. Reggy ! O Lord ! From fornication and all other deadly sins . . .

' Yes, darling ? '

' Reggy, it 's terribly wrong and wicked of us, but oh,' and her voice sank to an almost sacred tone of insinuation, ' if only we had the *right* to . . .'

Panic and Purfleet at that moment were indistinguishable. All his wits and devices abruptly deserted to the enemy. He was speechless and almost without thought. Marry Georgie ! ' Marriage was ordained for the . . .' O God, O Montreal ! Get me out of this, ye Fates, and never again, never again !

' Don't you think so, Reggy ? '

Somehow or other she must be made to shut up. In
desperation, conquering a surprising amount of repug-
nance, he kissed her. At least she couldn't say ' Reggy '
in that awful Marie Corelli way while she was kissing.
He wished he could gag her with a kiss.

Georgie disengaged herself, and tried to look into his
eyes. He wasn't having any, and gazed with Spartan
determination at the fire. She remained quite still for
a few seconds, and then abruptly got up. The sigh of
relief which immediately rose from the very depths of
Mr. Purfleet's heart was unfeigned but uncourtly. He
moved his stiffened legs with grave solicitude. Georgie
was fumbling as she put on her hat. He noticed that
her hands trembled slightly, and that she looked as if she
were going to cry. Purfleet hardened his heart. Now
that crushing physical weight was off him, he felt better,
more in control of the situation. She mustn't leave like
this ! Moreover, best avoid a scene.

' Don't go yet,' he said, with feigned cordiality.

' I must,' said Georgie tonelessly. ' I . . .'

And, to Purfleet's intense discomposure, she began to
cry, not melodramatically or ostentatiously, but just an
irresistible flow of tears, with an occasional broken little
sob, like a child's. Purfleet was consternated. His sen-
sualist's good-nature battled hard with his selfishness.
He couldn't bear to feel that he had caused those childish-
suffering tears ; on the other hand, he could still less
bear to pay the price of drying them. Purfleet married !
And to Georgie Smithers, an illiterate she-bumpkin of
the sportin class ! Intolerable Götterdämmerung !

' I say,' he stammered, ' don't do that. Please don't.
I 'm awfully sorry. What a terrible fiasco ! If I 'd
known you . . .'

Georgie miserably blew her nose into a damp hanky, which somehow had never before seemed so little and useless and comfortless. With an effort, she mobilised all the Stoic forces.

' All right. Don't worry. It 's nothing. I shall be all right in a minute.'

Purfleet stepped forward, as if to put his arm round her.

' Please don't touch me,' she said. And somehow he didn't dare.

She blew her nose again, with a sad little snivelling noise.

' There ! ' she said, with almost nurse-like false optimism. ' That 's all over now. I 'm so sorry. I didn't mean to.'

' I 'm sorry too, dreadfully sorry. I 'd no idea. No, you mustn't go at once. I insist. Someone will see you 've been . . . Sit down.'

He forced her into the arm-chair, and poured her out a glass of sherry with a rather shaky hand. Then he drew the curtains and half-opened the window. The rain had diminished to a fine mist, and the clear thrush-song came into the room. It sounded so impersonal, so inhuman, like snow-crystals made audible. Its pure senselessness and utter absence of feeling made all that had happened seem fancifully unreal.

' Lovely that thrush is,' said Purfleet with feigned composure. ' Such cold commentary on the bird-and-beer school of poets, don't you think ? '

' Yes,' said Georgie, who thought nothing at all, never having heard of the school in question.

Purfleet burbled on, regaining confidence as he went. He chatted, forcing every ounce of power out of his

mental engine.   She listened, answering only by a word
or two.   Once she laughed at something crude enough
to strike her as amusing.   But when she rose to go
a second time, he didn't try to stop her.   God-awful
strain !

'Can I lend you another book ?' asked Purfleet as
they moved from the room, almost abjectly anxious to
curry favour and placate her.

'No, thanks, I . . . I don't get much time for
reading.'

'Oh, all right, but do please remember that you 're
always welcome to borrow any you want.'

'Thanks.'

They had reached the front door, and Purfleet's fingers
were on the knob.   He paused.   Gallantry, common
decency, elementary humanity forbade that they should
part in this dismal and almost hostile manner.   He suddenly clutched her, and kissed her clumsily, like a bash-
ful cousin, first on one cheek and then on the other.

'There !' he said.   'I 'm awfully sorry, and I
apologise.   I didn't mean that you should be unhappy.'

Georgie laughed, but unhappily.

'Oh, it 's quite all right.   Please don't say any more
about it.'

'Well, look here—er—can't we meet again soon ?
Can't I come to see you some time next week ?'

Georgie looked at him.   With her it was now *final*
that there should be no more degradation.   Did he think
she would go on, after this . . . ?

'Will you come to tea—with Mother and me—on
Tuesday ?'

Purfleet saw the rebuff and the determination.   His
heart leaped up like any bird.   It was worth the bore-

dom of an hour to gain peace with honour in this war against his liberty.

'Tuesday?   All right.   I 'd love to.'

'Good-bye, then.'

'Good-bye.'

He watched her walk down the path, a strapping figure of a girl in her shiny raincoat.   A pity, a pity. He waved his hand as she went through the gate, but she did not respond.

Mr. Purfleet shut the door, stood still and rubbed his chin thoughtfully, went upstairs and washed his hands, came down and lighted a cigarette, rubbed his chin again even more thoughtfully, poured himself out a large brandy and soda, and returned to the adventures of Cupid and Psyche.

v

The wedding of Tom and Lizzie, that mystic cere- mony which somehow made all right everything which had been all wrong, was not much of a success and pleased nobody, though it might have provided enter- tainment and instruction to an anthropologist studying the persistence of magical practices and ceremonial cos- tumes in civilised communities.   Most of the gentry stayed away ;   in fact they were only represented by Fred Smithers and Purfleet.   For a moment, the Colonel had caressed the project of stunning the village with full regimentals and a row of medals, but all his finer feelings as a gentleman immediately told him that they could only be worn at the wedding of a *lady* marrying into the Army.   He and Purfleet both exhumed morning clothes and top-hats, alike in that both suits through the passage of time had become rather too tight for the owners, the

Colonel's having been purchased in 1912 and Purfleet's in the expensive days of 1919. Also, in the frenzy of getting off, Curzon had handed Purfleet his opera hat instead of his silk hat, a horrible solecism which Purfleet only discovered—with a gasp of horror—as he entered the Church. However, the eyes of the village were not used to these distinctions, and gazed with appreciative awe on these displays of upper-class elegance and luxury.

Lizzie was all of a fluster, and looked embarrassingly corpulent, while her white veil only emphasised the redness of her heated countenance. Tom was gawky and ineffective, giving exactly the impression of a large calf decked for ceremonial slaughter and uneasily aware that something unpleasant was pending. Maggie's postman acted as best man because Maggie had already gone the way of all hizzies. He had done a good bit of celebrating beforehand, and disgraced everybody by hiccuping with vulgar persistence through the most sacred and important part of the service. Only Mr. Judd looked and felt ' pretty middlin' comf'table ', as he put it. He wore the black suit which he used for funerals, a form of social entertainment which greatly appealed to Mr. Judd since it combined dignity of emotion with solemn lessons on the dangers of existence in an under-policed country. But since a wedding is, after all, supposed to be a festive affair, Mr. Judd wore a pink tie with a pearl pin, his best tan boots, and displayed his alberts nearly as ostentatiously as the Colonel would have liked to display his medals. He gave the bride away with almost indecent alacrity and cheerfulness. The bridesmaids, who frequently giggled, formed a Futurist composition of very short skirts and very pink legs. Mr. Carrington looked worried—he had heard that Sir Horace was in communication with the Bishop, and unfortunately the affair of the Canonry was not yet definitely settled.

Confetti was thrown as the bride and bridegroom sheepishly departed, but rather half-heartedly.

Purfleet returned from the ceremony in a state of acute depression. This travesty of what might be a rehearsal of his own fate filled him with uneasy foreboding. It would be an exaggeration to say that his conscience awoke, for it was extremely doubtful if Mr. Purfleet had a conscience, but the instinct of self-preservation which did the work of a conscience for him was very much awake and insistent.

At the moment of his parting with Georgie the day before, he had felt that he was out of the wood, that Georgie had accepted the fact that this particular fox had got clean away, and therefore the hunt was all up. So much so, that in his confidence he had been chiefly concerned to let her down lightly. But, on reflection, he was not so sure that she had accepted defeat. The more he thought about it, the more he disliked this tea invitation which he had rashly accepted. What did Georgie mean by bringing Alvina into the situation? Granted that their relation as respectable mother and daughter made any frank confidence impossible, still, one never knew. . . . Women have mysterious methods of inter-communication and invariably act as allies when not rivals. One woman, Purfleet felt he could deal with successfully, but two . . . Who could tell what he might be duped into? And, as he thought of Georgie and the Smithers family and their connections and all they stood for, he was appalled at his own rashness in trying to bring a little colour and comfort into Georgie's life, while he sweated with apprehension at the pictures of paying the price which obtruded themselves on his inward vision in more and more frightful forms.

By Sunday morning he had imagined so many ghastly possibilities that he looked positively haggard, and felt as if he were on the verge of a nervous breakdown. Even the arrival of a case of wine and a large parcel of second-hand books had failed to distract him. Curzon observed his depression and, diagnosing the probable cause with shrewd soldierly insight, mixed a strong dose of Epsom salts with Mr. Purfleet's morning tea, in accordance with the best Army practice in the treatment of melancholy recruits. Purfleet in his distracted state drank half a cup of the revolting mixture before he discovered how awful it was. The terrifying thought occurred to him that Georgie might have confessed everything to the Colonel, and that Curzon, from military obedience and loyalty, might now be trying to poison him. He rang up McCall to consult him about the symptoms and make him a confidant, but McCall—ever obedient to the whims of distinguished patients like Sir Horace and his Lady— sent word through the telephone by the housemaid that he was out, and did not know when he should be back.

In desperation, Purfleet returned to his books. But they had lost all their savour. The Muses fly from the uneasy heart; and even the Boucher Diana seemed to have taken on a sneering and menacing look, as if threatening him with the fate of Acteon. His instinct for flight drove him from his room into the air. It was a pleasantly bright morning, all twinkling leaves and soft wind and lush meadows and swishing motor-cars. But Mr. Purfleet, absorbed in his panic-stricken gloom, scarcely even noted that the sun was shining. He tramped across country on foot-paths, then got to a road, and eventually came to the bridge over the little river. Here he found Mr. Judd lingering at the end of his Sunday morning walk, contemplating the stumps of his elms with bitter resignation and occasionally spitting thoughtfully into the water. Mr. Judd looked up as Purfleet drew level.

' Mornin', Sir,' he said cheerfully.

' Morning, Judd,' said Purfleet in listless tones.

' Now this is what I call a day,' said Mr. Judd enthusiastically. ' If it wasn't for the women and them there moters I should reckon we was in Paradise. English weather, Sir, there ain't nothin' like it.'

Purfleet felt inclined to agree, especially about women and English weather, but all he said was :

' Yes, I suppose it *is* fine. I hadn't noticed.'

And then he looked so depressed and agitated that even Mr. Judd noticed something. A chain of cars, motor-cycles and a lorry or two began to crash over the bridge with raucous hoots and loud moanings of engines. Instinctively they began to walk back towards the village.

' If you 'll pardon me a-sayin' so, Sir, and takin' the liberty,' said Mr. Judd, ' you ain't lookin' your best this mornin'.'

' No, no, a little off colour, bit run down.'

' Ah ! ' replied Mr. Judd compassionately, ' it ain't to be wondered at, Sir. All them books o' yours and settin' there readin' mornin', noon an' night wouldn't do no good to no-one. Un'ealthy, I call it. In'uman. It 's a wonder you ain't gone melancholy mad or gone to 'orspital with gallopin' consumption.'

And Mr. Judd gazed at him with deep and benevolent compassion.

Purfleet laughed.   Already Mr. Judd was doing him good.   It was soothing to be with people who live elementary lives with elementary wisdom, rather like going to the Zoo à *la* Samuel Butler.

' Well, what would you do, Judd, if you were in my place ? '

Mr. Judd considered this question with his usual ponderous gravity.

' Well, Sir, if I was a genl'man of independent means and all your book-learnin', I should go into Parl'ment.'

' Into Parliament ! ' exclaimed Purfleet, who had all the horror of an active-minded man for the intellectual sloth of practical politics.   ' And what on earth would you do there ? '

' Ah ! ' said Mr. Judd meaningly, ' I shouldn't do nothin' at first, Sir.   I should keep me eyes and ears open, and get to know all them hanky-pankies that goes on be'ind the scenes.   That 's what bringin' the Country down, Sir.'

' And when you 'd found 'em out, what could you do ? '

This was rather a poser, and Mr. Judd meditated again.

' I should get all the facts, Sir, an' take 'em to Scotland Yard.'

' But suppose Scotland Yard turned out to be one of the hanky-pankies behind the scenes ? '

Mr. Judd gasped at such an impious supposition, but bravely retorted :

' Then I 'd put 'em afore *John Bull*, Sir.   I reckon 'e 'd show 'em up and 'elp to Save the Country.'

Purfleet felt he could not destroy Mr. Judd's last shred of belief in human nature and the Country by hinting that there might be some hanky-panky behind the scenes

even of popular journalism. So he was silent. Mr.
Judd went on persuasively :

' Be'in' as 'ow you aren't interested in Parl'ment, Sir,
'ow would it be if you was to get married ?   Take my
word for it, Sir, a man doesn't know what active life is
until 'e 's got a wife an' children.'

' That 's exactly what I 'm worried about,' said Purfleet in a burst of confidence, ' and the one thing I want
to avoid.'

' Indeed, Sir ? ' said Mr. Judd, too polite to make
any comment or try to force further confidence. Purfleet
was silent for a moment, and then made up his mind.
Consult the Judd oracle—rather like Panurge with Tri-
boulet. This literary illustration cheered him up still
further, and convinced him that he was recovering
mental equilibrium.

' What should you say, Judd, if I told you I had got
entangled with a girl, and didn't quite know how to get
out of it ? '

' Entangled with a girl ! ' repeated Mr. Judd with
amazement. ' Well, I shouldn't 'a thought that o' you,
Sir, I reelly shouldn't.'

And Mr. Judd shook his head with grave moral dis-
approbation.

' The point is that I feel perfectly certain she 's trying
to marry me, and I—er—I 've been foolish enough to
give her some encouragement—got myself in a confoundedly awkward position.'

' Oh ! ' said Mr. Judd, recovering much of his serenity.
' Then it ain't our Lizzie ? '

' Lizzie !   Good Lord, no ! '

' I 'm glad o' that, Sir,' said Mr. Judd apologetically.
' We don't want no more of 'er carryin'-ons now she 's

married and comf'table.   It 's a wonderful thing to me,
Sir, 'ow that girl 'as men buzzin' round 'er like flies
round a bit o' bad meat.   Fascinates 'em, she does,
fascinates 'em.   First that p'liceman bloke, then young
Tom, then Mr. Smale 'oo oughter 'a known better at
'is time o' life.   I suppose it 's what you 'd call the fatal
gift o' beauty, Sir.'

' *Dono infelice di bellezza?* ' murmured Purfleet,
struggling to smother the laugh which would have
offended Mr. Judd.   ' No, it isn't Lizzie.   I rather wish
it were.   It 's an unmarried girl of—er—about my own
class, and I feel I 'm the present marked-down victim of
her matrimonial ambitions.'

' Um,' Mr. Judd cogitated.   ' You 'll pardon me
haskin', Sir, but is the young lady in the fam'ly way ? '

Mr. Purfleet raised his arms in emphatic denial :

' Good God, no ! '

' And you ain't committed yourself, Sir ?   You ain't
said nothin' definite about namin' the day or seein' Parson
about a licence or settlin' down in a nice little 'ome ? '

' No, certainly not, nothing of the kind.'

' And you ain't given 'er a ring nor nothin', nor writ
'er no compromisin' letters ? '

' No, Judd, not a word, not a trinket, not a scrap in
writing.'

' Well, you are a one, you are, Sir,' said Mr. Judd
admiringly.   ' I shouldn't 'a thought you was as smart
as that, considerin' all them books.   But, if you ask my
opinion, Sir, I should say that there isn't a jury in the
land as 'd convict you, especially since she ain't in the
fam'ly way.'

And Mr. Judd emphasised this judicial verdict with a
very grave and learned puff of his pipe.

'It isn't any sort of legal action I'm afraid of,' said Purfleet rather impatiently. 'There's no question of that. What I am afraid of is . . .'

He paused, wondering what exactly he *was* afraid of.

'Yes, Sir?' said Mr. Judd encouragingly.

'I'm afraid that she and her mother between them may arrange things in such a way that I'm betrayed into a false situation, made to look as if I were making definite advances as a suitor. You know what women are, Judd.'

Mr. Judd nodded in cordial agreement.

'Women are wonderful creatures, Sir, wonderful. There's nothin' like 'em. The only way is to treat 'em rough. Don't stand no nonsense, and treat 'em rough. They always appreciates it, Sir, and looks up to you for it. But if you come the soft stuff with 'em and let 'em get an advantage of you, you'll be 'enpecked all your life, Sir.'

Purfleet felt quite certain he would be, if he ever gave a woman the chance, and shuddered at the thought.

'Then you don't believe in more freedom for women, Judd?'

Mr. Judd halted, so great was his emotion.

'More freedom for women! Why, what more could they 'ave? 'Aven't they got into Parl'ment? 'Aven't they got the pubs shut 'arf the time and the price o' beer up somethin' crool? Don't they 'ave all our money to spend? Ain't every other shop a women's clo'es shop? Look at 'em, smokin', and showin' off of their legs in pink stockin's, like them young 'ussies at Lizzie's weddin', an' carryin' on all ways. It's ruinin' the Country, Sir. What I always says is, a woman's place is the 'ome.'

Borne down by this tempest of eloquence and original thought, Purfleet attempted no reply. They walked on, and when he saw by the regularity of Mr. Judd's puffs of smoke that some calm had been re-established, he said :

' What would you advise me to do, Judd ? Tell me frankly. I 'm really very worried about it, and at my wits' end to know what to do.'

Mr. Judd considered.

' Lemme jest get it straight, Sir. You 've got entangled with a young lady, and you 're afraid 'er and 'er Ma atween 'em 'll catch you out, an' get you into Church afore you knows where you are. Is that it, Sir ? '

' That 's it, Judd, exactly.'

' Well, Sir, 'course, I don't know the young lady. Maybe if I knew 'er, I should say to you : " Go in, Sir, and win." The population must be kep' up, Sir. But seein' as 'ow you feel as 'ow you do, there 's nothin' for it but run away.'

' Run away ! ' exclaimed Purfleet in amazement.

' There 's a bit o' poetry I once read about that in the papers,' said Mr. Judd reflectively, ' but it 's slipped my mem'ry. Somethin' about fightin' agen, it was. But it 's common sense, Sir. If you can't stay 'ere and defy 'em, what else can you do but run away ? If the young lady 's made up 'er mind she wants you and if you 've give 'er some encouragement,—even if she ain't in the fam'ly way,—depend upon it, she and 'er Ma 'll be all over you, Sir. There won't be no gettin' away from 'em unless you 'ide in the cellar and give out you 've got the fever, and even then they might come and try to nurse you. You run away, Sir, and don't come 'ome till it 's all blowed over.'

' Judd ! ' said Purfleet excitedly ; ' what 's your favourite tobacco ? '

' Shag, Sir,' said Judd in bewilderment, ' Black twist, the kind that 'as a nigger's 'ead on the packet.'

' I 'll send you a pound of it,' said Purfleet, eagerly shaking his hand. ' Good-bye, and thanks for the advice.'

' Don't mention it, Sir,' said Mr. Judd politely. ' Always ready to 'elp a feller-creature in distress, Sir.'

On Monday morning Georgie received a letter, delivered by Mr. Judd's elder son, who insisted that it was to be given to her direct, and not to the new maid. The letter ran :

DEAR GEORGIE,

I 'm awfully sorry, but a most disagreeable *contretemps* must, I fear, prevent me from having the pleasure of drinking a dish of tea with you and Mrs. Smithers on Tuesday. My uncle, George Bunbury, is extremely ill in Paris, and has sent for me. I feel it is my duty to go, since the Bunburys have often been very kind and useful to me in my life. When my uncle recovers—as I sincerely hope he will —I shall take him to Salzburg to recuperate. (Mozart, they say, is wonderfully good for invalids.) So I fear I may be away for some time.

I need scarcely say how much I regret missing the tea-party and your conversation.

With kindest regards to Mrs. Smithers and the Colonel and, of course, to yourself,

Yours sincerely,

REGINALD PURFLEET.

PART IV

PART IV

I

BOTH National Pride and the Principle of Universal Benevolence would be gratified if the statement could be made that all the inhabitants of Cleeve lived up to the high moral standards set by leaders of society like Sir Horace Stimms, Mrs. Eastcourt and Mr. Smale. Unfortunately, the village flock —which Mr. Carrington was about to abandon so reluctantly at the Call of Duty and a Canonry—not only contained speckled and ring-straked lambs like Georgie and Mr. Purfleet, but a family of genuine black sheep.

The Wrigleys were not native Cleevites. They belonged to that less solid and static part of the community, which, owing to such improvements as cheap transport and the Great War, has more and more tended to swamp our native yeoman breed, and remains savagely indifferent to the civilising influences of Maypole dancing, folk songs and village crafts. Not that these were introduced with any particular fervour to the people of Cleeve, for Sir Horace did not believe in pamperin the poor. But even if there had been Maypole dancing, the Wrigleys would not have civilised themselves by gravely capering round that cheery phallic emblem. The Wrigleys were lacking in religious tradition. And they continued to lack religious instruction owing to a curious circumstance. Although their cottage was at the far end of one of the rows in which Craigie stabled his hands, the bull's hide of land on which it stood was exactly on the boundary of the three parishes of Cleeve, Mary-

hampton and Pudthorp. Consequently each of the
three clergy concerned felt that the cure of the Wrigley
souls was the province of his other two brethren, and
none of the three was anxious to be responsible for the
evident failure which would attend any preaching of the
Word in that quarter.

Nobody knew where either of the Wrigleys came from,
but one thing was certain—Mrs. Wrigley was a gipsy.
She was therefore regarded with extreme dislike and
horror by all the Cleevites who had lived there for more
than one generation, and particularly by Mr. Judd, who
belonged to that haughtiest of all aristocracies—the
British upper working class. A gipsy, being one who
has not where to lay his head and who openly consorts
with publicans and sinners, is naturally abhorrent to all
the fine feelings of a Christian community. It is just
possible that this universal hostility and dislike—however well grounded—may have had something to do
with the especial blackness of Mrs. Wrigley in particular
and all the Wrigleys in general.

You had only to look at Mrs. Wrigley to see that she
was a gipsy. Though reasonably and from an immoral point of view seductively plump, she was as
tough as a windy heath. She had glassy black eyes of
depthless cunning, black rather curly hair and a distinctly dark complexion. When engaged in household
tasks, which she disliked very much, she looked in-
credibly sluttish in a filthy old grey dressing-gown and
dishevelled petticoat, with her black hair greasily disordered about a fiery and sullen countenance. But when
she had occasion to display herself *in fiocchi*, the village
gasped at the gaudiness of her scarves and hats, the
elegance of her skirts, the provocative lowness of her

blouses, and the lavishness of her red and powder. If she needed to use the arts of persuasion she spoke with a glib flattery which (alas!) induced many an otherwise upright man to cross her palm with quite a lot of silver ; and when she was offended or felt impelled to express herself forcibly, she showed herself a mistress of fluent and indecent abuse. All her female neighbours were very much afraid of her, but like the perfect ladies they were, they did not attempt to retort her insults (in which they would almost certainly have been worsted) but kept theirselves to theirselves.

It seemed curious that so splendid a creature should have allied herself with Mr. Bert Wrigley, a ferrety little ugly man with enormous philoprogenitive tendencies. Perhaps the tendencies had something to do with it, but possibly, again, her gipsy blood was fascinated by his fundamental dishonesty and shiftiness. Between them —with perhaps a certain amount of outside assistance— they had produced almost every brand of child and adolescent known to science. There were noisy and filthy babies, red-haired little girls with dark eyes and black-haired little boys with blue eyes ; there were fair growing lads and gawky dark lasses. But in spite of their astonishing physical differences, they had this in common—they were all most skilful thieves. Even the babies stole things from other babies as soon as they could crawl, while the older children had an extremely wide range of petty larceny. Until the Wrigleys came to Cleeve, this sort of offence to property was unknown ; but almost immediately after their arrival, the tramps, who had hitherto behaved with exemplary honesty, began to pillage the neighbourhood. The police were warned, several innocent but indigent persons tramping from one workhouse to another were arrested and severely sentenced ; but the thefts went on.   Now Mr. Judd would lose a young porker, the apple of his eye ; now Margy's pear trees would appear one morning wantonly robbed and broken ;   now the Colonel's vegetable patch, of which he was very proud for he did no work in it himself, presented the appearance of a Somme battlefield. Eggs, chickens, milk, vegetables, pheasants, partridges, rabbits, hares, mysteriously disappeared ; and although the tramp-hunt was conducted with renewed vigour and severity, there was no alleviation.   Mr. Purfleet was reduced to silent agony by the loss of all his strawberries and asparagus.

Remarkably enough, nothing ever vanished from the grounds of Mr. Craigie—the Wrigleys' somewhat unwilling landlord—or from the immediate demesne of Sir Horace, who, without actually knowing it, was the Wrigleys' protector, at least indirectly.   This aristocratic, if unwilling and involuntary, patronage was a solid tribute to Bess Wrigley's charms and wits.   The mother of a large and rapidly increasing family must obviously do something to provide for them, especially when the father, in spite of his shiftiness, is both ineffective and unsuccessful.   Mrs. Wrigley did not intend her children to starve, if she could help it.   No great believer in education—she herself could barely read and write—she viewed with suspicion the intervention of the State, and managed to avoid the attention of School Inspectors by frequent and judicious changes of address. What she wanted for her children was not the chilly, abstract and doubtful blessing of the three Rs, but good solid material comforts.   What she knew she taught them—lessons which they learned with native aptitude and put into practice with the success already noted. But such additions to the family income were inadequate, if welcome, and Mrs. Wrigley for many years had been forced to add a supplement of her own.

Prolific ladies, whose husbands are unsuccessful or ill-rewarded, turn their thoughts towards charing and the taking in of washing. Not so Mrs. Wrigley. Possibly that wild gipsy blood which was pumped through her brain was less viscid than that of more respectable people. At any rate, she had made one or two observations on human society, as constituted by Law and consecrated by Religion. She had observed that if you are poor the way to remain poor is to work hard and efficiently at some essential but unpleasantly useful task, such as washing dirty clothes or cleaning house at a shilling an hour. It was just like the War, where a man got a shilling a day and discomfort for fighting in the front line, and two pounds a day plus field and fuel allowances for remembering the General liked Oxford marmalade for breakfast. With womanly intuition she also perceived that if you could not pretend you had Capital—that sacred totem which compels poor boobs to work for us—the only way to acquire money easily was to amuse mankind or to flatter its vices. So Mrs. Wrigley went into the mercenary siren trade in a small but energetic way.

The question arises immediately: Did Mr. Wrigley know of this, and supinely acquiesce? Unfortunately the early history of the Wrigley family is lost in obscurity. They are first discovered in a cheap but unpleasant suburb of Cricton, where Mr. Wrigley regularly every morning went out to look for work, and punctually returned every evening without having found anything but a strong odour of beer and shag. Consequently at that time Mrs. Wrigley plied the siren profession with extreme diligence, and, like the pelican, fed her young with the spoils of her own flesh. Mr. Wrigley was so much occupied in looking for work and so much worried at not finding it, that he failed to notice how frequently Mrs. Wrigley dressed up in all her finery and left her home for periods of several hours at a time. He took his weekly pocket-money from her without so much comment as a ' Thank you ', but was heard to remark that Bess ' managed wonderfully ' on the unemployed pay.

Quite how it happened is uncertain, but there can be no doubt that in the course of her self-sacrificing career of providing for her family, Mrs. Wrigley formed a connection with one Mr. Jeremiah Gould, a relative of the Gould who cut down Mr. Judd's trees. This Mr. J. Gould was obviously very susceptible to the charms of gipsy wit and insinuation, for after enjoying Mrs. Wrigley's conversation in the bar of a large but low pub, he hired a private room so that they might converse more freely and intimately. This was almost immediately followed by an outbreak of new clothes in the Wrigley family, while sausage and mashed with bottled beer became almost a commonplace.

But Mrs. Wrigley had also observed of human society that if you wish to make money easily in the siren line, you must add the power of evoking fear to that of flattering human weakness. Just about the time when Mr. J. Gould would have been very happy to get rid of Bess Wrigley, she developed a deep clinging passion for him and at the same time an exquisite sensitiveness of conscience. No, she said, she could *not* give him up ; he was in her blood, and when a real woman gets a man in

her blood, the tigress robbed of her whelps is not more
savagely possessive. At the same time, she hinted,
passion had purified her spirit. She felt she ought to
tell her husband of this newcomer, this fascinator, who
had overwhelmed her virtue ; and, at the same time, she
felt she ought to tell Mrs. Gould. Why should there be
deception and concealment ? She was not ashamed of
him, she gloried in him, she would like the whole world
to know that she had found a Man among men.

In his agonised perplexity, Mr. J. Gould consulted his
Cleeve cousin, who used his influence with that mysterious body known as ' the Council', which seems to be
so potent in village affairs. There were consultations
and comings and goings. Finally, the Wrigleys were
installed in a cottage belonging to Craigie, and Mr.
Wrigley was duly inducted into a post under the orders
of ' the Council'. This was a healthy out-of-door job,
suitable for a Public School or other uneducated person
of refined tastes, and consisted in the keeping up of the
paths and by-lanes of the parish. In the warmer
months it was a job of an almost ideal kind ; and in the
colder months Mr. Wrigley's delicate health kept him a
good deal at home. It was a job much coveted in the
village, since ' the Council ' paid more than twice the
wages of an ordinary agricultural labourer for services
far less arduous ; and it was supposed to be the reward
for uncommon virtuousness and boot-licking of the
Squire. Great then was the indignation when this plum
of office, with its aura of virtue, was bestowed upon
Mr. Wrigley, one who had not even been born in
the village and who had never touched his hat to Sir
Horace. But the Goulds and ' the Council ' carried
all before them, and Sir Horace, while approving their

actions in general, did not even know that Mr. Wrigley existed.

But a modest competence, even when supplemented by the lucky finds of the elder children, did not satisfy Mrs. Wrigley. Possibly the siren trade was in her gipsy blood ; and she might have carried it on as a distinguished amateur even in the midst of opulence. The fact is that soon after they arrived at Cleeve, Mrs. Wrigley bought a bicycle on the hire-purchase system, and frequently rode into Cricton to do her shopping—over which she spent an unconscionable time, and generally returned with a good deal more money than she had carried when starting. Since Mr. Wrigley was away all day, earning the living of himself and his enormous family by the honest if frugal sweat of his brow, he naturally knew nothing about these excursions.

It was a brave and gallant spectacle to behold Mrs. Wrigley setting forth on her bright clean bicycle—polished up for a shilling by one of the children—in all her various finery. Over the combed and frizzled black hair was a plum-coloured hat ; beneath it dangled imitation gold filigree ear-rings. A canary-coloured jumper joined a very well-cut tweed skirt (much better than Georgie's and Alvina's), and bright pink stockings led to excellent brogue shoes. A double necklace of large artificial pearls was supplemented by imitation diamond rings of the first water. In cold weather she added a lapin sealskin coat. But whatever the weather, she invariably carried her wedding-ring, not on her finger, but in her hand-bag. Her simple gipsy mind attributed mystic properties to that symbol of wedded life. By removing it she seemed to feel that she was temporarily divorced from Mr. Wrigley and from her obligations to him ; while by replacing it, she once more wedded him in the sight of God and man.

When good fortune comes to us, we should accept it gratefully but with suspicion, examining the Greek gifts of the gods for that ironic something they have devised for our destruction. Bess Wrigley, setting forth in her splendour, was beheld by Harry Reeves, a middle-aged farmer of some substance, with a wife and three children. Bess at first felt it was a bit of real luck to have found a friend with money so near home. And she continued to think so, even when her gipsy blood should have warned her that the luck was weighted with a curse. Briefly, the misfortune was that the farmer fell wildly in love with her, and she with him. At least, in her case, it would be more accurate to say that passion and the lure of immediate financial gain blinded her to her real interests and the longer view. At any rate, an extraordinary thing happened. Farmer Reeves deserted his land and family, and ran away to a neighbouring village with Bess Wrigley, who was accompanied by half a dozen hastily selected specimens of her younger children.

The village first learned of this dramatic event from Mr. Wrigley in person. Mr. Wrigley was not popular. He went his quiet and leisurely way with a peculiar sort of smile on his face, which somehow exasperated the village, as if it were a perpetual gloat of triumph over the Council job. At the beginning of Mrs. Wrigley's acquaintance with Farmer Reeves, a step-up in the social scale which must have been highly gratifying, Mr. Wrigley's smile was, if anything, more pronounced.

Mr. Wrigley did not frequent either of the village pubs. Somehow his delicacy forbade him to parade his good fortune in front of hungry envious eyes, and then

Bess always kept a bottle of Scotch in the house. After she had filled a large pocket-flask for an excursion, the remainder was always abandoned to Mr. Wrigley.

Conceive then the surprise when one evening Mr. Wrigley suddenly burst into the select company in the tap-room of the Fallow Buck. He had no hat, his hair was disordered, his clothes were muddy as if he had fallen down, his eyes stared glassily, and he displayed other symptoms of violent emotion.

He reeled rather than walked to the bar, and exclaimed in a thick hoarse voice :

' Gimme a pint o' gin.'

' Eh ? ' said the startled landlord.

' I mean, gimme a double beer. Quick.'

' 'Ere,' said the landlord indignantly. ' 'Oo d'you think you 're coddin' ? '

' You keep a civil tongue in yer 'ead,' retorted Mr. Wrigley, ' an' gimme a drink quick.'

And Mr. Wrigley fell heavily into a chair, and glared wildly and miserably about him.

' Whasmatter, Bert ? ' asked three or four eager voices. ' Anything gone wrong ? '

' Muck 'em all,' said Mr. Wrigley enigmatically. ' Gimme a drink.'

' Give 'im a pint o' beer, Joe,' said someone to the landlord, who drew it very reluctantly and kept an exceedingly sharp eye on Mr. Wrigley. Overcome with the joyous expectation that something unpleasant had happened to him, and sizzling with impatience to hear it, the customers crowded round Mr. Wrigley, who for the first time in his life found himself the centre of public interest and temporary flattery. He drank three-quarters of the pint at a draught, wiped his sordid moustache, and glared again, occasionally jerking his head and body in a remarkable and threatening way. At first he made no reply to the chorus of affectionate ' What is it, Bert, ole man ? ' and ' You can tell us, ole sport, we 're all pals 'ere ', and ' Come on, Bert, we 're listenin' ', except to mutter or shout ' Muck 'em all '.

' Muck 'oo ? ' shouted impatient voices.

' 'Er and 'im.'

' 'Oo 's 'er an' 'im ? '

' That feller Reeves. If ever I catch 'im, I 'll wring 'is bloody bleedin' neck for 'im, straight I will. Gimme a drink.'

' What 's Farmer Reeves done to you ? '

In his agony at losing Mrs. Wrigley's earnings, Mr. Wrigley sprang to his feet, cast his empty glass mug on the floor with a terrific crash, and clenched his fists.

' 'E 's run away with my wife, 'e 'as ! '

In a second the tap-room resembled a back-benchers' scene in the House of Commons. There were roars of ribald laughter amid shouts of ' Serve 'im right '.

' Good ole Reeves.'

' Chuck 'im out.'

' No, no.'

' Give 'im a drink.'

' Well, I 'm blessed.'

' Muck 'em all.'

' 'Oo was yer with last night ? '

' Cuckoo ! '

The intoxicated and heart-broken Mr. Wrigley, indignant at this heartless reception of his misfortune, assaulted those nearest him. The landlord dived under the bar-flap, seized Mr. Wrigley by the coat collar, shook him violently, and hurled him into the road, shouting :

' You 're drunk !   Out you go ! '   and slammed the door.
Hilarious faces crowded the pub window, to watch what
happened.   Mr. Wrigley sat for some time rubbing the
back of his head, and muttering to himself.   A motor,
which passed perilously near him in a rapid swerve,
brought him to his feet ; and after shaking his fist unsteadily at the jeering company, Mr. Wrigley staggered
back to his ruined and desolate Hearth and Home.

II

Georgie was not at Cleeve when this violent episode
occurred in Mrs. Wrigley's lifelong struggle to provide
her children with a little jam to put on the dry bread of
existence.   She had gone, or rather had been affectionately but firmly sent for a nice little holiday with Alvina's
relatives, the Empsom-Courtneys, of Bulawayo Bungalow, on the South Coast.

The reason for this was that Georgie had been
decidedly seedy, down in the mouth, off colour, and not
up to snuff ; even the Colonel noticed that she was
peckin at her oats, instead of clearing them up stolidly
in a genteel and indifferent manner.   Alvina, who was
never unwell herself, always felt that illness in others
was either feigned or the result of gross carelessness—in
either case, the patient was to be treated with a mixture
of indifference and scorn.   Fred, on the other hand, still
kept a compact travelling medical case, and dearly loved
to prescribe for ailments.   On this occasion, he diagnosed Georgie's indisposition as ' a touch of malaria ',
although Georgie had never had malaria and to the best
of everyone's knowledge had never even been bitten by
a mosquito.   But Fred was absolutely certain of it when,

on the day after receiving Purfleet's letter, Georgie had
a slight fever with fits of shivering. The Colonel immediately ordered her to bed, and gave her such a
swingeing dose of quinine that she was dizzy with headache for a couple of days and would inevitably have
miscarried had she been in a condition where it was
possible.

At first glance Georgie had taken the letter at its face
value : A Mr. Purfleet (no longer Reggy) had been
called away on urgent family affairs and wrote politely
to express regret &c. But as she thought it over, and
read and re-read the letter more carefully, she discovered
something unpleasant in its tone, a sort of frivolous
mockery which was in the very worst taste. Who was
this uncle Bunbury he referred to ? Purfleet's mother
(now with God) had been a Miss Wilkins, and Georgie
had never once heard him or anyone else refer to the
Bunburys. And why drag in Mozart, who was somebody you used to do in music lessons ? There was
something about the letter, she felt, which was both
contemptuous and too cheerful—as if he didn't think
much of her and was glad to be going away, instead of
coming to tea with Alvina and herself. She took the
letter into the garden, and read it again, sitting on a
' rustic ' bench (*i.e.* one made of unnecessarily crooked
pieces of wood) underneath the large walnut tree. Her
cheeks slowly grew very hot and red, as she realised that,
in fact, Purfleet had run away from her. It was only
too obvious—he was afraid of getting entangled with
her. And she . . . Torrents of shame and misery
seemed to rush through her—oh ! oh ! *oh !* how dreadful, how degrading, how weak !

The wind rustled pleasantly through the walnut leaves, and lovely sparkles of sun slipped through the moving canopy and splashed on the rank grass, where the crocuses and daffodils grew almost wild in spring. The odd-jobs man was mowing the lawn. She could not see him, but heard the deep moaning whirr of the machine which ended in a sharp rattle of knives as it was lifted from the grass for a turn. This ordinarily rather peaceful and drowsy sound seemed melancholy and almost sinister to Georgie at that moment. Almost more melancholy and disagreeable were the sounds from the Colonel's room, where he was working out cricket averages and persistently whistling : ' If you were the only girl in the world and I was the only boy'. Georgie wished, wished, *wished* he would stop. She felt too languid and unhappy to move. She tried not to think, but there was Carrington and there was Purfleet and all the disgraceful and disgusting things she had done, and oh ! if only one could die quickly and be out of it ! She was surprised to find how very much she disliked Purfleet, always had disliked him, disagreeable conceited little fellow with his airs of superiority ! She felt inclined to agree with Coz that Purfleet *was* a bounder. Yes, a bounder, who needed to be taken down a peg or two. . . . And she found herself plotting meetings and dialogues with him, in which she triumphantly took him down, and showed him just *how* paltry she thought him and *how* much she despised him for his odious behaviour to women. And then the thought of his odious behaviour made her flush again.

The result of twenty-four hours of acute self-reproach and disturbed emotions and a sleepless night was the

' malaria ', so skilfully treated by the Colonel. The
overdose of quinine made Georgie feel really ill, and
rather alarmed about herself. Odd and disagreeable
fancies haunted her. Undoubtedly God was punishing
her for allowing Purfleet to be so wicked. She had
heard that people who allowed such things either went
mad or contracted some shocking disease. Now she
was paying the price. And yet, she reflected, Lizzie had
not gone mad, and Lizzie had been far far more wicked.
The thought cheered her enormously (the effect of the
quinine was wearing off) and, though she immediately
fought it off as a relapse into wickedness, she even dared
to think for a moment that perhaps, after all, the little
passages with Mr. Purfleet might not be so extraordinary and flagrant a sin.

Georgie, in fact, was undergoing an over-rapid process of deflation, like a swollen currency injudiciously
and too rapidly restored to the gold standard of what-a-
young-girl-ought-to-be. It was a very painful process,
mentally and morally. Self-reproach is the hell of
tender minds, and there are silent but immense suffer-
ings unknown to the tougher and coarser world. As
Georgie lay in bed, still dizzy with quinine, she forced
herself to face two or three facts, although it was so
contrary to her training ever to face a fact. She admitted frankly to herself that she *had* made advances to
Carrington and to Purfleet ; she admitted that Lizzie
had made her almost envious and determined, if not
exactly to go and do likewise, at least to get a little away
from her protracted and dreary adolescence ; and she
admitted that what with Carrington and Lizzie and
Purfleet (especially, alas, Purfleet) life had been more
amusing, and now had somehow slid back to the old

emptiness. What would have happened (she wondered)
if her conscience had not forced her to remind Purfleet
that he had omitted any reference even to an engagement ?   She preferred not to follow that line of thought.
It was plain that she had erred and strayed like a lost
sheep, and had been duly if severely punished. Repent,
and sin no more. . . .

But Georgie was not to be allowed to lie quietly in bed,
and wrestle with the Angel of the Lord. As ever in a
land of charity, there were good and pious souls ready to
put themselves to inconvenience to visit the sick and
afflicted. Naturally, as soon as Mrs. Eastcourt heard
that Georgie was in bed with a temperature, she freely,
fully and sweetly forgave her all the wrongs she had
done Mrs. Eastcourt in the Lizzie business. Besides,
there were matters of public interest to enquire into—
Mr. Smale, for instance, and the sudden absence of
Mr. Purfleet.

Georgie started from her self-communings almost
guiltily as the door opened sharply and Alvina's voice
said with that clear optimism so irritating to invalids :

' I 've brought someone to see you, Georgie.'   An
immense female form clad in grey silk bulged through
the door, rather like a threatening mastodon squeezing
in upon an affrighted cave-dweller, and a well-known,
hated and unctuous voice said :

' Well, my dear, what is all this I hear ?   Not well ?
Dear, dear !   What a shame in all this lovely weather ! '

' Oh, it 's nothing ! ' said Alvina, with a bright little
cackle, ' just a little chill.   She 'll be up and running
about as merry as ever in a day or two.'

Georgie could not help thinking that her mother had

odd ideas of what constituted a merry life, but she said
nothing.   Mrs. Eastcourt waddled stickily across the
room, and laid a white, disgustingly pudgy hand on
Georgie's forehead.   It felt exactly like a lump of moist
dough.   Georgie shivered, and turned away her head.

'Ah!' said Mrs. Eastcourt, noting this instinctive
expression of dislike with deep satisfaction.   'Quite a
little fever.   Now whatever *have* you been doing, my
dear?   If I were your dear mother, I should be quite
troubled about you.   I'm sure whenever Martin is ill I
have to be up day and night with him until he's better.'

Alvina rather resented the insinuation that she wasn't
looking after Georgie, but could think of nothing to say
in reply, except remarks rather too rude to address to a
sister in Christ religiously visiting the sick.   So she said
nothing.   Mrs. Eastcourt sat down puffingly in a chair,
with her back to the light and a full view of Georgie.
She could feel how Georgie simply longed for her to
go, and therefore determined to stay.   She patted her
bulging corseted bosom with an expression of deep self-
commiseration, and said:

'Dear oh dear, this hot weather affects my heart so
much, but I felt it wouldn't be neighbourly if I left you
lying here lonely in bed, my dear, with no one to talk to.
I said to Martin at lunch to-day: "I feel I *must* go and
visit poor Georgie Smithers on her sick-bed, I feel in my
bones that she *needs* me."   So here I am, my dear, *all*
ready to cheer you up.'

'It's very kind of you,' said Georgie, who felt quite
paralysed and all weak inside under Mrs. Eastcourt's
basilisk gaze.

'I'll go and get you a cup of tea,' said Alvina.

'Oh, please, no!' exclaimed Mrs. Eastcourt.   'You

really mustn't go to any trouble for *me*. Besides, I don't think it's good for my heart.'

But Alvina had already vanished. She knew very well that if she didn't give Mrs. Eastcourt tea, she would go about saying : ' And do you know, my dear, I struggled down there through all the heat, with my poor heart beating, and they never even offered me a poor little cup of tea ! '

Georgie almost shrieked : ' Mother, come back ! ' For a moment she felt as panic-stricken as a child who loses its parent in the tiger-house of the Zoo. Oh, please Mrs. Jaguar-Eastcourt, don't bite me too hard !

' Now, my dear,' said Mrs. Eastcourt, whose muscular jowls *were* rather like a jaguar's, ' I feel there is more in this illness than meets the eye. People don't catch cold in August. Do let *me* be your confidant. You know you can rely on me, and I should be so, so happy to *help* you.'

' What a funny idea ! ' said Georgie with an imitation laugh and a sinking feeling inside. ' Of course it's nothing. Just a little cold.'

Mrs. Eastcourt shook her head with a kindly expression of if-only-you-would-trust-me-how-easily-it-would-all-come-right.

' I feel you must be tired out,' Mrs. Eastcourt went on, with a sinister purr in her voice. ' So much has been happening recently, hasn't it ? And you *have* worked hard and splendidly. I thought it so good of you, so really neighbourly, to take so much trouble about your maid and her young men. Of course, in my young days, young ladies didn't know about such things and . . . By the bye, my dear, how is dear Mr. Smale ? '

' Quite well, thank you.'

' Still away at the seaside ? '

' Yes.'

' What a long visit !   It almost looks as if he liked it
so much he 'd decided not to come back.   Ha ! Ha !
Wouldn't that be funny ? '

' He 'll be back next week,' said Georgie, helplessly
raging.

' Will he ?   Dear, dear, that *will* be nice for you.
There 'll be so much for you to talk over and compare,
won't there ?   I 'm so fond of dear Mr. Smale, he 's
such a *true* gentleman.   Do you know *another* dear
friend of yours is leaving the parish for good ? '

' Oh ! ' thought Georgie.   ' Has Reggy really gone
away for good ?   He must have been a little in love
with me then.'

She said :

' No, who ? '

' Mr. Carrington, the *Reverend* Carrington.   I don't
want to hurt your feelings, my dear, but after that really
disgraceful sermon he preached (so indelicate) I felt he
would not remain here long.   We have our faults in
Cleeve, but we do *not* want Modernists and Atheists in
our pulpit ! '

' Where has he gone ? ' asked Georgie imprudently.

' Ah, my dear, I 'm afraid you 'll have great difficulty
in tracing him, but I 'll do my best to help you by finding
out.   Of course, he gave out that he 'd been appointed
to a Canonry, but I don't believe it, not for one moment.
He was trying to cover up his disgrace, as I said to Sir
Horace only yesterday.'

And Mrs. Eastcourt smiled happily as she thought of
Sir Horace and his millions.   Georgie said nothing.
She was perspiring freely, and ready to slay Alvina for

being so slow about the tea.   Why didn't she make the
girl get it ?   What was Mrs. Eastcourt saying ?

' Have you seen dear Margy Stuart lately ? '

' No—no, I haven't,' and Georgie realised that she
had not seen much of Margy recently, except to ask her
for assistance in Purfleet's schemes.

' She 's such a dear girl, in spite of her dreadful
manners and, I fear, morals.   But, there, it seems to
be expected nowadays.   What I can't understand is
her tolerating that dreadful Mr. Purfleet.   Oh, I 'm
sorry, my dear, I forgot that he 's now *quite* a friend
of yours.'

' I only saw him once or twice about work for Lizzie's
husband,' said Georgie lamely, only too conscious that
she was reddening perceptibly under Mrs. Eastcourt's
gimlet stare.

' Oh, I thought you were as thick as thieves ! ' exclaimed Mrs. Eastcourt, with a dreadfully sinister
snigger.   ' It appears *he 's* gone away too.   I thought
you, if anyone, would be able to tell me why.'

' No, I—I don't know—why should I know ?—I
didn't know he was going until he wrote to me.'

' Oh, he wrote to you, did he ? '   Mrs. Eastcourt
pounced eagerly.   ' Didn't he say why he was going,
and where ? '

' He only wrote to apologise for not coming to tea
with Mother and me, because he had to go and see his
uncle who is ill in Paris.'

' Why then you *do* know why he 's gone ! '

Georgie went deep red with confusion—what a silly
mistake to have made !

' Gone to visit an uncle in Paris,' Mrs. Eastcourt
went on.   ' I didn't know he *had* an uncle.   I always

understood he was a charity boy or out of Borstal or something of the kind.'

At that moment the servant-girl came in bringing an immense silver tray, covered with tea-things and plates of bread and butter, sandwiches and home-made buns. Like so many persons of social eminence, Alvina almost invariably fed her enemies better than her friends ; not, indeed, on exaggerated principles of Christian charity, but because she feared the satire of her enemies more than she prized the comfort and appreciation of her friends. Alvina was obviously a born hostess. In accordance with the rules of the game, as played in Cleeve, Mrs. Eastcourt was to examine the offering as sharply as an inspecting martinet looking for faults, while at the same time she was to utter little cooing protests at such luxury being lavished on her, a poor old woman of no importance. All of which these two skilled practitioners went through with the speed and nonchalance of an old priest reciting Mass with a bored acolyte eager for dinner.

Georgie felt exhausted, and her retreating headache returned with vicious fury. Mrs. Eastcourt talked in her dawdling poor-old-lady voice, uttering remarks of the most desperate malevolence in tones of saintly resignation and piety. Georgie felt as if two old devils in grey silk were hammering at her temples. Even Alvina noticed how pale she looked, and managed to get Mrs. Eastcourt away sooner than she wanted. In fact, there can be little doubt that the old hag would have remained there saying nasty and hurting things until she fell asleep from sheer inanition, if Alvina had not almost forced her from the room. The affectionate leave she took of Georgie was therefore doubly bitter and unkind.

They found Martin downstairs engaged in a very one-sided conversation with the Colonel, who was off on a very long raid with his mounted infantry in South Africa. As the ladies entered, he was saying : ' And so I got on my gee-gee and rode over to Kitchener, and told him I wasn't goin to stand that sort of thing from a feller like French, don't y' know.' The Colonel with regret saw Martin leave with alacrity. A ceremonious procession to the front gate was formed, in accordance with the etiquette of the Versailles class in Cleeve. Mrs. Eastcourt whispered to Alvina :

' How poorly dear Georgie looks—all her lovely colour gone. My dear, I 'm *sure* she has something on her mind. I always get Martin's little secrets out of him, because it 's such a help to children if they can confide in their parents, isn't it ? I feel sure it would help Georgie if she would tell you her girlish griefs. I don't like the look of her at all. I remember I looked just like that and felt exactly as she describes when dear Martin was coming. . . . Good-bye, dear, good-bye.'

Alvina was speechless with rage and resentment. She gazed after Mrs. Eastcourt's retreating fat duck waddle as if putting a spell on her that would reduce her to ashes *instanter*, while the Colonel still politely held his hat in his hand.

' The old brute ! ' said Alvina vindictively, ' I—I—I 'd like to scratch her back hair down ! '

' Eh ? ' said the Colonel, both startled and scandalised. ' What ? What ? '

Alvina did not answer, but walked hastily into the house.

Almost at the same moment that Mrs. Eastcourt left, Dr. McCall drove his fast little two-seater down his small but neat drive lined with salvia and calceolarias, and turned the bonnet in the direction of Holly Lodge. He drove mechanically, thinking. In his pocket was a letter he had received that morning from the confiding Purfleet, who had not yet realised McCall's perfidy and appeared to find it necessary to let the cat out of the bag to someone—and that in spite of his proud boast that he was not a gentleman.

The letter ran thus :

606 Russell Square,
Bloomsbury, W.C.

Dear McCall,

What the devil have you been doing these past few days ? I tried very hard to see you before leaving, but like Baal, you were either hunting or sleeping or gone a journey. I hope it only means that you are successfully combining your two hobbies of love and sacrificial murder.

I wanted to see you as a father-confessor. The truth is I left Cleeve at a rake-helly gallop, having involved myself awkwardly and indeed perilously with our young friend, *la fille du régiment*, whom we have more than once discussed. In the absurd kindness of my heart, I took up the cause of our young Joseph, Mr. Strutt, and his amiable donah. This led to interviews with the Young Lady of Quality (?) and Virtue (??), whereof thou wottest. I can't tell you what Asmodeus then possessed me, but the undoubted fact is that she most openly invited, and I most foolishly but charitably supplied, certain pretty privities. Nothing serious, of course, a mere running up and down the scale. But she has a devil of a temperament, coupled with an indecent passion for per-manence and respectability. At the second of our stolen treats in the infants' jam cupboard, she grew devilish serious and popped the question in no uncertain terms. Naturally, I executed a skilful flank movement, and endured stoically the inevitable tears and reproaches.

Virtue, or possibly vanity, so far prevailed above this new and delightful hobby, that she not only made it plain that she would not continue without the information and necessary action of Church and State, but positively invited me to meet the formidable and fox-hunting Mamma. In a weak moment I accepted, but reflection and the consultation of an oracle of genius convinced me that I must not venture into that covert again if I was to keep the proud brush of unwedded felicity. So I fled, ignominiously perhaps, but certainly with swiftness and prudence.

In my farewell letter—a little gem in its way—I gave out that I was Bunburying in Paris and Salzburg. In fact, I am here lying *perdu* at the house of a learned and amiable friend, an Anglo-Catholic of staggering chastity who believes that this is a felicitous moment for effecting my conversion. I have amused myself—and deeply pained and scandalised this respectable Aristides—by twice relating to him (under pretence of repentant confession) all that occurred, with every lurid circumstance and numerous bawdy frills. He thinks I am drawing very nigh unto God.

London society is very pleasant, but now so exceedingly cultured that it cannot bother to read even the new books it condemns with such wit and superiority. The whole place is crowded with genius, for my friend here is the high-priest of a sort of cult, whose object is to get the Pope recognised as King of England. I am, of course, all in favour of it, and shall stay here until things have cooled down a bit at Cleeve. I rely on you to act as a spy in the land, and to let me know when the young lady has been sufficiently diverted from her infamous project to allow me to return safely to my lares.

Farewell, sweet imp.

R. P.

McCall had read and re-read this modest epistle, which was beautifully calligraphed in Purfleet's neat mean handwriting, which he had formed with immense pains on that of Tasso. Many of Mr. Purfleet's literary graces were wasted upon that solid Scotch intellect, but McCall was deeply interested in the main facts of the case and more than curious to know how Georgie felt

about it. Of course, a doctor has to be devilish careful,
but even in the learned professions Heaven has its little
arrangements. He would, at any rate, drop in for tea.

III

It was on McCall's advice that Georgie took a holiday
with her relatives at Bulawayo Bungalow.   Alvina and
Fred agreed that he had been wonderfully sympathetic
and really remarkable in his refusal to send in a bill for
all his visits.   From the moment he found her lying
in bed with a headache (and possibly a heartache) he
had done things handsomely.   A call every day, and
two thorough overhauls—in which no possibility was
neglected—did not exhaust his kindness.   Though
neither he nor Georgie ever mentioned Purfleet or any
of the other little complications of life, she felt he understood how hard things are for a girl.   She became quite
enthusiastic about medicine and surgery and the noble
life of self-denial voluntarily undertaken by the
members of the Medical Association for the good of
humanity.   Doctors, Georgie said, were like Crusaders ;
they did not merely *talk*, they did things, and their un-
sparing devotion was not wasted on merely superstitious
aims but given to the Real Betterment of the world.
(She had borrowed a copy of the *Lancet*.)

McCall discussed Georgie's case with her parents, not
in a dry professional way, but with that human understanding and shrewd insight which is so characteristic
of the General Practitioner.

' No, Mrs. Smithers,' he said, ' there 's nothing seriously wrong with Georgie at all.   I 've given her two
thorough examinations to make sure, and I can give you

my word that she's as healthy and well-made and clean-blooded a girl as I've ever seen.'

' I'm glad of that,' said the Colonel. ' Never did like ailing women—confounded nuisance.'

Alvina gave him a haughty and suspicious glance, and then turned sweetly to McCall :

' Then what do you think is wrong with her, doctor ? '

McCall coughed, and spoke slowly, choosing his words very carefully :

' Nothing is wrong—organically wrong, I mean. But there are psychological disturbances—yes, psychological disturbances. The Colonel, who has had to look after large bodies of men, will know what I mean. It's a question of morale, isn't it, Colonel ? '

' Yes, yes,' said the Colonel authoritatively, though he hadn't the slightest idea what McCall meant, ' yes, yes, morale, morale.'

' That being so,' said McCall, ' there's no need what-ever for physic and medical treatment in the ordinary sense, is there, Colonel ? '

' None whatever, certainly not,' said the Colonel. ' Morale, morale.'

' But what are we to *do* ? ' asked Alvina.

' In a sense you can do nothing,' said McCall. ' I—er—I feel she has had a shock of some sort. . . .'

' Carrington,' thought the Colonel ; ' that pig, Coz,' thought Alvina.

' But the main thing is,' McCall went on, ' how shall I put it ?—she needs interests, distraction, amusement. As the Colonel puts it, it's a question of morale. What I advise is that she should go on a little holiday—just a fortnight or so—to give her a change, and then, when

she comes back, I 'll take her out in my car, so that she
gets a little jaunt occasionally.'

Both Alvina and the Colonel were almost abject in
their thanks (the doctor again positively refused to send
in a bill) and the visit to the Empsom-Courtneys was
decided on at once. There was no need to consult
Georgie—Mother, if not Father, of course knew best.

McCall wrote very briefly to Purfleet:

WHITE WILLOWS, CLEEVE.

DEAR PURFLEET,

Thanks for your letter. The lady you mention is now in
my hands professionally. I think she has suffered a considerable shock, and will take some time to recover. I think
that in every way you will do well not to return for some
time. I 'll let you know when I think all is well.

Yours sincerely,
MALCOLM MCCALL.

To which Mr. Purfleet frivolously returned the following reply (unsigned) by telegram:

Over you go and the best of luck.

Georgie did not really want to go to Bulawayo
Bungalow, but on the other hand she was quite glad to
get away from Cleeve. Alvina was worried about her—
twice in the week preceding her departure, Georgie came
down to breakfast looking pale and very drawn and dark
about the eyes. Alvina felt the child was suffering from
lack of distraction, and invited everybody she could
think of to tea. It was very hard, she thought, that
Georgie seemed ungrateful, and even complained
about it.

Bulawayo Bungalow was beautifully situated on well-
drained chalk subsoil in one of the most aristocratic and

unspoiled of our Southern Beauty Spots, overlooking the Channel, and within five minutes of Church and Post-Office, bus passes the door. There had once been a village, but this was now lost in the eruption of highly-desirable freehold residences replete with every modern comfort and convenience. Grey chalk cliffs broke raggedly above a long row of bungalows and cottages, whose toes were rather roughly bathed by high spring tides. A triple row of detached gentlemen's residences sullied the cliff-top, and two dilapidated hotels (with very dilapidating prices) and a Temperance Boarding House were apologetically insinuated among them. The hundred and twenty large houses had one hundred and twenty-five tennis-courts appertaining to them; there was an eighteen-hole golf course; and a row of seventy-two wooden bathing-huts enabled residents to enjoy the delights of sea-bathing with purity and comfort.

The place was really rather made for the Georgies of Greater Britain, and she would have enjoyed it if the Empsom-Courtneys had been more youthful and lively. There was Mr. Empsom-Courtney (aged sixty-eight), who had spent a long and useful life administering justice to Basutos and Zulus who had a deep-rooted and constitutional dislike for legality. There was Mrs. Empsom-Courtney (aged sixty-two), who had been faithful to her husband for thirty-eight years, and prayed nightly for The Empire. There was Miss Empsom-Courtney, Mr. Courtney's elder sister (aged seventy), who subscribed to the Navy League, and during the European War knitted three hundred and twenty-two pairs of thick unwearable woollen socks for Our Troops in the tropics. Miss Empsom-Courtney was also a

member of the local committee of the S.P.C.A., and
took a keen interest in reformatories. She crocheted all
her brother's ties, and had raised him a bountiful crop
of corns with her hand-knitted socks.

They were kind, very kind. Amazing how kind such
people are ; the one thing more amazing is their dullness and stupidity. But—from him who hath not, even
that which he hath shall be taken away. Thus it was
with the Empsom-Courtneys. What little wits they had
ever possessed had been lavishly poured down the
Empire's drains, and now they dully existed, pensioned
ghosts of an abortive past, Joey Chamberlain's semi-
human legacy to posterity. None of them now played
tennis, and they seemed not to know anybody under
fifty in the place. Consequently, Georgie never once
took her tennis-racket out of its case during her visit.
Mr. Empsom-Courtney played nine holes with her, but
this brought on so acute an attack of sciatica that he was
forced to give up all thoughts of golf for some weeks.
Miss Empsom-Courtney taught her how to crochet ties
—' It will be so nice for you to be able to make them for
your future husband, my dear '—and took her to see a
reformatory, which made Georgie almost ill with compassion for the unlucky victims of philanthropy. Mr.
Empsom-Courtney talked to her seriously about the
Empire and about the Duty of Us All to Carry On—but
it was so much like Father, that Georgie almost went to
sleep. However, she enjoyed the bathing and went for
long walks on the cliffs by herself, gathering the hare-
bells and the knapweed and other wild flowers. She
got quite sunburned, and the occasional dark patches
under her eyes were almost invisible under the tan. She
wrote home twice a week, and answered a letter from

McCall which was filled with good advice and easy badinage.

But the real delights of Bulawayo Bungalow were the car and the wireless set. If you belong to the Age and generation of gadgets, it is hard luck not to have them. A sixteenth-century Italian Georgie would have pined for a Titian and the story of Amadis in woven tapestry and silks of Florence and brocades of Genoa and elaborately chased jewellery and a monkey and a jewelled dagger and a poet of the school of Messer Bembo and a really ostentatious rosary and a lute and a lover. Our twentieth-century British Georgie wanted none of these things, except possibly the silk, the monkey and the lover—and the last two would have been more embarrassment than pleasure, unless the lover were serious. But she did want a good sporting dog and a hunter and a fast little run-about and a gramophone and a wireless set and a mah-jong in mother-of-pearl and electric light and golf-clubs and a new gun and labour-saving devices and a large mascot-doll and a cigarette-lighter and a good hand-bag—and at least thirty-five other gadgets small and large, less expensive and more expensive. The most essential, perhaps, were the run-about, the gramophone and the wireless ; it was no good having a horse if you couldn't afford to keep it ; golf-clubs were valueless if there was no one to play with and you couldn't afford the subscription to a decent Club (*i.e.* one which refused all tradesmen and their wives and the lower orders generally) ; and labour-saving devices were spiritless without a home of one's own.

So Georgie spent a good deal of time at Bulawayo Bungalow listening in with head-phones on. The set was a rather primitive crystal one and the aerial was not very good, so the transmission was extremely faint. However, Georgie learned quite a lot about adjustment and earth-returns and cat's-whiskers, and sometimes heard what was being broadcasted. She disliked the lectures and highbrow music, but loved the children's hour and the brighter bands. She especially loved it in the late evening when the Savoy Orpheans were turned on. She listened to the faint, almost ghostly tinkle of the band with its jig-jigging rhythm (rather like a message from a planet of musical cretins) and thought how lovely it would be to dance at the Savoy under the bright lights with the large room filled with really decent people, all in evening dress. . . .

And Mr. Empsom-Courtney took her for drives in the car. The caution incident to the legal mind was in him reinforced by the cooling passions of age, and he impressed upon Georgie the golden rule of Safety First— that last straw of persistence clutched at by old men, old empires and old gods. Mr. Empsom-Courtney never allowed the car to run faster than twenty, and consequently was a menace to almost every other car on the road, and always escaping destruction by a hair's-breadth. After each of these agonising experiences, when Georgie's heart and breath and being had been suspended in expectation of what seemed an inevitable collision, Mr. Empsom-Courtney, supremely deaf to the cries, curses and insults of the other driver, would point out how Safety First had enabled him to avoid the consequences of the other driver's carelessness and ignorance. And Georgie really believed him, but thought that if *she* had a car, she 'd go just a *little* faster.

She missed the sea-bathing and the wireless very much when she returned to Cleeve. Although she did

not know it, more than one family council had been held
in her absence, and there was quite a determined and
concerted effort to amuse and distract her.   McCall had
suggested that Georgie might like to attend an Art
School—he understood there was a good one in Cricton,
which was almost entirely attended by the daughters of
' good families '.   Alvina was at first in favour of this—
she had vague traditional memories of the days when
English young ladies acquired accomplishments, such
as the harp, corkscrew curls, a passion for the Peninsular
and painting in water-colour.   But the question of
expense was a difficulty, which was solved by the un-
desirability of nude male models.   It was decided that
Georgie should ' learn paintin ' from Coz, and that her
pictures, if bad enough, might be sent to the Royal
Academy.   Coz also practised a mysterious art, unknown to the post-War world, and called by him
' cristoleum work.'   You stuck a photograph on a piece
of glass and treated the glass with some chemical ; then
you painted the photograph on the other side of the glass
with appropriate colours, removed the photograph with
more chemicals, and lo ! you had a bee-autiful picture.
Privately, Coz decided that Georgie would ' do better '
at cristoleum work than at water-colours.

The possibilities of a small car were freely discussed,
but a very tenuous bank balance and a couple of years
of debt pushed even the babiest of baby cars off the
Smithers horizon.   The Colonel was ' very keen on
gettin the child one of these whatycallums for listenin
in ', but Alvina was firm that the house of gentry must
not be disfigured by aerials, and the cheapest loud-
speakers then cost forty pounds.   In the matter of the
car, McCall afforded some relief by promising to call for

Georgie occasionally and take her on his rounds.   The
wireless was shelved, but Coz and the Colonel privately
ordered (on tick) a miniature billiard-table which they
had long coveted—a sportin girl ought to be able to
play a decent game of billiards.   The Colonel also
suggested that he might teach Georgie ' map readin ',
and when this was received (by Alvina) with wounding
coldness, fell back on bezique.   Against this Coz protested ; he said the only decent card game nowadays
was Bridge, and he 'd often wondered why they didn't
make up a four in the house.   And the Colonel said,
certainly, b' Jove, the girl ought to know how to play
Bridge—it was played in every decent Mess in the Army.
So that was agreed to.   And then Alvina said that,
although, owing to the extravagance of certain persons,
any regular entertainment was impossible, she would
arrange that more people came to tea.   McCall said that
was an excellent idea, and promised to come regularly.

Georgie was touched by these efforts, but somehow
found she was taking part in the amusement and distraction far more to please them and to avoid hurting
their feelings than to please herself.   The thirty or forty
years which lay between her and them was too wide to
be bridged by any amount of goodwill.   She fell into a
state of apathy, mitigated by a strong instinctive
physical dislike for McCall ; this, however, did not
prevent her from accepting a drive in his car whenever
he called for her.   Georgie was so obviously gloomy
that even Mrs. Eastcourt did not raise much protest over
the motor-driving.   In fact, perceiving how really
antipathetic McCall was to Georgie, Mrs. Eastcourt
felt it would be an excellent match, and worked most
unselfishly in that sense.

IV

Mr. Wrigley, though possibly not so exquisite a Man of Feeling as Mr. Purfleet, was undoubtedly a Man of Honour. The tenderest part of his honour was his Wife. Should Mr. Wrigley sin, an almost unthinkable contingency, he was, like the divine-right monarchs, responsible to God alone. But Mrs. Wrigley was responsible to God and her husband ; in fact the two were almost indistinguishable. It would be an exaggeration to say that Mr. Wrigley was a man of Calvinistic principles ; indeed, as we have seen, he was always ready to allow his wife any lawful (if profitable) liberty. But from a long line of obscure though doubtless saintly Calvinist ancestors, Mr. Wrigley had inherited the precious gift of always being in the right, of knowing innately (if not by revelation) that the ordinances of God and Man always coincided with his own interests, and the certainty that strong professions of righteousness would allow him to behave almost as he liked towards a sinful spouse. His attitude from the first was unassailable. He was ready to forgive and forget, if Mrs. Wrigley would return immediately to his roof (bringing, naturally, all the spoils of Farmer Reeves with her), and he was even prepared to allow her all her former liberty (including, so kindly and tolerant was he, permission to meet Farmer Reeves at stated intervals) so long as she remained under the said roof and did her bit in providing for her husband and family.

In his interview with the Reverend Thomas Stearn, that dissenting divine of high principles, Mr. Wrigley to some extent dissembled. The question of interests was not mentioned, but Mr. Wrigley laid great emphasis on the distress and misery of a motherless and wifeless home. He was overwhelmed with anguish and astonishment when Mr. Stearn gently reproved him for having connived at the gipsy exploits of Mrs. Wrigley. It was the first *he* had ever heard of them, but the Minister of course knew best ; however, if only Mrs. Wrigley would consent to be forgiven, he knew that such things could never occur again. The Reverend Mr. Stearn melted with charity, and promised his aid ; but his interview with Mrs. Wrigley was tempestuous and unsatisfactory. Among many other unsavoury epithets she called him ' a stinking bible-puncher', ' a measley drab-begotten ditch-delivered creeping jesus ', ' a dram-drinking old hypo-crite', and divers other unapostolic and less quotable things. Mr. Stearn re-read John Knox's *Monstrous Regiment of Women* and denounced her and her loathly paramour (naming no names, however) in good set terms from the pulpit. Mr. Wrigley, who had never before been guilty of such excess, attended Chapel twice every Sunday, and gave such evident tokens of regeneration that he might almost have qualified to recite his sins for the edification of out-of-door sects. But though Mr. Wrigley obtained sympathy and moral support, which spread even to those of other persuasions such as Mrs. Eastcourt, he was no nearer to getting Mrs. Wrigley back. His life, he felt, had become stale and unprofitable ; and he looked forward with alarm to an existence of unremitting toil and penury.

Things were indeed going badly. Deprived of a loving mother's care, the younger children were looked after by an elder sister, a housemaid imperiously summoned home by telegram from the best situation she had ever had. This girl, who had been disciplined into

cleanliness and order by sharp-tongued upper housemaids and cooks, discontented the rest of the family by
imposing a similar discipline on them. Mr. Wrigley
had to take off his boots and leave them outside the back
door when he returned home ; he was not allowed to
spit, even in the fire ; he was allowed no whisky, and
shrank appalled from the invective which followed the
most innocent visit to a pub ; the best food was given to
the children, and they were sent regularly to school,
though Mr. Wrigley was comforted to find that they
were chips of the old block, and often played truant.
Worse than this, bills kept coming in for Mrs. Wrigley,
and her distracted husband was made to understand
that the unjust judges of the land held him responsible
for her debts. Things were so bad that in his despair he
felt he would fall upon his pick, like Saul, or cut his
throat with his own billhook.

Something, he felt, must be done, and quickly. His
pathetic if illiterate letters remained unanswered. He
took a Saturday afternoon off and tramped eight miles
to see her ; but the two children he interviewed told him
Ma had gone to the pictures with ' Dadda ' and the
other children, and they were going next week, and they
had lovely food and ' Dadda ' had given them such lovely
toys, look . . . ! Mr. Wrigley's fatherly and husbandly
heart nearly burst with grief at the revelation of this
luxury so cruelly withheld from him, but he went empty
away. For a week he cogitated, and then, putting half
a brick in one pocket and some bread and cheese in the
other, he started off early in the morning.

For some time he hung about the village, undecided
what to do, and feeling himself scarcely up to a contest
with both Bess and Farmer Reeves, who was muscular,

even if sensual.   He drank a pint of beer, but remained
uncertain ; and walked the whole length of the village
in deep perplexity.   But God, who deserteth not the
righteous, favoured him.   As he walked back towards
the cottage of Sin, he saw Mrs. Wrigley and the farmer
driving towards him in a muddy dog-cart drawn by a
fastish cob.   Mrs. Wrigley was superbly arrayed and
looked, as they say, radiant.   From a distance Mr.
Wrigley waved his arms in frenzied denunciation and
called on them to stop.   Mrs. Wrigley said something
to the farmer, who laughed with great heartiness and
scorn of Mr. Wrigley.   Stung to the heart, the Man of
Honour and Feeling plucked the half-brick from his
pocket and flung it with frantic energy.   Guided by
divine providence the brick hit Farmer Reeves on the
left side of his face, just at the moment when McCall's
car, complete with Georgie, turned out to pass the
dog-cart.   A scene of amazing simultaneous confusion
occurred.   Farmer Reeves fell senseless and bleeding
into the road ; Mrs. Wrigley alternately screamed and
uttered horrid blasphemies against her lawful husband ;
a passing Harrovian, overcome by admiration, exclaimed : ' Good shot, Sir, good shot ' ; people rushed
out from the cottages, caught the cob before it could
bolt, and surrounded the prostrate adulterer ; McCall
stopped the car, and pushed his way bag in hand
towards the sufferer, followed by Georgie.   Mr. Wrigley,
after gazing open-mouthed, at first with surprise and
joy, then with alarm and horror, at the apparent murder,
turned and fled, pallid and trembling.

Everybody talked at once, asking unanswered questions and uttering unnecessary exclamations.   Mrs.
Wrigley went on screaming and cursing with a rich

obscenity of phrase which made Georgie tremble almost
more than the sight of blood shed by a civilian. McCall
took charge of the situation. He ordered four of the
inevitable unemployed men to carry Farmer Reeves into
the cottage, and told another to take the restive cob back
to the stable. He sternly ordered Mrs. Wrigley to be
quiet, whereupon she called him a low, unfeeling brute,
burst into tears, and asked to be buried in her lover's
grave. And he ordered Georgie to get back into the
car, and to wait for him.

Georgie did not wholly like waiting alone in a strange
village—the people stared so. However, she endured
their disapproving inspection quite well, for there is
something about sitting in a car which gives a superiority over starers, such as no one could feel if merely
sitting on a milestone. McCall was a long time away,
or seemed so. Finally he came back, looking rather
cross, and started the car with a certain violence.

' I get awfully sick of these people,' he said. ' They
live like pigs, and the panel doctor is their slave. And
not so much as a thank-you.'

' How is the man ? ' asked Georgie timidly. ' He
wasn't killed, was he ? '

' Lord, no ! He recovered consciousness before I left,
but he 's had a nasty shock. His jaw is broken, and
I 'm afraid he may lose his eye too.'

' Oh ! ' Georgie gave the appropriate little shiver of
refined shrinking from others' pain. ' Poor man, how
dreadful ! Whatever made the other man do such a
horrible thing ? '

McCall paused a moment—should a doctor tell ? Oh
well, she might as well know a little bit about life, might
help to save her from insinuating bounders like Purfleet.

'The man who threw the stone was Wrigley, the woman's husband,' he said deliberately. 'And the man who was hit keeps her and some of the children.'

'Oh! How dreadful!' Georgie repeated, again with a coy shrink—of modesty this time.

'Haven't you heard about it? No, you were away, but it was quite a nine days' tit-bit of scandal.'

'She—she left her husband,' asked Georgie, quite goggle-eyed with excitement, 'and went to live with another man?'

'Yes.'

'How dreadful of her! And what a beastly man the other man must be! And how sad for poor Wrigley! Of course,' she went on virtuously, 'I don't approve of him trying to kill the other man like that, but I do think there is *every* excuse in such cases. But I think the woman ought to be punished. Only a bad woman would do such a thing.'

'Um?' McCall, thinking of Purfleet, gave a side glance which revealed only a countenance of surprisingly virtuous indignation. 'I don't think anything can be done to her, but I shouldn't be surprised if Wrigley got three months for assault.'

'No! Do you really think so? Wouldn't they realise how he must have loved her and suffered to do such a thing?'

'Well, I dunno about that. You see, Mr. Wrigley himself is not such an exemplary character, and if the wife liked she could get him into very hot water indeed.'

'What a shame! How dreadfully unfair! Even if he did drink, I don't think she has a right to go off like *that*.'

Georgie was all out for serious people sticking together until death do us part; obviously, since it was none too easy to find a serious man, it was wasteful and ridiculous excess to throw him over for another who might prove not to be serious at all. McCall felt she would certainly prove herself one of the wives of the bull-bitch breed.

' Oh, it wasn't drink, though I daresay the gentleman doesn't recoil from a glass of liquor when it 's good. I was thinking of something which the Law might take rather more seriously.'

' What ? '

McCall took one hand off the steering-wheel, and rubbed his chin with his gauntlet.

' I hardly know how to put it politely, but rumour has it—and I 've no doubt it 's true—that the virtuous husband you pity so much was not above living on his wife's immoral earnings.'

' " Immoral earnings " ? ' asked Georgie, rather thrilled to know that even earnings could be immoral. ' What does that mean ? '

' Do you really mean that you don't know that ? '

' No, I don't know.'

McCall whistled :

' Well, I 'm blowed ! It 's truer than ever that one half the world doesn't know how the other half lives.'

' I know I 'm dreadfully ignorant,' said Georgie pathetically, ' but how *is* a girl to learn things, about life and immorality and important things like that ? I don't like to ask Father and Mother, though there are lots of things I want to ask, and girls are always so silly and giggly, and clergymen always say that nice girls must be shielded from the world, and I don't *want* to be shielded from the world, I want to know about it ! '

'Well, well, it's natural enough,' said McCall, a little surprised by this outburst. 'But,' he added maliciously, 'I should have thought you might learn a great deal from our friend Purfleet.'

Georgie flushed very red.

'He talks the greatest nonsense, and I think he's a *cad*, and I don't want to ever see him again!'

Ho-ho, thought McCall, so it went as far as that, did it? Methinks the lady doth protest too much.

'Mr. Wrigley's offence, which I think is considered rather serious by the Law, is this,' he said, carefully concentrating on the road to give her blush time to evaporate. 'He allowed his wife to associate with other men, and to take money from them which he shared.'

This was too much for Georgie to accept all at once.

'I don't quite understand. I—do you mean Mrs. Wrigley did *that*—with other men—for *money*?'

'Yes.'

'Oh! And he *knew* it, and took some of the money?'

'How could he help knowing? He knew his wife nearly always had plenty of money for a woman of that class, and he knew perfectly well she couldn't earn it honestly.'

Georgie hunted vainly for words to express her horror and amazement; one of the many drawbacks in belonging to the sportin aristocracy is that you have no vocabulary, and are forced to use the same expressions for a hair in the soup and the sacred horror of incest.

'I think it's perfectly beastly,' she said emphatically. 'It's—it's *degraded*.'

'It's pretty low,' McCall agreed coolly.

'I can scarcely believe it,' Georgie went on indignantly. 'I thought it was only the most dreadful street-women who did such things, and the Wrigleys are married people, with children! They ought to be turned out of the place.'

' They 'd probably only go and create worse trouble elsewhere,' said McCall philosophically. ' And though they 're more than a little crude in their methods, I don't know that they 're by any means unique.'

' What! You don't mean there are other people like that? I don't believe it!'

' My dear young lady,' said McCall rather impatiently, ' I don't want to be offensive, but you are almost desperately ignorant of life.'

' I know I am,' said Georgie, humbled immediately, ' but I simply can't believe it 's true.'

' It 's true enough. Many a man rises on stepping-stones of his dead loves to higher things. Strange secrets lurk behind many an undeservedly successful career. I don't say that such things exist among the honest goops of the world, the people whose integrity keeps the wheels going round. No one would dream of imputing such a thing to a man like Carrington or to Judd or most of the villagers, but as you see by the Wrigleys it exists even here. But in what you might call the world of careerism, it 's by no means exceptional, it 's almost the rule.'

' The world of careerism?' murmured Georgie in bewilderment.

' I mean the world or the circles where people more or less live by their wits, and the other circles where they are determined to get on by any means, good or bad.'

' But you said Wrigley had committed a serious offence! Why aren't they locked up?'

McCall sighed with weary impatience.

'You don't suppose that people of the jewels and motor-car class behave with the crass brutality of the Wrigleys, do you ? There are ways, and ways. I 'm thinking of the up and coming business man who introduces his pretty wife to the impressionable but powerful man-who-has-arrived, and doesn't enquire too closely into what they say to each other, so long as his new Company is recommended in the right quarters.'

'Oh ! Business men ! ' said Georgie with all the contempt of the military aristocrat for what he knows nothing about.

'And not only business men ! Successful business men doubtless have more opportunity, because they have more money ; but the wise ones are prodigiously cautious about what they do. I 've no doubt they spend a considerable amount of time running away from unwelcome offers, much as publishers have to hide away from designing females behind a rampart of office boys and devoted typists.'

'Now you 're talking just the sort of nonsense that Mr. Purfleet talks ! ' cried Georgie. 'I don't believe you.'

'All right, don't. But feminine charms may be powerful, even without going to the lengths of " that ", as you call it. There 's no essential difference. There aren't many men who could honestly swear that they have never advanced their interests through their wives' sex appeal. Why, the most austere politician gets votes through his wife's winning smile and gracious ways. It 's a question of degree.'

'Politics in this country have been thoroughly corrupt since 1906,' Georgie declared oracularly, quoting shame-

lessly as her own one of the Colonel's favourite pro-
nouncements.

'Well, they may be,' said McCall calmly, slowing
down as they came to Holly Lodge, 'but even the
immaculate Army is not exempt. Staff appointments
are not *always* the result of the highest merit.'

'I don't believe it!'

'Then,' McCall retorted, 'I fear you can't read the
newspaper very carefully or know anything about the
noble art of wire-pulling.'

V

McCall's crude revelations made Georgie feel a little
sick and more deflated than ever. True, in the case of
the Wrigleys, the course of moral turpitude had not run
particularly smoothly, but it was distressing to realise
that but for Mrs. Wrigley's back-sliding into romance,
they might have gone on unscathed until their children
were old enough to keep them, thus making Sin unnecessary except as an agreeable hobby. Still more distressing to her were McCall's allegations about the more
or less upper or successful classes. She didn't quite
believe him, any more than she quite believed in Divine
Providence, but she couldn't help thinking of what he
had said. What a world!

She determined henceforth to be pure, and went to
hear the preaching of the *locum tenens*, who had temporarily replaced Carrington. He was a dumpy little man,
with a whisky-red face, and an air of diffidence and
bewilderment—which was not remarkable, considering
that he was always gently sozzled and always in terror of
being unfrocked in consequence. Georgie came away

uncomforted, for the man of God was so afraid of giving offence that he spoke of the mysteries of his Faith with the air of an abashed apologist, and devoted the major portion of his discourse to an incoherent exposition of the symbolical meaning of vestments. Luckily for him, much of what he said was inaudible; otherwise, Mrs. Eastcourt would inevitably have accused him of poisoning their minds with Popery.

It was regrettable, Georgie felt, that Mr. Carrington had departed so abruptly and, as it were, had deserted her in the midst of a warm action with the Powers of Evil. But the scenes with Sir Horace had become so violent that Carrington had packed off in a hurry to avoid a scandal, which Sir Horace doubtless wished to provoke in order to discredit a parson who had had the confounded effrontery to oppose him. In her own, rather mawkish phrase, Georgie 'felt very low', and spent a good deal of time moping in her 'den', contrary to all good manners and Girl Guide discipline. She was not roused to cheerfulness even by the merry chaffing of Coz, who had returned from his exile like a gelded ass vainly endeavouring to look haughty. The schedule of amusement and distraction was carried out with an implacability which would have crushed a less stoical spirit, and even Georgie felt like screaming sometimes, when Coz summoned her to the delights of cristoleum painting or Alvina lost her temper over a game of Bridge which Georgie hadn't wanted to play and couldn't for the life of her learn properly.

But this, she decided, was life; and if she was being punished it was because she had endured, even connived at, her degradation by the abominable Purfleet. The excursions with McCall practically ceased; and his scientific interest in this remarkable patient evaporated as rapidly as it had formed ; one or two tentative advances in the direction of further degradation had been repelled so very decisively that McCall had written quite warmly to Purfleet, informing Georgie's cad that it was now quite safe for him to return.   It was a great shame, she thought, that she should feel so low when the weather was so beautiful, but with nothing to do of any interest, ' feeling low ' was almost inevitable.   She found that she had a great disposition to cry, and indeed meditative weeping in her den became quite a consolatory hobby.

She wished there would be another War, which would once again bring out all the highest qualities of the Nation.   She would immediately join up as a V.A.D., and before the War had lasted three years she would certainly be in charge of a hospital.   She would give herself unflinchingly and unsparingly in the national cause, and work the flesh from her bones to give of her best to wounded heroes and return them fresh and fit once more to a man's real work in the firing-line.   Any attempt at familiarity—let alone degradation—from doctors, orderlies or convalescents she would repel, gently at first (many of them would hunger for a mother's or sister's love), but then sternly if they persisted.   And yet . . . It might happen in this way. There would be a Captain, a tall handsome man and a pukka Regular, badly wounded while winning the V.C. as he charged, sword in hand, at the head of his men. Better let him be a cavalryman, they are bound to be good riders, and always the cleanest and most sportin men.   Yes, and he would come in on his stretcher, pale but very handsome, and open his clear blue eyes as she

bent over him, and whisper : ' It 's all up with me,
Matron. Don't bother about me, look after my gallant
men.' And she would say : ' Nonsense, Captain
Dalrymple ' (having read his name of course on the
label), ' nonsense, you 'll be back at the front in six
months.' And a look of hope and valour would flash
into his eyes, the warrior's wistful longing to be back on
the field of honour. But, of course, he would be very,
very seedy indeed, and would in fact die, if Georgie
didn't devote herself night and day (not neglecting her
other patients, of course) and snatch him back from the
very jaws of death. And he would get better and better,
and be able to sit up, and get back from slops to solids,
and she would give him her arm to help him walk, as he
limped along unsteadily, with a gay brave smile, leaning
on a stick. There would be no familiarity, of course, yet
sometimes he would look at her with his whimsical but
manly blue eyes, and it would seem as if he was trying
to say something, but always checked himself, as an
honourable man always does under these circumstances.
But when he went back to fight once more for the
Glorious Cause, he would take her hand and say gently :

' Miss Smithers, I owe you my life ! '

And she would say :

' Nonsense, Captain Dalrymple, you owe it to your
excellent constitution.'

' No, no,' he would say, ' it was your unflinching
devotion, and, if I may say so,' here his voice would sink
musically, ' your flattering interest in me, which gave
me strength to recover.'

She would say nothing, but lower her eyes, and then
he would ask if he might write to her and if she would
write to him, and she would reluctantly agree, but warn

him she was a very busy woman, and then he would write twice a week regularly, and she would answer. And then three or four years later the War would end with a Tremendous Victory. She would be sitting alone in her Matron's snuggery, apart from the somewhat riotous scenes of rejoicing, when suddenly the door would open, and a bronzed young Colonel of hussars with a row of medals and bright eyes would come in.

' Miss Smithers ! Georgie ! '

' Colonel Dalrymple ! . . .'

' Geooor-gie ! ' came Alvina's shrill voice from the garden, ' Geooor-gie ! Where are you ? '

Georgie rushed from her den to the shrubbery and then into the garden, following the sound of the ' Geooorgies ', which grew shriller and more impatient.

' Here I am, Mother. What is it ? '

' Wherever have you been ? I was looking for you everywhere. Here 's a wire from Geoffrey Hunter-Payne to say he 's at Marseilles and is coming straight through to us.'

' Oh, is that all ? ' said Georgie rather crossly.

' All ? ' retorted Alvina, with a reproving cackle. ' All indeed ! A relative and a guest ! And when your father said we were to treat him as if he were a brother officer as well as a connection of the family ! I want you to come and help me to get things prepared for him.'

' All right, Mother,' said Georgie submissively.

Captain Dalrymple, eyes and all, vanished into regretted nothingness as Georgie followed Alvina into the house. Yet she did not feel quite so resentful as she expected, and even some of the ' lowness ' vanished. After all, here was something to do, and even something

to look forward to, though it was no more than a vague
relative returning from the Colonies on leave.

Alvina calculated the time of Geoffrey's journey from
Marseilles on the basis of the old happy days, when she
followed the troopship in a P. and O.   From Marseilles
(which Alvina remembered unfavourably as being distinctly within the dago belt) to ' the Gib ' (renowned for
domestic architecture and good hotels) was two days ;
and from the Gib to Tilbury was two more.   Add a day
and a night in London for a Turkish bath—men will be
men—and it would be nearly a week before he arrived.

Heated by an animated debate with a low tradesman,
who impertinently and unreasonably demanded that a
six months' bill should be settled on the spot or they 'd
get no more of him, Alvina returned to a complicated
task.   She was trying to ' get the linen straight ' and at
the same time dictate the week's orders for tradesmen to
Georgie.   Both ladies were flushed and cross with the
repeated altercations which always ensue when two
people try to run the same show and each is convinced
she can do it better than the other.   They did not even
hear the front-door bell ring.   The servant suddenly
thrust her head into the room and said :

' Please 'M, Mr. 'Unter-Payne's in the drawing-
room, 'M.'

' Eh ? ' exclaimed Alvina, so sharply that the maid
half-withdrew her head as if expecting something to be
thrown at it.   ' Good God ! '

' You 're sure it 's Mr. *Geoffrey* Hunter-Payne ? '
asked Georgie.

' Yes, Miss.'

' I 'll go and talk to him, Mother.   How ever did he
get here so soon ?   Nelly, go and tell Colonel Smithers

and Mr. Smale that Mr. Hunter-Payne is here.   I'll
slip away and see about his room presently, Mother.
Come down as soon as you can.'

Alvina gazed after her with some disrelish.   The
impertinence of the young nowadays !   A chit of a gel
like that giving orders to her own Mother, if you please !
And Alvina uttered a throbbing snort of disgust, a remarkable unconscious imitation of a horse snuffing
its oats.

As Georgie went downstairs she composed her countenance and her opening speech.   She would walk right
up to him and say, with just a shade of reproach for this
unheralded and premature arrival :

'How do you do, Mr. Hunter-Payne ?   I'm Georgie
Smithers.   How ever *did* you manage to get here so
soon from Marseilles ? '

But in the drama of life it is generally useless to map
out one's part too minutely.   Georgie did indeed open
the door, but she failed to enter or to speak.   Facing
her, in the centre of the room, stood the Captain-Colonel
Dalrymple of her day-dreams, a tall wide-shouldered
young man dressed in the most elegant plus-fours
Georgie had ever seen.   His face was rather too plump,
but most interestingly bronzed.   His nose was as ugly
as Georgie's own, his ears were large, and his teeth were
rather bad, but he owned a positively Byronic head of
brown curls, and eyes which were nearly the authentic
day-dream blue.   His subaltern's moustache was relentlessly cut down to a half-inch smear of stub under
the nostrils.

'Hullo ! ' said the young man, after they had gazed
at each other for nearly half a minute in silence, ' I'm
Hunter-Payne.   I suppose you're Georgie ? '

'Yes,' said Georgie weakly, almost submissively. She didn't know how to speak to this colonial Hermes in plus-fours. They shook hands in silence, and Georgie almost drooped into a chair. She had seldom felt more embarrassed, even when being thoroughly overhauled by McCall. A phrase from her prepared speech uttered itself automatically :

'How did you get here so quickly ? '

'I got fed up with the ship,' he said cheerily (just as Colonel Dalrymple would have said it, Georgie thought), 'and took a 'plane from Marseilles to London. Got to Croydon at four yesterday. Bought a damn good second-hand Bentley and drove her down here this morning in two hours and a quarter. Pretty good going, considering I didn't know the road, what ? I say, are there always so many cars on the roads in England now ? '

'I—I think so,' Georgie stammered, not knowing really what she thought, perceiving only the sound of his voice (so pleasant and manly and unlike Purfleet's rather high-pitched intellectual squeak !) and her own fluttered self-consciousness.

'There was a chap in a Sunbeam,' Geoffrey began, but at that moment Fred Smithers came in. Oddly enough, the plus-fours, the eyes and the voice seemed to have no ill effects on the Colonel's composure. In fact, he recollected his prepared speech extremely well.

'My dear boy,' he said, grasping Geoffrey strenuously by the hand to show the restrained but deep emotion always felt by brother Empire-builders when they meet, 'I 'm delighted to see you, lookin so well too. Welcome to the Old Country! Best of the bunch, eh what? You must consider this house as your own home as long as you want to use it. Knew your dear mother well—fine figure of a woman and a damn good seat in the huntin field.   Sit down, my dear boy, sit down, and let's have all your news.   Things goin well in your district ?   No trouble with the natives or any nonsense of that sort, what ?   I want to hear all about new developments and all that sort of thing, don't you know. . . .'

Impossible to say how long the Colonel would have continued this slightly incoherent monologue.   The old man was not a little excited, and half-lost in his own dream that this might have been the home-coming of the son he had never had.   This vague figure somehow intervened between him and the real Geoffrey, making, so it seemed, just the right answers, so that the Colonel hardly noticed Geoffrey's hearty *clichés* or even the properly deferential ' Sir ' he used with slightly osten-tatious good-breeding.   But the Colonel was interrupted by the entry of Coz, who had to get off his own little speech about the best of the Country's blood keepin up the old traditions, and welcome home, welcome home ! And then Alvina arrived, rather hot and bad-tempered and hoity-toity ; but the hyacinthine locks and the wide shoulders succeeded with her too (though not with the *coup de foudre* which had smitten Georgie into silence) and she too forgot her prepared speech.   Instead of sweetly-acid *surprise* (in the best Cleeve-Eastcourt tradi-tion of innuendo) that he had arrived so *soon*, she found she too was only expressing her pleasure at seeing him. Obviously Geoffrey was a success.   And obviously he was placidly pleased, though not surprised, to find him-self so warmly welcomed.

Georgie sat in a semi-daze, listening to the exchange of compliments without actually comprehending them, and occasionally glancing shyly at the materialised day-

dream in the well-cut tweeds.   She did not dare meet
his eyes, not that there was anything improper or particularly expressive about them—indeed they had just
the pukka gentleman's right degree of expressionless-
ness, which always seems on the verge of imbecility, but
never quite touches it.   No, Georgie simply felt that if
she let him gaze directly at her, she would blush, and
look as adoring and pathetic as a lonely-souled poodle.
. . . She became aware that Alvina was frowning at
her, and tossing her head in an impatient and horse-like
manner.   Good heavens, the room wasn't made up !
Georgie sprang to her feet with such guilty alacrity that
she trod heavily on Coz's toe and educed an agonised
scream from that corn-afflicted gentleman, who was
most eloquently discoursing on the relationship between
the Hunter-Paynes, the Smales and others of the
aristocracy.   With a very hasty ' Sorry, Coz ', Georgie
fled blushing from the room.

' What the diggins is the matter with the girl ? ' asked
Coz petulantly, as he strove to soothe a burning foot.
' She came down on me like a ton lorry.'

' I wanted her to do something for me,' Alvina checked
him frigidly.

The door shut gently behind Georgie, who handled
the knob with extreme delicacy as if trying to atone
thereby for her other clumsiness.   She put her hands to
her cheeks, and felt how hot and flushed they were.
Upstairs, in the spare room which she already called to
herself ' Geoffrey's room ', she looked at herself in the
mirror.   A frightened-eyed, almost blowzily flushed
Georgie looked back at her.

' You fool ! ' she whispered.   ' You clumsy ass !
My hat, how ugly you are ! '

And she gave her nose a tweak, as if she wanted to pull it off and substitute something more appealing or classical, a neat little snow-white Pompadour nose, or one of those straight Greek noses which connoisseurs think so beautiful but which Georgie always considered a little cold and mannish. But it *was* a misery to be born with a nose like, well, rather like an old horse out at grass. Perhaps, thought Georgie, if Mother hadn't been so keen on horses, I 'd have a more human nose. Her eyes began to overflow with tears of vexation, confusion and self-pity, and she thought how more than ugly she looked when she began to cry. Yet, in stories, the heroines always looked ravishingly attractive when they cried, and the hero was generally at hand with sympathy and a nice lace-fringed hanky.

' You fool ! ' she said again, and then added rather inconsequently, ' Don't be a fool ! '

She suddenly recollected that Geoffrey also had ' the family nose ', as Alvina called it, to excuse her own aesthetic deficiencies in making babies and their appendages. ' I ought to have been a boy,' thought Georgie dismally, ' then it wouldn't have mattered so much. *He* is really handsome.' She couldn't quite recollect how Geoffrey's nose went or indeed quite how he looked, for he was still rather mentally confused for her with Colonel Dalrymple. She must have a good but surreptitious look at him. Perhaps since he had the family nose, hers mightn't be so bad after all. And, half-consoled, she rang for the servant and began the task of making ' his ' bed comfortable.

That evening was by far the most animated Georgie had ever known at Holly Lodge. Preparations of un-

precedented magnificence were made for dinner to
honour the scion of Empire, who unfortunately was
completely unaware that anything special was intended
and only hoped to God that they did not always fare as
badly.   The Colonel slipped out judiciously, and returned from the pub with a bottle of whisky and a bottle
of alleged port.   Unluckily, he had to pay cash for them
—otherwise he would have bought a great deal more.
As he sneaked along—awful disgrace if someone like old
Ma Eastcourt saw him carryin a brace of bottles—he
deplored his own lack of economy and regretted the
London excursions and the too numerous bets on ' certs ',
which had proved so expensive.   It would have been
pleasant to see that the boy had his cocktails, and a
decent claret, and some good old port and brandy afterwards, and, yes by Jove, they ought to have cracked a
bottle of fizz over his return.   When he returned to the
drawing-room, after secreting the bottles in the dining-
room corner cupboard, the Colonel remarked that the
heat seemed to have touched up his wounds a bit, and
he must be careful what he had for dinner.

Urged on by Georgie, Alvina went to unprecedented
lengths of luxury.   The best silver—all Alvina's own,
and sadly diminished in quantity since her wedding day
—was exhumed from the box lined with green baize,
which Alvina always kept under her bed.   A dinner-
service of white porcelain with a florid red pattern and
gold rims was committed to Nelly's charge, with threats
of fearful reprisals in case of damage.   Georgie somewhere discovered pink crinkled paper-shades for the
silver candlesticks.   Then Alvina decided that they must
have a chicken in addition to the unsucculent mutton
chops supplied by a sullen and reluctant butcher.   She

therefore ordered Nelly to murder one of the youngest of the cockerels with a chopper. And when Nelly, flatly refusing, threatened to follow Lizzie in the ' screamin' 'ysterics' line, Alvina most gallantly performed the deed —and a very tough young brute the victim turned out to be. And Georgie got flowers from the garden, and, as she went upstairs to dress, thought how pretty the table looked with the clean white cloth and the silver and the best glasses and the flowers and the lamp-shades. She made a specially nice arrangement of roses for Geoffrey's place. As she put on the only ' decent ' evening dress she had, she was distressed to find that it was getting rather too tight—that meant she 'd been getting slack and needed exercise, perhaps she 'd get more now there was someone to walk with. She hadn't a necklace she really liked, so she put on the old-fashioned gold pendant with the seed pearls. Mr. Purfleet and his ways were so far from her thoughts that she never for a moment re-collected—so serene is feminine forgetfulness of the inessential—that she once, not so long before, put on that same pendant in order to discuss Lizzie's affairs more lucidly. She did not even think of Lizzie, though that siren was now near her time.

Geoffrey chattered and laughed a great deal at dinner, after cheering the Colonel immensely by spontaneously remarking that he never drank anything but whisky and soda with his meals—he couldn't stand French wines, he said, because they all tasted like vinegar to *him*.

' Hear, hear,' said Coz, with a wistful eye on the bottle, which the Colonel strategically kept as far from him as possible. ' No use spendin money on foreign messes, and encouragin foreigners, especially when our export trade 's none too good.'

' But I s'pose if they 're to buy from us, we 've got to buy from them,' said Geoffrey, with a shrewd political-economist smile, and a glance at Georgie to see if she ' got his point '.

' Stuff and nonsense,' said Coz bullishly. ' Empire trade, my boy, that 's the line. And *you* should know it.'

' I always think,' said Alvina, tactfully changing the subject, ' that a life like yours is a real man's life. Soldierin and developin our great overseas possessions —that 's the work for *men*.'

' Yes,' said Geoffrey, gravely accepting the compliment, ' this development of the backward nations seems particularly the Englishman's job.'

' Yes, yes ! ' they agreed heartily.

' Of course,' he went on, with the right gentlemanly self-depreciation—mustn't put on side, ' you may say that plantation work 's a bit tame and, you know, not quite . . .'

' No, no ! ' they protested, and Alvina remarked, unnoticed, that she had *always* said it needed real men.

' I don't say it 's difficult work,' said Geoffrey modestly, ' but it 's interesting. It 's no good going out there with book knowledge and all that sort of thing, you know. What we need is the power of command, the authority which comes naturally to the best type of public school man. Fr'instance, myself, I don't bother much about the technical side of things—we 've got a Scotchman who attends to that—but I patrol the estate pretty regularly. Always on horseback, of course.'

' What do you wear ? ' asked Georgie almost breathlessly, with the air of one who expects a description of splendid panoply.

' Oh, the usual thing, sun helmet, light breeches and

gaiters.   But I always carry a good heavy ridin crop.
The natives know what that means, and I can assure
you there's no slacking on our estate.'

'Bravo,' said the Colonel, 'bravo ! That's the way
to treat 'em.   They won't work unless they're made to,
and in their own interests we must see that they *are*
made to.   It's no good our tryin to develop the country,
and then let the natives idle about and live off us.   The
Government's too slack about it.'

'Funny thing,' said Geoffrey ; 'a month or two before
I came on leave, I was talking to a feller who'd lived in
the French colonies in North Africa.   He said it was so
beastly, it positively turned his stomach, and he got out.
Would you believe it, he told me that instead of keeping
a proper distance between the whites and the natives,
they actually pal up with 'em, and you can see *white
women* sitting in the same cafés with the native sheiks ! '

'*No !*' exclaimed Alvina.   'Really ?   How disgusting !   But aren't they always having risings ? '

'According to this chap, they didn't,' Geoffrey admitted reluctantly, 'though I can scarcely believe it.
But, of course, they're new to the game, not old hands
like ourselves.   S'far as I can gather, they've no idea of
colonial life at all.   Now, the Englishman when he's
finished his day's work, jumps into his bath, and has a
jolly hard game of tennis or a strenuous round of golf.
That gets him ready for dinner, and he turns in feeling
as fit as a fiddle.   But according to this chap I mentioned, the French just sit about with their women, and
talk a lot of twaddle about Paris and theatres and music
and those beastly dirty books of theirs—oh, sorry,
Mrs. Smithers.'

'Ha !   Ha ! ' laughed the Colonel uproariously.

' Not play games and sit about with the women and talk about . . . ? Ha! Ha! Ha! Have some more whisky, my boy? No? Well, when the ladies leave us,' here he frowned and did a sort of silent turkey gobble of annoyance in the direction of Alvina, ' we 'll have a spot of port.'

Geoffrey held the door open for them.

' Don't be too long,' whispered Georgie. ' When Father gets started on one of his stories . . .'

' All right,' and Geoffrey looked at her—she could scarcely believe it—not only with the regulation school-boy complicity, but with quite a glance of admiration. Then he completed her amazement by adding : ' As a matter of fact, I 'd rather come with you than stay here.'

Georgie gave him a look, in which perhaps intense gratitude came next to amazement, and fled.

After a few smutty chestnuts from Coz, and a pre-Georgian limerick from Geoffrey which had not yet reached Holly Lodge, the Colonel branched forth on a long story of complicated manœuvres whereby he had worsted the administrative side of the Army Remount Department. After three-quarters of an hour's patient listening, Geoffrey suddenly slapped his thigh :

' I say, excuse my interrupting you, Sir, but I 've left the Bentley in the road outside. Have you got room in the garage for it ? '

' Tch! Tch! ' exclaimed the Colonel, a little testy at being interrupted, and still more so at the reference to his non-existent garage; ' there 's plenty of time for that. Now, where was I ? '

' If you don't mind, Sir,' said Geoffrey firmly, ' I 'd like to get it under cover at once. There 's a heavy dew to-night.'

'Oh, all right,' grunted the Colonel. 'You young fellers nowadays treat your confounded machines as if they were as valuable as horses. Go and find that gel of mine, she'll show you where to put it.'

'I'm afraid there's only an old barn,' said Georgie apologetically, as she got into the car beside Geoffrey. 'We haven't got a garage or a car, though I'd *love* to drive one.'

'Oh, I'll soon teach you on this old bus. It's as easy as anything when you've got a little gumption.'

'Will you really? How lovely! I've been dying to —turn right, now, yes, through the gate, shall I hold it for you?'

'No, I can manage. Straight ahead?'

'Yes, follow the old cart-track. Now stop.'

Georgie jumped down, and tried to open the huge door of the barn, which sagged and whined on its rusty hinges. By a terrific effort she managed to shove it open without having to call for Geoffrey's aid.

'I'm afraid it's only an old barn,' said Georgie again.

'It'll do splendidly—why, there's room for half a dozen cars!'

He stopped the engine, switched off the lights, and dragged the old door shut.

'It's wonderful,' he said, as they walked back under the mellow summer sky, with its misty wisps of stars, and the soft rustling of the huge solemn elms, 'it's wonderful to be back in England.'

'It must be.'

'A man gets very lonely " out there " sometimes, you know.'

'Are you very cut off?'

'Three miles from the nearest house, and twenty-five from the nearest town, if you can call it town.'

'Oh! How you must long for home sometimes!'

'Not so much home, as company. It's different, of course, for the men who have wives, but the poor devil of a bachelor has a thin time. Do you know, you're the first girl—white girl, that is—I've known for close on two years?'

'Really?'

'Seems funny, doesn't it? I couldn't help looking at you in that nice fluffy frock of yours with the gold pendant, at dinner. I hope you didn't mind?'

'I—oh, of course not—but I didn't notice—I . . .'

'Oh, naturally you wouldn't be thinking about *me*, but I couldn't help thinking how much we chaps lose through not having the society of decent well-bred girls. Makes us uncouth, you know.'

'Oh, but it *doesn't*, I . . .'

'You don't mind me saying that, I hope?'

'Of course not! Why should I?'

'Thanks. I—I hope we shall be good pals while I'm here—it's awfully good of your people to ask me.'

'I'm *sure* we shall,' said Georgie, with something like a paean of triumph in her voice. 'Why ever shouldn't we be?'

And she ran into the drawing-room with a clear laugh, which made Coz look up in disgust, Alvina glare slightly over her spectacles, and caused the Colonel to reflect that if a man can't have a son, well, it's a comfort to have a happy daughter about the place.

VI

Grave as a politic convocation of arch - wizards, Mr. Judd, Mr. Strutt and Dr. McCall sat together in the poky little parlour of Tom's cottage, awaiting the arrival of Lizzie's contribution to the human species. McCall was in a slightly snappy temper. His suggestion that Lizzie should go to the County Infirmary had met with unexpected opposition both from herself and from Mr. Judd. Lizzie's objection was irrational; she asserted that you were never sent to the 'Orspital unless the doctor thought you were going to die, and even if the doctor didn't think so, the callous hospital people saw that you did die, because they were only interested in making fatal experiments with patients. Mr. Judd, as is well known, objected to institutions on principle; besides, there was a sufficient cloud already over this coming grandson, without his having the insult of ' charity kid ' or ' workus brat ' thrown at him in later life. So argued Mr. Judd, who strangely but obstinately considered all social services as charity, and immediately connected them with the Workhouse. So here was Lizzie, having her baby in her own house like a lady, but with a lamentable insufficiency of equipment. And then the new District Nurse, rather nervous and uncertain of herself, had summoned the doctor too early, but not so early that he felt he could go away. Mrs. Judd, in paroxysms of inefficient anxiety to help, alternately over-boiled water with a tremendous hissing in the kitchen, or sat on the top of the stairs with her apron over her head and her fingers in her ears, waiting to call the doctor.

Having exhausted the weather and news of the fac-

tory, McCall sat in rather bad-tempered silence. He
glanced round the parlour, which Lizzie had worked
hard to beautify with inadequate materials. The oil-
cloth on the floor figured a pattern of green tiles with
ornate but undistinguished yellow arabesques on them ;
and this, horrible enough in itself, grated painfully
against a wall-paper of enormous pink peonies tied by
true-lovers knots of strong mauve on to a fanciful lattice-
work of Du Barry blue. Bits of furniture spared from
the Strutt and Judd households were mixed up with
Lizzie's choice from the Edwardian stocks of second-
hand dealers in Cricton. Thus a terracotta head of a
Mexican girl with a real cigarette in her mouth stood on
a worn but dignified chest of drawers of the late eight-
eenth century ; and two very creaky and new-looking
basket arm-chairs affronted the six fiddle-back walnut
chairs from the Judd parlour. McCall, who had furnished his house throughout with sham Jacobean and
Tottenham Court Road Sheraton, on the hire-purchase
system, could naturally afford to feel contemptuous
and almost Wildeishly depressed by this lamentable
ugliness.

Tom Strutt sat on one of the more uncomfortable
chairs, leaning forward gloomily, with his hands clasped
between his open knees. Mr. Judd, outwardly very
placid and dignified, inwardly highly agitated and
excited, occasionally creaked the chair as he puffed at
his pipe. The cloud of shag smoke began to afflict
McCall's throat and lungs—he never smoked when on
duty—and he began to cough.

' What 's that gunpowder you smoke, Judd ? '

' Shag, Sir. 'Tisn't exactly the regular brand I
smokes, but it was give me by Mr. Purfleet. He give

me a pound afore he went away, and another pound
when 'e come back last week.'

' He did, did he ? Well, he might have given you
something less dangerous to your own and other people's
lungs.   Do you mind if we have the window open ? '

' Tom,' said Mr. Judd, still continuing to smoke and
placidly ignoring a hint he considered too pointed, ' open
the window, open 'em both wide.   It 's a remarkable
thing to me, what 's only a intelligent observer, Sir, 'ow
the doctors does change their mind like.   When I was
a nipper, there wasn't no panel doctors, there was on'y
an old genl'man usto drive out from Cricton in a dog-
cart.   I 'member 'im well, because 'e 'ad a two-foot
beard that smelt o' baccer and brandy somethin' crool.
Well, Sir, I mind 'im sayin' to my old Mother that 's
gone now, " Mrs. Judd," 'e said, " you keep the child
well wrapped up and keep them winders closed.   Don't
let 'im get in no draughts," 'e said.   Now it 's all the
oppos-ite.   Doctors is all for fresh air, as they calls it.
I don't 'old with it.   Always slept with my winders shut,
I 'ave, and always shall.   But when I goes to work in
the mornin's, blowed if I don't see all the gentry 'as
their bedroom winders open.   It 's temptin' Providence,
Sir, besides puttin' extra work on the p'lice, what with
all them cat burglars.'

' Ump,' grunted McCall, ' so you think it does your
lungs no harm to poison them with the carbon dioxide
of your own breath as well as with foul tobacco ? '

' I dunno, Sir,' Mr. Judd replied cheerfully, ' but
when I don't feel no 'arm, I don't 'oller.'

At this moment Mr. Judd eructated so loudly that his
apologetic cough failed to cover the lowly sound.

' Beg pardon, Sir, beg pardon.   It 's them fried

onions as Mother would give me f' tea.   They always
repeats with me.'

'Try a soda mint or a pinch of bicarbonate of soda in
a little warm water,' said McCall gruffly.

'There's another thing I don't 'old with,' said
Mr. Judd amiably, 'if you'll pardon me a-sayin' so,
Sir.   Drugs.   Drugs is a dangerous 'abit, Sir.   I'm
always readin' in the papers about them film actresses
and folks in 'igh society bein' took off to the Workus
'Orspital sufferin' from drugs, or else committin' suicide
'cos they can't break the 'abit.   No, Sir, I've never took
no drugs in my life, 'cept a bit of a pill and that there
Lions Mixture for my back.   Ah!   That's wonderful
stuff that is.   Ain't it, Tom?'

'I dunno,' said Tom.   'My old Dad always give us
Dutch Drops, same as 'e give the 'orses.'

'Drugs,' said Mr. Judd crisply.   'You stick to Lions
Mixture, my boy, outside and inside application,
guaranteed pure of all deleterious drugs.'

McCall, grumpy as a wizard of another clan, refused
even to discuss the methods of these inferior illuminati,
and greeted the remarks of Tom and Mr. Judd only
with an occasional grunt or puff of disdain.   Sickening
for a man of scientific education to have to deal with
these ignorant and pig-headed yokels.   He listened
hopefully for the step of the Nurse coming to call him,
but heard nothing but a smothered shriek from the
unfortunate Lizzie, who was biting the sheet hard in her
pains.   Mr. Judd also heard the shriek, and winced.
He went on bravely making conversation.

'I suppose you've 'eard, Sir, as Mrs. Wrigley 'as
gone back to that there ferrety-eyed 'usband of 'ers?'

'No!' exclaimed McCall, interested at last.   'Has

she really ?   But it's what one might have expected.
It was a bad day for the village when they were allowed
to come here.'

'Ah, it was that, Sir,' said Mr. Judd gravely, ' and
you mark my words, there's worse'll come of it.
Didn't I ketch one of them young barstards—no dis-
respeck to you, Sir—goin' off with that young Bert of
mine to pinch some of Colonel Smithers's apples ?   I'd
'ave give 'em both the strap if I'd 'a ketched 'em.
Proper goin's-on for a respectable man's son.   But I
reckon young Bert won't be in such a 'urry next time.'

'You don't happen to know how and why Mrs.
Wrigley went back, do you ? ' asked McCall.

'Well, Sir, I never was one to 'old with scandal-
mongerin',' said Mr. Judd, settling back in his chair
with a gossip's deep content, ' but, 'course, a man of the
world can't 'elp 'earin' things, can 'e, Sir ?   It appears
that in cons'quence of you treatin' of Farmer Reeves, 'e
lost 'is eye, and Mrs. Wrigley, she couldn't abear the
sight of 'im.   Old Mrs. Reeves, 'is wife, was always
sendin' 'im letters to come 'ome, and the two daughters
was always comin' down an' makin' scenes, and the
children cryin' and Mrs. Wrigley cussin' and blindin'.
Proper 'ell it must 'a bin, Sir.   And they do say, Sir '—
here Mr. Judd lowered his voice to the awed whisper
appropriate to the recital of unspeakable turpitude—
' that 'er an' Wrigley 'ad made it up, private like, and
she was on'y stayin' on to get money out of Reeves.
All a reg'lar plant, Sir.   An' I don't disbelieve it, 'cos
my young Bert told me they'd got a lot of new toones
for the gramophone up to Wrigley's cottage, and I saw
one of them wenches myself with a new 'at and skirt on.
Where'd they get the money from ? '

'Very likely, very likely,' said McCall, 'they're a bad lot.'

' Ah, that's as true as you're settin' 'ere, Sir,' said Mr. Judd, starting slightly as a rather dreadful moan came from upstairs. ' Anyways, she 'ung on with Reeves until 'is money give out or 'e wouldn't let 'er 'ave no more. So two days ago one of the children at 'ome was took ill mysterious like—least, that's what they give out. An' Mrs. Wrigley went to the Reverend Stearn and made a 'igh ole business about 'avin' sinned and repented, and 'er conscience tellin' 'er that 'er place was by 'er sick child, and wouldn't 'e—meanin' Reverend Stearn—get 'er 'usband to take 'er back. And there she is, Sir,' Mr. Judd concluded abruptly, hearing a clatter of feet on the stairway, ' there she is—large as life and twice as impudent ! '

The door had opened sharply, and Mrs. Judd said in tones which bleated with nervous excitement :

' Please, Sir, you're wanted at once, Sir. Oh, please come quick, Sir, the pains is somethin' awful.'

McCall got up very deliberately and calmly, looked through his bag for something he didn't want, and said with a composure which his indignant audience thought callous :

' Plenty of time, Mrs. Judd, no need to fuss. Just see that there's plenty of hot water, will you, and bring it up when I ask for it.'

Mr. Judd and Tom were left together in a room which seemed extremely empty and unfriendly. Mr. Judd hemmed several times to give himself a countenance, and then refilled his pipe with rather shaky fingers.

' It's a wonder Miss Georgie ain't been round to enquire,' said Mr. Judd unsteadily. ' Did you 'member to tell Nelly to tell 'er, Tom ? '

' Yes, I told 'er, and I told the postman to tell Maggie, 'cos Lizzie wanted 'er to know. Nelly said Miss Georgie was busy, 'cos they 'ad comp'ny up to the Lodge.'

' Ah!' said Mr. Judd. 'That must be the genl'man I saw, wearin' one of them tweed suits with legs like small beer barrels. It's to be 'oped 'e marries Miss Georgie, afore she turns yeller and sour-like. But she might 'ave 'ad a thought for Lizzie. Still, what can y' expect of the gentry ? '

Tom had no comment to offer, and they sat in silence, listening. Mr. Judd fidgeted in his chair.

' Life,' he said, rendered philosophical by agitation, ' life 's a rum thing, Tom. There 's bein' born and there 's dyin', an' that 's about all any of us knows, even them 'igh blokes up to Cambridge and Oxfud and such-like. It 's pretty middlin' easy to get a gal in the fam'ly way, but it ain't so easy to be a good 'usband an' father. Love-makin' 's all very well, I don't say nothin' against it. It 's natchral like. But it 's the 'oney on the poisoned cup, Tom. Leastways, I don't exactly say as marriage is poison, but 'tain't all 'oney. It 's the re-sponsibility that weighs on a man. 'Ow do you feel, Tom, now that you 're just about father of your first son ? '

' What makes you so darned sure it 's goin' to be a boy ? ' asked Tom, anxious to avoid further enquiry into his own feelings.

' 'Course it 's goin' to be a boy—shs ! ' Mr. Judd broke off and listened, but there was no sound but the occasional moving of feet overhead and Mrs. Judd snivelling on the stairs. He proceeded : ' There 's circumstances in this case as makes it certain.'

Out of regard for Tom's feelings, Mr. Judd did not

specify what were the ' circumstances ' in question, but
when Mrs. Judd had earlier in the week asked him why
he ' knew ' it would be a boy, Mr. Judd had replied with
stately definiteness : ' A baby with two fathers is
always a boy.'

Tom got up and began to walk uneasily about the
small room. Mr. Judd watched him with intelligent
scientific interest.

' You don't feel no pains yourself, do you, Tom ? ' he
asked with intense curiosity.

' No,' said Tom shortly, ' I don't. But if you want
to know, I feel all of a shiver like, and I wish 'twas over
an' all well.'

' They do say,' remarked Mr. Judd reflectively, ' as
the real father always feels pains like the mother, no
matter where 'e is.'

' Well, I don't feel none,' Tom almost snapped at him.

' I never felt none meself,' Mr. Judd admitted magnanimously, ' but I 've knowed men as said they did.
But what I always says is, when it comes to women, a
man don't know whether 'e 's on 'is 'ead or 'is 'eels. To
'ear 'em tattle, you 'd think they was all reg'lar sieves
as couldn't keep nothin' to theirselves, but d'rectly
they 've a secret of their own to keep, they 're closer than
oysters. If a man was to live a thousand years an' get
more artful all the time, I lay a penny 'e 'd be reg'lar
flummoxed and took in by the first wench as 'ad a mind
that way.'

' Ah, I reckon 'e would,' said Tom vaguely, still per-
ambulating uneasily.

' Shs ! ' exclaimed Mr. Judd. They listened, and
then Tom began to walk about once more.

' If I was you, Tom,' said Mr. Judd benevolently, ' I

sh'd sit still and take it calm like. It don't do no good you meanderin' about as if you was a p'liceman lookin' the other way.'

' I dessay I should sit still if I was you,' Tom retorted acrimoniously, ' but bein' me, it 's different.'

' I 'm sorry your good Dad an' Ma wouldn't come down t'night. They might 'a let bygones be bygones, and join the fam'ly when their first grandchild 's bein' born. It 's in'uman to bear grudges against your own flesh and blood.'

Tom grunted uneasily. He didn't like any reference to the fact that his own parents disapproved of his marriage with Lizzie—' a reg'lar young strumpet light-o'-heels,' as his mother called her—although they had grudgingly given him some of their furniture.

' They 'll come round in time,' he muttered.

' Well,' said Mr. Judd, feeling he might have lowered his dignity by remarking on an absence which was a criticism, ' I dunno as they 're any such loss, no offence to you, my boy.'

' That 's all right,' said Tom, not quite knowing what he meant, but with a dismal feeling as he spoke the words that somehow it was all wrong. To be married and a father at twenty-one, with a long highway of virtue before him where the years would go by as monotonously as milestones—that was not the happiest of prospects. Was he even sure that Lizzie's baby, just gasping its way into life, was his ? It occurred to Tom's slow wits, a little late perhaps, that throughout the whole business everybody had thought of Lizzie and her reputation and future, and nobody had thought of him —except his own parents, who had merely made themselves unpleasant. After all, was he so much more to

blame than Lizzie? Hadn't she rather insisted on
intimacy, even when he told her it was dangerous?
Now both caught in the trap for life. . . . It might have
been better to let things go, and not be so impatient for
respectability. . . .

He became aware that Mr. Judd was speaking.

'Yes,' Mr. Judd said, rather as if meditating aloud,
'it's all a rum business, I can tell you. We don't ask to
be born, but there we are, and soon as we're shakin'
down an' gettin' a bit comf'table like, blowed if we don't
start 'avin a fam'ly what didn't ask us to 'ave 'em.
Then you goes on, day in, day out, year after year, 'avin'
more of 'em. Sometimes the Missus is pretty middlin',
but mostly it's washin' day, and 'er as snappy as an ole
dog with worms or summat. Well, you goes on workin'
an' you goes on 'opin', and thinkin' pretty soon the
kids 'll be growin' up to be a prop to your old age like,
and maybe bring in a few shillin's a week to 'elp the
Missus. And afore you knows where you are, blessed
if they don't go and do it too. Don't seem no hobjeck
in it, as you might say.'

Tom almost groaned assent. Mr. Judd was expressing his own feelings with almost painful accuracy.

'Still,' Mr. Judd continued, more optimistically,
'what I always says is, it's a pore 'eart as never re-
joices.'

After listening carefully to make sure nobody was
coming, Mr. Judd conspiratorially drew a small bottle
from his pocket.

'I slipped into the Buck afore I come along,' he
whispered confidentially, 'an' got a quartern o' rum.
There's nothin' like rum for facin' the tragedies of life.
Jest you nip into the kitchen, Tom—mind Mother ain't

there—and bring in a couple of glasses, some 'ot water and a few lumps of sugar.'

Breathing heavily from mental concentration, Mr. Judd mixed two glasses of rum and hot water, and sipped one of them experimentally.

' Tisn't what it usto be afore the War,' he said, ' but it isn't so bad neither. 'Ere 's good luck to your son and my grandson, bless 'is 'eart, though 'e wasn't wanted.'

' Good luck,' said Tom.

' What I always says is,' remarked Mr. Judd, pursuing his path of philosophy, ' what 's the use of takin' on and frettin' yourself ? If I 've said that once to Mother, I 've said it a thousand times. But—would you believe it ?—it don't seem to 'ave no more effect on 'er than if I said nothin' at all. Frettin' and worryin' and goin' on she is, mornin', noon and night. Leastways, she would, if I didn't put a stop to it pretty smart. Don't you let Lizzie start them grousin' and grumblin' ways. If you do, there won't be no way out, 'cept to pretend you 're deaf, and she 'll pretty soon rumble that.'

' I don't see 'ow you can stop 'em,' Tom objected.

' Firmness,' said Mr. Judd dogmatically, ' the iron glove on the velvet 'and, as they say. Fetch 'em up smart like, and laugh 'em out of it. You mark my words, Tom, it isn't no good keepin' your nose in stinkin' fish, jest as it ain't no good pretending that pound-notes grows on gooseberry bushes. A good steady man wants a good steady life, and no nonsense. Let 'im mind 'is own business, get on with 'is own job, and not owe nothin' to nobody. I don't 'old with all this idea of bein' 'elped 'ere and bein' 'elped there, and Gov'ment aid an' all the rest of it. A self-respectin' man 'elps 'isself, and don't ask nobody else to 'elp 'im, no, not even the Lord A'mighty 'Igh Chamberlain or the King 'isself, long may 'e reign !'

' But . . .' Tom began, when he was interrupted by the sudden opening of the door, and the entrance of McCall, carrying what looked like a squirming and hairless red monkey of extreme age wrapped in a piece of blanket. Mr. Judd and Tom gaped at it, as he held it forth to Tom.

' Here you are, Strutt,' said McCall with feigned cheerfulness, ' salute your first-born. It 's a girl, and the mother insisted I should say it 's to be called Georgina, after Miss Smithers.'

' A girl ? ' exclaimed Mr. Judd, recoiling a step in horror, ' a girl ! Mark my words, that means more trouble for somebody.'

PART V

PART V

I

GEORGIE was in love, 'really-and-truly' in love—there could be no doubt about it. Occasionally Nature does appear to do things handsomely—especially when preparing a dirty trick. Georgie might have advertised for weeks in the more expensive dailies and have interviewed thousands of applicants from the unemployable public school men who are 'fond of outdoor life, able drive car, go anywhere, do anything', without discovering anyone so suitable for her vacancy as Geoffrey. If she had suffered from the temperament of Joan of Arc, she would have heard heavenly voices saying gently but unmistakably : ' Georgie ! Be Mrs. Geoffrey Hunter-Payne.' And if Heaven had imposed that duty upon her, how cheerfully she would have obeyed !

But no voices came from Heaven.

Nor—more annoyingly—did Geoffrey propose.

And yet, after all, was not that reticence one more perfection to add to his great sum ? Was it not further, if supererogatory, evidence of the true English gentleman, that he preferred to allow matters to ripen slowly down from precedent to precedent, rather than to rush hectically into an engagement, which he would be too honourable ever to break, before he was *quite* certain of himself and *quite* certain of Georgie ?

To be just, Georgie herself was too happy in her happiness to nourish sordid projects of matrimony—perhaps unwisely, for the best of men need an occasional prod. While everyone round her adopted an offensive attitude of beaming fatuity towards the pair, and inwardly awaited the declaration with a fever of expectation which became almost intolerable, Georgie herself was perfectly happy ' being pals ' with Geoffrey. That was the right way, wasn't it ? Pals first, then real pals, then old pals with an understanding, then a shy and preferably clumsy declaration—and then, on with the orange-blossom and till-death-doth-part !

That, at least, is how Georgie understood it.

Starting from pals on the first night, they were about a fortnight in arriving at the confessed status of real pals. While exact calculations are impossible, about six or eight weeks should have brought them to the height of old pals with an understanding—from which Geoffrey would have found some difficulty in retreating. Georgie really had plenty of time, though it was unfortunate, on purely tactical grounds, that Geoffrey came home in the early autumn and not in the beginning of spring. The summer months are more convenient for those leisurely courtships which alone mature into the fruit of perfect marriage. At least, Georgie thought so, and it was nobody else's business to run her love affairs for her.

She was an honest girl, still with much unschooled faith in human nature.

At first, Nature and mankind seemed to conspire for her felicity. A wettish summer was followed by a superbly mellow autumn, with that slight nip of frost in the early morning which Georgie had been induced in childhood to believe that she liked. Long before midday, the thick white pools of mist vanished from the meadows and half-shorn grain-fields, and hung in a

faint blue haze over the distant woods on the low hills.
The whirr and rattle of the distant reaper going round
and round a twenty-acre field came through the still air
like a chord of familiar music, somehow reassuring and
tranquillising. The swifts, which all summer had
darted and screamed round the church tower and above
the lanes, had already gone, but as the afternoon grew
yellow with diffused sunlight the swallows gathered on
the telegraph wires in larger and larger lines of little
twittering creatures in evening dress, with white waistcoats and russet bibs. The elms changed their heavy
summer green for tarnished yellow, the beeches came
out ostentatiously in gold, the oaks were flushed with
dull red, and a large solitary maple tree flamed out an
exotic crimson. The willows began to drop their thin
dried little spear-heads, and the horse-chestnuts littered
the paths with their great sprawling spatulate leaves.
At evening the sun set in solemn cardinalate splendour,
and the bats went restlessly up and down, like frightened
cavalry patrols, through the gathering mist which
blurred the stars.

It all made Georgie feel breathless and exalted and a
little ashamed. She couldn't make out whether the
autumn was really so much more splendid than any she
had ever lived before, or whether it was looking at things
with Geoffrey which gave them this magical glow and
strangeness. How curious that she had never found
things so interesting before ! And how funny that she
should find herself thinking a silly old reaper and binder
sounded like music, and that the swallows were in evening dress and the bats like cavalry patrols ! And how
strange that silly little things like that made her feel so
happy, so alive, so—well—so just right and settled and

contented !   Of course, she didn't tell anyone about it, not even Geoffrey.   Even he might think her silly and putting on side, and, even if he didn't, he might accidentally let out something to Coz, and then there 'd be a weary stack of chaff to eat in humility of spirit.   Georgie felt she just couldn't be humble.   It was all so splendid, so—so really top-hole.   She had to check herself because she found she was always starting to sing, even when she sewed.

And she had even stranger fancies.   When she gathered dahlias and chrysanthemums for the table, she felt she wanted to press them against her lips—the shiny almost scentless dahlias and the fluffier chrysanthemums with their musky pungent autumn scent.   She wondered if trees had life, and thought if she put her arms round a smooth beech trunk and held it tight against her cheek she might hear the very slow, very distant beat of a heart. Then she thought that if she lay on the grass in the sun, she would feel the bright sun-rays plunging into her and the dark earth growing up and round and about her, so that she would be all sensation compact of gold fire and dark earth.   She was afraid to do any of these things— someone might see her, and they would be sure to laugh at her.   But one evening as she stood with Geoffrey on the lawn he put his arm through hers—as old pals do— and she was caught up in an ecstasy.   They were looking up at the new moon, and it seemed to Georgie that she felt the huge roll of the earth through space, all the fields and houses and woods and roads and people rolling through the stars with inconceivable majesty and speed. She was afraid to speak, and her eyes filled with sentimental tears.   Geoffrey said nothing, and they stood there for at least five minutes, until the strange feeling of godlike movement gradually disappeared. What he felt she never knew, but suddenly he lifted up her hand and kissed it—the first time he had ever attempted any caress—and then suddenly went away, as if afraid of something. Georgie felt a little lonely and lost at his going, though she was thrilled by the touch of his hot mouth on her hand. She wished he had stayed, she wished he had—what did she wish ? She wanted to hold his head in her hands and look at him, and—well, give that *pure* devotion which she had kept for him. How happy she could make him ! But patience, all in God's good time.

The guardian angel, as pleased as punch, strutted about with his chest thrown out, and shooed away all the little devils who tried to whisper : ' What about McCall and those—you know ? ' ' How 's Carrington, eh ? ' ' Been to tea with Purfleet recently ? He ! He ! '

But it is scarcely necessary to say that these morbid and unhealthy fancies occupied a comparatively small part of her time and thought. Usually she was just a happy, healthy English girl, ready for any game that was proposed. She found everybody exceptionally amiable. God, who after all must have some decent instincts, afflicted Mrs. Eastcourt in the rheumatic line, so that she was nailed, grousing, to her bed, and could not interfere. The Colonel turned up when he was wanted, and disappeared when he wasn't. Coz must have received severe orders, for he scarcely dared open his lips. Alvina, rather feeling the strain, maintained a frontispiece of almost agonising sweetness, relieved Georgie of all household duties, and twice bicycled into Cricton herself rather than interrupt an extempore game of tennis on the bumpy and undersized lawn. Purfleet and McCall kept graciously out of the way, and Purfleet bet five to one Georgie was engaged before Christmas and two to one that she married Geoffrey within six months. McCall, after a canny weighing of probabilities, refused to take him. Mr. Judd, ever optimistic, journeyed to Cricton and bought a new hat and another albert for his watch-chain, against the wedding.

The whole village had a sort of illustrated Christmas card feeling about Miss Georgie, and wished her as much luck as if she had been the robin in the snow under ye olde English churche.

Georgie seemed suddenly to have acquired in reality the theoretical status of a medieval monarch—she could do no wrong. A less obtuse person—if such could be found—would have perceived that her bit of England expected her to do her duty, and would spare her no expense in seeing that she did it. A few days after Geoffrey's arrival, when he chose to spend the morning in his shirt-sleeves, getting hot and filthy under his Bentley in the delusion that he was making the machine more efficient, Georgie cycled into Cricton. She returned after a considerable absence with a number of parcels containing tubes and bottles and pots. Later, with a shock Alvina observed, with self-restraint refrained from denouncing, the fact that Georgie's dressing-table was no longer virgin of cosmetics. To make quite sure that she missed nothing of importance, Georgie bought all the aids to beauty she had ever heard of, from the glycerine and cucumber, praised by Lizzie as sovereign for chapped hands, to Madame Bernhardt's Superior Vanishing Cream, once negligently recommended by Georgie's dissipated aunt in London.

Georgie had thought of writing to this almost fabulous relative for advice, but on consideration felt it best to trust to her own woman's instinct, and not to sully love with the probably unwholesome counsels of low lust.

It is impossible to estimate accurately how much (if anything) Georgie owed to these various compounds of refined lard and perfume, and how much to her own state of mind and, perhaps, unperceived glandular secretions. But the fact is that she underwent a startling if temporary change, and became almost pretty. Nor was this wholly due to alterations in her manner of dressing. True, it was a distinct advantage that she abandoned black stockings for *tête-de-nègre* and fawn ones of artificial silk, and wore shoes that were less sensible and of a more erotic cut. Again, the almost new dresses, which the generous Margy insisted on her taking and slaved over for two days to adapt to Georgie's robuster figure, were a startling improvement on the overgrown schoolgirl wardrobe of Alvina's choosing. And then everybody except Alvina and Coz (who nevertheless dared not criticise) highly approved of Margy's rearrangement of Georgie's hair, which she made into two plaits and then braided into a couple of neat little interwoven wheels over the ears. Not exactly fashionable, of course, but the best which could be done with a girl who was afraid to have her hair properly cut, and certainly good enough for Cleeve and a savage just returned from some ghastly outpost of Empire very much east of Suez.

All these helped, no doubt ; but the main miracle is that Georgie's face changed, or seemed to change. She no longer made you think of a painted stucco cherub puffing an invisible trumpet. Was it the refined lard or

was it feeling happy or was it unperceived facial massage
on the part of the guardian angel when she was asleep,
which somehow softened the contours and modified the
hues of those too opulent cheeks ?   It may have been
the powder, of course, but certainly even her nose lost
that painful milkmaid Marion blush, and attained a
more sober harmony of form and colour.   The childish
eyes and mouth stayed childish, but developed some sort
of promise ; just a little light in the eyes instead of an
owlish dullness, and—was it merely a delusion that her
lips silently ' cherry-ripe ! ' themselves did cry ?   If you
had considered the old Georgie as merely an overgrown
child, you would have said that she had become a young
woman in a week ; or if you had considered her as a
grown woman uncomfortably retaining all the gawki-
ness of adolescence, you would have felt that she looked
five years younger.

The one person who remained totally unaware of this
modern addition to the Metamorphoses was Geoffrey.
Having taken two complete courses of Pelmanism—the
second to remind him of what he had forgotten of the
first—he was naturally almost idiotically unobservant.
What he perceived when he looked at her over the dinner
table on his first night at Holly Lodge was merely ' the
White Girl '.   You might really have thought that he
only became aware of her with the good old Lawrentian
dark abdomen, and not with his rational senses at all.
When he told Georgie that she was the first white girl
etcetera, it was not wholly false.   His feeble and awkward efforts to establish intrigues with one or other of
the wives of his brother Empire-builders had proved a
miserable failure.   On the ship coming home, he had
spent most of his time sleeping, losing money at poker,

diving in the swimming-bath and playing an extraordinary variety of deck games with other men. The
women on the boat were mostly rather liverish-looking
matrons, worried with the cares of a family. So that
Georgie really *had* seemed rather a vision of delight on
that first evening. But, obviously, this state of be-
dazzlement could not last. In a very few days the feeling of delighted amazement over ordinary English life
wore off, and Geoffrey ceased to be the backwoodsman
in the settlements. As he drove about he saw other
women that they were comely, so that all Georgie's
amazing and indeed inexplicable changes for his benefit
only resulted in her barely maintaining the position
which she had jumped into at the first meeting.

Yet, for Georgie, the wonderful experience was not so
much becoming almost pretty (she was scarcely aware of
it) or even her own emotions and remarkable discoveries
about the world. What fascinated her was growing
acquainted with Geoffrey. You must remember she
had no brothers and had scarcely ever been in the least
intimate with a male of her own age and prejudices.
While this undoubtedly left her happily ignorant of a
good deal of stupidity and aimless domineering, it also
left her with a human hemisphere to discover and
explore. Since she might not unreasonably have been
said to be determined that Geoffrey should please, there
may seem nothing extraordinary in the fact that he did
please her. But it surprised her ; and it surprised Coz,
who more than once interrupted their chatter at meals—
how different from the old silences or the grim chaffing !
—by saying : ' Well, I 've heard of people gettin on
like a house on fire, but it beats me where you two find

so much to talk about '.   And then Georgie would look
appealingly at Alvina, and Alvina would gallop Coz
into silence and flight as if she had been a big stallion
and he a little stallion after her pet mare.

Geoffrey did not tell her unpleasant things about life
and human conduct, like McCall ; nor did he touch her
in a way which made her feel violated.   Geoffrey talked
a good deal, but his conversation, unlike Purfleet's, was
never a tissue of allusions and ideas she couldn't understand.   Indeed Geoffrey never liked an idea until it had
been well desiccated and sterilised by much use.   Nor
did Geoffrey suffer from the professional caution and
indeed prudery imposed on the established clergy.   It
was grotesque to imagine that he would waste a *tête-à-
tête* tea-party in the desperate camouflage of prayer.
On the other hand, Geoffrey never made any moves in
the direction of degradation ; in fact, seemed to have no
tendencies that way at all.   He kept up the real pals
pose so scrupulously that a less smitten Georgie might
have been a little disappointed.   Indeed, there were
moments, such as that pleasant half-swoon which pre-
cedes sleep, when Georgie was astonished to find that
if Geoffrey had chosen to emulate Mr. Purfleet she
would not have felt degraded at all.   Life is very
puzzling for a girl.

They motored a good deal.   Geoffrey wore a very
peaked check cap, pulled slightly to one side, and was
desolated whenever he was passed by a higher-powered
car.   He did not forget his promise to teach her to drive.
But Georgie made no great progress, in spite of her
efforts.   It was often necessary for Geoffrey to put his
hands over hers on the steering-wheel to avoid a spill,
and this somehow paralysed while it thrilled her.   As

she felt his firm indifferent clutch, intent only on the steering, she forgot everything, and only wished he would go on. And then she was stupid about the pedals, pushing down the accelerator when she wanted to change gear, or the brake when she wanted to accelerate. And consequently more than once Geoffrey had to grab her ankle to pull her foot away. Georgie wished it didn't make her go so red in the face. And, then, in spite of all this Geoffrey obtusely remained a real pal, and never even hinted at becoming an old pal with an understanding. Life is very difficult for a girl.

Geoffrey said the lawn was too small for tennis, and they ought to have clock-golf instead. So he and Georgie motored up to London and lunched at the Trocadero, where Geoffrey used to go when he was on leave during the War. And Georgie asked very shyly and diffidently :

' Were you—were you always alone ? '

' No,' said Geoffrey, frowning a little, ' I was generally with some of the other chaps, you know.'

' But wasn't there—anyone you were fond of ? '

' Well,' Geoffrey admitted, ' as a matter of fact, there was a girl . . .'

Such a sharp little pang of jealousy, Georgie was quite startled !

' . . . I *thought* I was a bit gone on. *You* know what it was in the War.'

' Was she very pretty ? '

' Oh, so-so,' said Geoffrey with male perfidy. ' Quite a nice little thing—I 've really forgotten what she looked like, ha, ha ! '

' Weren't you very fond of her ? '

Geoffrey hesitated, and then determined to do the George Washington—to a certain extent.

' As a matter of fact,' he hesitated. ' Well, we were engaged for a time . . .'

Another sharp little pang !

' . . . But it all fizzled out. You know how it was in the War.'

' I was with Mother,' said Georgie simply.

And then Geoffrey was very nice, and said it had all been nothing and he had even forgotten the girl's name. He said he wished he had known Georgie then, it was odd how you sometimes missed the very person you 'd have liked to know. And Georgie said yes, it was, and how much she wished she had seen more of the War, but Mother's Hospital was right in the depths of the country, and you had to work so hard you never saw anybody. And Geoffrey said it was a confounded shame, and he wished to Heaven he 'd had a real girl-pal like her to think about in the line, and honest Injun he 'd never known a nicer and more sporting girl in his life. And Georgie felt terribly pleased and happy and somehow ' nearer ' to him, but there was just a small after-pang because he said nothing about engagement or anything like that or even hinted at an understanding.

After lunch they went to Gamage's, and Geoffrey bought the most expensive clock-golf outfit he could find, although Georgie said it was wrong to spend so much money. But Geoffrey pointed out that he made eight hundred a year and didn't spend half of it ' out there', and that soon after he went back he expected to rise to a thousand. And Georgie felt all cold and sad at the thought of his ' going back out there', and yet a little hopeful, on account of the thousand a year. Many a man, she reflected, had to marry on far less nowadays. And she questioned Geoffrey closely about expenses and conditions 'out there', and privately felt that two people could manage very well indeed. And even though there was no understanding, still, she felt sure that Geoffrey must know something of what she felt about him, and he *had* said she was the nicest and most sporting girl he had ever known. He was quite right not to be too precipitate. After all, if they became regularly engaged he would have to leave the house—you couldn't possibly sleep in the same house with your *fiancé*, even if your mother was there. It was all stuff and nonsense, of course—people were so much more broad-minded nowadays—but Mother and Father would think it was right for Geoffrey to leave, if only because Mrs. Eastcourt would say the most horrid things if he didn't.

They drove back in the evening, and while Geoffrey concentrated on the task of beating his previous record from London by at least a minute, Georgie leaned back in her seat and watched the slow fading of coloured light from the sky. It was wonderful to rush steadily and swiftly through the air, with the black road coiling and uncoiling in front, and the fields and trees and villages swooping towards you and then suddenly shooting out of sight as you whizzed past. Geoffrey was such a good driver! She felt such complete confidence in him. How different from those awful 'safety first' drives from Bulawayo Bungalow! She was quite sad when they drew up at Holly Lodge with a cheerful hooting of the klaxon by way of announcement. How lovely if they could have driven on like that for ever, just real pals together, without all the complications and worries and too frightening intimacies.

Georgie and Geoffrey were both tired, and went to bed early.   Coz retired to work on his huge patriotic stamp design, which he intended now should be his wedding present to Georgie.   Fred and Alvina were left alone in the drawing-room, with its odd mixture of oil seascapes by unknown masters, faded water-colour sketches by great-aunts, large modern arm-chairs and old brocaded chairs, and queer trophies on curly-legged marble-topped tables stood against the wall.   Alvina, with her spectacles on, was trying to sew something.   The Colonel was meditating, with his eyes open—for a wonder—and was gazing at the flower-pattern painted on the paravent in front of the empty grate.

' They seem to have enjoyed the trip to London,' said Alvina, stitching away steadily and as if with a hint of some ulterior purpose.

' Yes,' replied the Colonel, still gazing at the flowers, which certainly would have made a most handsome bouquet if real.   ' It 's very decent of Geoffrey to buy Georgie that clock-golf set.   It 'll be exercise for all of us.   I must remember to give 'em a hand with the lawn to-morrow.'

' You certainly will *not*,' said Alvina decisively.

' And why not, if you please, Ma'am ? ' asked Fred sarcastically.

' Because they 'd rather be alone,' retorted Alvina promptly and rather tartly.

' Umph,' said Fred, rather quelled ; and he went on gazing at the flower-pattern—not so unlike the bouquet Alvina had carried at their wedding.   He noted with faint surprise but resignation that few of the hopes he had felt that morning had been realised.   That slender, clear-eyed, clear-voiced girl he had married was now the rather cantankerous old lady stitching with such infernal persistence by his side.

' And if you want to know *why*,' Alvina broke the silence almost vindictively, ' it's because they're in love.'

The Colonel was uneasily startled by this brusque assertion.

' I say, I say,' he protested. ' Come now, it hasn't gone as far as that yet, has it ? '

' I don't know what you mean by " as far as that ", snapped Alvina, ' but anyone who wasn't half-besotted with porin over cricket scores would have seen it long ago.'

' But he hasn't been here a month ! ' cried the poor Colonel, making no effort to defend himself from her cruel aspersion.

Alvina sniffed haughtily.

' As if that mattered !   I *know* it's true.'

' How do you know ?   Has Georgie said anything to you ? '

' As if it were always necessary to *say* things ! ' Alvina sniffed again. ' Haven't you noticed how the gel has changed, how happy she looks ? '

' Well, yes,' Fred admitted. ' But what does that prove ? '

Alvina stopped stitching, and laid the sewing in her lap.

' When two young people are about together mornin, noon and night ; when they're always chatterin to each other at meals, and always goin off together to have more talk ; when the young man casts sheep's eyes at the gel every time she moves, and the gel is either singin about the house or sittin quiet as a mouse in a brown study—what do you think that means ? '

The Colonel rubbed the end of his prominent nose.

' It certainly looks like it,' he confessed.

' Of course it looks like it,' retorted Alvina, taking up her sewing again.

There was a short pause, and then the Colonel asked :

' What ought we to do about it ? '

' Nothing at present, of course. Geoffrey's a perfectly eligible young man, related to the family—so we know all about him—and in a very decent way of life. If Georgie likes him enough to marry him, that's her business.'

' But do you think it's safe ? ' asked the Colonel apprehensively.

' Safe what ? '

' I mean safe for them to go about together so freely ? Mightn't there—er ? '

' Nonsense ! ' said Alvina decisively. ' Geoffrey's a gentleman and the gel's a lady. Besides, she's perfectly innocent and pure, I know. She'd be utterly shocked at the slightest improper suggestion.'

The Colonel pondered over this piece of information with his heavily-moving Staff mind, and then remarked :

' Well, if that's the case, and you think she's likely to be married soon, oughtn't you—er—to give her a little advice, don't you know ? I shouldn't like my little gel to be shocked and frightened on her wedding night.'

' You're sentimental about your daughter like a lot of other silly old men,' said Alvina offensively. She felt a deep if inexplicable resistance against ' giving advice ' to Georgie on such matters. It was the husband's duty, not the mother's.

' But,' the Colonel persisted in his heavy way, but

with that slow authority in his voice which Alvina always found, to her annoyance, that she obeyed, ' I think she *ought* to be prepared.   I don't say you should tell her anything which might wound her—her delicacy.   But I think that from time to time you should drop a little hint, you know, something just put before her with feminine tact, eh what ? '

' It might be premature,' Alvina objected weakly.

' Just now you were all the other way,' said Fred. ' If you 're so sure it 's going to be a match, *I 'm* sure the child shouldn't go into it quite unprepared.'

' Oh, all right, I 'll speak to her,' said Alvina shortly.

There was another silence, broken only by the sound of Alvina's stitching, the flutter of autumn moths against a window-pane where the curtain had been withdrawn, and the slightly stertorous breathing which had come upon Fred with age.

' The house will be lonely without Georgie,' he said slowly.

' Umph,' said Alvina, not wholly pleased by the implied slight to herself.   ' It 's quite time she was married and had a home of her own.   You mustn't be selfish about it.'

' No, no,' said the Colonel hastily.   ' No, no. Mustn't be selfish, of course.'

Again there was a silence, while the Colonel once more contemplated the painted flowers.   What had Alvina done with the diamond brooch he gave her as a wedding present ?   Oh, of course, lost it on the liner coming back from the Cape, the time when she was so infernally interested in that R.A.M.C. bounder.   Just like her to go and lose the most important relic of their happy days.

'I'm sorry,' he said slowly, ' that we can't do more for the gel.'

'How do you mean?'

'In the way of money and all that.   I'd like to be able to start her decently and—and settle something on her.'

'Well, if you can't, you can't.'

'I'm afraid I've been a bit extravagant,' said the old gentleman regretfully, ' and the Army certainly hasn't been very profitable.'

'What can you expect from *politicians*?' Alvina asked the rhetorical question with an extraordinarily vindictive stress on the last word.

'I don't expect anything,' replied the Colonel calmly, ' and I certainly don't get it, not even a K.C.B.—and most of the survivors from my time at Sandhurst have got that.'

Alvina made no remark—she was weary of proffering consolation for this unbestowed honour, the lack of which afflicted the Colonel more than his poverty.

'Still,' he said more hopefully, ' we might do something.'

'What!   On our income, with all our debts?'

'I'll give up smoking,' said Fred energetically, ' and not a drop of whisky after Geoffrey goes.'

'That'd be a blessing,' Alvina admitted, ' but it won't save much.   What about betting and London?'

The Colonel thumped his fist on his bony knee.

'Not another bet—except next week, I've got an absolute cert there.   And we can raise another hundred or so by a second mortgage on the house.'

'Um?' grunted Alvina doubtfully.

'And,' said the Colonel, now thoroughly roused, ' I'll—I'll resign from the Club!'

Alvina gazed at him, speechless with surprise. That
Club, about which there had been such quarrels and
tears ; that Club, which the Colonel had clung to as the
last remnant of military splendour ; that Club, whose
annual subscription of twenty guineas had always been
such a wrench—he was proposing to give up the Club !
No more trips to London to meet those strange-scented
Generals and Admirals !

She stitched on in silence, and the Colonel continued
to gaze at the flowers in deep thought. Finally, he
yawned and stood up in his stiff awkward way.

' Good-night,' he said.   ' I 'm sleepy.'

' Good-night,' replied Alvina, without looking up
from her sewing.

Georgie was nearly asleep when there came a peremptory tap at her door. She started up, with the
feeling that something must be wrong.

' Come in ! ' she exclaimed agitatedly.   ' Who is it ? '

Alvina half-opened the door, and looked in, her head
curiously illuminated by the candle she was carrying.

' Only me.'

' Mother !   Do you want me for something ? '

' No, dear.   I . . .'

Georgie waited, wondering what on earth was coming.
Alvina made a terrific effort.

' Georgie ! '

' Yes, Mother.'

' If you 're ever married, remember that unpleasant
things happen. But pay no attention to them—I
never did.'

And she was gone.

II

Georgie and Geoffrey worked hard to get the lawn smooth enough to make clock-golf a pleasure as well as a religious rite. That was one of the things Georgie felt was so ' unique ' about Geoffrey—it was always such fun to work at something with him. He always knew exactly what ought to be done, and could do it so well himself ; and he always gave her something interesting and not too difficult to do, and if she made a mistake he didn't get ratty or chaff her, but came and put it right, so nicely and patiently.

As they worked, they talked. Georgie found she nearly always agreed with Geoffrey. And when she didn't, they had such *interesting* discussions, which invariably ended by his converting her to his point of view. What mildly surprised Georgie was to find the number of subjects about which she had no fixed opinion at all, so that it was sufficient for Geoffrey to indicate what *he* thought, for her to become convinced that he was right. And in all the matters about which she felt dogmatic, where there could be no yielding to heresy, Geoffrey most delightfully thought exactly as she did.

They discussed religion. Geoffrey said he hadn't much use for it, a feller ' out there ' couldn't help seeing that there was a deuce of a lot in the world which the parsons didn't know and which wasn't mentioned in the Bible. Besides, after all, dash it, there was Science—a feller couldn't believe all that about Adam and Eve, and Jonah in the whale's belly, could he ? Georgie was a little shocked by this, and said that you must look at the spirit not the letter of religion, and there must be a God because things had to start somehow, and anyway people needed something in their lives.

'Exactly,' Geoffrey agreed. 'That's the point I was leading up to. There's no need for *educated* people like you and I to believe all the old rigmarole, but religion's necessary for the working classes. It helps to discipline 'em. Keeps 'em in their place. But the missionaries are a nuisance—putting all sorts of ideas in the natives' heads.'

'I always did think missionaries were silly old busybodies,' said Georgie, working away with her trowel.

''Fernal nuisance,' said Geoffrey, taking up a spade and beating the lawn with almost sadistic energy, as if he were hitting a missionary's head. Presently he stopped, a little out of breath.

'Don't you believe in *anything*?' asked Georgie, rather awe-struck by so much infidelity in one so beautiful.

'I don't see it's a question of believing. There's what we know, and what we don't know—what's the good of *believing* a lot of old tales nobody can prove or disprove? What a chap's got to do, is lead as straight a life as he can and do his bit for the Empire and make enough to keep himself and his dependents in comfort. 'Course,' he went on magnanimously, 'I don't say it mayn't be different for a woman. If religion helps her to go *straight*, I'm all for it.'

'I used to go to Church a lot,' said Georgie, prodding vigorously.

'And you don't now?'

'Oh, sometimes, to please Mother,' she lied with cheerful unconsciousness. '*You* know what old people are about such things.'

' I haven't any parents living myself,' said Geoffrey with proper wistfulness, ' I wish I had.'

' You poor thing ! ' said Georgie tenderly, and then with a ray of hope, ' Aren't you *very* lonely ? '

' Sometimes,' said Geoffrey, missing her point.

Georgie sighed.   There was a pause.

' Lots of people,' Geoffrey remarked presently, ' think poetry is all rot.'

Georgie was just going to say : ' Yes, *isn't* it ? ' but checked herself and said :

' Do they ? '

' But I don't agree,' Geoffrey said stoutly.   ' Naturally, there 's lots of old-fashioned stuff which nobody wants to read nowadays.   To tell you the honest truth, I think Shakespeare 's over-rated, don't you ? '

' Oh, yes, I can't bear him.   We always had to do him in school, and I loathed it.   But I love Kipling.'

' He 's fine ! ' Geoffrey said.   ' I always like that bit —how does it go ?—dash it, I can't remember—you know, the bit about the feller with a bullet in his spleen. That 's *real* poetry.'

' Yes,' said Georgie doubtfully, ' *I* always like the Jungle Books.   Do you remember Rikki-Tikki-Tavi ? '

' Rather !   I say, what a lot you 've read ! '

' Oh, I 've read awfully little,' Georgie protested. ' I don't really like books much, you know.   I 'd always rather be out of doors or playing some decent game.'

' So would I,' agreed Geoffrey, ' but I think an educated chap ought to read a few books now and then. Sometimes out there it 's too hot even to move, and there 's nothing to do but read.'

' I 'm very fond of painting,' said Georgie, on the

defensive, and anxious to get away from dangerous ground—Geoffrey was obviously far beyond her in matters of literature.

' Are you ? I 'm afraid I don't know anything about it. But I used to know a chap who was cracked about it—feller who went to the National Gallery and had all sorts of photographs of pictures. You know, Botticelli and that sort of stuff.'

' Oh, I *hate* old masters ! ' said Georgie. ' What I was thinking of was Wyllie—he paints such lovely pictures of battleships, every detail correct, Father says. And then there 's a man named Mullins or Muggins who paints race-horses, and they 're so real, you expect them to walk out of the canvas. It 's wonderful.'

' Yes,' said Geoffrey, ' I think I 've seen them in the illustrated papers. Do you know, I was afraid you might like those Cubist chaps.'

' Oh ! ' exclaimed Georgie. ' How could you ! I 've never seen *any* of them, but I think they 're perfectly horrible.'

' They may be all right for foreigners,' said Geoffrey, being broad-minded, ' but you 'll never get English people to tolerate that sort of thing. We may not be a very brainy people or very *artistic* and all that sort of thing, but we 've got too much healthy common sense to be taken in by such stuff. They can't be any good as painters if they can't make their pictures look like what you see, can they ? '

' No, of course not ! '

' That 's one thing I like about you,' said Geoffrey, shifting to another part of the lawn, ' you 've got so much common sense. You 're intelligent and up-to-date and well-dressed and all that, but you haven't got mixed up in any of these perfectly foul cliques in London.'

Georgie looked at him in silent adoration—so many compliments, all meant too, in one sentence !

' Of course, they aren't *real* Society,' Geoffrey proceeded, ' though they do get themselves into all the papers. They 're just the rotters and the wasters, sort of froth thrown up by the War. One of these days the Country 'll get sick of 'em, and kick 'em all out. Sooner the better, I say. *We* 've made the Empire, and what we have we 'll hold. And we 're not going to work for a set of immoral skunks like that. Take the Old Man's son, now . . .'

' The old man ? ' Georgie interrupted.

' The Old Man 's the Managing Director of my Company,' Geoffrey explained importantly, ' owns more than half the shares, and really founded the whole estate. I should say he must make a good eight or ten thousand a year, if not more. Well, he sent his son to one of the Universities, and he got in with a foul set there—you know, degenerates.'

' Degenerates ? ' Georgie echoed again.

' Oh, it 's a beastly thing—I can't tell you about it,' said Geoffrey hastily. ' Anyway, this young blighter absolutely refused to go out to the estate, and hangs about London trying to get a job as an actor ! Just think of that, with the opportunity he 's got.'

' How dreadful for his poor father,' said Georgie.

' So there you are,' Geoffrey concluded, though where exactly they were Georgie couldn't quite make out. And she hadn't time to ask Geoffrey to explain further, because Alvina came and called them to tea. But Georgie felt they had had a most interesting and valu-

able talk—it really *was* a comfort to have somebody
intelligent to discuss things with.

A talent for intellectual conversation was by no means
the only endearing trait Georgie discovered in Geoffrey.
He shared with her the common but essentially mystic
passion for gadgets—the white man's mechanical grigris.
It seemed scarcely worth while Geoffrey's making his
tremendous mental efforts to free himself from the
slough of religion, since he immediately fell into the
much older and more nauseous bog of magic. And
this gadget-worship found its echo in Georgie, in whom
it was inextricably woven with the primitive feminine
worship of trinkets.

You could see that Geoffrey was a typical machine-
worshipper, because he spent more time tinkering with
a gadget than using it, and because no sooner had he
acquired one ' convenience ' than he wanted another.
Within a very short time of his arrival, he quite trans-
formed Holly Lodge. The Colonel had told him to
consider the house as his own home, and he treated it
accordingly. He introduced a portable gramophone and
spent a lot of time taking it to pieces and reassembling
it—a feat which he successfully performed, thereby
showing his mechanical genius. Georgie and he passed
happy hours going through catalogues of records, and
deciding which they would get in Cricton. Nor did
Geoffrey limit himself to dances and songs from recent
musical comedies. On the contrary, he enriched their
repertory with Grieg's Dance of the Gnomes, Wagner's
Ride of the Walkyrie and an astonishing rendering of
Verdi's *La Donna è mobile* by an Italian tenor of the
New York Metropolitan Opera House. He bought the

first because, as he said, it is the most top-hole piece of music ever written ; but the other two were acquired for purely mechanical reasons—they were at once the loudest and yet clearest recordings ever made. The Walkyrie had a range of three hundred yards, but the Italian tenor went to nearly a quarter of a mile. In the evening, on the rare occasions when the gramophone was not undergoing skilled dissection, he put on fox-trots and taught Georgie to dance under the benevolent gaze of the Colonel. Alvina refused either to listen or to dance. Geoffrey tried hard to get her a record of a hunting-field scene, but failed. Even his gift of Mr. Masefield's splendid and British ' Reynard the Fox ' failed to placate her—she said huntin was too serious a thing to be made fun of by long-haired poets.

But all Alvina's deepest sense of maternal responsibility and finest gifts of self-control were needed to prevent an outburst when Geoffrey suddenly turned up one afternoon carrying an enormous coil of shining copper wire and an instrument which looked to her like a devilish and complicated telephone set. Without so much as a by-your-leave, Geoffrey turned a gentleman's house into a low suburban-looking villa by rigging up a most conspicuous aerial. Georgie was delighted, and almost with tears begged Alvina not to be cross about it. Alvina set her lips tight and performed the most unusual feat (for her) of taking a long solitary walk ; but she stoically said nothing. The wireless set was infinitely better than the Bulawayo Bungalow contraption ; but Georgie did not get quite so much fun out of it as she hoped, because Geoffrey was never satisfied with the reception and was always fiddling with valves and whatnot to improve it.

The absence of both telephone and electric light from
Holly Lodge grieved and pained Geoffrey. Finding
the Colonel alone in the garden one morning, Geoffrey
tactfully brought the matter up.

' Lovely morning, Sir.'

' Beautiful,' said the Colonel, who was listening to
the distant pops of Sir Horace and party shooting.
' I 'm sorry we can't give you any shootin, my boy.
Splendid day to be out with the guns.'

' Oh, that 's all right, Sir, I daresay we 'll be able to
do something about that presently. But, I say, don't
you find it confoundedly awkward not having a telephone ? I had to drive to the post-office yesterday to
get a call to Cricton.'

' I 'm sorry you had the trouble,' said the Colonel
mildly, ' but it would be a useless expense for me to have
the telephone. You see, there 's nobody in particular
I want to talk to or who wants to talk to me.'

' Awfully useful for shopping and all that,' urged
Geoffrey.

The Colonel shook his head. He wasn't going to
admit that he couldn't afford to have the telephone, even
to spare Georgie's legs and Alvina's memory.

Geoffrey changed the subject.

' I noticed the other day that there 's a very neat little
dam and power-house on the river with a wire leading
up to the Squire's house. Why don't you get him to let
you run a wire along here—we could install all sorts of
things. I could do most of the installation myself if we
only had the power.'

' It 's very good of you, my boy, but, no, no.' The
Colonel shook his head sadly, and continued in a con-
fidential tone : ' As a matter of fact, I was on quite good

terms with Stimms, and then my wife offended him in
some confoundedly tactless way, just like her.   But he
wouldn't like it anyway.   He's one of these chaps
whose property's gone to his head, if you know what I
mean.   He thinks the river's all his because it runs for
a mile or so through his land, and he wouldn't dream of
allowing anyone else to use his electric power.'

' But you could offer to pay,' Geoffrey remarked.

Offering to pay what he couldn't afford to pay had
been an active disease with the Colonel all his life, but on
this occasion he quite definitely refused.   He said he
was too old to start rows with his neighbours, especially
the very rich ones ; he left that sort of thing to young
and plucky birds like Mrs. Eastcourt.   So Geoffrey
went empty and disconsolate away, and consoled himself by taking Georgie, or Georgie and Coz, to the
pictures.

Geoffrey preferred the cinema to the stage.   He said
it was because the cinema was more up-to-date and
lively, but what he really liked was its being mechanical.
He told Georgie that if he had more money he would go
into the business himself—it had a great future, and the
old stage was dead.   It was true, though he did not
refer to it, that he twice or thrice went off by himself to
London and spent the night there in order to ' see a
show '.   On each occasion he returned late the following
afternoon, looking tired but contented, and was exceedingly vague about which show he had seen.

For Georgie the cinema was joy, although it was long
before the days of talkies.   Neither the Colonel nor
Alvina ' objected ' to the cinema *qua* cinema, but they
just were not interested.   Georgie hated going with Coz
—he always said such silly and offensive things at the

most touching moments—and somehow she seldom went
alone.   It wasn't much fun, and then you do get into a
rut in the country, so that everything out of the routine
becomes an effort.   Now, she and Geoffrey went to see
every ' new ' film which came to Cricton—new to them,
since Cricton was as far behind London as London is
behind New York.

They nearly always went in the afternoon, because
Georgie thought that Mother and Father mightn't quite
like her going off at night with Geoffrey and not getting
back until midnight. Geoffrey was sometimes extremely
critical of the films and pointed out all sorts of defects
which had been, and generally remained, invisible to her.
She laughed very heartily at the comic ones where
people got so amusingly knocked about, and became
flushed and excited over the mystery and crime ones,
and very much interested in the high life ones, and was
greatly moved by the sentimental costume ones.   But
what she liked best were the Wild West or Mexico ones,
where there were Indians and lots of shooting and wild
pursuits and flights and charges on horseback, and men
were always drawing guns from their embroidered flaps
and banging off like lightning, and where the girl was
rescued just in time from dire peril to her honour by the
manly-faced hero.   She clutched Geoffrey's hand, and
gasped with excitement at the flights and horsemanship,
and quivered with apprehension when the hero or
heroine were in danger, and wept unfeignedly over all
the tender and pathetic parts.   And how she thrilled
when the young hero sent his fist right smash on the chin
of the would-be raping villain and knocked him sprawling ! She could have cheered. And how she more than
thrilled when the slim figure with its dangling guns and

firm chin and glorious eyes strode forward and took the
girl in his arms, and they looked into each other's eyes,
and then she quivered and shut her eyes and turned up
her face, and he kissed her, and all the horrid little
urchins in the sixpenny seats hooted and jeered, and
then it said ' The End ' and the lights turned up before
Georgie had time to wipe her eyes and blow her nose.
That's another reason why she hated going with Coz—he
always chaffed her for weeping, and she simply couldn't
help it, because the flicker of the films tried her eyes.
But Geoffrey was always frightfully decent, and pretended not to see, and then talked to give her time to
recover.   She felt that the cinema was the greatest
invention that had ever been made, the really great art
which went direct to the heart.   She was very proud of
that phrase.

They discussed the film they had seen as they drove
back to dinner—Georgie loved the cinema so much that
she didn't even mind missing her tea to see it.   They
looked at the matter from rather different standpoints,
and yet they nearly always agreed.   Geoffrey was interested in the technical side—how did the camera-man get
such and such a shot, how did they manage to move the
camera without blurring the film, why was a close-up
usually so much more effective than a long shot ?   At
times, he almost felt as if he would sacrifice some of his
leave, and return ' out there ' by way of California, in
order to have a week in Hollywood, the gorgeous-with-
gadgets. (This wish he did not communicate to Georgie,
however.)   She, as a film critic, was wholly interested in
the human and moral side.   What she liked was the
clean moral—almost ' teaching ' you might call it—and
the insistence on the great stable human feelings, real

love, manliness, virility, mother-love, the sacredness of
the home.   She was very severe towards the men who
tampered with a girl's feelings or tried to force her in-
clinations, and even more severe towards the female
vamps.   If they were not always proved wrong, she
said, it would be criminal to show people that such
women existed.   She talked as if the personages were
not shadowy projections on a large white sheet, compounded by cynical men for money, but as if they were
real—and after all they did *look* real, and the camera
cannot lie.

Yet with all this intimacy and soul-communion,
day after day passed and still Geoffrey made no move
towards the definite felicity of matrimony or even towards the more indefinite but almost equally comforting
'understanding'.   The Colonel and Alvina looked en-
quiringly at each other and spoke vague comfort con-
cerning the strange ways of young people nowadays,
but still — they must arrange things for themselves.
Alvina once hinted that Fred might 'say something' to
Geoffrey, but the Colonel most resolutely recoiled from
so dangerous an assault.   Coz worked less ardently and
rapidly at his great design, and was inclined to be a bit
satirical.   The rest of Cleeve was almost derisive.   What!
Georgie had had the man all to herself for weeks, fair
field and no competitor, and hadn't managed to hook
him yet ?   A most incompetent girl, unworthy of sympathy.   Serve her right if she had to lead apes in hell.
Even Georgie was at times a little impatient, a little
uneasy, a little melancholy.   Was there someone else ?
Those trips to London !   Had he really forgotten the
' other girl' ?   Was she one of those fascinating vamps

who have such power over men that they are able to draw them, weak as water, from true love ? Georgie hated the vague images of insubstantial but triumphant rivals which foisted themselves on her imagination. She wished Margy were not away. Never mind, she would be back soon, and would give Georgie the most helpful advice. . . .

The reasons for Mr. Hunter-Payne's prudence were really very simple. The simplest and most important was that he was not anything like as much in love with Georgie as she with him. He was extremely flattered by her very evident devotion, and he certainly had formed a higher opinion of her charms and endowments than any other eligible male. But he had no very strong feelings, and was quite incapable of falling in love with anyone with Georgie's brooding intensity. After all, why should he be so quixotic as to marry a penniless and not even pretty girl, simply because she happened to fall in love with him, especially when there must be scores of handsome creatures with money who would be only too glad to secure so fine a specimen of Homo Insapiens, Subspecies, Col. Brit. ? Naturally, *she* was eager—the whole bargain was in her favour. She had everything to gain and nothing to lose by marrying such a damn fine chap, but what had he to gain but a none too comely responsibility, even if she was virtuous and devoted ? Even those admirable qualities, pushed to excess, might become a nuisance. Still, Geoffrey didn't say no. He thought it was about time he married, and if he didn't come across anyone more suitable before the end of his leave, he thought he might as well have Georgie. A feller could do worse. Meanwhile, she was happy enough, and why be in a hurry ? Before he finally

decided, he 'd take a couple of weeks' trip alone in the
car, and look up a few of the Old Man's connections.

Towards the end of September rain and gales drove
off the lingering sun and badly shattered the scenic display of coloured leaves.   Then came the last lull before
the long dreariness of winter—a few very still days of
misty sun and light frost.   Georgie and Geoffrey went
for a long walk together, because the car was in dock
recovering from Geoffrey's skilled tinkerings.

They both wore tweeds and carried walking-sticks.
Georgie had on an old pair of sensible shoes—there was
still a lot of mud after the rain—but wore a new cloche
hat and a new coat and skirt from Margy's dressmaker,
very smart and becoming.   Geoffrey said at once that
she looked most awfully well, tweeds suited her down to
the ground.

They walked along a side road, then struck across
fields, and came to the river just outside Sir Horace's
estate.   The heavy misty air was so still that it seemed
valedictory, an end to something, rather than a transi-
tion or a beginning.   The fields of young winter wheat
and overgrown mangels were wet and glistening with
melted frost.   Peewits stalked, stiff-legged and crested,
over the wet earth ; or gathered overhead in huge cir-
cling flocks which flashed white as they turned their
undersides to the sun.   The caw of a passing rook was
startlingly loud, almost menacing.   The yet unfallen
leaves hung heavily and soddenly from wet boughs,
quite motionless.   Occasionally, for no apparent reason,
a leaf fell silently and was swept away by the river or lay
inert and anonymous on the wet heaps of its predecessors.
The only moving things were the birds and the stiff reeds

which wagged monotonously in the passing water and the slow, writhing, softly gurgling river itself. Occasionally a gun banged in the distance, where some farmers were shooting rabbits.

Georgie felt it all intensely, and wanted to cry. It was as if the earth were being gently abandoned by life and light, gently but quite relentlessly, and were slipping helplessly into the miserable apathy of winter darkness and death. No more sun, no more clear sky, no more flowers, no more gay green leaves. It gave her the feeling that there might never be another spring, but always rain and cold and fog and dispiriting gloom. It was so long till April, and in April Geoffrey would be gone.

They sat down side by side on the trunk of a felled tree. Geoffrey sat blinking at the misty sun, which looked like a blurred gold gash in the grey-blue sky. Georgie prodded little patterns in the muddy path with the end of her stick. She said :

' How quickly the time has gone recently.'

' Yes, hasn't it ? But I s'pose it always does when you 're on leave.'

' Will you—will you mind very much—having to go back—out there ? '

Geoffrey stretched himself, and yawned slightly with his mouth shut.

' In a way, yes. And in another way, no. It 's tremendous fun being in England, of course, and it 's been wonderful of your people and you to be so nice to me. I 've enjoyed myself immensely. But I like the tropics and the life there. If I could take what I like best in England back with me, I should be quite happy.'

Georgie's heart fluttered at the phrase ' take what I like best in England back with me ', although it was ambiguous.   She glanced up at him, but he was looking hard at the swirling water, and seemed not to notice her. She said :

'And what do you mean by what you like best in England ? '

'Oh, you know, the jolly life and the people and the cars and all that.   It 's not much use having a car out there, because the roads are still so few and bad.   And people get slack.   If it wasn't for the fresh ones coming out from England, do you know I sometimes think the old hands would go rotten like the natives, and let things slide.   It 's hard to explain, and it seems ridiculous here —but there 's something in the tropics that gets people down.   They get un-English, if you know what I mean, lose their moral sense and don't care whether they make money or not.'

'Yes,' said Georgie.   This was not exactly the line she had wanted or expected him to take.   She was silent, and prodded hard with her stick.

'You 'll be gone before it 's spring,' she said.

'Yes, end of February or beginning of March.'

'We shall miss you.'

'It 's jolly decent of you to say that.'

'I shall miss you very much.'

'Will you really ?   That *is* decent of you.   I say, I hope you don't mind, but—well—there 's something I 've been wanting to ask you for a long time, and didn't dare.'

Georgie's heart soared and sank, like a car swooping over a raised culvert.   Was it coming at last ?

'How silly of you ! '   She laughed.   'What is this dreadful thing you want me to do ? '

'Well,' said Geoffrey apologetically, 'I 'm afraid

you 'll think it awfully presumptuous of me and all that, but I should be awfully bucked if you 'd promise me something.'

Unconsciously Georgie put her hand to her chest—it was quite difficult to breathe. But with the true stoicism of the Colonel's daughter she showed not a trace of emotion, and her voice was quite calm and ordinary as she said :

' Of course, I 'd be glad to do anything.'

' How awfully nice of you ! As a matter of fact, I 've been thinking that it would be a great boon if you 'd write to me sometimes, once a month or so, and tell me what 's going on in England. A feller feels so cut off out there, you know.'

Georgie laughed—a rather pained little laugh, but a very brave one.

' Of course I 'll write.'

They were silent again.

Said Geoffrey :

' I say ! '

' What ? '

' You know I think you 're a top-hole girl, absolutely topping.'

' I 'm awfully glad.'

' I never knew anybody I liked so much.'

' Really ? Not even the girl during the War you were engaged to ? '

' Oh, her ! That 's nothing *now*. You 're different.'

' How different ? '

' Oh, I don't know, more sporting and all that. You know, the kind of girl a feller *trusts*.'

' Oh.'

Geoffrey took her hand and held it in his. They both

gazed silently at the coiling river, whose dull muddy water was rippled with gold from the setting sun. Their embarrassment was quite terrific.

' I say,' said Geoffrey presently.

' What ? '

' May I kiss you ? '

' Why ? '

' Oh, I don't know. It's just—well, I say, do let me ! '

Georgie turned and looked at him. She was reminded of the end of the film they had seen, where the caption ' Her eyes were stars radiant with promise ' had been flashed on before the close-up of the final kiss.

Rather clumsily Geoffrey kissed her. Georgie shut her eyes, and with one hand clutched the lapel of his tweed coat, like a semi-damned soul clinging to the cross. Presently Geoffrey said, rather calmly :

' Hadn't we better be going ? You mustn't catch cold.'

' Yes,' said Georgie in a very shaky voice. She stood up, and was amazed to find her knees were trembling violently, while she felt as if she were melting away.

They walked home hand-in-hand, almost silent.

That evening, as they were dancing, with Coz and Fred looking on, the gramophone suddenly began to run down with most mournful groans. Geoffrey rushed over to wind it up.

' I say,' he said rather petulantly, ' it 's an awful bore having to stop and wind all the time. I wish we knew more people. If we had a little crowd, the dancing would be more fun, and somebody could always stand out and keep the old machine going.'

' Margy 's back,' said Georgie. ' And I think she 's

got some people with her. She asked me to bring you to see her some time. Suppose we go and see her to-morrow, and ask them if they 'll come round in the evening ? '

' Top-hole,' said Geoffrey, putting on the needle.

III

Margy Stuart had peculiar talents as a hostess. She liked to have a couple of stars for a week-end perform-ance, but owing to a somewhat superficial observation of human life, she frequently invited two sub-eminent persons who were violently antipathetic to each other. Them she would surround with a miscellaneous collec-tion of youth, picked up more or less at hazard over the telephone at the last minute, and usually so ill-assorted that the stars hated the chorus nearly as much as they loathed each other. And then Margy complained that people weren't a bit grateful for what you did for them, and wondered why the sub-eminent so rarely came twice. It was, she felt, very mysterious ; and she sometimes almost suspected that there must be some sort of plot or conspiracy against her among older and longer-estab-lished celebrity-hunters.

At various times Margy had collected Sport and the Peerage, the Bar and the Stage. But her K.C.s were inevitably those who are not starred in the newspapers, and her Juniors were of the careful type who took third-class tickets to Cricton and then first-class to the next station where the car was waiting for them. During the Stage period her drawing-room was a green-room of un-recognised talent, or perhaps more like the ante-room of a dramatic agency filled with restless resters. She was not coarse and drunken enough to succeed with the ephebes of Sport, and the pukka Peerage wouldn't have her. The best she ever did was an English Dowager from Northumbria and a profligate Irish Earl, whose house had been burned by the Sinn Feiners ; and that was a failure, because the Dowager refused to speak to the Earl on account of his having been mixed up in a divorce case as a witness against one of her nieces.

During Mr. Purfleet's flight from Cythera to London, Margy had been seduced by him into the society of the Arts. Purfleet pointed out quite frankly that the Arts don't cut much ice socially in England, at least until the practitioners thereof have become so senile as to be practically harmless as well as totally uninteresting ; but, he added, it wasn't a bad wheeze for sneaking up the back stairs of celebrity, for the simple and obvious reason that a good deal of newspaper social gossip was supplied and even written by the Artists in question. Purfleet did not take Margy into the intellectual Anglo-Catholic circle of which he had given McCall so delighted an account—this was a treat he kept for himself, a little hobby for the winter months. Besides, they were far too serious and well-informed to put up with Margy; and they always pretended to be utterly furious if their names appeared in the ' social columns ' to which Margy aspired. Like Georgie in other circumstances, they felt it a degradation.

So Purfleet steered Margy on less lofty courses. And since Margy was well-off and generous and had a car and was lavish with drinks, she soon acquired what is known as an enthusiastic following. On the particular week-end when Georgie and Geoffrey came in search of dancing partners, Margy had convened her wild-beast show without consulting the infallible Purfleet. As soon as he entered the room, he saw at a glance that Margy had made another of her unique *gaffes*. The stars of honour were a Poetess of fragile genius with a loud lilting voice, from Hampstead ; and a burly Parodist from Chelsea. The Poetess was married, to a Chartered Accountant ; but, though they inhabited the same large and slightly musty house, they rarely saw each other, and He was never introduced to Her friends. It was generally understood that the shock of his wife's publishing a book of poems-which-were-worthy-of-Keats-and-gave-marvellous-promise had so preyed on the poor fellow's mind that he was drinking himself to death with dog's-nose, a vulgar drink compounded of gin and beer in almost equal proportions. This was regretted by the friends of the Poetess on scientific grounds. No one had ever seen her without a hat on, always the same hat, or at any rate one of a series so alike as to be indistinguishable. And the friends were simply dying to ask the husband if she wore the hat in bed and in her bath—if, indeed, she ever took baths.

The Parodist was a husky fellow with prodigious long arms and prognathous jaws, which surprisingly gave utterance to a mild almost squeakily infantile voice. He wore rough tweeds reeking of peat and a shirt as green as a billiard cloth, to show his devotion to the Irish Cause —though why the Irish Cause should have been so important to a person of unblemished Cockney descent is a mystery. But it was important, so important that it had prevented the Parodist from taking any active part whatsoever in the late lamented European War. Having failed rather badly as a poet, he had scored an immense success quite unexpectedly by a volume of parodies of

such late Victorian poets as were still vaguely familiar to
the Educated Public. This book had first been intended
as a volume of original verse, 'designed to show that
the great English tradition of poetry still lives in our
midst'. But an astute critic, on being shown the manu-
script, had said : ' Publish 'em as parodies, old man.
Stick in a few funny bits, and put 'em over as parodies.'
The unknown Poet took the hint, and thereby became
the famous Parodist.

At first the Parodist had been mightily in favour of
the Poetess. Indeed, he had written that her famous
sonnet :

'I must not come to you ; but you, my dear . . .'

was one of the greatest poems in English, nay, in all
literature. But suspecting her of treachery to the Irish
Cause, he had fiercely parodied her. The Poetess was
so much upset that she had to go to Bath for three
months to recover, under the kind ministrations of an
aged but omniscient critic. Her admirers were furious.
As one of them said, slightly ambiguously, at the time,
' it was an ape calling the Madonna black '.

And now as Georgie and Geoffrey—*pur sang* Philis-
tines—almost gate-crashed into Margy's drawing-room
to add further troubles to her distracted mind, there sat
the Poetess at one end and the Parodist at the other,
while a gathering of the charming youth of the time
circulated about them, acutely anxious that the rag
should continue. There were maidens—no, girls—all
shingled and shorn, and young men in nicely-waisted
coats who looked haughtily down their noses and gobbled
faintly, like emasculated turkeys. They were drinking
cocktails, and running about, and making offensive re-

marks meant to be overheard, and lying on couches and kissing, and generally comporting themselves as befitted the cream of culture.

Margy felt the rag would become a battlefield if the party were allowed to know that two such innocents had joined it. In her despair she plumped Georgie down beside Purfleet—of all people!—with an appealing glance which said : ' For Heaven's sake keep her away from the others ! ' Purfleet saw the agonised appeal, and nodded reassurance. Margy took Geoffrey off to a remote window-seat, out of Georgie's line of vision, and engaged him in a conversation which languished at first, but soon became animated, and then absorbing.

' You 're looking extremely well,' said Purfleet genially, quite unabashed, and genuinely amused at Georgie's embarrassment. ' What have you been doing to yourself ? Upon my word, you look like Euphrosyne in tweeds among all these freaks.'

' Thanks,' said Georgie sharply. ' You needn't chaff me.'

Purfleet protested :

' Hinkipable of sech a haction, lidy—as the man says in Shaw.'

Georgie made no answer, and looked away from him at the seething room, with her head held at what she felt was a proper angle of disdain. Purfleet refused to be silenced.

' You 're watching Margy's Famous Performing Menagerie ? Quaint birds, aren't they ? '

' I don't like to judge people hastily,' said Georgie, ' but I don't think I like them very much. Who are they ? '

' A brace of the intelligentsia who 've got their names

into the newspapers.   The loquacious old geezer in the battered Roman helm by the fireplace is a famous poet. The hardy youth with the green chest who looks like a very tame gorilla is also famous—he makes unfunny parodies which are alleged to be spiteful.   The rest are a chance selection of *la jeunesse dédorée*—gingerbread supermen with the gilt knocked off early in life.   Squits and squitees, I call 'em.'

Georgie did not know what to say.   As usual she found more than half of what Mr. Purfleet said irritatingly incomprehensible.   She became aware that a young man and woman on the opposite side of the room were staring at her.   Each held a cocktail glass.   The young man, with his head held loftily back, was smoking a cigarette with a flourish, holding it with the back of his hand turned to his face, like a girl.   The young woman said in a loud penetrating voice, obviously meant to be heard :

' I think she 's too *fermentingly* hideous ! '

Georgie couldn't catch what the young man said, he spoke in such a curious gobbling way.   It sounded like :

' Snotspoisnoussees.'

Georgie felt hurt, angry, and somehow ashamed. She found she was blushing, and did not know where to look, as the couple continued to stare at her and obviously discuss her.

' Nice young angel in the house, isn't she ? '   Purfleet remarked genially.   ' Sweet seventeen, and already at her third lover. They get off the mark early these days.'

' I think she 's very rude,' said Georgie, still blushing.

' 'Course she is,' Purfleet agreed.   ' Amazing how early they catch the Guardee manner.   But they 've got to do it or be conspicuous nincompoops.'

' What did the young man say ? ' asked Georgie. ' I couldn't hear—he spoke in such a funny way.'

' I think,' said Purfleet, ' mind you, I only think, I wouldn't be sure, that what he meant to say was : " She is not so poisonous as he is "—one for me, you know. But I wouldn't guarantee the accuracy of my translation without first consulting a native interpreter.'

At that moment there was quite a terrific clamour. Someone, to keep the rag going, had poured the dregs of a cocktail inside the Parodist's green collar. There was a stampede to hear what he would say in this interesting circumstance, and the movement revealed to Georgie something which had been hidden from her by intervening legs and bodies. A young man and woman, rather touzled as to the hair, were lying in each other's arms on a sofa, the lady displaying a broad black pleated ribbon garter and a fair prospect of pink silk knicker.

' Oh ! ' exclaimed Georgie.

' What ? ' said Purfleet, a little startled. ' What 's the matter ? '

' Those two over there ! '

' What two ? Oh, you mean those two worshippers of Astarte on the couch ? That 's nothing. You 'll soon get accustomed to that. You ought to be thankful that at least they have the decency to belong to different sexes.'

'It 's dreadful ! ' said Georgie. ' However did Margy come to invite such people ? I must go and tell her, so that she can make them stop.'

The female amorist half-rolled over and slapped the face of the gentleman, who cowered behind a sheltering arm and whimpered : ' *Don't* be such a sadist, Joan ', and she replied : ' You know you like it, you horrid little homosexual masochist!' and then, sitting up, powdered her face with great indifference.

The horror-stricken Georgie was about to rush off in search of Margy in order to quell the scandal, but Purfleet resolutely pulled her back into her seat.

'Sit still and keep cool,' he said. 'It isn't our business, and if Margy doesn't choose to object—well, leave it alone. We can defeat their exhibitionism by not looking.'

Between amazement and horror Georgie sat in scandalised silence, while Purfleet continued to give off what he considered witticisms at her elbow. She scarcely heard him, and certainly did not notice what he said. She looked round for Geoffrey to take her away from this Armida's garden of light loves, but he was nowhere to be seen. What was he doing? Wherever could he have gone? And where was Margy? What could she have been thinking of, to invite such dreadful people? Life, she reflected, was too awful nowadays. First, you had Lizzie and her polyandry; then Purfleet and his—his degrading influence; then the doctor, who was really *not* the sort of man who ought to be trusted with a girl undressed; then the Wrigleys; and now these awful people who seemed to think it right not only to show off their rudeness, but to do in public what a nice girl thought twice about doing even in private. How thankful she was that she hadn't brought Mother! It would have meant a break with Margy for ever, and Georgie couldn't believe that Margy even knew, let alone approved, of what had been going on. Anyhow it was probably only a regrettable exception—two mad people. But to her horror, no sooner had the couple abandoned the couch than their vacant places were taken by another

pair, who immediately displayed the most unequivocal
signs of close intimacy.   It was too dreadful, a positively
disgusting nightmare.   Georgie turned to Purfleet, who
was gazing at the couple with benevolent cynicism, and
said firmly :

'Will you please find Mr. Hunter-Payne.'

'Eh ?'

'Will you please find Mr. Payne for me—the man who
came with me.   I want him to take me away.'

' 'Fraid I shouldn't recognise him if I saw him,' said
Purfleet coolly.   'Don't be in a hurry—he 'll turn up
sooner or later.'

Georgie was just going to insist, when a girl came up
to them.   She had very golden hair cut very short, very
thin cheeks beautifully reddened, and very large appealing eyes.   She was so tubular and thin, and dressed in
such wispy clothes, that Georgie felt as if a puff of March
wind would have blown her away like a lost hat.   She
was smoking a cigarette in a long blue holder.

'Who 's your friend, Reggy ?' she said.

'Let me introduce you,' said Purfleet without getting
up.   'Georgie Smithers—Dolly Casement.   She 's just
your sort, Dolly,' he added maliciously.

Dolly sat down vivaciously on the sofa, and took both
Georgie's hands in hers.

'Darling !' she exclaimed, 'I 've been simply *dying*
to know you !'

'Me ?' asked Georgie in wonderment.

'Oh, don't pretend !   I 've heard lots about you—
haven't I, Reggy ?'

'Don't appeal to me,' said Purfleet.   'You know jolly
well I haven't told you anything about her.'

'Isn't he a *pig* ?' said the young creature vivaciously,

pressing Georgie's hands and squeezing up against her
in a way which made Georgie feel vaguely embarrassed.
' Men *are* horrid, aren't they ? '

' Sometimes,' Georgie admitted.

' I knew you 'd feel that ! ' And she squeezed Georgie's
hands again.   ' As soon as I saw you I said to myself,
" She looks so sensitive and fine, I 'm sure she *hates*
men ".   Don't laugh like that, Reggy ! '

' But I 'm sure you can't have heard about me,' said
simple-minded Georgie, ' unless it was from Margy ? '

' Oh, *Margy* ! ' Miss Casement somehow managed to
express a titanic contempt for Margy in the tone of her
voice.   ' You know, darling, she 's not sound, honestly
she isn't.   I saw her talking away like anything with a
man just now behind the window curtain.   Quite *beastly*.'

Geoffrey ! thought Georgie, with a pang of jealousy.
She said :

' Well, if it wasn't Margy, I don't know who it could
have been.'

' Let me see,' and the creature cast up her appealing
violet.eyes, and displayed a very slender Modigliani neck
which sank into a very flat bosom.   ' Oh yes, you must
know Heather Salisbury ? '

' No,' said Georgie.

' You don't ?   However can you have missed her ?
Oh, *I* know, you belong to the other set, of course.   I
must have heard about you from Lady Trenton.'

And she pressed so close and gazed so ardently and appealingly into her eyes that Georgie felt as embarrassed as
Alice when all the animals crowded round her.   Purfleet
watched them with subdued but intense merriment.

' No,' said Georgie, shaking her head in a puzzled
way, ' I 'm afraid I never heard of her.'

' Then you aren't one of *us* ? ' cried Miss Casement, throwing Georgie's hands back at her and gazing at her with intense indignation.   Purfleet intervened :

' You may as well give it up, Dolly.   Miss Smithers has led a sheltered life, and doesn't know a Colette from a Cocteau.'

Miss Casement stood up, gazed at Georgie with an air of extremely refined *hauteur*, and walked away.

' What a queer girl ! ' said the bewildered Georgie. ' But she 's very pretty, isn't she ? '

' Very,' said Purfleet drily. ' I call her the lily of Malady that grew in secret mud.   You know, one of the lilies of Les——   Good Lord, what are you doing here, Maitland ? '

This last remark was addressed to a man with a lined, weary-looking face, who stood smiling at them.   Purfleet introduced them, and whispered in Georgie's ear : ' Awfully stout chap in the War—didn't even get an M.C.'   Maitland sat down in the place just vacated by Miss Casement, but neither pressed Georgie's hands nor squeezed up against her.   Georgie felt grateful, for she wondered if everyone did that in this queer topsy-turvy society.

' Forgive my curiosity if it 's indecent,' said Purfleet, ' but I really should like to know how you got here.   I never expected to see you in this particular gang.'

' It is odd, isn't it ? ' said Maitland laughing.   ' But you see, Stuart was D.A.A.G. to my Division during the War.   I met him at the Club recently, and he asked me to run down any week-end I liked.   I didn't know he was away.   But I must say his daughter has been extremely kind and hospitable and all that.'

' Oh, she 's all right,' said Purfleet.   ' This singular

agape is only one of her innumerable wild oats.   She 's
a nice girl, isn't she, Georgie ? '

'Very nice,' said Georgie, without much convic-
tion.   Wherever was Geoffrey ?   What *could* they be
doing ?

'Cheery sight this,' said Purfleet, gazing at the party,
which grew more tumultuous as the cocktails flowed.
'It must warm the cockles of your heart to see the world
made safe for democracy.'

'I honestly don't care a damn,' said Maitland.

'You don't ? ' enquired Purfleet.   'Now I take a
sociological interest in it.   It seems to me that from
time to time I hear a distant if metaphorical rolling of
tumbrils.'

Georgie wondered what he meant, but the other man
seemed to understand.

'You 're an optimist,' he said.   'Who do you think 's
got the guts to drive them ? '

'Oh,' said Purfleet airily, 'the inevitable *tiers état*, the
vile rabble, the pornophilous proletariat.'

'I 've become a confirmed spectator at an early age,'
said Maitland.   'It 's a matter of complete indifference
to me what they do.   Let 'em get on with it.'

'You 're a nice pillar of the Empire,' mocked Purfleet.
'I 'll tell the Staff about you.   But, seriously, Maitland,
what do you want, what do you think ? '

Maitland offered Georgie a cigarette, which she
refused, and lit one himself.

'What do I think ? ' he said slowly.   'I suppose I
think a good deal, but I don't choose to let it be known.
I think the most complete moral bankruptcy of history
—1914—has been remarkably favourable to the growth
of unpleasant human weeds.   I think the only thing for

chaps like me to do is to be missing, believed killed. And what I want is to be let alone.'

'A quiet passage to a welcome grave?' said Purfleet. 'Well, well, I wasn't one of you hero boys, and I confess I'm curious to see the show.'

'You're welcome,' said Maitland, shrugging his shoulders. 'I don't think you'll see much worth seeing. Does it matter how they fornicate and what muck their vanity feeds on?'

Georgie found this talk very depressing, and she didn't like the man using a word which was only proper in the Litany. Thank heaven! There were Geoffrey and Margy at last! She jumped up.

'Good-bye. There's Mr. Payne. Good-bye.'

'Who is that plain but rather nice girl?' asked Maitland, looking after her, as she joined Margy and Geoffrey.

'Daughter of a retired professional Army man,' said Purfleet. 'You know—born in a barracks and bred in a dug-out. I once thought of rescuing her—in a purely immoral way of course. But she's hopelessly virtuous.'

'Is she engaged to the beefy fellow in plus-fours?'

'Ah! That's one of our local crime mysteries. A few weeks ago I offered to bet five to one she'd be engaged to him by now. But nothing has been announced. She must have played her cards with consummate clumsiness. You'd think even a fool like Georgie could have driven her nail into that Hindenburg head.'

'He seems extremely interested in our hostess.'

'Yes, by Jove, so he does!' said Purfleet with more interest in his voice. 'How like our dear Margy! She never does see anything in a man until another woman

wants him.   Really, this Americanisation of England is
being carried too far.'

Georgie stepped from the light of the Stuarts' hall
into the swathing darkness of a foggy October night.
Geoffrey took her arm, and they groped their way
through the shrubbery to the open road where the darkness was less overwhelming.   But he still held her arm.
At any other time she would have been thrilled, but now
she felt that the ' something ' between them had been
injured, if not wholly destroyed.   She even rather wished
he would let go, but hadn't the strength to repulse him.
Superficially it would be true enough to say that she was
jealous, but was it wholly jealousy ?   Her mind was in
too confused a tumult for her to know.

She had only her instincts to go on.   If she had tried
to explain them to the wily Purfleet, he would have had
no difficulty in disposing of her childish arguments—but
something inside her would have remained unconvinced.
It was not only the stuffily indoctrinated Colonel's
daughter, but the possibilities, the potentialities of a
complete woman, which were instinctively revolted by
the scenes of trumpery tumescence she had just observed.
This fiddling about, this pose of sexual sophistication
made her feel impatient, as well as uneasy.   And the
awful thing was that Geoffrey seemed to enjoy it, as well
as the cocktails which he had consumed freely.   As soon
as they could walk without stumbling at every other step,
he began in a loud spirituous voice :

' I say, I am glad we went there to-night.   What an
awfully jolly party !   Haven't enjoyed myself so much
for years.'

A little instinctive shudder ran over Georgie—grey

goose walking over my grave, she thought mechanically.
But she did not speak.

' Really priceless rag,' Geoffrey went on loudly and
alcoholically. ' I say, did you see the feller who poured
the cocktail down the other feller's neck ? I thought I
should have died of laughing ! Quite too superb ! '

Georgie winced. That last was one of Margy's
favourite *clichés*.

' I couldn't see where you were,' said Georgie. ' What
were you doing ? '

' Oh, just amusing myself. I say, what a topping girl
your friend Margy is, isn't she ? '

' Yes,' said Georgie loyally, if with a shade of doubt.

' I thought she was a bit high-hat at first. You know,
rather upper-ten and all that, but she soon dropped it
when she found I wasn't having any. I think she 's
awfully nice.'

He did not add that he had arranged to take Margy
out to tea in the Bentley next day, even though it did
mean running away from her guests for two or three
hours.

' What did you talk about ? '

' Oh, all sorts of things. I say, she knows an awful
lot about theatres and actors and all the writing people
in London. And she knows packs and packs of people
—made me feel quite provincial. You know, that was
really quite a distinguished gathering. Margy told me
a lot about most of them. And what awful good fun
they were ! I 'd heard that people of the best sort are
very broad-minded and all that nowadays, but I didn't
know they let themselves rip in such a jolly way. I *did*
enjoy it. And Margy was awfully decent, asked me to
come and see her in London, and go the round with her.'

If Geoffrey had not been three parts drunk, he would not have talked so brutally or have given himself away so fatuously.   But with half his controls out of action, he simply babbled out what was in his mind.   Georgie felt chilled and miserable.   How easily and confidently he talked of ' Margy ' !   And here he was approving that ' froth thrown up by the War ' which he had denounced so contemptuously on the lawn !   Why had he changed his mind so completely and so suddenly ?   Was it because then ' the froth ' wouldn't have him, and now had accepted him ?   But no, that couldn't be, that wasn't like Geoffrey.   And, after all, perhaps it was only Margy's fondness for her which had made her be especially nice to Geoffrey. . . .

They came to a bend in the road, where heavy, slowly dripping trees made a darker shadow.   Flown with insolence and gin, this very recently adopted son of Belial pulled Georgie almost roughly towards him, and began kissing her and fumbling with her person.   She felt his hot alcoholic breath in her face, and he clutched her so tightly with one arm that it hurt her.   How different from the respectful and tender Geoffrey who had kissed her so gently as they sat on the fallen tree !   Yet, even so, in a different mood, in different circumstances, Georgie might not have ' minded ' ;   but now it seemed to her that he was doing this, not because he cared for her, but simply because of what he had seen at Margy's party.   This, she thought primly and wretchedly, is lust, not love !   O Geoffrey, Geoffrey !   Yet still she did not repulse him—after all, she *was* in love with him.   Only when a clumsy but brutally precise gesture startled her almost to terror, did she tear herself away from him.

' Geoffrey ! '

' Don't be silly,' said Geoffrey thickly. ' Come on. Where 's the harm ? '

Georgie stamped her foot in a kind of paroxysm.

' Don't touch me ! Don't ! If you loved me and wanted to marry me, it would be, it would be—— But you don't. You just think I 'm like one of those dreadful girls—Oh ! '

To his dismay Georgie broke into uncontrollable sobbing. Geoffrey, his temporary ardour all gone, stood in front of her with his arms hanging limp, trying to see her face in the darkness.

' I say ! ' he said awkwardly. ' Don't do that. I 'm most awfully sorry. I didn't mean—— I say, do stop. I—I—I apologise most frightfully.'

' It 's, it 's so awful,' sobbed Georgie. ' It 's worse than, worse than degrading. You must have known I —I cared for you. I thought you were so wonderful— so different—so fine—I—I thought you cared for me too. Oh, I do wish—wish I was dead ! '

Geoffrey stood stock-still without uttering a word. He didn't know what to do or say, and only wished impatiently that she 'd stop and get the scene over. How awful these unsophisticated country girls are ! He felt sure Margy wouldn't have made such a ridiculous and lamentable exhibition of herself. Yet he couldn't help feeling a bit ashamed somewhere inside him. If he hadn't felt so much ashamed he might have been able to do something, and save the situation.

Presently Georgie began to walk slowly in the direction of home, still sobbing. Geoffrey walked about half a step behind her. Twice he tried to make her stop, began a halting apology ; but he found each attempt brought on so alarming an increase of weeping that he desisted. In this melancholy manner they reached the gates of Holly Lodge. Georgie made an effort, dried her eyes, and controlled herself. In a surprisingly normal manner she said :

' Go in and talk to Father and Mother. Don't say anything to them. I wouldn't have them know for worlds. I 'll be down in a minute.'

' All right,' said Geoffrey, sheepishly submissive.

But though, when Georgie came down from her room five minutes later, she had carefully washed her red eyes and powdered her flushed puffy face, even Fred and Alvina felt that something was wrong. And this impression was confirmed by the awkward silences and still more awkward dabs at conversation of a slightly drunk-pale Geoffrey, whose eyes looked vague and terror-stricken. Georgie soon said she was tired, and went to bed. A quarter of an hour later Geoffrey said good-night and departed to his room. He stood for a minute or so outside Georgie's door. He had a feebly alcoholic impression that if he went in and apologised, it would ' be all right ' ; in fact, his previous mood somehow got the upper hand, and he optimistically thought that she might even let him stay the night in her bedroom. He gently turned the door-knob, and found to his surprise and chagrin that the door was locked. Twice he tapped —gently, so as not to be heard downstairs—but Georgie made no reply. He hesitated, made a grimace in the darkness, and walked to his own room.

Downstairs, the Colonel hobbled off to see if Geoffrey had locked and bolted the front door. He hadn't. In the hall, Alvina had just lighted a couple of candles.

The Colonel took one of them, and began trimming the wick with a spent match.

'What was the matter with those two ? ' he asked. ' I thought the gel looked upset.'

' Oh, just a lovers' quarrel, I expect,' said Alvina with feigned brightness. ' They 'll make it up to-morrow.'

Fred threw away the match, examined the wick with a more meticulous care than seemed necessary, opened his mouth as if about to speak, and said nothing. Alvina took her candle and started up the stairs. She looked back over her shoulder.

' It 'll be all right,' she said. ' It 's just the usual sort of tiff. They 'll get over it.'

' I expect you 're right,' said Fred, and then was caught with a bad paroxysm of coughing. ' Dash it ! ' he gasped, struggling for breath, ' I wish I could shake off this cold—one of the worst I ever had. It 's so painful.'

IV

To assert that Georgie lost her almost-prettiness in a single night would be melodrama. And it would be equally sensational and untrue to claim that she there and then gave up all thought and hope of Geoffrey, and resigned herself to the gritty paths of virtuous celibacy. In fact, she missed the martyr's palm of matrimony by the narrowest of margins, entirely due to the caution and misplaced delicacy of the guardian angel who most officiously opposed the advice of her own enlightened self-interest. If Georgie had let Geoffrey in when he tapped at her door, she might indeed have lost some technical prestige all round, but Geoffrey would have let himself in for the devil of a situation—seducing the daughter of

distant and honourable relatives who had welcomed him
with a hospitality they couldn't afford !   It is hard to see
how he could have escaped the toils.   He was too recent
a convert to brightness and lechery not to feel some
qualms of conscience.   And even if he had tried to sneak
off like a bright young gentleman, a family council and
the threat of an appeal to the Old Man would have certainly yanked him back.   But that was Georgie—all
good intentions and no tactics, always trying to do the
abstract right thing and never succeeding in squaring
her morality with her interests.

My beloved put in his hand at the door.   When
Geoffrey tried the door handle, Georgie was in bed.
When he tapped the first time, she was standing in her
night-dress with her hands clasped and her arms clutched
with unnecessary violence over her breasts, debating
wildly with the almost frantic angel.   When he tapped
the second time, she was hunting for her dressing-gown.
And when she softly opened the door, he had gone.
What is your beloved more than another beloved ?

During a long uneasy night Georgie's brain was a
battle-ground of confused and warring feelings and
thoughts unholy.   She never quite lost consciousness
and yet she was never wholly awake, but lay in a sort of
stupefied delirium.   She staged innumerable scenes between herself and Geoffrey, and invented countless
dialogues which tailed off into nothing.   Over and over
again she re-lived the party and the walk back, sometimes blaming herself, more often feeling a passionate
resentment against Geoffrey and still more against
Margy.   The disproportion of night thoughts afflicted
her with visions of awful calamity and shame, while
twice in her mental wanderings she got out of bed to go

to Geoffrey's bedroom and ask him to forgive her.   If
only it had not happened that way, if only they could be
back at the gentleness and nearly-serious-understanding
of the kiss by the river !   Each time she got back into
bed, and accused Georgie Smithers with relentless
insight. Who was she to blame Geoffrey, after Carrington, after McCall, above all after Purfleet ?   And then
with an almost Baudelairian self-loathing she found
herself thinking that if Geoffrey let her down, she might
still go and see Purfleet on wet afternoons. Violently
she tried to calm herself ; and at last lay exhausted,
rather than asleep.

It was quite late, even for Sunday morning, when
Georgie, looking infinitely weary, came down to breakfast. She found Alvina sitting alone over the tail-end
of buttered toast and marmalade, reading the Sunday
newspaper.

' Where 's Geoffrey ? ' Georgie asked impulsively, unable to conceal her anxiety.

Alvina, she noticed, looked tired and worried too.

' He went off early in the car and said he wouldn't be
back till this evening,' said Alvina indifferently.   ' He
wouldn't let me wake you.   I hope he gets over his bad
temper.   I 'm ashamed of you both, worrying your
father with your quarrels when he 's ill.'

' Ill ! ' echoed Georgie in surprise.   ' Why, what 's the
matter with him ? '

' His cold 's gone to his lungs,' said Alvina sharply.
' And he constantly complains of acute pain in the chest
and back.   I 've sent the gel up for the doctor.'

' Oh ! ' exclaimed Georgie, all remorse in an instant.
' Poor Father !   I 'm so sorry.   I 'll run up and see him.'

' You'll do nothing of the sort,' replied Alvina, with a mixture of jealousy and authority. ' Sit down and have your breakfast—it's nearly cold as it is. He's resting now, and I don't want him disturbed until the doctor has seen him.'

Georgie began on a semi-cold sausage sitting in con-gealed fat and a cold fried egg which had probably seen better days. Alvina returned to her printed horrors, and Georgie ate in silence, deep in thought, not noticing the taste of anything. She drank cups of strong luke-warm tea to drive away her headache.

In a way, she reflected, this illness of Father's was also Geoffrey's fault, although he had meant well. But what an upset Geoffrey had made in their quiet lives ! Father unwell, her own heart broken, Coz still sulking in bed, and Mother coming up over the top of the newspaper like thunder 'cross the Bay. And yet, when Geoffrey had told her his plan, she had felt so happy and had thought how good it was of him and how affectionate towards them all.

Geoffrey had been struck by the Colonel's wistful remarks about shootin and the lack of cordiality be-tween himself and Sir Horace. After consultation with Georgie, Geoffrey had driven into Cricton and sent a long cable to the Old Man. The Old Man was not exactly on the Stimms scale, but they had more than once Jolly Rogered in the same boat, so to speak. Three days later a footman had come down from ' The House ' with a letter requiring Mr. Hunter-Payne's presence at dinner. And Geoffrey had done the young Empire-builder so successfully and presented the Colonel's case so tactfully, that he returned with an invitation for him-self, Fred and ' one of the ladies ' to Sir Horace's next shoot. The Colonel's joy when Geoffrey communicated this news was touching. He immediately began a long story of how he had waded up to his waist for six hours in a paddy-field and killed prodigious quantities of birds ; branched off on to a shooting anecdote of Sir Hector Macdonald and King Teddy ; and spent the rest of the day in filling cartridge-belts, cleaning game-bags and pulling through guns. He had insisted that Geoffrey should take the best gun—his own—and made Georgie take the next best, Coz's. He himself took Alvina's, though, as he said, it was a bit awkward for a feller to get used to a woman's gun.

The morning of the shoot was damp, and threatened rain, while the Colonel had a slight cold. Alvina begged him not to risk his health for the sake of a day's shooting, but the Colonel had been highly offended at the suggestion that he was not just as fit at nearly seventy as he had been forty years earlier. And Fred had thoroughly enjoyed himself. He greeted Sir Horace with a warmth in which there was not the least trace of ill-feeling, only an ease of good manners which made the plutocrat feel rather irritatedly small. In spite of Alvina's gun, he had massacred an astounding number of pheasants, and tramped through long wet grass and damp steaming coverts with unflagging spirits. But at dinner that night he had fallen fast asleep over an anecdote of exceptional length and complexity, and Alvina had had to put him to bed. And now, here he was, laid up with a cold which might last the whole winter. Georgie knew what that meant. Alvina might snub her off from going to him at once, but when the Colonel was ill, the nursing all fell to Georgie. Somehow Alvina's presence in the sick-room annoyed him, and sent up his temperature.

In private he once confessed to Georgie that Alvina had
such a confoundedly professional cheerfulness that she
made him feel as if he was having a baby—which, he
said, was a damned unpleasant and ambiguous feeling.

It was nearly ten o'clock at night when Geoffrey returned, in high spirits but with some of the apprehension
of a cool welcome which haunts a schoolboy who has
dodged compulsory games. In the morning he had
driven far and fast, and had lunched by himself in
Oxford. By three o'clock he had been back at Cleeve
to pick up Margy. They had had an awful comfy drive
and a snack of tea, and had then returned to her house,
where he had stayed for dinner. There had been a
topping rag, and Geoffrey had been made quite free of
the sofa, in the company of Margy, after he had been
ferociously turned down by the young lady with the
violet eyes, who called him a filthy toad of a man.
Geoffrey was already full fathom five deep in love with
Margy. There was a girl for you ! He felt she really
understood him, in a way which was impossible for
Georgie with her provincial upbringing. And then the
contrast ! Georgie could not for an instant endure the
comparison. Margy was pretty, lovely, beautiful, en-
chanting ; she was exquisitely dressed, fashionable,
confoundedly intelligent, broad-minded, and open-
armed. And she was rich—couple of thousand a year
of her own and heiress to a fortune. How it would
stagger the Colony if he went back with a wife like that !
In fact, if he married Margy, he could run his own
plantation, or, better still, remain in England. Divine
prospect ! He never stopped to enquire what he had to
offer her in exchange, or reflected that her immediate

willingness to indulge in amorous privities not only
betrayed an extensive practice but hinted that she might
not be so eager to commit matrimony with him as he
with her.   Does true Love ask these questions ?   As to
Georgie—what he now felt about her was simply that
she was remarkably prudish and unattractive.   He felt
quite ashamed of having made advances to her, but
excused himself on the grounds of his long absence
abroad. . . .

Geoffrey found the front door bolted, and the façade
of Holly Lodge dark and silent.   Ridiculous bumpkin-
ism !   Fancy having the house shut against him before
ten, when he had torn himself away from a most jolly
party which was only just beginning !   With a slight
pang, he hoped that Margy was not now occupying the
couch with the green gorilla—apparently the only other
male of the party with reasonably normal sexual instincts.   He rang the bell with a slightly intoxicated
feeling of superiority and authority.   Presently he saw
the faint moving gleam of a candle through the fan-
light ; the bolts were withdrawn ; the door opened and
revealed Alvina astoundingly garbed in the full dress
uniform of a hospital matron.

' Hush ! ' she said, putting her fingers to her lips.

' Eh ? ' exclaimed Geoffrey, gazing owlishly and
without comprehension at this dramatic transformation.

' Hush ! ' she repeated.   ' Fred 's very ill.   The
doctor has just left, and says he must be kept quiet.'

' Ill ! ' asked Geoffrey, still stupefied.   ' What 's the
matter with him ? '

' Double pneumonia.   Come in, but come quietly.
Have you put the car to bed ? '

' No, but it can stay where it is. Doesn't matter. I
say, I 'm awfully sorry. I hope it isn't serious ? '

Alvina had closed the door, and they were talking in
whispers in the candle-lighted hall. She did not answer
his question.

' Would you awfully mind leaving your boots downstairs, and going to bed on tiptoe ? He 's asleep, and
mustn't be wakened. Georgie 's with him.'

' Of course,' said Geoffrey, all deference and the-
right-thing at once. ' But, I say, if he 's really ill, I
think I ought to go at once.'

' No, no. Go to bed now, and we 'll see how he is in
the morning. The doctor 'll be here first thing. Fred
would be dreadfully upset if he thought you 'd been
turned out. You know, he almost thinks of you as a
son. Good-night. There 's a candle on the table.'

' Good-night,' whispered Geoffrey. The phrase about
thinking of him as a son made him feel sheepish and
uncomfortable.

McCall arrived at eight the next morning, an exceptionally early hour for him, but in his way he was rather
fond of Fred Smithers. It was a dark rainy morning,
with a growling wind and a nasty sting of winter cold.
Everything seemed cheerless and unhappy to Georgie
as she waited alone in the dining-room for the examination to end. Geoffrey had not come down yet, and Coz,
after wandering about fretfully, had retired to his room.
At last she heard the doctor and her Mother on the
stairs. She heard him ask : ' Where 's Georgie ? ' and
Alvina reply : ' In the dining-room, I think '. Then
they said good-bye, and McCall added something
encouraging in a cheerful tone. A moment afterwards

he came into the room, sat down beside her and leaned his chin on his hand.

'How is he this morning?' asked Georgie anxiously.

McCall did not answer her question, but rubbed his chin hard and distractedly.

'Look here, Georgie,' he said slowly, watching her carefully. 'You're the only responsible person left in this household. Smale is a useless fool, and your Mother so occupied in playing the part of an inefficient matron she hasn't time to face realities. You'll have to.'

'What do you mean?' stammered Georgie.

'I mean this. Your Father is very seriously ill. Both lungs are badly affected, and—well, he isn't a young man. He must have had it on him for days—I ought to have been called in long ago. Now listen to me. You've got to turn this house into a nursing-home —he's far too ill to be moved. First, we must get a trained night nurse—I'll see to that. Next, you must turn Smale and Payne out at once. We can't have them about the place. Then you must get extra help in the kitchen—I daresay Lizzie can leave her baby. Anyway, I'll see about that. And you must keep your Mother out of the sick-room as much as possible, you understand? Invent things for her to do, but don't let him see much of anybody but the Nurse and yourself.'

Tears were running silently down Georgie's face.

'He's as ill as that! Is he going to die?'

McCall rubbed his chin again, as if he wished he could rub it off.

'It's touch and go,' he said. 'We may just be able to save him, but . . . Well, anyhow, I swear to you I'll do my damnedest for him, but it wouldn't be fair to you to say there's more than a slender chance. Don't let

anyone else know, especially the patient—we must keep
him as cheerful as possible.   But don't let him talk.
I'm sorry—I—I'll go and telephone for the Nurse.
Remember, you're the one person who can save him.
Turn those two fools out at once.   I—good-bye.   I'll
be back at two.'

And McCall fled.   Georgie put her face in her hands
and tried to push the tears back with her finger-tips.
So it had come to this.   While—she could scarcely bear
to think of it.   How selfish she had been, how wrong !
How awful if she had allowed Geoffrey into her room
with her Father dying in the house !   If only he wouldn't
die.   What did all the little tiresome things about him
matter now ?   He had always been so kind, so affectionate in his funny old-fashioned way.   And how
nearly she had let him down !   Purfleet, that party,
Geoffrey—how hurt he would have been. . . .

She suddenly sat up.   It wasn't helping him to sit
there crying and sentimentalising.   If he was to be
saved, she must act.   ' Remember, you're the one
person who can save him.'   The doctor said that, and
he wasn't playing the fool.   She dabbed her eyes hard,
rolled the wet hanky into a ball, and stuffed it into her
pocket.   First, she must get those two men out of the
house.

Grumblingly Coz packed his bags and left.   Awkwardly Geoffrey listened to her explanations and
apologies, and awkwardly he departed, without a word
of tenderness or promise, only an ill-concealed gladness
to be gone.   She waited in the hall, hoping he would say
something when he went out, give her something to live
for, make her feel that he cared for her and would come

back and not forget. She heard him go to his room to pack. After an immeasurable time, the door opened and he came out. She heard him put down his bags to close the door ; and then he walked along the corridor, away from her, down the servants' stairs to the kitchen, and out towards the barn. She listened. She heard the faint whirr of the engine starting up in the distance, then the car bumping across the field track into the side road. The gear changed as he came towards the house ; with gathering speed the car swished past the front gates, hooted as he turned into the main road, and then the roar of the engine slowly faded away into complete silence. . . . It was several days later that she found he had taken the gramophone and records and the receiving set with him.

McCall returned at two, bringing a Nurse ; returned at five with Lizzie ; and came in again at nine. He gazed at the Colonel fighting for breath, at Alvina in her ludicrous costume, at Georgie, pale and agonised. He beckoned the two women, and left Fred alone with the Nurse. Downstairs, he addressed Alvina :

' Mrs. Smithers,' he said flatteringly, ' we shall need all your help to-morrow. Will you take my advice ? I know I have less experience of sick-rooms than you, but after all, the doctor 's the doctor, isn't he ? '

Alvina cackled in a pleased way.

' What do you suggest, doctor ? '

' I think you should go to bed at once, so that you can take over early to-morrow. I think our patient will need you then.'

' All right. Come along, Georgie.'

' No, just a moment, please. I should like to give

Georgie some routine instructions for the night.   Good-night, Mrs. Smithers, *good*-night.'

Reluctantly Alvina went to her room.   Georgie and McCall faced each other in silence.

'Well?' asked Georgie, looking up at him.

'If I could do anything by staying, I'd stay,' said McCall unsteadily.   'The crisis will be to-night.   If he pulls through that, he'll probably be all right.'   He paused, and coughed.   'The Nurse is a good one—I took her off another job to come here.   And—er—don't worry about the expense—that'll be seen to.   Er—give him anything he asks for.   I'll come at eight to-morrow.   Good-bye.'

He bent hastily forward and kissed her awkwardly on the forehead.

'You're a good girl,' he said, and went out.

Georgie went silently back to the Colonel's room, and sat down at one side of the bed, with the Nurse on the other.   The old man fought for breath, as the disease gained on his lungs, and Georgie watched him helplessly, wishing she could give him some of the air which flowed so easily in and out of her own lungs.   From time to time, the Nurse moistened his lips with a feather dipped in brandy and milk.   Sometimes the Colonel slept, sometimes muttered with open unseeing eyes.   He was quite delirious, and did not recognise even Georgie. She listened to his mutterings :

'Well done, Sir, well ridden !   By Jove, he's cleared the water-jump !   Eh ?   What's that ?   Nonsense, I won't hear of retirement !   Tell them to bring the guns up.   I won't have it, I won't have it.   What ?   I wish I could understand what's happening.   I think I must be

wounded, but . . . I say we *can't* leave those men there.
Orderly ! Orderly ! Tell them . . . Oh, there you are,
Sir ! We can't let them down like that, Sir. You must
let me attack, Sir. . . . I think you 'd better get me a
stretcher, Orderly, but remember my orders are . . .
Well, Sir, I may have made a mistake, but I did my best,
and I didn't spare myself. . . . Poor Georgie, I might
have done more for her.'

So he went on hour after hour, mixing up War and
Sport and Georgie and references to his past life which
she didn't understand. In between these fitful mutterings came periods of awful speechlessness when his
breath rattled horribly, and he rolled unseeing eyes in a
frightening way, and kept pulling at the sheets. At
last, after hours, he fell into a sort of stertorous lethargy.
Georgie went on tiptoe to the Nurse and whispered :

' He seems to be asleep now. Do you think he 's past
the crisis ? '

The Nurse shook her head, and said nothing. She
dipped another feather in neat brandy and brushed it
over the Colonel's lips.

' We ought to have had oxygen,' she whispered, ' but
it 's too late now.'

' Eh ! ' exclaimed the Colonel with surprising vigour.
' Go to the devil, Sir ! I tell you she 's my daughter.'

The heavy gasping suddenly ceased.

' He 's asleep ! ' whispered Georgie hopefully.

The Nurse took the shaded lamp and held it over the
Colonel's face. Then she turned to Georgie.

' I think you 'd better go and call your Mother, my
dear.'

As Georgie stood on the landing, she saw the panes of

the large skylight above the hall were turning a dirtyish
grey, and heard the faint drumming of a steady rain.
She was surprised that it was already dawn.   The night
had seemed timeless, at once interminable and very
short.   She was feverish with lack of sleep and concentrated anxiety, but so dazed with shock that at
present she hardly perceived anything but immediate
sensations.   Above everything she desired to be alone.
She could not bear even the anticipation of saying to
Alvina: 'Father is dead', and of hearing Alvina's vain
lamentations and recriminations at not having been
called.   Along the corridor she could see the blank
darkness of Alvina's door, with a thin straight line of
light at the foot—it looked as if someone had ruled it on
with a luminous pencil, she thought.   In the vague
dawn, the banisters up the stairway and round the open
space above the hall were unfamiliar and unfriendly, as
if the ordinary banisters of day-time had gone and their
places had been taken by a sort of night-guard of hostile
doubles.   She heard the Nurse moving about in the
room, and faint sounds came from the kitchen through
the monotonous grumble of the rain.   It all seemed
remote and unreal, yet, even so, nearer and more real
than her own life. . . .

She tapped at Alvina's door, and opened it without
waiting for a reply.   Alvina was carefully adjusting her
hospital uniform in front of a very ill-lighted mirror.
How ridiculous, how ridiculous, thought Georgie ; why
must we always be bothering about the right clothes ?
Soon it 'll be mourning.   And the word ' mourning ' in
her mind brought the first stab of realisation.

' How 's the patient this morning ? ' asked Alvina
with an important cheerfulness, which did not hide

her feeling of terror as she saw Georgie's remote white face.

Georgie did not answer the question. She said :
' The Nurse wants you at once.'

Then she went and locked herself in her bedroom. With its drawn curtains letting in the unfamiliar dawn, its undisturbed bed and complete tidiness, the room looked cold and mortified, as if sulking at her absence. The window had been left wide open all night, and the rain had splashed over the sill and trickled down the wall-paper, making marks like straight worms of wet. She went to the window and looked out, hearing the distant crow of cockerels and the jangle of a milk-cart coming from one of the farms. Outside the sky was compact and livid, and the world was soaked and softly gleaming with moisture. The tall almost leafless trees were drenched to the root, and water dripped and trickled from them on to the sodden ground. The last chrysanthemums, she saw, had nearly all collapsed, and dabbled their large fleecy heads in the mire.

How quickly it had all happened, how swiftly and disastrously her life had crumbled about her ! Only four days ago, she had been so happy, so sure that Geoffrey's kiss meant that he ' understood ', that it was all right between them, that life would be heaven. And then—she felt as if someone she trusted had suddenly turned on her with a devil's look and smashed her in the face twice with his fist. ' I don't believe in God,' said Georgie half-aloud, ' I don't, I *don't*.' Even if Geoffrey ' came back ', it would be useless. She couldn't leave Mother all alone. Now, if Geoffrey said those so eagerly awaited words about marriage, she would say, she would have to say : ' No '.

V

At the funeral everyone noticed how ill and miserable Georgie looked, and how rapidly she was losing the illusion of prettiness which Geoffrey's coming had brought her.

' Poor lass ! ' whispered Mr. Judd to his wife, thinking of the undutiful Lizzie. ' There's one that cares about her Dad goin'.'

' Ah ! ' whispered Mrs. Judd.   ' And maybe she isn't thinking of the young gentleman that went off and left her in the lurch like ? '

' Ump,' grunted Mr. Judd, and returned to the service for the Burial of the Dead, which through long familiarity he knew by heart. Mr. Judd's enjoyment of the funeral, which was enlived by a Union Jack and a great many cheerfully valedictory flowers from Sir Horace (not present), was utterly marred by the fact that the victim was the Colonel.   Even so, its splendour fell far short of Mr. Judd's anticipation. He did not realise that since the Colonel was merely a half-pay officer without money and connections, the Garrison at Cricton couldn't possibly afford to send a Bearer and Firing Party and a bugler. So they didn't even sound the Last Post over the Colonel's grave.

Georgie's mourning looked nearly as miserable as she. It was an old frock hastily dyed black, an old velours hat with a bit of cheap crape round it, the old black cotton stockings and the old sensible shoes. The Smithers were now not merely gentry poor, they were poor. Even before the coffin had left the house, bills and threatening letters started to pour in, and soon flowed in an avalanche which terrified Georgie. How could they ever pay all this money ? Ten pounds here, twenty pounds there, forty pounds here—the sum made a monstrous total. And that with the Colonel's pension gone too !

Alvina turned weak and helpless-sentimental. She sat for hours looking at the Colonel's medals and reading old faded letters, and when Georgie came to her with a new batch of post and worries, she said :

' You open them, dear. I 'm sure you can take that little worry off me. It 'll be all right. Poor Fred ! '

And then she would weep, and Georgie would have to comfort her before going on to the task of dealing with these dreadful letters. Some of them puzzled her extremely, especially one which was signed ' Mabel ', and began by enquiring archly why the writer had seen nothing of the Colonel recently, and ended up with an almost peremptory request for a ' tenner to go on with '. And there was another from a solicitor, containing some reference to a child which needed money for its launching in the world. It was terribly upsetting and confusing.

Then tradesmen began coming to the door and demanding to see Alvina ; and each time the servant arrived with such a message Alvina melted into tears and told the maid to go to Miss Georgie—she 'd deal with it. And Georgie did deal with it, quite efficiently. She listened patiently and politely to the half-insolent, half-threatening, inevitably similar tale of the ' long-outstanding account ' ; and composed a little speech in answer. With very much the offended lady's air, she replied that of course everything would be paid in full ; but they must realise, if they had any knowledge of such things, that there were many legal formalities to go

through before Colonel Smithers's estate was available
for distribution (she was very proud of that phrase), and
that the family solicitors would deal with everything.
And thus she ushered them away, half-protesting, half-
apologising.

But, to herself, Georgie wondered what on earth they
were to do.   There seemed to be no money coming in,
and a prodigious demand for money to go out.   She
wrote one urgent letter after another to the firm of
solicitors who had vaguely had charge of the Colonel's
very unprofitable affairs, and at last they sent a clerk
down to see her.   He was a Cockney, who had grown
old in the narrow cynicism of the Law, and seemed to
take a perverse if melancholy pleasure in revealing un-
pleasantness and foreseeing disaster.   But he was
shrewd, and had not been in the house ten minutes
before he fully realised that Alvina had determined to
allow all responsibility to fall on Georgie—and to her
he addressed his remarks, as they sat round a table
littered with bills, documents and letters.

' The will ? ' he said, in answer to an anxious enquiry
from Georgie.   ' Got a copy of it 'ere, Miss.   You can
see it, if you like.   All open and above-board, life-
interest in estate to widow with remainder to only
daughter.   Executors, Generals, since deceased.   So
the Firm 'll 'ave to see to that.'

' Does that make a great difficulty ? ' asked Georgie.

' That can be got over, Miss, but . . .' the clerk
coughed in a slightly intimidating way.

' But what ? ' asked Georgie.

' Well, Miss, as far as we can see, the estate won't no
more than meet the debts against it, if it does that.   The
deceased wasn't a good business man, and it 'asn't been

easy for us to estimate the extent of the liabilities, but they 're 'eavy, Miss, very 'eavy.'

'Then,' said Georgie bravely, ' you mean we have nothing ? '

The clerk held up his hand in protest, as he had seen the Head of the Firm do on important occasions.

' I don't mean nothing of the sort, Miss. Please don't jump to 'asty conclusions. What I 'm instructed to say is that the Firm is doin' its best, and will expedite matters as far as possible. But it 'd be misleadin' you, Miss, if I was to 'old out 'opes of anything much comin' to you from the deceased's estate. It 'll all be swollered up, or pretty near, in meetin' liabilities.'

' Why, then, we have got nothing ! ' cried Georgie impatiently.

' Wait a minute, Miss, *wait* a minute ! First, there 's the furniture, valued four 'undred and fifty, and belongin' to the widow by a properly executed deed dated 1905.' He turned to Alvina. ' That was the time you sold the shares, Madam, to pay the racin' debts, and the solicitors insisted that the furniture should be made over to you.'

' Yes ? ' said Alvina haughtily. She had forgotten all about it long ago.

' Then,' he continued, ' there 's a 'undred and fifty a year secured to the widow in 'er own right. And whatever pension she 's entitled to as a Regular Horfficer's widow. And there 's a 'undred a year, Miss, comes to you from your maternal grandmother, 'itherto in accordance with your instructions paid into the deceased's account.'

When, Georgie wondered, had she given instructions about an income she didn't know she possessed ? It must have been that deed which Father asked her to sign on her twenty-first birthday ! How queer that he should have done that.

The clerk coughed again.

' There are one or two private little matters outstanding which the Firm 'll deal with,' he said. ' Meanwhile, they 're makin' arrangements to sell the 'ouse—but it won't fetch much more than what it 's mortgaged for, if that. And they 'll realise on anything else, Miss, if there 's anything to realise.'

' But how are we to live?' asked Georgie. ' Can we draw any of the income you mention ? '

' The Firm instructs me to say, Miss, that they advise you to look out for a small, 'ealthy cottage in the district, at not more than twelve and six a week. As soon as possible, they 'll arrange for the sale of the furniture you don't want, and that goes to Mrs. Smithers, of course. Thinkin' you might be 'ard up, the Firm are willing to advance you fifty pound on account of monies accruin' provided you 'll both sign this receipt and an undertakin' to accept responsibility for all legal expenses not covered by the deceased's estate. There you are, Miss.'

Georgie and Alvina looked helplessly at each other, and Alvina nodded. They signed, and Georgie received the money.

' You understand, Miss, that 's not to be used for payin' any debts—it 's for your own personal use. You won't be able to run up no more debts in the deceased's name, so I 'm instructed to say you should pay cash for everything and live very economical like. And look out for that cottage as soon as possible.'

So that was indeed that.

Georgie understood vaguely from the clerk that some

sort of official would come down to 'take over' the duties of executor. The clerk warned her that nothing was to be touched or destroyed, under pain of grievous legal penalties. But Georgie thought that there might be things among her father's papers which he would not like strangers to see. As soon as the clerk had gone, she took her father's keys, and locked herself in his room. It was very still and desolate and pathetic, as a dead person's room always is; and the dust was already settling on the scattered papers and silent mementoes, which seemed already as pointless and sordid as the rubbish in a cheap second-hand shop. She opened the window slightly, to let in a little air.

The papers lying about, she felt, would not be very private. If there was anything to be saved from prying eyes it would be in the drawers of the roll-top desk. She was some time in discovering how it opened, but at last the roll shot up with a jerk and revealed an enormous mass of letters. Georgie looked at some of them, and found them monotonously alike: To Account Rendered; We beg to call your attention to enclosed Account now long overdue; Your *earliest* attention to enclosed will enable us to clear our books and oblige. She left this discouraging mountain of arrears, and turned to the drawers. Two were crammed with minute statistics of cricket scores. Another was filled with newspaper cuttings about race-horses and notes of their form. The next one was entirely empty, except for a stick of sealing-wax and a very small file of receipts.

The top drawer on the right contained the large MS. book in which the Colonel had been going to write his life and adventures, and a great number of Ordnance Survey maps, battle orders, Field Service Message

books and memoranda. The next drawer contained a
supply of blank paper, such as the Colonel had used for
his expert investigations of cricket statistics. So far she
had found nothing which justified her search ; but the
third drawer down did not open with the key which
fitted all the others. It seemed to have had another
lock put on it. One by one she tried the keys on the
two crammed bunches—most of them utterly super-
annuated keys of despatch boxes and official record
boxes which had long ago passed from the Colonel's
possession. At last she felt the lock turn, and pulled
out the drawer.

The first thing she saw was a large cigar. A piece of
paper was tied to it with a ribbon, and on it was written
' Given to me by his late Majesty, King Edward VII.,
then Prince of Wales, on the occasion of the Regi-
mental Dinner, September, 1895. Fred Smithers.' This
Georgie put reverently into a large clean envelope to
preserve as a family souvenir. The succeeding finds
left her more and more bewildered and concerned.
There was a box containing a number of curious objects
made of thin rubber, whose purpose Georgie could not
imagine. Then came a large envelope containing three
smaller envelopes, each of which held a lock of different
coloured hair, with a different female name written in
faded ink on each of the smaller packets. From a piece
of thick folded paper fell a gold locket with a little wisp
of pale hair in it. Inside the paper was written :
' Georgie's. Aged 2.' Georgie tucked that inside the
front of her blouse.

After that, each successive find was consternation and
acute distress. There were bundles of old letters in
women's angular writing, beginning ' Darling Fred ' or

' Dearest Freddie ' or ' My own naughty boy ' ; there were signed photographs of unknown young women in dresses dating from 1880 to 1915 ; there was a large collection of post cards and photographs which made Georgie blush red to look at, though something forced her to look at every one ; and finally there was a small collection of books, curious and facete, mostly illustrated with cuts of exceptional crudity and frankness.

The last drawer, which Georgie opened with almost feverish haste, was quite empty.

She sat helplessly in her father's arm-chair gazing at the mass of objects from the drawer which she had piled round her on the floor.   What was she to do with them ? She could not leave them for Mother to see ; or, worse still, for the prying mean eyes of some horrid little official, who would perhaps use them to disgrace Father's memory.   And how could she destroy them without being noticed and without leaving ashes for Alvina's suspicious eyes?   For a long time she sat there wondering how she could conceal those compromising objects from a derisive and censorious world.   At last she had an idea.   She hunted round the room until she found a large piece of brown paper and a ball of string.   Then she carefully made the books, the post cards, the letters and the other things into a neat square parcel, tied it hard, and sealed all the knots with the stick of sealing-wax.   On it she wrote in large printed letters : ' Strictly Private.   To be destroyed unopened at my death. Georgina Smithers.'

She locked all the drawers and shut the desk ; listened at the door to make sure there was no one in the corridor ;   then sneaked along rapidly and guiltily with the parcel in her arms, locked herself in her room, and

hid the parcel in a trunk along with her large but nearly
empty jewel-case.

And during these days Georgie had not thought of
Geoffrey ? On the contrary, she had thought about
him a great deal, all the more since she had determined
that, even if he did ask her to marry him—which somehow she felt was improbable—it would be her duty to
refuse. Father, she felt, would have wanted her to look
after Mother, because she had always depended on him,
and now that he was gone it was for Georgie to carry on
his high standards of duty. Still, she was hurt that
Geoffrey had not come to the funeral, and still more hurt
that he had gone away without a word to her, and had
not sent a message or a line since leaving. It seemed
very callous and—well, ungentlemanly—just to run
away from another person's life like that. She could
not help wondering a great deal what Geoffrey was
doing, and whether he still wanted her to write to him
after he went back ' out there '.

But Georgie was very busy, and day after day ran
past with a host of occupations—and no word from
Geoffrey. Men came down from London on official
business, and people arrived to look over the house to
see if they wanted to buy it, and generally went away
looking discontented and saying how shabby and out of
repair it was. She had to cycle all round the neighbouring villages looking for a cottage ; and when at
last she found one, there was the business of packing
trunks and selecting furniture, and arguing with Mother
that one simply could *not* afford to take some huge
lumbering piece of ugliness along simply because it had
belonged to Great-Aunt Smale. And then she had to

go to London with Alvina to see the solicitors, and listen to a lot of dry if well-meant advice, and discover that when the remains of the ' estate ' were gathered together and invested, they would not yield more than another twenty pounds a year. And she had been forced to apologise to the lawyer because Alvina had suddenly flared up in a temper and had demanded to know what had happened to all the family money—they were gentle-folk, and there always had been money and there *ought* to be money now, where was it ? And privately the lawyer told her that they ought to be very thankful there was anything at all left over. They only had the few hundreds remaining because several old Army men, hearing that the widow and daughter had been left badly off, had generously cancelled I.O.U.s they held from the Colonel. Georgie did not quite know what an I.O.U. was, but she asked the lawyer to thank the officers ; and he said he would. . . .

They had a dreary journey back on the last train to Cricton in a third-class carriage, filled with working men carrying large baskets of tools, who spat and ex-changed jokes which Georgie could not understand. Alvina kept nodding off to sleep in the corner, and her hat got tilted over her nose in a ludicrous and undigni-fied way. And even when they reached Cricton, quite tired out, they had to get their bicycles, light the horrid oil wicks which simply *wouldn't* catch alight, and bike back through the mud and fog to the half-unfurnished Lodge.

The servant had left the table laid, and some cold supper for them ; and by one of the plates was laid a letter addressed to Georgie. At the first glance she felt

sure it was from Geoffrey, and slipped it into her pocket.
Over supper, Alvina most unobligingly woke up, and
began to make all sorts of voluble plans for their future
in the cottage.   She would do this, and Georgie would
do that, and they would do this that and the other together, and be very happy and comfortable.   Of course,
Georgie was glad that Mother felt more cheerful and
hopeful.   It showed that Georgie's doing her duty had
not been wasted.   But she did wish Alvina would stop
talking and go to bed.   The high rather senile voice and
the loud cackling laugh gave Georgie a throbbing
neuralgia in the temples.   And then she did so much
want to be alone and read Geoffrey's letter.   Perhaps,
after all, it might still be possible ; perhaps somehow
things could be arranged ?   If he *really* cared, he surely
wouldn't mind Alvina coming ' out there ' with them
both, for the few years she had to live ?

Georgie locked herself in her room, and opened the
letter.   It *was* from Geoffrey !   She read :

My DEAR GEORGIE,
    I was awfully cut up when I heard of the Colonel's death
a few days ago, and wished I could have been of some use
to you.   But as it was then all over, and you had seemed to
want me to go, I felt there wasn't anything I could do.   I
shall always remember the very jolly way you all greeted the
homeless orphan on his return to England !
    I wonder very much what you will do now ?   I enclose
with this the firm's address in the City.   If you write to
them, they 'll forward to me.
    For the past two or three weeks I 've had a really top-
hole time motoring, although the weather has been far from
good.   However, we 've managed to see a good deal of
England, and now we 've arranged to take the Bentley over
to France and run down to the Riviera for a bit.   By ' we ',

I mean Margy and myself.   That 's another thing for which
I can never thank you enough—introducing me to Margy.
If it hadn't been for you, I might never have met her, and
have missed the most superb experience in life.   She really
is quite too wonderful.

I tell you all this, because I feel almost as if you were my
sister.   You see I haven't got any near relatives, and it
would be awfully nice if you would let me think of you as
my sister, and confide in you.   Will you ?

As a matter of fact, I am very puzzled about Margy.
Though she has given me everything a woman can give a
man, she laughs every time I ask her when we can be
married.   She puts me off by saying : ' I 'm only training
you ; if you must marry someone, go back and marry
Georgie.'   But, I know you will feel that is impossible.
My own feeling always was that you and I were like brother
and sister, and that neither of us expected or wanted anything else of the other.   At least, it always was so with me.
And I feel sure Margy is only joking.   Sooner or later she
must realise that the only thing to do is for us to get married.

Apart from that anxiety, which I feel sure will right itself,
I feel perfectly fit and happy.   I hope you are too.   I seem
to have filled this letter with myself, and not to have said
anything about you.   But then I expect you to give me
your news in exchange for mine.   Do write and tell me
what you are doing, and what your plans are for the future.

Is Smale with you or has he left permanently ?   In any
case, remember me to him when you see him.

With my warmest regards to Mrs. Smithers (whose hospitality I shall never forget) and with all affectionate and
(may I say ?) brotherly greetings to yourself,

Yours ever,

GEOFFREY.

P.S.—I find I left a pair of pyjamas and a hair-brush in
the hurry of packing.   Would you mind very much sending
them to me at the address I give ?   Thanks awfully.   G.

Georgie read the letter through hastily, standing
beside the lighted candle on her table.   She sat down,

and read it again very slowly and carefully. Then she put it neatly back in the envelope, and locked it in her jewel-case beside the large packet from the Colonel's desk. When she was in her night-dress and ready for bed, she looked carefully at her face in the mirror, holding up the candle to get its full light. Then she blew the flame out, pulled back the curtain to open the window, and got into bed.

.   .   .   .

Towards the end of April, Mr. Purfleet felt that London was becoming a bore and that the time had arrived when one should re-read the pastoral poets in the country. He sent Curzon to Cleeve to get the cottage ready, and motored himself down from London the next day, stopping to lunch at an Inn which, he had heard, specialised in a revival of good local cooking. He sent a post card to his gastronomic friend, containing the brief but irrefragable verdict : ‘ Succulent but gross. R. P.’

The afternoon was really charming, yes, positively he had to use that over-worked and mis-used adjective. The soft air, the gentle sunlight, the wide misty prospects of meadows and trees coming into bud and hedges like green waves breaking in a foam of hawthorn, even the monotonous and unfashionable song of birds—all combined to make up *charm*, the unemphatic but undeniable charm of English landscape in spring. At least, so Mr. Purfleet thought, as he stood at the top of Cleeve hill beside his car, and looked out across the country. There was no vulgar picture post card effect of sunset ; no horrible grazing Royal Academy cattle in the foreground ; best of all, no lamentable peasantry about. It was all discreet, subdued, delicately graded in scale and values. The ordinary uneducated and tasteless admirer of landscape would have passed it over as insufficiently picturesque. What the deuce did they mean by their ' picturesque ' ? Something obvious, something violent in form or colour, or desolatingly sentimental. Nature uncorrected, he mused, is seldom satisfactory. At best, she can only conform to a good school and mimic its style.

He spent some little time trying to determine exactly how to classify the scene he was looking at. It was obviously English landscape school between 1770 and 1840, and probably a water-colour. Yes, it must be a water-colour, for only water-colour could ' get ' those very damp-looking white clouds with darker borders and the rather mottled look of the distance. Turner was too obvious, too much a martyr to the picturesque. Constable, perhaps ? Yes, very much Constable, in a way, but there was a touch of Bonnington in the handling of the middle distance, and quite a Crome-ish bit in the foreground. And then that line of ruffled willows at the foot of the hill was distinctly exotic and en Corot. The analogy was commonplace, but if Corot would specialise in fluffy willows *ad nauseam*, how on earth could one avoid thinking of him when a perfect little bit of Corot appeared in a landscape . . . ?

Mr. Purfleet became aware that a dark figure was toiling up the long hill on a bicycle. A woman. By Jove ! Georgie Smithers coming back from Cricton with the shopping to that wretched little cottage of theirs on the other side of Cleeve. Purfleet hadn't seen her for months, and gazed at her intently as she came nearer and nearer. She had obviously been thinking absorb-

edly about something, for he saw her start as she abruptly
recognised him. He noticed that she was dressed in
rather shabby semi-mourning, and that her face was
very red with exercise or embarrassment. As she came
toiling up level with him on the crest of the hill, he lifted
his hat, took a step forward, and said :

'Hullo, Georgie ! How are you ? '

She was panting with the exertion of riding, as if she
had been determined not to get off and give him an
opportunity of speaking. At any rate, she made no
answer to his greeting, but gave him a curt little peck of
a nod, and rode on. Where the road began to slope
down, she ceased pedalling and free-wheeled. Mr.
Purfleet gazed after her retreating dark figure until she
swept round a corner, and was hidden from sight by the
hedge. Then he put on his hat, nodded his head once
or twice, and said aloud :

'Poor Georgie.'

EPILOGUE

EPILOGUE

Enter Bim and Bom

THE Shelleyan paper-boat of the moon was entangled in the leafy boughs of a huge solitary elm, and seemed to have difficulty in floating free. Light dew-drops of stars seemed ready to fall at any moment; or perhaps a grand discharge of silver rockets had become suspended indefinitely in misty ether. The pointers of the Great Bear discharged their shafts of light with tiresome accuracy several degrees away from the mark they are supposed to hit every time. A nightingale monotonously Toti del Monted.

It was about eleven o'clock on a late spring night, possibly the evening of Derby Day in post-War England. In the distance the searchlights of many cars passing on the main road formed slightly terrifying phantoms of light, like the luminous ray battles of deep-sea fishes fought under medieval auspices. The occasional grunt of a klaxon or coughing growl of a changed gear interrupted the nightingale without putting him off. The remarkable phenomenon of a moaning star slowly moving horizontally across the sky was correctly assumed by both Relativists to be a night-flying airplane.

Bim and Bom sat facing each other inside a pair of Soccer goal-posts, situated in a small outlying field of a large park. Sir Horace Stimms, the grease prince, had with reluctance ceded this otherwise useless field to keep up the spirit of manly sport in the village hobbledehoys. The Russian clowns had adopted suitable costume for this important occasion. Bim wore a Harlequin shirt,

351

plus-fours, and white tennis shoes; Bom sported a red
hunting coat, running shorts and football boots. In
further deference to English taste each had on the
ordinary clown's white cone hat. Bim's was inscribed
'H.M.S. Knarr'; Bom's 'K.O. Borderlines'. They
were hungrily eating sandwiches from paper bags, and
drinking bottled Bass à même le goulot. Both ate and
drank with vulgar relish. Presently Bim sighed, and
said:

'Well, what about it?'

'What?'

'All this. What are we doing in the land of Baldwin
the Boujois? I tell you what, Bom, I'm nervous. I'm
afraid of these bloodthirsty Whites. Suppose a band of
fox-hunters came along—they'd certainly kill us with
their dreadful spears.'

Bom picked his proletarian teeth with a stiff and pro-
testing stalk of aristocratic English grass.

'We're under diplomatic protection—for what that's
worth from the Whites. We're the Epilogue.'

'Are we to enjoy ourselves?'

'I don't think so. I believe it's not allowed in
England. They don't like it. It's bad form. They
have a huge organisation to prevent it. Lord Watch and
Ward, Lord Chamberlain, Viscount Chadband, The
Earl of Copper and Prince Beak are all members of their
O.G.P.U. If they caught you, Bim, they'd geld you.
None of your smutty jokes here, my lad.'

Bim shuddered, and hastily assured himself that the
threatened organs were in position. He whimpered.

'I wish you'd get us out of this, Bom. I don't like
it at all. You know I never wanted to be a missionary
in savage lands—why should they put us on propaganda

work?   It's frightfully dangerous, and I think it's boring.'

  'Of course, but you've got to remember that every-thing here is ages behind the times.   Why, people still go to Church here.   Hence this clandestine gathering by moonlight.   After all, it's much worse for the intelli-gent English than it is for us.   Everything's topsy-turvy here.'

  Bom drank half a bottle of Bass with rapid gurgles, and smeared his hand across his wide grin.   Bim scratched inside his plus-fours.   He yawned.

  'Well, I say, let the English get on with it.   Why don't they turn the whole island into a 19th-century Museum?'

  'They will.   You'd be surprised, Bim, if I told you half the things that go on here. . . .'

  'Surprised, but not interested.'

  'I'm sorry, Bim, but we've got to go through with this.   The author explained his intention to me, and I promised we'd do it.   Besides, look at all the Bass he's given us!'

Stately Homes of England

  The elm tree suddenly released its hold on the moon, which shot free with a little curl of white mist-foam at the prow.   The nightingale shut up, at least two hours after the local closing time.   The electric lights which had been shining haughtily over the dark village from every window in the distant mansion were suddenly extinguished; the wealthy but thrifty host possessed a switch to turn off every light in the house at twelve sharp.   Waste not, want not.

Bom called Bim's notice to this.

' *Attention !   The Lord of the Manor has dowsed the glim.   This pop-eyed crustacean, who looks as if his face had been boiled scarlet in his own juice, is a splendid though far from unique specimen of the modern British star performer in financial cat-burglary and the reception of stolen goods.   Like the hermit crab, he excels in the art of shoving his fat white behind into other people's shells.   In fact, he is less considerate, and seldom waits for the demise of the occupant.   Get it now is his motto —and he gets it.*

' *Sir Horace is a baronet, Bim.   Think of that, Bim ! That means he's one o' them way up ones, Bim.   If he caught us unlawfully consuming Bass between his goalposts at midnight, he'd have us in the parish stocks in two shakes of a J.P.   You don't know what a Baronet is, Bim.   He paid at least a thousand chervonetz for a coat of arms—a pocket picked proper, I expect, on a field shady with a past sinister.   That means he's one of the gentry, Bim, a leader of the nation.'*

' *Ah, ha !' said Bim, ' I get you.   One of the intelligentsia.   A Shavian Menshevist ? '*

' *No, Bim.   Not one of the intelligentsia.   Intelligence doesn't pay here—they go in for high hats and low cunning.   But listen to me, Bim, and don't drink so much of that Bass or you'll go to sleep.   As in many similar instances, the foundations of yonder stately home were laid by the son of a needy military adventurer who joined the Crusade of William the Bastard.   There his descendants abode, living and hunting on the land for which they performed military service or paid scutage. Sir Horace, I may say, has invariably paid scutage, particularly during the years 1914-18.   I interject here*

*something you may be surprised to learn, Bim ; which
is, that the very landscape we are sitting in or upon was
the model for that recruiting War poster which depicted
a highly coloured English village, with the superscrip-
tion : " Is this worth fighting for ? "   I am instructed
to say that the answer is : " Undoubtedly, but not to
give it to Horace ".   You get that point, don't you,
Bim ? '*

*Waking suddenly from a Bass-y snooze, Bim failed to
cover a gentle snore with an apologetic cough.*

' I 'm very tired, Bom.'

Bom spoke sharply :

*' Bim, attention ! Put that Bass down.   At once !
You mustn't go to sleep, d'you hear ? Pinch yourself, or
I 'll pinch you, hard too.   Cretin, louse, beer-swigger,
blackleg, stick to your guns, you son of drowsy marriage
blankets ! '*

' A' right, Bom, don't be too hard on me, Bom.'

*' Hard on you ! I 'll shove a steel backbone into you,
brother ! Sit up and listen !*

*' Thrice that house has been rebuilt—when it was
turned from a fortress to a mansion under Elizabeth,
after it had been burned by Essex's pikemen, and finally
in 1765 when the Lord had grown rich on English farming.   Unwisely for them, the family stood out against
the Whig industrialists.   The last scion of that noble
house, an orphan, served in the European War as aide-
de-camp to a general of specialised morals.   In 1921 he
was served in his turn with a* lettre de cachet *of exile.
He is now an inferior decorator in München.   The
mansion was on the market—dirt cheap, for the young
laird was a bloody fool in the hands of crooks, and there
was a hell of a trade slump.   In comes me master*

Horace, and snaps it up with an easy and shark-like grace.

'*Behold our grease merchant, who sells his axle-grease as margarine in packets, and his margarine as axle-grease in tins, installed as Lord of the Manor, duly seised of the manors of Pudthorp, Cleeve-on-the-Hill and Maryhampton, with rights of soc and sac, infangthief and outfangthief—why didn't he put a noose round his own neck?—and divers others which escape my memory. By the year he may dispend in current coin, chiefly paper, of this demi-paradise, this royal throne of kings, this fortress built by Nature for herself, the equivalent of half a million chervonetz roubles at par, cable exchange on London. And why? In that he has trafficked in other men's goods, other men's lives and the labour of other men's hands and brains; in that he bought cheap and sold dear; in that he dodged the column in the ranks of the Young Indispensables; in that he practised craft, leasing, simulation, legalised fraud and adroit adulteration; in that he was a furnisher or contractor for supplies to the Imperial Forces of His Majesty serving beyond the seas. Think not, O Bim, that I asperse His Sacred Majesty. The King, an't like Your Grace, is as honest a man as any in Christendom . . .*'

'*Is that meant as a compliment, Bom?*'

'*. . . and handleth an arquebus right royally. Ra, ta, ta, will a' say, bounce will a' say. Would that His Majesty, of his mere will and pleasure and loving-kindness to us his loyal subjects, would let off some of those unerring lefts and rights in his own House of Peers in solemn session lawfully assembled. Gentlemen, the King! God bless him!*'

'*Goblessim,*' said Bim. '*Shan't we give him three times three in Bass, Bom?*'

'*No! Put that bottle down! Put it down, I say!*

'*Doubtless, O Bim, you grow weary of Sir 'Orace, as he sometimes unguardedly calls himself, even as I myself. But this gear must be handled mainly. And think not, O Bim, that I am moved by mine own privy displeasure in this matter. I declare myself guiltless of all special, private and personal hatred and malice towards his person or fortune. Setting aside his manhood and margarine, he is not a bad man. He cleaveth to the wife of his bosom and provideth dowries unto his typist handmaidens that are big with child; punctual in the service of God, he diligently and piously approacheth His Sacred Table; he relieveth the poor, through contributions lawfully paid unto the Overseer of the Workhouse; when men cry "Noël, noël!" and neighbourly love and charity soften the heart, upon each and every of his tenantry doth he bestow a coney from his own broad acres. Nor is he overweening in pride, but courteous and winsome with all men. Unto this farmer, he crieth of a morning: "Good-morrow, Giles! How dost thou, man? How fareth Marion, my godsib, thy fat wife? But tush, man, I must deal roundly with thee. Right is right. And thou payest not thy lawful quit-rent come Michaelmas, the Law shall deal 'twixt thee and me, and thou and thine must trudge." Cometh the Sabbath and my Lord goes forth to breathe the delicate fine air of evening. But what sees he? A man and a maid playing the two-backed beast under one of my Lord's own hedges. What doth he then but fetch me the varlet a stout thwack o' the rump with his good ashen cudgel, crying: "Up, thou losel, thou harlot! What, do ye profane the Lord's Sabbath by lewdness and wanton play? Will ye breed bastards upon my lawful acres beneath my legitimate hedge? See that ye are joined in wedlock ere next month be sped, or—there is Law in this land—that hovel of thine shall lack its tenant. Avaunt ye, repent, and know that the Lord sees your lewd dealings!" Nay more, once in his discreet goings-forth upon his lawful occasions, he came upon a little weeping child—perchance of his own getting, who can tell?—and to quiet its whimperings did bestow in mere charity and compassion an unclipped penny of the Realm.'*

'By're Lady!' quoth Bim, 'a right courteous Lord, and a merry, and one that loves the poor. Yet I marvel, Bom, that our Lord the King hath not cherished him with titles of nobility nor called him to be about his royal person.'

'If you paid attention to what I say, Bim, you wouldn't pass silly remarks. Haven't I told you Horace is a baronet? You must not suppose that Horace has spent all his time fussing round the grease factory, rigging the market and playing the bluff old English Squire. He was a demon for recruiting, Bim, and his stern dignified methods of dealing with conchies were in the finest tradition of British justice and won torrents of enthusiastic approval from the Patriot Press. From O.B.E. to J.P. was but a step, an overdue tribute to a man of his substance. Alarmed in his conscience for the political liberties of his country, Horace made a handsome donation to party funds ; and in the next birthday honours his name appeared among the hereditary knights of England, Chevaliers sans peur et sans reproche, "*for eminent and unwearied services rendered*

during the War ". I prophesy. When His Majesty next issues writs for the election of knights and burgesses to the Commons, Sir Horace will stand forth as candidate for the representation of this constituency's interests, with which his own are so largely entangled. O.B.E., J.P., Bart., M.P., to what may this greasy Cawdor, this juggling Glamis not aspire? Right honourable, Bim, right honourable as himself shall be his title.'

This Realm This England

' *Bim, under my Russian blouse—which, by the bye, I am not wearing—there beats an English heart. Heart of my heart were it more, more should be laid at her feet. But I cannot away with Horace, Bim. Like an Athanasian mystery, he is not one but many. His name is legion. Britannia is a whore, and the Press is her pimp. Let Sporus tremble with shame, Horace will not. He and his pals have bewitched the wench. These beastly wizards have bolted to other people's castles with the spoils of War; and there comes no Red Cross Knight to wind a challenge at the portcullis. Age, age, Horatio. Let us be senile, and a while forget.'*

Ichabod—Thank God

Presently Bom began to chuckle; and gasped and snickered and choked with repressed laughter.

' *We 're a couple of bloody fools, Bim.'*

' *So we are, Mas'r Davy boy, so we are!* ' *exclaimed Bim with good old Peggotty false enthusiasm.* ' *So we are. Genel'men bore and bred. But why?* '

' It's a serious problem, Bim. Is it the air, the land-scape, the Bass? Or the adjacent population? In any case, we two cheery fools have undoubtedly been guilty of a solemnity which would reflect credit on "The Pillar" or a Justice of the King's Bench. Did you ever read " The Pillar", Bim? The highbrowest daily in the world, Bim, with a tradition, an aura of pretentious solemnity and affected dignity. The old-fashioned well-bred English gentleman, a little gone at the teeth, a little bare and bony at the occiput, keeping his pure cricket bags unsullied in spite of his woundy panic.

' I claim no originality for my portrait of Horace, Bim. Horace is universal, the 20th-century Homo esuriens in pink perfection. He is the heir of all the ages, the temporary summit of evolution, the peak quota-tion of human grandeur, one, Bim, for whom the visible world exists. There are Horaces all over the shop. Hence their importance. In London our particular Horace is rather lost in the mob of gentlemen who bank with ease. Sometimes, I admit, I have seriously con-sidered the advisability of getting rid of all the Horaces, but shrank appalled by the expenditure of rope and re-volver bullets. Acute shortage in the hemp and lead markets. I don't object to Horace qua Horace. He's as good a right to live as I have—better, for I never greased the wheels of Mars's chariot or the palms of the College of Heralds. It's his beastly pervasiveness I object to. You can't get away from him. He rules the roost. He is, so to speak, der Mond und der Sonnen-schein, the Alf alpha and dough mega, the mystic trinity of the el, the ess and the don. Horace has burgled the rainbow. He's Fafnir—one hell of a worm.'

Bim hummed a motif from the Götterdämmerung.

'*Precisely,*' *said Bom.* '*But as I remarked before in somewhat different symbology, where the blazes is Siegfried?* Non est inventus. *This field we sit upon, Bim, was filched from the commons of England some century ago by the simple process of putting a fence round it and a notice "Trespassers will be prosecuted". When the simple-minded villagers, who had been accustomed to pasture on it a few lean kine, asses and geese, called attention to this larceny by pulling down the fence and celebrating on one of Horace's predecessor's sheep, they were deported to Botany Bay with the stigma of crime on their honest bumpkin brows. No redressor turned up then, and I doubt if one will turn up now. It's the way of a man with a maid, Bim, which the Scripture oddly telleth us leaveth no trace. I beg the Scripture's pardon—it does, in both cases. Horace is now a gentleman, Bim, and a gentleman nowadays is one who practises the field sports of other people's ancestors. Horace justifies his slaughter of pheasants by well-bred hints about his Norman blood. He might consider the fate of Rufus. But granted that these hot-blooded aristocrats of the grease factory must expend their fierce energies in the chase, could not Horace take it out at the cokernut shies? A healthy sport, Bim, providing military training in bomb-throwing as well as moral improvement. Horace could still keep pheasants in the chicken run— where they ought to be—and improve his intellect and morals by skilfully wringing their necks. Meanwhile the village, which as you cannot see in the darkness, is uncomfortably huddled together on a motor-racing track called an arterial road, might have a chance to expand over Horace's chace.*'

'*Bom*,' said Bim, '*you'll excuse me, old pal, and all that you know, but between you and me and the goal-post I've heard all this before. Aren't you filching the wizard's wurzels?*'

'*Wizards are bright yet though the brightest fell*,' returned Bom brightly and promptly. '*I merely sketch you a hasty but faithful history of this rustic microcosm, this corner of an English field which is for ever alienate. Horace is the big bug in these parts. He's the whole shooting match, and the rest of the place exists by kind permission of Horace and Liddell on torts. (One of these fine nights, Bim, we'll have a symposium on Liddell, damn his ermine.) The unfortunate and prolific blackamoor at the Rectory, who has floured his face and hands and sugared his voice in an effort to prove himself a Nordic blond, is very much in Horace's pocket. Horace has the presentation of the living. What Horace blows through brass, the blackamoor breathes through the harmonium. Unless you agree with Horace, it's hell to live here.*

'*As a matter of fact, Horace didn't do so damn much. It was his old Dad from Camberwell who built up the grease business and left it to Horace, who merely nipped in at the right moment during the Great Ramp for Freedom. Horace is the dwarf standing on the shoulders of the Camberwell giant. Otherwise, he might be earning his own living. Even so, Horace is a better man than the wobbly giton he dispossessed. I assume you share the common prejudice that a cinaedus is superior to a pathicus? But why, in the name of Catullus, should Horace irrumate the whole damn place? Answer me that.*'

'*Dunno,*' said Bim drearily. '*Why not ask your*

broadcasting Uncle? Hang Horace, blow Horace, curse Horace, do anything you like with Horace, but let us dry up and get away from here. Methinks there is a lightening of yonder eastern sky and soon the lusty chanticleer will hail bright Phoebus' beams. If Horace catches us here, he'll have us tied to the stake, and the blackamoor will tomahawk us with the circumcision knife. By heavens, Bom, I tremble for you. Rash, imprudent, vain man, to what an abyss of peril hast thou brought thyself, and me too, the trusting partner of thy joys and sorrows? How do you know Horace hasn't secreted himself behind that elm with a couple of platoons of Scouts and Brownies, who will joyously beat us to death with their serviceable staves? You talk a lot about England, Bom, but you don't know it. Haven't you read the latest British atrocities in Isvestia? Let's hop it, Bom. Come on.'

' You exaggerate, Bim. Regrettable as my mansue-tude may appear, I don't believe the Boujois are as bloody as the comrades paint them. (Don't, however, repeat this, even in the privacy of your own cell.) Upon my soul, I am getting almost fond of Horace. Just now I felt sorry for him. He and his pals have made a con-founded mess of things, Bim, and they'll make a worse one. It's odd, by the bye, that Horace always suggests metaphors of filching to me—I wonder why? But just now I was thinking that he reminds me of an upstart and puny Hercules who has stolen a dozen of the man-eating steeds of Diomedes ; the reins are all mixed up, the steeds are getting restive and prancing and beginning to show their red teeth ominously. As a matter of fact, for all his bounce and brag, Horace is in a whale of a funk. He's as scared as a sissy boy on patrol. He'd give any-

thing for a quiet time. Safety first. But the safest way home may prove the longest way round. Horace is getting effete, Bim. His beard-singeing days are over. People have got wise to him, and he 'll find it more and more difficult to play his profitable little pranks. So far as Horace is concerned, the cry for the future is: Ichabod. Thank God. Whether, in response to the entreaties or rather challenge of the late William Blake, Petticoat Lane will arise and build a New Jerusalem in these cow pastures, I don't know. But Horace's number is up. Unfortunately, he has captured all the institutions, and it may be impossible to dislodge him before it's too late. So far as this rainy little gem is concerned, things look serious. Without so much as a by your leave, Horace has forced the inhabitants to back him to the last penny in the international Derby. But Horace is napoo, Horace is now a rank outsider, a broken reed. I fear this greasy Samson. Will he pull the whole caboodle down? This decaying microcosm of three parishes is a portent. You get me, Bim?'

'I'm sorry, Bom, I didn't hear what you were saying. Oh Bom, it is getting light, and I'm sure I noticed suspicious movement along that hedge. It's Brownies with jack-knives and thuggish scarves. Do let's go, Bom. Why won't you hurry?'

For once in his life Bim was right. There was a perceptible effort of light against darkness. A wind from the south-west started up, with little gusts that went hoo-ing miserably round the cottages. Clouds coming up too—another rainy spell. Poor old Ascot.

In his impatient terror, Bim dragged Bom to his feet and hurried him to the airplane which was waiting for them. Bim clambered in at once, and cowered in the *cockpit.   With one foot on the ladder, Bom turned and looked back at the dun fields and hunchy little cottages, silent and infelicitous in the rainy dawn.   He raised his hand.*

' *Farewell,*' *he said aloud,* ' *a long farewell. . . .*'

THE END